Prophecy of the Seventh Dragon

FIVE STAR

Prophecy of the Seventh Dragon

Tyler Blackwood

Five Star • Waterville, Maine

This novel is a work of fiction. Names, characters, places and incidents are either the product of the author's imagination, or, if real, used fictitiously.

First Edition
First Printing: September 2005

Published in 2005 in conjunction with
Tekno Books and Ed Gorman.

Set in 11 pt. Plantin by Al Chase.

Printed in the United States on permanent paper.

Library of Congress Cataloging-in-Publication Data

Blackwood, Tyler.
Prophecy of the seventh dragon / By Tyler Blackwood.—1st ed.
p. cm.
ISBN 1-59414-389-7 (hc : alk. paper) 1. Wizards—Fiction. I. Title.
PS3602.L3325P76 2005
813′.6—dc22 2005013397

Prophecy of the Seventh Dragon

Chapter One

Vashon Island, Washington, October 2002

The Bermudan water dragon had taken a human life.

One minute the old man was standing, the next he was on the ground, gasping for air, gnarled fingers clutching his bloodied neck. Whatever breath he'd had caught in his throat, and then he just died.

The dragon had been fast. Though several people milled about farther down the rocky shoreline, no one saw the small, scaly creature explode from beneath the water's surface. No one saw the razor-sharp talons breach the man's neck to take what it needed.

No one but Christopher Bartholomew. He knew the dragons sometimes hunted outside their boundaries if their normal, staple food was scarce. He also knew that this dragon, having discovered a rich, new food source, would have continued to hunt humans.

But no longer. Christopher had seen to the dragon's demise with a simple sweep of his double-edged dagger.

He closed his eyes and called his telekinetic energies into focus. His power was great, but summoning the heat was difficult and exhausting. And necessary.

It wouldn't do to have humans discover a slain water dragon. There would be too many questions, too many investigations. Too many ways for them to overlook important details and make a wrong decision. Better they not know about this hidden world. Easier for everyone.

He inhaled deeply, and let go.

The dragon's body exploded in a single, white-hot flash. Christopher took a step back, pulled dark sunglasses from his coat pocket, and put them on. The fire consumed the dragon in less than a second—before anyone even noticed—reducing it to soft, gray ash.

His people were dedicated to the destruction of the myriad unnatural threats to humans, like water dragons and demon wolves.

The battle was always waiting.

And he was always ready. Christopher was an Eskarian, an immortal warrior among humans. A protector of life. A Defender.

He bent to rinse off his dagger in the salty, black water of the Puget Sound. Sore muscles protested the move, but he ignored it. A small amount of Livendium would take care of that.

"Nice work."

Christopher sheathed his dagger, and faced his commander. "Easy, for the most part."

Blair Atkinson approached with Christopher's old wooden bow and quiver in his hands. "Everything should be that easy."

Christopher took the bow. The quiver he slung over his shoulder. "No kidding. I wish demon wolves were that easy. My life would be so much less stressful."

Blair nodded, scanning the surface of the water. "I can almost imagine what life would be like without wolves. Almost."

"I know exactly what I'd do, if they weren't around." Christopher scanned the calm waters of the Puget Sound, and drank in the transient calmness of the moment. A wisp of dark hair wafted over his eyes, carried by the afternoon breeze. Absently, he pushed it aside and scanned the ground. The shadows had become very long. Nightfall approached.

Soon, they would awaken.

"What's that?" Blair returned his obsidian gaze to Christopher. Sunlight caught in his eyes, highlighting the silver, iridescent rings at the outer edges of his irises, one of several unique attributes of their kind.

Christopher instinctively pushed his sunglasses farther up the bridge of his nose. The rings were visible only in bright light and, while he didn't expect to see any humans before the sun set, it was better to not risk exposure like that. Glowing eyes did not sit well with most people.

In fact, some got quite upset by it.

"I'd take off on a month-long cruise to Alaska," he said. "Just Ivan and me, for at least a month. No, make that six months. We'd do the inside passage. He'd love it. *I* need it."

Blair smiled. "Sounds like a good time."

"Yeah, it does." Christopher plucked a toothpick from his shirt pocket, popped it into his mouth, and thought about the Siberian Husky he'd rescued as a pup. Ivan's former owner had lost a battle with a demon wolf two years ago. Christopher couldn't bear to see the little guy homeless, so he took in the small black and white pup, gave him a name, and built an elaborate house for him.

Never mind that Ivan slept with Christopher most of the time.

"Sometimes I wish I had that luxury," he said softly. "Just drop everything and go without telling a soul." He waved away thoughts of responsibility and duty. Protection.

His gaze swung to a sailboat gliding out from the harbor. "I can't fight these demon wolves by myself much longer, Blair," Christopher admitted. "They breed like rabbits. Have you noticed that? I feel like I'm fighting a battle I can't win. It's starting to wear on me." He shook his head. "It was easier when they weren't so smart. Easier when they just morphed into animals at sunset. Now that they keep their human intelligence and emotion, it just takes too long to chase them down. What's worse, every time I corner one, I hear the human thoughts inside the wolf. I hear him plead for his life . . . It's difficult, even when I know that wolf has been killing humans. It's a hundred times worse when I know it's a woman."

Blair sighed. "I understand completely. Several Defenders from other regions have complained. They feel the same as you. The wolves are taking more and more of our resources. I've already put out a call for volunteers. Griffin, Jason, Alex, and Michael have responded. They should be arriving over the next few days. Randy and Aaron will come in the Northeast in a week or two. Unfortunately, I still need you here for a while longer."

Christopher nodded. "I knew you'd say that."

The demon wolf population was more concentrated in the Pacific Northwest than other parts of the country. Christopher's elite position in the Defender ranks was unchallenged, so it was logical that he'd have to remain and finish the job.

He spat the toothpick into the black water. Damn it.

Blair continued, "The sooner we can exterminate these wolves, the better off we'll all be—and the sooner you and Ivan can take that trip. But right now, we need your speed to gain an advantage over them. You'll work in teams for the next few days. I want you to pair up with Griffin." Blair paused and held up one hand. "I know what you're thinking, but I need you two to work together. You're both fast and accurate hunters. Our best. I need you to set aside your differences, at least for a little while. Let's see if we can wrap up this problem once and for all."

"Sure," Christopher said with a grim smile. He glanced at the bow, which had been carved in Rome a thousand years ago. Arden's Bow, named after the original owner, had seen enough blood and death over the centuries to last an eternity, much like its current owner.

Damn, but he was tired. And he didn't want to work with Griffin. Not now. Griffin McCallum was difficult to handle on a good day. On a bad day, forget it.

"Just make sure he keeps his yap shut. I'm in no mood for his blather," he added.

Blair nodded. "Understood. You know he won't, though. He only listens to Ian. I have control of him when he tolerates it, but that's seldom."

Christopher looked away. "Yeah, I know." Great. How many days would this hunt take? Like it mattered. Five minutes with Griffin was too much.

He removed a small wooden pipe and a baggie from the pocket of his black raincoat. Pulling out a few silver-tipped leaves from the baggie, he stuffed the pipe, and lit the leaves with his telekinetics. The herb, Livendium, was cultivated as a tool to center the mind and body, prepare for battle, and sharpen telepathic ability. He liked that it also dissolved the little worries that pestered him from time to time. Like demon wolves who thought they were clever enough to escape a Defender.

He inhaled deeply. The spicy-sweet fragrance, a mixture of sage and mint, drifted in long, smoky tendrils around him. His body quickly accepted the soothing elements of the herb, easing him into a relaxed state. Even his sore muscles felt better. He closed his eyes while he exhaled. "You know, for two days now, I've hunted that same wolf. I can't believe the damn thing got away last night. I just don't know where my head was."

"I'm sure you'll get it tonight." Blair paused and thought for a moment. "Have I ever mentioned that Jason said you'd end up one of our best warriors? He said that just after he started your training."

"You might've said something about it once or twice." Or ten times. Christopher drew on his pipe again and blew out a small smoke ring. Then he blew out a larger ring to encompass the smaller one and grinned at the results.

"It's a remarkable feat that you did it in only two hundred years. You're still quite the youngster."

Christopher shrugged again. "It's nothing, really."

Blair's eyebrows shot up. "Not true. Nonetheless, I know how tired you are. As soon as I'm able, I'll rotate you out to somewhere more sedate. Until then, Griffin and the others will do what they can to help." He placed his hand on Christopher's shoulder and offered a paternal smile. "I need to use you while I can. It won't always be like this."

"I'm sure." Christopher nodded, not really feeling sure at all. "Do you remember the Priestess of Aulterran?" He paused and thought about the vicious battle between the beautiful enchantress and himself. Her long fingers, tipped with retractable needle-like extensions, were lethal and fast. Good thing he'd been faster.

"How could I forget? Her idea of fun was bleeding the life-force from humans."

"Yeah, that's right." He glanced at the once-intricate carvings on the old bow, twirling it around absently. "Before I took out her heart, she told me I wouldn't always be alone."

Blair chuckled. "Of course not. Given your life span, it's hardly logical that you'd never find anyone."

"Maybe, but that was almost a hundred years ago and I've never come across anyone who did anything more than excite my hormones. How do you know I'll find her? Isn't it possible that some people are meant to be alone?"

Blair tilted his head. "Is that what you really think?"

"I don't know." He paused, then let out a snort. "I don't even know what I would do with myself if I wasn't a Defender. It's been my life for over two hundred years. I can't imagine waking up next to someone now."

"The day will come when you can't imagine *not* waking up next to someone."

Christopher paused to consider Blair's words. "I can't see it. I wish I could, though. I really do. I'm tired of always being alone."

Blair scanned the shimmering water. "That day will come, Christopher. Have faith in the gods."

Christopher waved his hand dismissively. He'd already lost faith in the creative force they referred to as gods. "We'll see, I guess." The long shadows told him the sun was about to set.

Time for another battle.

He lifted his boot and tapped the pipe against it to empty the spent contents. "Time for you to go. Anastasia would bleed me dry if anything were to happen to you."

Blair chuckled. "She probably would. Very well, then. I'll leave you to your work." He patted Christopher's shoulder, then hurried toward the large estate that sat above the marina.

Christopher's gaze lingered on Blair. The elder Eskarian had been the commander of the Defender forces for as long as anyone could remember. His authority was unquestioned and absolute. They all depended on him to keep the Defender ranks in order and functioning efficiently. Christopher hoped that never changed.

After all, Griffin was second in command.

Christopher shook his head. If Blair ever passed the torch

to Griffin, Christopher would leave Service in a heartbeat. Hell would freeze over before he answered to Griffin. That old coot was far too abrasive for Christopher's liking.

Griffin affected most everyone like that, except maybe old Nic. No one saw much of Dominic De Santo. Just as well. If Griffin was abrasive, Nic gave caustic new meaning.

Screw 'em. They could both rot.

Christopher stuffed his pipe into the back pocket of his faded blue jeans. With a quick shrug, he turned up the collar of his black raincoat and brushed a wayward strand of hair from his eyes.

Minutes remained. Despite the peaceful appearance of the island, the setting sun brought out some truly dangerous creatures.

Demon wolves.

Human by day, wolf by night. They sought human blood, sometimes banding together to take down a group of unwary travelers. Given the freedom, a single wolf could take one, sometimes two, human lives per night. Christopher's job was to make sure that didn't happen.

The problem was that the wolf could only be hunted at night, when there were fewer humans around to potentially witness or interfere. No evidence of the killings could remain. It was against Eskarian Code to allow humans to witness supernatural phenomena like that.

Better to do it at night.

As if on cue, his extraordinary hearing picked up the muffled cry of a man in pain.

The nightly transformation from human to demon wolf had begun.

Christopher whirled toward the sound, knowing that he had only seconds to catch the demon creature before it vanished into the woods.

Ensuring his double-edged dagger was safely sheathed and secured to his belt, he slung the wooden bow over his shoulder and headed toward the cry. The sound was faint, subdued. Most demon wolves knew they were hunted, condemned creatures. They knew they had precious little time to complete the terrible transformation from human to animal before a Defender came.

The man's cry set the nearby dogs to barking, a stark reminder that time raced against him. Humans lived in the surrounding homes. Families.

The wolf howled.

Time to hunt.

Christopher sifted through the brush beneath Maple and Fir trees for shredded clothes and blood, signs of the human's painful transformation. He scanned the area in all directions, his night vision perfect in the pitch of a moonless night.

A change in the wind allowed him to catch the scent of the wolf. He spun to follow it toward the water's edge. The beast had doubled back, and Christopher suspected it would use the water to hide its scent, but his sense of smell was so highly developed, tracking the creature would not be difficult.

He raced for the harbor over fallen trees, soft ferns, and leaves. Twigs snapped beneath his boots. Pine needles stung his face as he shot past. He soared over a fallen tree, startling two deer who hadn't heard his rapid approach.

Seconds later, he burst through the dense forest to the rocky shoreline.

He skidded to a halt, kicking up a rooster tail of dirt, rocks, and shells. The wolf wasn't on the waterfront as he'd suspected and now the scent was gone.

Christopher had made a novice's mistake and lost his target.

"Damn it," he whispered. Another mistake. He let out a slow breath and chastised himself again for being so tired.

Get over it. Find the wolf.

He turned an ear to listen for new evidence of the wolf, something to give away its position. If he didn't find it quickly, the next sound would be someone choking to death, caught in the powerful jaws of a wolf whose need for blood and soft flesh overwhelmed reason and logic.

The sudden rustle of dead leaves caught Christopher's attention.

Shit.

The wolf had attacked. He swung toward the sound, which came from a waterfront house set back into a natural landscape of trees, bushes, and ferns. With preternatural speed, he rushed into the forest surrounding the house and once again found the acrid scent of the wolf. Rounding the corner of the house, he caught another smell. Blood. The beast was close and it had killed.

There it was, in the middle of the yard. A tall, gray wolf.

He was too late.

"Damn it!" He slammed back against the wall in anger and shoved strands of dark hair from his eyes. Not again.

He peered around the corner. The wolf had indeed made the kill and was now feeding from the body of a young woman.

They were losing the battle. There was just no way to keep up.

Too many lives lost, too much blood, too little time.

The attack had been quick. The woman's face was calm, her glazed eyes cast upwards, as if she hadn't seen it coming.

Which meant this was a seasoned wolf who'd learned how to survive.

Without a sound, he slipped the bow off his shoulder and pulled an arrow from the quiver on his back. Drawing it back, he stretched the bowstring, and stepped away from the house. He aimed carefully at the center of the wolf's body.

A woman's voice distracted him. "Amy?"

Christopher lowered the bow, retreating into the shadows.

A young woman appeared on the other side of the house, dressed in torn jeans and a dark blue T-shirt, concern etched on her face as she searched for Amy. She was tall, and her fluid movements stole his complete attention. She walked from the porch toward the thick canopy of trees—toward the wolf. Wisps of long, black hair danced about her pale face. She was exquisite.

Something within him awoke.

Something with a fierce, dark hunger.

She ignited a yearning within him he hadn't ever felt before. His pulse quickened; he felt hot, sweaty, and unable to think straight. He steadied himself against the wall of the house and wiped the sweat off his brow. God, he was panicked. Why was this happening? Why now? He could even smell her from here. Lavender.

Who was she?

He peered around the corner. She was walking out into the open yard. The wolf and its victim were farther into the shadows, but it wouldn't be long before she saw it.

More importantly, it would be only seconds before the wolf saw her.

Amy had been the first kill of the night. Now the woman who searched for her was in danger. Even if Amy hadn't been the first, the wolf would most likely see this as an easy meal and take it.

Christopher closed his eyes and forced himself to focus on the task. Forced his emotions back to sleep.

He stepped out, once again, from the protection of the shadows.

The wolf raised its head, licking its bloodstained mouth.

Black eyes focused on the unsuspecting woman.

Powerful legs lunged toward her.

Christopher raised the bow, took aim, and released. The white arrow struck the animal's back, hurling it onto its side. The wolf tried to rip out the arrow with strong jaws, but Christopher's aim had been precise and calculated. That arrow wasn't going anywhere.

The woman's gaze swung to the wolf. She gasped, stumbled back, and covered her mouth with both hands.

The noise drew the wolf's attention again. Rising up on its forelegs, the wolf dragged its weakened hind legs in pursuit, teeth bared in preparation for the attack.

She screamed, spun on her heel, and fled.

Good. She didn't need to see anymore.

Christopher drew another arrow and nocked it. He carefully aimed for the wolf's throat and released. The arrow flew, striking its target perfectly, pinning the wolf to the ground. Blood oozed from the new wound, collecting in a black pool at the base of its neck. He slipped the wooden bow over his shoulder and trotted to the downed demon-creature. Poised behind it, he removed his double-edged dagger from the sheath. The long, engraved blade was used to cut and separate the demon wolf's head from the body. He raised the wolf's muzzle to expose its bloodied throat.

These wolves lived forever. There was only one way to ensure they remained dead.

Without a head, they'd stay dead.

"Get away from that wolf." The woman had returned, a rifle in her hands.

He met her gaze. "This isn't a wolf. It's an aberration of nature."

She peered over the sights of the rifle. "Then I want to study it."

Christopher shook his head. "I can't allow that."

"Allow? You're on my property. I don't give a rip what you think you should allow. Step away from the wolf, or you get the tranquilizer dart. Your choice."

He looked at her in disbelief. "Look, I really need to finish this."

"Fine." She took aim and fired the rifle.

A pink carnation struck Christopher's thigh. He took a step back, shocked by the pain of the thick needle embedded in his muscle.

A tranquilizer dart?

Warmth spread through his leg, up to his hip, then dissipated, a little too slowly for his comfort. Inhaling deeply, he bent and wrenched the dart out. He straightened, and though the rifle was still aimed at his body, he approached her, scanning her mind the entire time. If she intended to shoot, he'd know.

"These won't work on me." He held out the dart in an open palm.

Her emerald gaze dropped to his hand. She ignored his question. "How is that possible?"

He shrugged. "I'm not human. I'm an immortal warrior who exterminates things like this demon wolf."

She raised her eyebrows. "Excuse me?"

"Was that not what you wanted to hear?" He smiled and stepped back. "Sorry. I need to finish this." He turned and headed back to the wolf.

"Stop," she ordered.

"No." He knew what was coming next. Oh, yes, he knew.

She fired . . . reloaded . . . fired again. One dart hit the small of his back, another struck his calf.

Damn it. He plucked them out and dropped them on the grass, glancing back at her. "Are you done yet?"

"No, I'm not." She pulled more carnations from her back pocket. "How come you're still awake? You should be snoring by now."

"Like I said, I'm not human," he said over his shoulder. He ignored the silent threat of more darts and sank the blade into the wolf's neck, then sliced, viciously, to remove the head.

The dark-haired beauty gasped. Her knees buckled and gave out, dropping her to the grass. She wasn't supposed to see this. Now that she had, she'd made his night a little more difficult.

At least the damn wolf had had enough sense to keep quiet.

He glanced at her, then stepped back, eyes closed, and called his energy into sharp focus.

A second later, the wolf's body and decapitated head exploded into white-hot flames. Christopher watched the display, then wiped his dagger on the grass and sheathed it. The wolf's carcass, like the water dragon's, was consumed in a second, leaving only fine, gray ash.

Adjusting the bow over his shoulder, Christopher trotted toward the woman.

Her wide-eyed focus settled on the ashen remains. She covered her mouth with a trembling hand.

Christopher knelt before her with a forearm on his knee. "Are you all right?" His heart went out to her. His first instinct was to take her into his arms and tell her that everything would be all right. After that, maybe he'd whisk her away to some mountain hideaway on the other side of the world.

Damn it. He could do none of these things. Duty came first. Always.

He was so damn tired of duty.

She looked at him, fear in her eyes. "What are you?"

He shrugged. "I'm an Eskarian. A Defender." It didn't matter what he said. By morning, she'd have no idea what had happened.

"A what?" she asked, frowning.

"Forget it. The wolf is gone now. You'll be fine." Christopher gave her a reassuring smile. She smelled so fresh and inviting. Her beautiful, emerald eyes tugged at his heart, pulling him deeper into something he could not yet identify. Everything about her called to him, and he wanted desperately to answer.

"Amy." Her attention snapped back to her fallen friend. "Where's Amy?" She looked around, her gaze finally settling on the body farther out in the yard. "Oh my God! That wolf killed her, didn't it? Is that what happened? Could she still be alive?" She started to rise, but Christopher caught her shoulder, and eased her back down to the soft grass.

"You stay here. I'll check to see if she's still alive."

He strode to Amy's body, already knowing there was no way she'd survived. Demon wolves were quick and deadly.

Amy's throat and stomach were deeply scored, and some of her internal organs were either severely damaged or missing. The wolf had been extraordinarily quick. Yes, this one had lived the dual life a long time.

Amy had been taken from life too soon, and the wolf too late.

With a soft sigh, he rubbed his forehead. He'd grown weary of hunting, and tonight the burden was especially heavy. In the past, humans had occasionally seen him destroy whatever threat had come along, and to protect himself and his people, he had simply removed the human's memory of the offending event.

He looked back at her. This time, he didn't *want* to do it.

Didn't want to let her go, didn't want to say goodbye. *I want you to know who I am.*

He returned, knelt, and laid a hand on her arm. "I'm sorry. She didn't survive the attack."

"She's dead? Amy's gone?" New tears spilled onto her pale cheeks. She wiped them away with both hands and look at him with those gorgeous emerald eyes. "Oh, God. I don't believe it."

He raised her chin with a light touch, holding her gaze. "I'm sorry. I should've been faster."

A single tear found its way down her cheek. He brushed a thumb across her silky skin to whisk it away. He wanted to stay with her, but that was impossible. She was human and he was not. Her memories of the demon wolf and him had to be removed. "I wish it didn't have to be this way," he said softly. "You have the most beautiful eyes I've seen in a very long time. I could lose myself in them. I *would* lose myself in them. Willingly."

Her brow furrowed. "What? I don't understand."

He held her face in his hands and leaned closer, focusing his energies once again. "Shhh," he whispered. His powerful thoughts, capable of both telepathic thought and telekinetic movement, sent her into a deep sleep so he could steal back the memories she never should have had. When her eyes closed, he scooped her up and headed for the house. Inside, he carefully laid her on the couch, and swept aside her memories of the demon wolf and him. "Sleep, Beautiful." He brushed her cheek again with his fingers. Her skin was petal-soft, clear, and so warm, his own skin grew hot. Did that mean?

No . . . surely not.

Gently he brushed the hair from her forehead.

All at once, he caught the scent. The mark of the wolf.

Damn, he should've noticed it before now. He was more familiar with that smell than he cared to be. Leaning over the woman, he inhaled to find the wound.

There it was. Her left shoulder.

He pushed her collar aside to expose the bite. "No," he whispered, taking two steps back. "Not you . . ."

How many days did she have left? Two? One? How long before he returned to take her life?

Christopher stumbled back and turned around. Resting both hands on his hips, he gazed sightlessly at the ceiling while he thought about it. Duty required him to follow her until she made her first transformation. After she shifted, she was supposed to be fair game.

The hell with duty. He wouldn't do it. She was too beautiful and the way she affected him made him think maybe she was . . .

No . . . don't go there. Forget it. Don't think it. Don't say it. Just forget it.

The remote control sat on the coffee table. He clicked on the small television set to suggest she'd merely fallen asleep. She would remember only that Amy had left earlier in the evening.

What happened after that was up to the gods. He would not knowingly hunt her.

In the doorway, he stopped to watch the gentle rise and fall of her breasts. His heart truly ached to leave her, and the sorrow of what she would become almost overwhelmed him. Much as he wanted to scoop her up and leave all this, he couldn't. He'd already taken away her memory of him. It was too late now.

He took in a deep breath, then let it out slowly. One more thing to do and then he could leave.

Returning to Amy's body, he once again summoned his

power. Her body exploded into a white flash, and a second later, only ashes remained, which the night wind would scatter by morning.

His business here was now complete, yet he lingered. *Her* scent was on his hands, her emerald eyes forever carved into his memory, and his body was on fire. He didn't want to let go—just the simple act of feeling something was precious. She had awakened him.

But she was human and only days away from shifting into a bloodthirsty killer. He had to just forget her and move on.

He locked the door behind him. Adjusting the bow over his shoulder, he set out for home. The battle would have to wait another day. He needed sleep. Needed to try to forget the dark-haired beauty.

Things would look much different tomorrow.

Christopher, I must speak with you. Blair's voice inside his head was clear, the tone urgent, unsettled. Something terrible had happened.

He turned to see a large mountain lion pad toward him with eyes glittering like obsidian. At once, the lion shifted mid-stride from animal to man.

"What's wrong?" Christopher pushed a lock of hair back and moved to meet him.

Blair stuffed his hands into his coat pockets. The lines in his face had deepened with concern. "Ian needs to see you tonight. Griffin is already on the way."

"Griffin? Why?"

"He's flying in tonight. Anastasia will bring him to Ian's." Blair paused. "Have you ever heard of the Dragon Prophecies?"

"I heard about them over a century ago, but I don't really know anything specific. Why?"

"Seven prophecies were set in stone several thousand

years ago. They accurately foretold of catastrophic events in mankind's history."

Blair inhaled sharply, turning to watch the Seattle ferry skim through the water. "The seventh one is unfolding now." His obsidian gaze returned to Christopher. "This won't be easy, my friend. Come. Let me take you to Ian."

Chapter Two

Mackenzie Wallace bolted upright. "No! No! I haven't done anything!" she cried.

She looked around to get her bearings. Living room. Tan walls, dark hardwood floors. Soft, cushy blue couch beneath her. Old, blue La-Z-Boy falling apart in the corner. Okay, this was home. Now, why the hell was she sleeping on the couch? What time was it?

The clock on the DVD player said ten in the morning. She exhaled softly. The dream had been intense enough to frighten the bejeebers out of her, but now it was fading from memory. Something had been chasing her with the intent to kill . . .

The television was still on.

Mackenzie frowned. Her neck was stiff. She rubbed the nape and tried to remember when she'd sat down to watch television, and what time she'd fallen asleep. And why she didn't remember why she'd slept on the couch. Maybe Amy knew something.

"Amy?"

No answer.

Also bizarre. Amy was almost always home on Saturday morning. She loved to stay up late Friday night and work on her various art projects. Most of the time, she slept in until at least nine. She should be up by now.

Come to think of it, Mackenzie didn't remember seeing much of Amy last night. She scanned the living room again and realized she didn't remember *anything* about last night. The last thing she recalled was coming home from the work yesterday afternoon and then Amy going outside for something. *Nothing else.*

Then it was morning and some stupid dream had scared the shit out of her.

What had happened? She might forget a birthday, or what she ate for breakfast, but she'd never lost an entire evening. Even after a night of heavy partying, she just wasn't the sort of person who lost control like that. Something really weird had happened. "Amy, you here?"

Still, nothing.

Alarms went off in her head. She bolted off the couch and tore upstairs, looking for her roommate. Something was wrong. Really wrong.

The waterfront house had three bedrooms upstairs. Mackenzie looked in each one, starting with Amy's. The bed was still made, which meant Amy had been gone all night. The guest room was empty too.

Mackenzie flew downstairs, threw open the front door, and searched the front yard and the carport. Amy's car was still there. "Amy? Are you here?"

No response. She knew, though. She felt it deep in her bones. Amy wasn't coming back. Something awful had happened and Mackenzie was never going to see her again. "Shit. Come on, Amy . . . where are you?" she whispered. Until she'd exhausted every possibility, she wasn't going to give up. And that nagging feeling that Amy was gone forever? She'd ignore that, too.

Spinning on her heel, she jogged around the corner to the back yard. "Amy?"

What might've happened? Could she have been kidnapped? Mackenzie scanned the yard, searching for evidence of foul play. Not that she'd necessarily know what foul play looked like, but any information was better than nothing.

A dark patch in the middle of the yard caught her attention. Curiosity distracted her for a minute.

The grass had been burnt or singed. She crouched, passing her hand slowly over the darkened blades of grass. When had this happened? It wasn't like this yesterday, was it? And who'd done it? Did it have anything to do with Amy's disappearance? The questions turned over and over in her mind, but she wasn't sure if this was a clue, or something random. Who knew? Maybe lightning had hit the ground last night.

She studied the charred grass. No, it wasn't lightning. The burn pattern was oval, not round. Didn't make sense.

Might there be a note on the refrigerator? Maybe Amy had decided to spend the night at Scott's.

She trotted to the house. The kitchen was right off the back porch. She threw the door open and looked for notes everywhere. Table, fridge, countertops. Nothing.

Amy's cell phone was in the charging cradle, and her purse was strewn over the back of the kitchen chair.

She found Scott's phone number on the refrigerator door, and tapped in the number on the cordless. Two rings later, Scott answered.

"Scott, this is Mackenzie. Is Amy with you?" She chewed on a thumbnail while she waited for his answer.

"No. I haven't seen her since Thursday night. Why? What's going on?"

"She's gone. There's no note. Nothing. I saw her go out last night, but she was in her slippers. I thought she'd be right back." *Oh, and I have no memory after that, so who knows? Maybe we were both abducted by aliens and she's still on the mother ship.*

On second thought, better keep quiet about that.

"Could she have gone somewhere?" Scott asked.

"Her purse and car are still here. Scott, she never does stuff like this. Something's really wrong."

"Okay, let's give it a little more time before we call the cops. I'll start checking around with some of our friends. Let me know if you hear from her, 'kay?"

"Absolutely. You do the same." She turned the phone off and set it down on the countertop.

Amy had vanished.

Returning to the living room, Mackenzie fell back onto the couch to think about what she should do next. Something more useful than sitting around and waiting for Amy to show up.

The blather coming from the television was an irritating reminder that her world wasn't right. Amy's disappearance wasn't even the start of all this weirdness. The nasty wound on her shoulder had been her passkey to this alternate reality where nothing made sense. What she really needed was to find the exit. Post-haste.

She reached up to pull her collar aside and inspect the wound, inadvertently grazing it with her fingers. "Ow, ow, ow," she whimpered.

Damn. After two days, it still hadn't even scabbed over.

The injury, a series of deep scores and punctures from sharp teeth, throbbed in response. Instinctively, she sought to protect it, but caught herself before she actually touched it. Fighting the urge to look at it for the hundredth time, she steadied herself instead with a calming breath. Or two. Looking at it made her sick to her stomach.

After her softball game two nights ago, she and her brother, Sean, were getting ready to leave. She'd leaned against the back of the car to remove her cleats. Out of nowhere came a huge, black wolf. As if planned, the wolf launched an assault, locking strong jaws onto her shoulder and bearing down.

The attack had been so quick, she didn't even have a chance to react. Thank God her brother Sean had been there. He'd bashed the wolf in the ribs with a baseball bat, tearing it from Mackenzie's shoulder. The wretched beast had yelped, growled, and finally dashed off into the nearby woods.

She'd collapsed from the assault, in tears and bleeding. Sean had scooped her up and taken her to Urgent Care right away. Luckily, the staff wasn't busy when they arrived, so they'd tended her without the usual wait. Sean sat beside her while the doctor cleaned and stitched the vicious, gaping wound. There had been so much pain.

The worst part? The part she'd been unable to tell a soul about was the second the wolf's teeth had broken her skin. She'd heard words in her head. Strong words.

I love you, Mackenzie Wallace. I'd rather see you dead than with another man . . .

Mackenzie would've thought it random nonsense, but not two weeks prior, that's *exactly* what Vincent St. James had said to her.

Vincent was a veterinary assistant, and had been a damn fine addition to her staff. Until he started stalking her after work, of course. He didn't seem to understand that she'd been with Daniel for more than a year. Vincent didn't understand many things, she decided. *Like, don't bite the boss . . .*

But now the damage was done. The first night, she noticed that her hearing had improved and her night vision had sharpened. Last night, her sense of smell became acute. She knew instinctively the reason for the change was the wolf's bite, that something evil and poisonous now ran through her veins. She also knew there was nothing she could do to reverse what had been done. Her life was about to change.

She felt the taint of something not right, something . . . evil and dark.

"Mackenzie?" The screen door swung open with a creak, then closed with a thwack.

"In here," she answered.

Daniel Wilson, her boyfriend, strode into the living room. "Hey, gorgeous." He bent to kiss the top of her head, then fell back into the overstuffed chair beside her. "How's your shoulder?"

She carefully pushed the collar aside to show him.

He made a sour face. "Yuck. It still looks disgusting. You should stop taking the bandages off. Let me put on a new one for you."

She shrugged, frowning. "The bandage drives me nuts."

Daniel raised an eyebrow. "That thing needs to heal. I'll be careful, I promise."

Mackenzie conceded. He meant well. "Okay." With a tentative sigh, she smiled and stood up.

He followed her to the bathroom. After she switched on the light, she turned to face him. "Just don't touch it any more than you need to, and use warm water this time."

He gave her a sheepish grin. "Yes, ma'am."

She leaned against the vanity, pulled her long hair aside, and tilted her head away from the throbbing wound. Daniel leaned closer to inspect it. The gentle massage his fingers worked on her upper arm felt nice. Reassuring and comfortable.

He nodded. "It does look as if it's healed a bit."

"Maybe," she said with a thin smile. She wasn't sure she agreed.

Daniel kissed her cheek. "I'm sorry."

"Thanks. It would've been much worse if Sean hadn't

been there. I honestly can't say I would've survived without him. That thing had a tight hold on me."

He pulled the antiseptic and bandages from the cabinet. "I wish I could've been there to save you. I'm sorry I wasn't."

"I understand. You have clients. I know you can't just drop them." She paused to regard the wound. "This thing will take forever to heal, I just know it. It just blows me away that a wolf up and bit me. What the hell did I do to deserve this?" She shook her head.

His soft brown eyes drifted over her face. "Nothing, Mackenzie. It just happened."

Her thoughts drifted back to Vincent's words. *I'd rather see you dead . . .* How easily she could've died that day. "I don't know . . ."

"Why don't we just keep an eye on it? If it's not better on Monday, go back to the doctor."

"Yeah, okay," she said absently.

Daniel wrung out the washcloth and dabbed at her shoulder. Instantly she flung herself away, inhaling through clenched teeth as the pain ripped through her neck and arm. "I'm sorry, I'm sorry," she whispered quickly. "It hurts."

Daniel pulled her close. "Mackenzie, this thing needs to be bandaged. You need to have it covered to be sure it doesn't get infected."

"I know. I'm sorry," she said softly. "Please, continue. I'll stay still."

"If you don't, I'll have to tie you down to do this." He gave her an impish grin. "Hmm . . . maybe I'll do that anyway."

"Ha. You wish." She pushed against him with her good hand.

He caught it and brought it to his mouth, pressing a warm kiss to her palm. "Yeah, I do. I'd love to see you all helpless and at my mercy. Who knows what naughty things I might do to you?"

She grinned. "You don't need to tie me up to do those things. As long as it isn't completely weird, I'm game."

"I'll remember that." His gaze moved over her face again, lingering on her eyes and mouth, then he returned to the task at hand. "Hold still now, so I can finish this."

She sighed. "Okay, okay." Her eyelids drifted down as she gave herself over to his care. The washcloth felt like sandpaper as it scraped over her wound, but she managed to say nothing. She even held still as he applied the antiseptic, though it stung horribly. The worst part was when the liquid penetrated the tender wound. She fought back the tears in silence, impatient for the pain to stop.

With that much done, Daniel unwrapped a large bandage. "Now, that wasn't so bad, was it?"

Yes, it hurt like hell. "No, it wasn't too bad."

He set the gauze over the raw wound and secured it. "See? No big deal." He nodded after he'd inspected his work. "You're all done."

"Thank you, Daniel. I do appreciate this." She touched the edge of bandage lightly with two fingers. "Feels like you did a good job."

He nodded. "You're most welcome." He returned the bandages and antiseptic to the cabinet. "Can I take you to lunch?"

"Sure." Not that food sounded appealing.

Nothing did, really.

In the span of a few minutes, that wolf had changed her life. The wound was only the beginning.

Her body was shifting, changing somehow. She felt it and knew it, though no one had told her it was so. Maybe she was becoming a wolf herself.

The thought made her laugh out loud. She followed him into the hallway.

"What's so funny," he asked.

"Wouldn't it be something if I became a werewolf?" She laughed again.

He frowned. "Assuming there was such a thing . . . no. Can you imagine howling at the moon all night?"

I don't know. Maybe. Her smile faded. "I guess not."

"But maybe I should lock you up, just in case. You know, just to keep you safe. At the very least, I should tie you up. It'd be for your own protection, of course." He grinned mischievously.

She laughed. "What is it with you and rope?" She batted his arm playfully.

He slammed against the opposite wall.

Stunned, her hands flew to her mouth. "Oh, my God. I'm sorry, Daniel. I didn't mean to hit you so hard. I didn't think—"

"What was that all about," he growled, rubbing his arm.

"I don't even know how that happened. I'm so sorry. Really, I didn't mean it. I feel awful." She shook her head.

"No problem. It's okay." He threw her a hurt look and walked to the front door.

She locked the door behind her and followed him outside without a word. Made no sense what had just happened. She looked at her hands. Something was happening all right. But what?

Crawling into Daniel's SUV, she almost wished she hadn't made the lunch plans. The more she thought about it, the more it bothered her Daniel had suffered such a blow when she'd barely touched him. The werewolf idea crossed her mind again, but she shook it off, since there was clearly no such thing as a werewolf.

Was there?

"Where do you want to go? Do you want Mexican, Chinese, or Thai?"

Her stomach turned as she thought about food. "I don't think I can eat anything, Daniel. I'm not feeling well. Would you be upset with me if I took a rain check? I'd like to lie down for a while."

"You just got up." He pressed his hand to her forehead. "But you do feel hot. I'll stay with you for a bit, just to be sure you're all right."

"Thanks. I'll be grateful for your company." She meant it, too. He had such a big heart. "You really are very good to me. I'm not sure I deserve you."

He raised a brow. "Not true at all. You totally deserve me."

Upstairs, Mackenzie kicked off her sneakers, traded her jeans for blue sweats, and slid under the quilts. She still felt so tired, and just plain out-of-sorts.

Daniel sat down beside her. "Do you mind if I lie down with you?"

"No, of course not. Just don't expect me to stay awake, okay?" She turned to face him with a pillow bunched up under her head.

"Sure. I just want to feel you next to me."

She smiled and let her eyes drift shut. "You can't imagine how much I'd like that." She was fading already. The sound of his shoes being tossed aside echoed in the back of her mind.

He brushed gentle fingers across her cheek. "I love you," he said, his voice far away.

But you're not the one, Daniel.

Inside her mind, her true mate whispered soft words: *Do you understand what forever means?* His soft eyes held the color of a summer sky.

Daniel, I'm sorry. There is another . . .

She howled into the night. Then she stood in the midst of a large field, and listened for a response, three wolves at her side, her sisters in the battle for survival. She raised her nose to find prey, her young ones attentive, learning how to hunt. They would know how to hide from the unfamiliar animals, the tall ones who came and killed their kind. She would find a way to protect them from the painful death the unfamiliar ones brought.

She had scented a small animal only moments ago, but now another smell had distracted her from her prey. What was it? Unfamiliar. Not like the other animals. The scent was now behind her.

The unfamiliar ones.

Her gaze turned to the sound in the woods. Shadows all around. The moon provided ample light and she saw clearly in the dark, but the animals with the unfamiliar scent remained out of sight.

Time to run.

Muscular legs spun her around, dug into the soft grass under her feet. The moon at her back, she sought refuge from the foreign sounds behind her. The scent foretold of danger and death.

Suddenly surrounded, she stopped. Nowhere to turn. The tall, unfamiliar animals were all around. Their scent was foreign, hostile. Danger. At once she knew her time had come.

Blinding pain in her side. She cried out as the force of the strike pushed her off balance. Another strike sent her to the ground. The pain was more than she could bear. Wetness all around her legs, face, body.

No more time.

Mackenzie woke up drenched in sweat. Another dream. She shook her head. Not again. Another dream of being chased, hunted.

Her heart raced, filled with the terror that she'd run out of time, that her life was over already. She scanned the room, recognizing a second later that this was her own room. The celadon-colored walls were comforting. The off-white quilt had been given to her by her mother. Yes, this was good. Home . . .

Yet despite that, in the back of her mind that sense of dread persisted.

The sun was low in the horizon. She'd slept most of the day, and now she'd probably be up all night, something she absolutely despised. Remembering that Daniel had lain down beside her, she wondered if he was still around. His company would do her some good, she thought. It'd get her mind off the fear that time was not on her side. She rubbed her forehead, pushed the thought from her mind. Thinking like that wouldn't do any good at all.

No more time.

What did that mean, anyway? No more time for what?

Annoyed, she threw off the quilts, and sat up, stretched, and took in the scents of the late afternoon through the open window. Thick trees and lush ferns and bushes surrounded the house, wrapping her in a protective cocoon. All around her now, the scents and sounds of the birds and animals filled her with a sense of belonging, of oneness with all that was. At once, her fears disappeared and she smiled. She'd been foolish to think such thoughts in the first place, as she truly was a part of all this. Time was not an issue. Not at all.

She swung her legs over the bed and stood, sifting both hands through the long tangle of black hair. As she padded towards the stairs, she shivered; she was cold, though the room itself had been warmed by the sun. Nonetheless, she plucked a thick robe from behind the door as she passed by and threw it over her shoulders.

The sound of a sports game drew her attention. Good. Daniel was still there. She padded down the stairs on bare feet. If she didn't know better, she'd swear her step was somehow lighter, more swift and silent.

Like a predator.

Daniel was slouched on the sofa with a beer propped up on his stomach, engrossed in a college football game.

"Hi, Sweetie." She curled up beside him on the sofa, her long legs tucked beneath her.

"Hi." He scanned her face, concern etched into his handsome features. "How do you feel?"

"Fine." She hadn't eaten all day, yet her stomach was quiet. Propped up against Daniel's shoulder, she watched the game, or rather, stared absently at the screen. "Who's playing?"

"Huskies and Wildcats," he said, lowering the volume. He curled his arm around her shoulder. "Sure you're all right? You feel kind of warm."

She pressed her palm to her cheek. "I think I'm okay. A little out of it, but I think it'll be fine."

A moment later, she found herself unable to focus. The uneasiness she'd dispelled earlier crept back into her thoughts.

Daniel pulled her closer. "I'm glad you're awake. I was starting to miss you."

Mackenzie smiled. "Really?"

"Absolutely," he assured her.

He had the most amazing eyes. Sapphire blue. Wonderful. She should just try to relax and just enjoy her time with him. Everything *seemed* fine. Why did she feel so . . . ?

She sat upright. No, something was very wrong. Her skin tingled all over, as if the circulation had been cut off to her entire body.

She rubbed her brow, trying to calm herself, but the sensation persisted. Now she felt downright panicked. What was happening to her?

"What's wrong?" Daniel held her shoulders.

Time seemed to move in spurts. When had he taken her shoulders?

He drew her closer. "You're shaking. What's going on?"

"I don't know. Something's happening. I don't know," she said. Suddenly she burst into tears, unable to contain her emotions any longer.

Daniel's voice was frantic. "Honey, tell me what's happening. I don't understand why you're crying."

The tingling increased, and the deep ache in the pit of her stomach almost took her breath away. Her mouth opened to answer him, but no sound came. She searched his face through her tears, momentarily finding her voice. "Help me," she whispered. "Hurts."

"What do I do?" he asked. "Tell me."

At once, pain ripped through her body, searing her skin. Muscles became rigid, then flexed with uncontrollable spasms. She fell to the floor amid tears and screamed for relief, anything to take the pain away. Daniel knelt beside her to whisper soothing words, but she couldn't understand him anymore. Her hands balled into white knuckled fists, and fingernails dug into tender skin. Still the pain did not cease.

She prayed for relief.

And then she begged for relief.

Sharp pain tore through her stomach and chest, then spread down to her belly and legs as bones cracked and shifted. Over the length of her body, the skin rippled and shimmered to life with a short, downy fur. Her breath came in short, rapid gasps, yet she still felt as if she were suffocating. Certain she was about to die, she panicked, screamed again for it to end. Pain seared her internal organs, and she knew instinctively they had begun to change, to mutate into something foreign and dark.

Wolf.

Sharp teeth formed as powerful jaws extended from the once-human face. The ability to see colors disappeared as green eyes became brown and vision sharpened. Her spine lengthened, burning as vertebrae formed a long tail that whipped and snapped through the air. Sharp claws tore through hands. Fingers dissolved. She screamed for life, for Daniel, for mercy, for all that was not to be, no matter how much she pleaded, cried, or begged for the hot pain ripping through every fiber of her body to stop, stop, please God, *stop.*

Stop.

Where was Daniel?

She opened her eyes. No color. The room was awash in shades of gray and black.

Her thoughts became images with no words behind them. Then she raised her nose to the moon and announced her arrival.

She'd killed someone. No, there was more than just one. She'd taken three lives tonight.

Wolf.

Inside this lupine body, the desire for blood had been so strong, and she'd tried so hard, but just couldn't control it. Her life depended on it. She needed to feel it in her veins, needed the hot stickiness on her tongue. Ah, the scent had filled her so completely. It had been easy to pull them down and break open their throats to feed until the voracious appetite had finally been sated.

Her muscles were strong, her body sleek—she'd seen long

legs stretched out before her as she ran through the dense forest. Glossy, black fur now covered the once-human body, and she knew what she was now.

Wolf.

There was still so much she didn't understand. Why had that wolf—*Vincent*—come after her? Was she a wolf or a werewolf? Would she do this every night, or just when the full moon was out?

There wasn't a full moon tonight.

Then would she be a wolf from this day forward? Had her human life ended? Were the other wolves in the area once people, too?

Perhaps there was such a thing as a werewolf—and she was one of them.

Something new in the air caught her attention. Yes, there it was.

She could smell him.

Someone pursued her. She'd scented him earlier, just after she'd killed that couple. She'd run as fast as she could, but he was still behind her. His masculine scent was very different from the people she'd just killed. It wasn't just a different scent; it was a different *type* of scent.

He didn't smell human. Didn't smell like an animal, either. She didn't know what he was, but he was strong and fast.

The distance she'd wrought between them had diminished. His unusual masculine scent permeated her nostrils as if he were only a breath away.

Desperately, she sought to be home, back in her familiar surroundings, away from this madness and the hunter, if that was possible. Tired and frightened, she knew she had to keep going or he would find her, and what then? What were his intentions? She asked the question as if she needed an answer, but she didn't. Instinctively, she knew he meant to harm her. He wanted her life.

Why? Did he know what she'd done?

She headed for home. There was really no place else to go. If Death intended to take her tonight, then she at least wanted to be in a place of comfort, among things she loved.

In the dead of night, the old bridge was deserted and she crossed it without incident, but home was still two miles away. She stayed off the main road, within the protection of the trees, and hoped the hunter would lose her scent before she reached home. When she could, she doused her scent in the small backyard creeks. Darting in and out of private property, she tried to lose him, but the hunter's pursuit never faltered. Who was he, that he could track her with such tenacity? Such accuracy?

Oh, dear God.

She skidded to a halt.

She was cornered.

Shit!

Her neighbor to the north kept several cars in the back yard. She'd gotten confused, tired, and had somehow gotten herself in between the old rusted cars and a huge firewood pile. It was a mistake, and now she would pay for it with her life. She paced frantically. There had to be a way out.

A tall, masculine frame appeared, silhouetted by a porch light on the house, several yards away. This was the hunter who'd pursued her for miles. She knew him by his scent. Rich and spicy, it drew her attention. Captivated her. It was different from that of the humans. Tangy. *He* was different. And ultimately a thousand times more lethal.

His long, dark hair hung past wide shoulders. Muscles strained and rippled beneath a flannel shirt and faded denim jeans. Huge and deadly.

She backed into the corner. *Oh, no . . .*

The hunter stood before her and drew a double-edged dagger from his coat pocket—a blade meant for her.

God, there had to be a way out. She had no intention of hanging around to find out what those blades felt like. She would not die like this. Not like this: hunted, desperate, waiting for the end. No, she wouldn't go down without a fight. Mackenzie was no one's victim. Not now, not ever.

The hunter charged her. She flung herself upward and over the cars with preternatural speed, landing with a soft thud on the other side of the cars, away from the hunter. Her claws dug into the soft dirt and grass, propelled her closer to home. To sanctuary.

Almost there.

Her own porch light called to her, made her dizzy with hope of actually surviving the hunter's advance. Her legs were strong and agile. Fast. She should be able to outrun him. And yet, she knew he was gaining on her again. No matter how fast she ran, it wasn't enough. His scent still assaulted her and, in the distance, she heard his boot heels clash against grass and dirt. He was closing the gap at a terrifying speed.

Now another scent on the breeze told her someone else approached.

Another hunter?

Sudden, intense pain in her thigh threw her balance off. She tumbled down to the grass, skidding several feet from the velocity of the impact.

A white arrow protruded from her thigh, a slow, thick stain of blood forming around it. Seconds later, her body became heavy and lethargic.

There had to have been something on the tip of the arrow, some kind of drug. She couldn't move. Her muscles simply would not cooperate with her demands, no matter how much she struggled. There was no chance to escape the hunter now.

It was over.

Two men appeared at her side. The taller one carried the double-edged dagger, and now knelt behind her.

Mackenzie shivered. *I'm so afraid. If you must do this, please have mercy and make it quick.* She threw the thought out with every bit of mental energy she had. *Just be quick.*

He lifted her chin, pressed the blade to her throat.

"Griffin, wait." The other man knelt down. "I know that voice." He laid a hand on her shoulder, and at once she felt heat through her entire body, as if his touch sparked something within her. Something deep and primal. Elemental.

"Who is it?" Griffin lowered the blade from her throat.

"I tracked a wolf to this woman's home last night. She is . . ." He stood abruptly. "God, I can't believe this."

"What? Christopher, who is she?"

"She's the One, Griffin. I can feel it."

Griffin stood. "How can that be? She's a wolf. I don't think you can take a wolf as your benekeda."

"Not a wolf, no, but maybe the curse can be lifted. I know she's the one the Priestess spoke of. I know it in my heart."

"You're serious, aren't you?" Griffin looked at her.

Christopher pushed both hands through his hair. "I wasn't sure last night. I thought . . . I don't know what I thought, but I felt her lifeforce moving through me when I touched her. She is the One, and I have to find a way to change her." Christopher crouched beside her again, then looked back at Griffin. "I need to find out if she can be changed. Tell me you'll protect her if I'm not around. Give me your word that no one will harm her."

"Absolutely not. I'm not protecting a demon wolf. I'll give

you one day to change this. After that, she's mine. And I assure you, I'll have no problem cutting her throat, benekeda or not. You'll just have to find another one." Griffin sheathed his blade.

Christopher's gaze shot to Griffin's. "You'll have to cut mine first. It took me two hundred years to find her."

Griffin's head shook as he turned to head back to the shadows. "Consider yourself lucky, then. I'm almost a thousand years old."

"Then you'll understand more than most why I won't allow you kill her. I mean it, Griffin. Don't you touch her. Not now, not ever."

Griffin waved dismissively. "Take care of the problem, Little One, and I won't have to touch her. But, hesitate and I'll solve the problem for you."

Christopher's eyes flashed. Were they blue or green? She wished she could see the color. Either way, she knew they were incredible. Like captured daylight. Like a dream . . .

"Get the hell out of my sight. I'd be doing everyone a favor if I took you out right now."

Griffin's eyes, seemingly devoid of color, narrowed on his friend. "I am still your superior officer, Christopher. You will *not* disregard our laws. Not even for her."

Christopher's lips curled in disgust. "For now . . ."

"We'll see," his friend replied. "I'll be watching. Don't make the mistake of thinking you're above our laws." Griffin turned and headed for the darkness of the forest.

"Whatever, asshole." Christopher turned to her, his light eyes warming as he scanned her body. "You won't be able to move for a while yet. Let me tend your wound. I should have our sendagi—our healer—do it, but I think I can manage. I've done this before." He brushed her fur and smiled. "I didn't think I'd ever find you. Tell me your name."

* * * * *

Mackenzie awoke in her own bed. The late afternoon sun told her she'd slept most of the day. Again. It was long past time to get up, but when she tried to sit, sudden pain shot through her right leg. She spat out several curses in protest. Lifting the covers, she found the remains of an angry wound just below her bare hip. She whispered two fingers across it, studying it while she struggled to remember what had happened.

Her foggy brain was slow to bring last night back into focus, but a moment later she recalled the violence, the hunt.

The blade at her throat.

Nausea roiled in her stomach. Bile rose in her throat. Mackenzie covered her mouth and threw the blankets off her legs. She slid off the bed and immediately tumbled to the floor, pain ripping from her leg to her hip. Clutching her thigh, she crawled along the floor toward the bathroom. Her entire stomach threatened to turn itself inside out long before she reached her destination.

Clenching her jaw until it hurt, she forced her body's compliance long enough to grasp the wastebasket in the bathroom and lean over it, just as she lost control and heaved the contents of her stomach.

A moment later, she cringed at the bloody evidence of her first night as a wolf.

It was true then. She wiped her mouth with the back of her hand.

She didn't need a confirmation, but there it was anyway. Haunted by the knowledge that a man had died because of her, she relived what she'd done to his body. The need to take what she needed had overwhelmed her. Desire had consumed her. She'd been so hungry. It had been horrible.

But it wasn't *just* a man she'd killed.

God, it was Daniel.

And there were two more, strangers she'd never seen before. Her need to feed upon them had been unbearable, uncontrollable. For her, as well as the victims, there had been no choice.

But now who could she turn to for help? She didn't ask for this, didn't want to have taken their lives, yet that's what had happened. Who would console the killer now? Would anyone care that the half-human/half-animal was distraught from the memory of what she had done? Somehow, she didn't think it would matter to a single person, except one. Maybe.

And she'd just killed him.

She remembered being cornered and panicked. She'd searched for a way to escape the double-edged dagger that waited for her. The one named Griffin had pressed the blade to her throat after she'd been shot and drugged with an arrow. Christopher had shot her. Then he'd said she was *the one*. One what?

The one who had killed all those people in cold blood.

Griffin had allowed her to live, and Christopher had removed the arrow. She'd whimpered in pain, but he'd soothed her, stroked her fur, and spoken softly in a language she didn't understand. She'd been so afraid then. His strong hands upon her body had comforted her, if only a little. She'd spoken to him in her mind, asked for his compassion as she'd bled, and he'd understood what she'd said. He'd whispered such soft, sweet words. No, he wouldn't destroy her now, and he wouldn't let Griffin near her.

She belonged to him. She was his mate and he would love her forever.

Moments later, he'd carried her home and put her to bed.

That was real?

The contents of the wastebasket said it was.

The fact that she was completely naked suggested it was real, too. Mackenzie never slept in the nude.

She needed a shower.

Something normal.

She turned on the water and stepped into the shower. Under a spray hot enough to turn her skin pink, she welcomed the sting as if it were an old friend. After what had happened last night, she deserved nothing less and, in fact, deserved much worse. Her heart sank with the terrible guilt that she'd killed Daniel and fed from his torn body.

Daniel, for God's sake. What kind of monster does something like that to a loved one?

As the tears fell, she raised her head to allow the force of the water to wash them from her face. Daniel's death tore at her conscience; it was too much to handle. She sank down against the shower wall, head in hands, and sobbed uncontrollably. Whatever it took, it didn't matter, she needed the pain, the memory to just go away. She sobbed until the water turned cold and she shivered. Then she turned the water off and rose from the floor, hand on her thigh again.

The wound felt better now that she'd pelted it with hot water.

She numbly dried herself and dragged on an old pair of jeans and a faded T-shirt.

Downstairs, she found her robe on the living room floor. It had been ripped in several places—shredded, even. Her torn clothes were strewn about the floor, but she couldn't remember exactly how it had happened. All she remembered was the searing, exploding pain and then a need: a demand for blood.

She'd scented sweet, hot blood and found her boyfriend frozen against the wall.

Where was his body?

"Daniel," she whispered, new tears forming in her eyes. "I'm so sorry."

The screen door creaked and slammed shut. "Kenz? Where are you?"

"In the living room." She wiped her face as fast as she could. Sean didn't need to know about this yet. Or ever.

Sean rushed in from the kitchen. "I've been calling since yesterday. Where have you been?" The condition of the room caught his attention right away. He inspected the bloodied furniture and torn clothing with increased alarm in his blue eyes. "What the hell happened?"

How would she explain this?

Uncertain about how much to divulge, she sat down on the coffee table to compose her thoughts. "I don't even know where to begin." She looked up into his face. "You have to promise to listen to what I say, before you decide I need to be committed. Will you do that?"

"Kenz, you're scaring me. Tell me what's going on." Sean sat down on the floor at her feet, his blue eyes wide with concern and fear.

"Do you remember when the wolf attacked me?" She rubbed her left shoulder.

He nodded. "Yeah, I think I busted some bones when I cracked that thing with a bat."

"It did something to me." She was afraid to continue, certain he'd think she was crazy.

"What?" His brow furrowed.

When it came right down to it, she couldn't bear to tell him the truth. "I blacked out—for a long time. When I woke up, this." She pointed at the blood on the couch.

"What does that have to do with the wolf?"

"I don't know, but look at my shoulder." She peeled her T-shirt aside to reveal a smooth shoulder. No scar, no scab, as if it had never happened.

"It's totally healed," he said. "How is that possible?"

"I don't know that either." She leaned over to turn on a light. The sun was almost down. "I can't begin to tell you what happened here. I don't know whose blood this is." The lie continued. He would have her committed, being wholly unable to believe she'd physically become a wolf and killed three people. She could hardly believe it herself. Why would he?

Her skin started to tingle again.

Oh, God.

She knew this feeling. Soon, she'd be on the floor in tears. The pain would rip out her insides and change her body from human to something else. Something awful. Again.

Would this happen every night? There was no moon again, which meant she wasn't a werewolf. What was she, then?

The sun had just dipped below the horizon.

She had to get Sean out of the house. If she became a wolf again, his life was over, just as Daniel's had been. *Damn it.*

"Sean, I have some errands to run. Do you mind if I catch up with you later?"

"I'll go with you. I don't have anything going on," he said, shrugging.

She was frightened now, and unsure of how much time she had left. Sean had to be far away by the time the animal instincts were in control, or his life would be in danger. "Maybe tonight isn't the best time to hang out. I'm really not feeling well." That much was true.

Please don't let it happen again. Please, please . . .

Sean stood up and grasped her shoulders too tight. He was nervous. "Kenz, what's going on? You're acting strange."

Mackenzie tried to push him away. "Nothing. I, um, just don't feel well." Her lies sounded weak, even to her own ears.

How could she possibly expect her own brother to buy into what she said? "I'll be in the bathroom," she said quickly. The pain began in earnest now. It wouldn't be very long before her body altered from human to animal. Perhaps, if nothing else, the wolf could be contained inside the bathroom, at least until Sean left. "Don't wait for me," she said, swiping at the sudden explosion of perspiration on her brow.

The screen door slammed again. Both Mackenzie and Sean turned to the tall, heavily-muscled man that filled the entry way to the living room.

Mackenzie sat down hard on the coffee table. His sky-blue gaze captivated her when it found her, wide-eyed and amazed. How intense, those eyes. She couldn't pull her own gaze away from him. "You. I remember you. What are you doing here?"

Christopher turned to Sean. "You need to leave." His voice was soft, low, hypnotic.

Sean scrambled to his feet. "Like hell I do. Who is this guy, Kenz?"

"Sean, I . . . I can't explain now. It's too complicated. Please do as he says and leave. Really. Trust me on this, please." The pain had spread now to every part of her body. She wrapped her arms around her stomach, as if that might keep her insides from exploding.

As if anything would.

Christopher stepped into the living room, then leaned casually against the wall. "You were attacked by a wolf a few days ago. After that, your hearing changed, as did your night vision. The third night, you survived your first transformation into a demon wolf. And then you killed people you loved. You'll transform like this, every night, from now until the end of time. And you'll take lives, just like you did last night."

Oh, God. He knew. What did he say she was? Demon wolf?

What the hell was that?

Sean glared at Christopher. "Exactly what are you accusing my sister of?"

Christopher's gaze shot back to her. "I'm not surprised you didn't tell him. Eventually, you'll have to, you know. Can't keep the secret forever, Mackenzie."

Sean stepped in front of Mackenzie, arms folded across his chest. "In case you're too stupid to figure it out, you're trespassing on private property. Get the hell out of here *now*, or I'm calling the cops."

Christopher's gaze slid over to Sean. "Back off, big brother. This doesn't concern you."

"The hell it doesn't." Sean's body shook with fury. "You're not coming near her. Try, and I swear I'll kill you."

Mackenzie rested one hand against Sean's shoulder. "Now is *not* the time to play hero, Sean. I need you to leave. Please, *please,* do as I ask. I don't think Christopher is here to hurt us."

He shrugged her hand off and acted as if he hadn't heard her at all. "Get out of this house. Last warning."

Christopher smiled and reached into his breast pocket to pull out a toothpick. He stuck it in between his teeth, then rolled it to the side of his mouth. "Is that right?"

The dead calm on his face made Mackenzie take a step back. "I don't think this is a good idea, Sean."

And then the next wave of pain hit. She doubled over, fists in tight balls pressed against her stomach, and when the pain ripped through her, she screamed, dropping to the floor. Her knees shot up to her chest.

Sean crouched beside her. "What's wrong? Kenz? What's wrong? Tell me."

Christopher moved with lightning speed, picking Sean up by the arms and pinning him to the wall. His feet didn't touch the floor. "Your sister needs help. I need you out of my way. If you fail to do so, I will make you go to sleep. Do you understand? If you think I can't do it, just try me. If you think your sister isn't in serious trouble, go look in her wastebasket upstairs."

"No!" Mackenzie cried, reaching blindly for Sean. "Don't . . ."

Sean's wide eyes darted from the cold, blue gaze to Mackenzie, in tears on the floor with her arms wrapped around her stomach. "Don't hurt her."

Christopher shook his head. "I won't." He let go of Sean and stepped back. "Believe it or not, I'm here to help."

Sean landed on his feet with a soft grunt.

Christopher spun on his heel and bent to scoop Mackenzie up in his arms. Taking long strides, he carried her upstairs to the bedroom with Sean only two steps behind. He laid her gently on the bed, then turned to her brother. "You stay out." He pressed a hand to Sean's chest and gave him enough of a shove to send him out to the hallway. The door slammed in his shocked face.

Immediately, Sean pounded on the door, shouted curse-filled demands to be let back in. Christopher threw a quick, seemingly annoyed glance towards the door. The pounding stopped and seconds later, a soft moan and a thud against the door suggested Sean had indeed been sent to sleep.

"You didn't hurt my brother, did you?" she asked, her voice barely a whisper.

"Not really. He might have a bit of a bump on his head from hitting the door, but that's all."

"And what of me?" The weakness in her voice drove her crazy, but she was helpless to change it. The pain stole her breath.

He sat on the bed beside her. "I'm not going to hurt you,

either. But, I need you to trust me with no questions, just yet. I can stop the transformation for tonight only and give you some time to sort things out."

Mackenzie frowned. "Why can't I ask any questions?"

Christopher brushed a strand of hair from her forehead. "You can, just not right now. Do you understand what I told you about the demon wolf?"

"Yes, I just don't understand why."

He shrugged. "There is no why. The wolf wanted to bite, and you were there. It's that simple. Most of the time, it's the males who bite. Maybe he found you incredibly beautiful and thought he'd make you part of his world. I don't know. It doesn't really matter now, does it? You have to live with what he's done. That's why I'm here."

She realized what he was saying. "You hunt them. You were hunting me."

"Yes. Tonight, I'm here to stop the wolf from claiming your body."

He took a small ceramic pot from his coat pocket and set it down on the nightstand. From the other pocket he produced a small bag of silver-tipped leaves, which he crumbled into the tiny pot. While he shook his coat off and tossed it onto the chair, the leaves in the small pot smoldered, seemingly on their own. The spicy scent wafted into the room and was somehow soothing. "Will you allow me to do this for you?"

Mackenzie wiped her tears away. She was certain her body would explode at any moment now, even though she held her muscles tightly clenched. It exhausted her, mentally as well as physically. "Yes. Please, make it go away."

Chapter Three

"What's your brother's name?" Christopher rolled up the shirtsleeves of his white cotton shirt. Muscles rippled beneath the unusual golden skin. Gorgeous skin.

"Sean," she answered. The pain was unbearable. Mackenzie's muscles were so tight, it only added to the pain, but she was afraid to let go. Not much time left. "What are you going to do?"

Christopher shook his head. "Don't worry about that for now." His blue eyes met hers and his features softened. He touched her face with two fingers. "Sean will sleep while you and I talk. He'll be fine, as will you. Now, I want you to follow my instructions without question. When it's done, I'll tell you what you need to know. Do you understand?"

She sighed and sank back into the pillows. "Yeah . . ." *Hurry . . .*

"Good. Roll onto your back." Christopher smiled. His face seemed young and old at the same time. It was in the eyes, she decided. While his golden skin was smooth and youthful-looking, his eyes told her he'd seen many things.

Mackenzie quietly obeyed. It would be only moments—seconds maybe—before the inner wolf exploded and everything inside her broke and shifted.

He straightened. "I'll need to touch you to stop the transformation. Close your eyes now. No questions."

She nodded her consent as her eyelids drifted down. Whatever burned in that little pot, she liked it. The scent was spicy and sweet at the same time, a combination that soothed her nerves and gave her a much-needed respite from the fear and pain of the transformation. "Is that incense you're burning?"

"No, it's Livendium," he answered. "An herb we grow. Do you like it?"

"It's nice. Very soothing." She inhaled again.

"I'm glad you like it. Relax for me. This won't take very long."

Mackenzie's muscles tightened again. She didn't know what to expect and wasn't entirely comfortable trusting a stranger. She did know Christopher was very strong, a hunter of wolves. He seemed so sure of every move, every word, and knew what she'd become.

And was not afraid.

But what did that tell her? Nothing, really.

Part of her wanted him closer. Part of her wanted to run. The wolf inside her knew he was a dangerous man. In every way.

Christopher leaned over her. The mattress sank near her head where his hands supported his large frame. His scent was wild and masculine, sweet and seductive to her senses. She remembered that smell from last night, when he and the one called Griffin had hunted her.

His dark brown hair brushed her face. His breath, hot against her neck, was shallow and rapid, just like hers. As if he sought to calm her, his lips caressed the skin of her neck and shoulder in a pattern so slow and gentle, she couldn't do anything but surrender.

"Don't be afraid," he whispered.

But she was afraid. Exactly who was this sorcerer with the icy-blue eyes? How could anyone have so much sexual power that the mere press of his skin upon hers ignited her body and transformed it into a living pyre?

No one had ever done that before.

The warmth of his body so close to hers brought to mind images of passionate kisses, the scent of damp skin, and long nights spent making love. Her pulse raced with his words. Even her own newly-ignited fire surprised her with its intensity. Wholly unprepared for the power of her arousal, she squeezed her eyes shut. She braced herself against the hard wall of his chest, not to push him away, but to ground herself. She was terrified of her own thoughts and feelings. All she could think of was how perfect his body would feel upon hers, how right and amazing he would fit inside her. Treacherous thoughts.

His mouth found her pulse. "No fear, Mackenzie."

Her breath caught in her throat, and muscles clenched as sharp teeth pierced her neck. The contravention of skin and veins unsettled her. This was not what she thought he might do to stop the wolf.

When his mouth began to pull blood from her body, it left her both revolted and sickened. What kind of man would do such a thing? What was he? Some kind of vampire?

Eskarian. His voice whispered seductively inside her head.

His voice? How did she know it was his voice and, more importantly, how could she possibly hear someone else's voice inside her head? What Eskarian might be was not something she cared to consider just yet. Later. Maybe. "Don't take it all," she heard herself whisper.

I have to. That's how I'll stop the transformation. There it was again, that magical voice inside her head. Pure and clear. She heard it as easily as if he'd spoken aloud.

"How do you talk inside my head?" she asked softly.

Sleep, Beautiful. I'll take care of you. He continued to siphon the blood from her body.

Nausea and exhaustion washed over her. It seemed he was taking too much. She had no choice but to sleep now, even if for just a little while.

Eventually, his warm mouth left her skin. How much time had passed?

Her mind drifted away from the soft voice that whispered in a language she didn't understand. Didn't care what he said, though his voice—ah, his voice was a mesmerizing beacon that pulled her, called her back from the deep, black ocean that teased her with promises of relief.

Dizziness washed over her. Was she spinning? Maybe it was just the room that spun. She could've spun away for all it mattered to her now, but the sound of his voice kept her at his side.

Water slowly dripped beside her head. The sound of a single drop became the sound of a thousand drops, like rain all around her. Her body felt lighter. Was she floating? Warmth surrounded her, enclosed her inside a safe cocoon. She didn't know what was happening, but it felt all right.

And then, finally, there was no pain.

No fear.

No emotion.

Nothing.

"Mackenzie."

Christopher's voice startled her. She didn't know where she was, but sensed that he stood nearby. Her breathing was slow, shallow, her heartbeat weak and irregular. She was dying. She felt herself drift away and didn't care.

Better this than taking lives. Better that this demon pass quietly into the blackness than tear her body to pieces night after night.

"Open your mouth." Christopher spoke gently, as if addressing a child. "You're not going to die tonight.

Relax, Mackenzie. It's all right."

Was it? How would she know? Her lips parted just enough that a small amount of liquid could be poured into her mouth. She moaned softly as it burned her tongue and throat.

Hot.

"Swallow."

She obeyed, lacking the will to do anything else.

"This is my blood. It will keep you alive until you regain your strength."

Mackenzie swallowed more hot, sizzling liquid.

Blood.

Hurts, she thought. *Hot.* Why was blood burning her mouth?

He leaned closer. "Our blood is very hot and tends to do that to humans," he said, pausing. "It's normal. Rest now. You'll be fine in a few minutes. There'll be no transformation tonight."

Mackenzie's eyelids fluttered. Her head turned toward him, but her eyes didn't open. A drop of blood trickled from the corner of her mouth. She felt it, but still didn't care.

Christopher was still speaking to her again in that strange language she couldn't identify. She listened to it, felt his breath against her cheek and lips.

She became aware of wolves. The spirits of several surrounded her. She could even see them in her mind. Some were black and others gray. Tall, short. There were so many. They sang to her in rich, sweet tones, a welcome reprieve from the terror of this night.

Their song drew her to them. She thought she should go to them, and yet she didn't, couldn't. A moment later, even the wolves were far away. They were leaving her.

Wait for me, she called in her mind, but they continued to run. Did they not hear her?

Yes, they heard. It was not her path to follow them. Not tonight. Christopher had seen to that. He'd taken her pain and replaced it with a dream.

Thank you for saving me, she thought.

"You're welcome," he said softly against her lips.

Her brother's voice filtered through the fading reverie, curled around her; a comfort when so much seemed strange and frightening. She bade the wolves farewell with an unexpected tinge of sorrow that her place was not with them, then opened her eyes.

The bedroom door was open, and Christopher stood in the doorway, his back to her. As if to impede Sean's entry, Christopher's muscular body filled it. His fingers casually curled over the top the doorframe, the thumb of his left hand tapping against the wood. The lazy tilt of his hips suggested he was at ease, but Mackenzie suspected that under his relaxed posture lay a fierce protector. Yes, that's what he was. Fierce. Dangerous.

Christopher leaned forward. "I need a little more time with her. Do you think you can behave while we talk, or should I send you back to sleep now?"

"No, don't send me back to sleep. I'll wait." Sean took a step back.

Mackenzie rolled onto her side. "I need to see my brother," she said softly. Her voice sounded weak. She cleared her throat. "Let him in."

Christopher stepped aside to allow Sean to pass. His gaze followed her brother as a predator might watch prey. Very dangerous.

Sean crouched on the floor beside her. He took her hand in his and held it to his chest. "How are you feeling?"

Her gaze moved from her brother to Christopher, who leaned against the wall behind Sean, hands stuffed into the pockets of his jeans. She allowed her gaze to rest on him a moment. His tousled, collar-length hair framed his face, while long bangs hung over his blue eyes. Even though he'd just taken her blood, she thought he had a kind face. A sexy, handsome face.

He grinned. He'd heard her thoughts again. *Yes, I did hear you. I like listening to you.*

Damn.

Her cheeks got very hot. Busted.

Still, she liked the way he filled out his cotton shirt. Long legs completed a very nice package. For a vampire, anyway.

"Kenz?"

She had too many questions about all that had happened. And he himself raised a completely different set of questions, ones she wasn't sure she had the courage to ask.

"I'm okay." Her attention returned to Sean. "What happened? How long have I been asleep?"

"Only about a half-hour. I've been sleeping myself, evidently. He told me he took a lot of your blood and gave you a little of his own, which is really bizarre in and of itself, but he did it to save you, not hurt you, or so he says. Supposedly, there's a hunter coming after you, whatever that means. Why would a hunter be after you? Does this have anything to do with the blood all over the couch?"

Mackenzie thought about that. "That would be Griffin, I guess. Yeah, it does."

"Whose blood is it? Amy's? And who's Griffin?" Sean sounded tense again. He was the consummate big brother, often looking out for her.

"No, not Amy's." How could she tell him the blood on the couch was Daniel's? She still wasn't convinced that she wouldn't end up in the mental hospital. And then what? "Griffin is Christopher's friend, I suppose. Or maybe he's a co-worker. I don't know what they are." That was true enough. She really *didn't* know what they were.

"And what's this about you being a demon wolf? What the hell is that?"

Mackenzie shrugged one shoulder. "It's a nightmare. I don't understand it myself, but this Christopher seems to understand it quite well."

"Tell me what's been going on, Kenz. This is scaring me. What I'm seeing here is all really bizarre." Sean glanced back at Christopher.

"Ask him," she said, waving a hand dismissively. "He knows more than I do, anyway." Mackenzie would love to hear the explanation as well. One that made sense this time.

"I don't want to talk to him. I don't like him." He leaned close to Mackenzie. "Everything about him is weird and, honestly, Kenz, I really don't want him near you. God only knows what he could do. He's not right, that one."

"He already took my blood. If he was going to hurt me, I think he would have already done so. It appears neither you or I can stop him from doing whatever he wants, anyway, so I'm not certain there's any point in worrying about it." Whispering two fingers over the place where he'd taken her blood, she felt the residual welts. They'd healed already. "He's got some teeth, that's for sure." She shook away the thought. "Whatever. I can't think about vampires with all this wolf stuff going on."

Christopher leaned to the side. "I'm an Eskarian, not a vampire. There's no such thing as vampires."

Mackenzie looked at Christopher, but her focus was on her brother. "Sean, I need to talk to him. Things have happened to me—things that really scare me. Can you give me some time with him now? Please?" Her gaze found Sean's face again, and she smiled. She wanted to reassure him, even though she herself was uncertain. Exactly what was Eskarian?

"I don't know." Sean threw a glance back at the tall Eskarian who leaned casually against the wall. "I *really* don't like him. I'd prefer that he just got out of the house and out of our lives."

"I'd like that, too." She propped herself up on an elbow. "The thing is, Sean, my life *has* already changed in ways I don't understand. *He* does. I need to find out what's happened to me, and I can't have you in here doing your macho thing. Please, just give me a few minutes. I swear to you, I need this. I'll be fine. I don't believe he wants to hurt me."

"Fine. I guess. I'll be just outside the door, if you need me. If I hear anything out of the ordinary, I swear I'll bust that door down and take a bat to that guy's head."

"Fair enough. Let's hope it doesn't come to that." She brushed his light brown hair, then touched his shoulder. "Thank you. And thanks for wanting to protect me."

Sean straightened. "Always, Kenz." He strode to the doorway where Christopher still leaned against the wall. "I'll come after you, if you hurt her."

Christopher nodded. "I know."

Mackenzie sighed. "Sean, please . . ."

Sean glared at him a moment, then stormed out of the room. Christopher was a little taller and a lot more muscular. It wouldn't have been much of a contest between the two, and she didn't want her brother hurt.

Christopher closed the door and knelt before her. His elbow rested on his knee. He fished a single toothpick from his shirt pocket and popped it into his mouth. Somehow he always looked comfortable, relaxed. His movements were graceful, feline, like a large panther. "How are you feeling now? Can you sit up?"

"I'm okay, I guess. Tired." She sat up a little, then leaned back against the pillows. "Listen, there's one thing I need to know. What happened to Daniel's body?"

"I destroyed all the bodies last night after you fed, so no one would ever find them. Part of what we do is clean up after the wolves. It's best to keep them as much of a secret from humans as possible. Everything we do, really, is kept from the human world. Each year, people just disappear, without a trace. For some, this is the reason they've disappeared." He paused. "Others face even worse threats. You see, there's always something out there, and it's always deadly. That's why I'm here. I get rid of the threat as best I can."

He looked away. Light from a nearby lamp caught in his eyes, which made them suddenly shimmer with their own light. She studied them and realized there were light blue rings around the edges of his irises, something she'd never seen before.

Light rings around his eyes? Eskarian? From the planet Eskaria?

"Now, let me tell you about the demon wolf. It's been around for many thousands of years, but a few years ago, a new strain emerged. This one is really a cursed creature: human by day, wolf by night, and all it does is feed on the human body. It serves no other purpose. And of course, it propagates by infecting other people with its saliva. The incubation process takes three days, as you well know." The shimmer in his eyes faded when he turned from the lamp. "We began tracking you last night after you killed that couple. Like I said, that's what I do—get rid of problems."

She swallowed the lump in her throat. "Yes, you and Griffin were hunting me. I remember that."

"Yes." His gaze lowered.

"And Griffin was going to cut my throat."

"He was, yes." Christopher shifted a little, as if he were

uncomfortable. He laid his hand on her forearm. Long fingers traced gentle circles on her skin. She liked his touch. Liked the trails of heat.

"Why did you stop him?"

He looked at his hand. "Do you feel that heat?"

Mackenzie glanced down at his hand then back up again. "Yeah, I do. What is that?"

"That's the reason you're here." He shrugged.

"Hmm . . ." She nodded, uncertain about what she should do with that. "Then you said the priestess told you I was the one. One what?"

He shook his head. "It'd be better if I didn't answer that. Not right now."

Her brow furrowed. "Why not?"

"For the moment, it's not really important."

"Okay. But you stopped the transformation to give me time. For what?" Pulling the quilts over her legs for warmth or comfort—she wasn't sure which—she tried her best to hide the fact that she was afraid. Really afraid.

Once again, she watched his fingers trace the circles on her forearm. Her thoughts drifted back to the moment he'd first touched her, and the heat that had resulted. His touch now heated her skin in a way that made her think of things lovers did behind closed doors. She remembered his body close to hers, remembered how he'd set her on fire. How was that possible? They'd just met and already she felt somehow connected to him through that fire. Made no sense and, honestly, she wasn't sure she thought it was such a good thing.

Her gaze returned to his face. He simply watched her, his blue gaze clouded, a hint of a smile creasing his features.

"Are you all right?" she asked. She didn't know why she'd asked, or if she was even interested in the answer.

"Yeah, I'm fine. I'm glad I found you." He gave her a

warm smile and touched her cheek.

She pulled away. "You almost killed me. Actually, you don't need to touch me so much."

"*Actually,* I do, but I'll wait, for now. You need to understand what happened to you." His gaze dropped to the floor. Sinfully thick black lashes shadowed his sky-blue eyes. "Had you been anyone else, we wouldn't be having this conversation. We would've killed you. Our job is to destroy the wolves, but I chose to break the rules for you. I had to, but I'll explain more about that later. Now, there is an alternative to the curse of the wolf. Admittedly, it may not seem like much of a choice, but it's the best I can offer."

Mackenzie rubbed the back of her neck. This didn't sound good. "Okay, tell me. What's the alternative?"

His blue gaze met hers. "Become like me."

"And what are you?" she asked, raising her eyebrows.

"As I've said, I'm an Eskarian, an immortal. I look human, but I'm not. I was born human a long time ago and, after a nasty accident almost ended my life, Blair gave me a new one." He paused to sit on the bed beside her. "Our people have lived along with yours since the beginning of time, protecting you—humans—from things like demon wolves, and usually much more serious threats. I have done this for almost two hundred years. I am what my people call a Defender."

"A Defender." She nodded. "I see. You're like a monster hunter."

"Well, yeah, I guess you could put it that way." His brow furrowed. "Sort of."

She shrugged. "Okay."

He studied her face. "You don't believe me, do you?"

"I don't know. You talk inside my head and those teeth are pretty sharp. You drank my blood, which is gross, by the way.

But, it did stop me from turning into a wolf again. I don't know. I've never heard of Eskarian. Sure you're not just a vampire wannabe?"

"No, I'm not a vampire wannabe. I'm an Eskarian." Now he sounded irritated with her. "Do you really think I came here to play make-believe? How do you think I stopped you from becoming a wolf?"

Mackenzie couldn't think of a good response. "I don't really know. I can't explain that." Well, maybe he was telling the truth. "Okay, assuming I do this, which is a *huge* assumption, then what becomes of me? I know nothing about you. For all I know, you turn into a pumpkin at midnight. So, tell me. What happens after I become like you?"

He took in a deep breath and seemed to relax a little. "There would be no limitations to what you could do. You become whatever you want."

"I want to be human again." There, she said it. Yes, that was what she wanted. "I want to know that the sun can set and I won't turn into a bloodthirsty wolf who takes the lives of people she loves. Can you do that for me?"

"I can take the wolf away, so no one will hunt you." He tilted his head. "But no one can restore your humanity. You can only go forward from here." Christopher shifted again.

"I don't know. I'm not sure I buy this immortal Eskarian thing." She crossed her arms over her breasts. "I think it would be better for me to stay as I am. At least I know what to expect, and I'm still who I am, essentially. Sean will help me deal with this wolf business, I'm sure. There has to be a way to feed without taking lives."

He shook his head. "There isn't. And you forget—Griffin will be looking for you. He *will* find you, just like I did."

"No, he won't," she insisted. "I'll have myself caged."

He exhaled softly. "I don't think you understand."

Now it was her turn to be irritated. "How hard can it be? I'm a veterinarian, Christopher. My life is all about caring for animals. If I can't figure out how to deal with a wolf, I need to go back to school."

"Demon wolf. They aren't animals. They're vicious, insatiable, immortal killers."

"Fine. Look, I don't know how you did what you did, but I thank you for it. I'll talk to Sean and, together, we'll figure out what to do." She nodded toward the door. "My brother will show you out."

He straightened with all the fluid grace of a large panther. Everything about him, down to the feral glow of his eyes, was feline: movement so liquid and sensual, it almost took her breath away.

"I'm sorry you feel that way." He walked to the door, but stopped two paces away, with his head lowered, as if he were thinking about something. Turning to face her again, he leaned against the wall.

The light caught his eyes again, highlighting the iridescent ring around his irises. Definitely not human. She accepted that much as the truth. Planet Eskaria was still not out of the question.

"Come outside with me," he offered. "Maybe it was foolish of me to ask you to accept so much on faith. Let me show you what I'm talking about."

Her eyebrows shot up. "Forget it. I'm not going anywhere with you."

A smile creased his face. "You sure? There's a whole new world out there. I'd love to show it to you. Is it possible you might like it?"

"Doubt it," she snapped.

"We'll see then, won't we? I might not be as easy to forget as you would like to believe."

She snorted. "You wish."

He departed quietly, but the lazy smile never left his face.

Several minutes passed before Mackenzie moved. She was afraid he might have lingered, and she didn't want to see him again. Ever.

She slid off the bed, padding silently to the bathroom. The mirror reflected what she knew already to be true, but it startled her just the same.

The pale stranger with black hair and soulful green eyes had seen too much, done too much. Taken lives.

Mackenzie touched the healed remains of the punctures Christopher had left on her skin. Her eyes closed. Her fingers traced a slow path from the front of her throat down to the hollow of her neck. The feel of Christopher's mouth and tongue on her skin made her warm, made her wonder what they'd feel like on her body. And after that, how would he feel inside her?

Like heaven.

She shook her reverie aside.

She scowled at her pallid counterpart in the mirror. "What are you thinking? You don't know anything about him. Don't let that pretty face affect your judgment."

She pushed away thoughts of Christopher and his incredible, soft mouth, dragged a comb through her hair, and headed downstairs.

Sean sat at the kitchen table, beer in hand.

"Is he gone?" she asked. She stopped abruptly, her gaze settling on the brown bottle in his hand. "Isn't it a little early for beer?"

He offered a sheepish grin and shrugged. "Yeah, I suppose it is, but I don't care. After what just happened, I deserve it. I need it. Christopher left without a word, thank God. I hope that's the last we see of him."

"Me too." And just like that, her thoughts shot back to the memory of his mouth on her skin, his warm body close to hers. Treacherous thoughts. She shoved them aside.

Absently, she set the tea kettle on the burner. While she waited for it to boil, she leaned against the doorway. Pushing both hands through her hair, she took a deep breath and let it out slowly.

"You okay?" Sean glanced at her while he pulled another beer from the refrigerator.

She nodded. "All things considered, I suppose I am. That *man* just irritates me the more I think about him."

"He ought to play for the Hawks. That's one big guy." He leaned against the counter. "What's a demon wolf, Kenz?"

A nightmare. Christopher had given her one night's reprieve. Mackenzie was grateful for that. "A half-human, half-wolf thing that will live forever and take human lives, or so I'm told."

"And you believe this?"

"Unfortunately, I know some of it is true." She rubbed her forehead. "Look, can we just drop it for a while?"

Sean's hand shot up. "I'm just asking. You don't have to bite my head off."

"I know. I'm sorry." She turned to the stove. The water hadn't gotten hot yet. Her thoughts drifted back to Christopher. Dark brown hair, eyes like liquid daylight. Strong, powerful. Protector. She closed her eyes and realized, to her chagrin, she needed to feel his body close to hers. Yes, she *wanted* his body on hers.

Ah, God.

Horrified, she pushed the thought away, as if it were poison. How could her feelings betray her like that? Daniel hadn't been gone but a day, and she was already thinking of another man.

But not just a man. An *Eskarian.* And she was thinking about what he would feel like inside her.

The water still hadn't gotten hot yet. She looked at the stove controls and realized she hadn't turned it on. "Aw, crap."

Christopher had distracted her completely. She pressed both palms to her forehead. One evening with him and now the man haunted her. This had to stop. "I need some air, Sean. I'll be out back for a bit."

Sean finished his beer and belched. "Don't stay out too long."

"I won't." She stepped over the threshold onto the porch. Her new, distinctly sharper senses immediately gave her information about the night. Leaning against one of the posts, she allowed the cool air to waft over her and listened to the surrounding sounds. The breeze, and the myriad calls of night creatures soothed her frazzled mind and seemed to welcome her as one of them.

Her night vision had changed. Though the colors had dulled, she saw just as well at night as she did during the day.

The breeze sifted through the trees. She felt a part of the night again—a part of the feral world around her. The memory of running as a wolf last night didn't seem quite so bad, now that her need for blood was gone, at least temporarily.

In the distance, she heard the call of a lone wolf.

She scented Sean's blood in the house, beckoning to her, but no, she didn't need to heed its call. Not tonight.

She stepped off the porch and walked out into the yard. With outstretched arms, eyes closed, and her face to the stars, she twirled around and around. She took in the earthy aromas of the soil, plants, and animals, and felt one with it all. At peace, as if she belonged, not as a human, an observer, but as one who truly lived as part of this secret world. The night spoke to her of need, then of blood.

Blood.

Licking her lips, she remembered the sweet, hot stickiness of blood and shivered. She'd last tasted it a little more than an hour ago and *liked it.*

A small raccoon scurried by, jolting her back to the moment.

Sating her need for blood brought death to others. Would she kill again tomorrow night? Christopher had said she would. The wolf would return then, but she was hopeful Sean would help her contain the beast. He had to help.

Mackenzie touched her lips with her fingers. Sean just *had* to help.

This was to be her life for all eternity then. Uncertainty washed over her, brought tears to her eyes. She really had no idea how she would keep the beast from taking lives. And what if Sean *didn't* understand? What if she revolted him? What if he refused to help?

What if Griffin found her?

Mackenzie no longer wanted to be outside, for the night now seemed more like an enemy: the bringer of change, of death.

She started toward the back deck, but stopped abruptly, breath caught in her throat.

Only a few feet away, a wolf stood with glistening black fur and gleaming eyes focused on her. This was the first time she was able to get a good look at one.

Terrible.

She took a step back. Would it attack, knowing they were one and the same? Surely not.

My sister, I am truly sorry. Your blood calls to me and I must answer. I cannot stop it anymore than I can stop the sun from rising in the morning.

The wolf charged, but she remained perfectly still. She'd never outrun it. She closed her eyes, terrified yet somehow willing to accept the inevitable.

The animal yelped.

She opened her eyes to see the wolf tumble to the ground, a white arrow protruding from its side. She looked around, but saw no one. Didn't matter. She knew a Defender was close. She scented him now. *Christopher.* He'd returned.

Chapter Four

"We always destroy them at night, when the demon is in control." Christopher emerged from the trees and crossed the grass toward the wolf. "They're still intelligent, but not able to fight as well. I use a bow, with arrows dipped in a solution our sendagi created. It doesn't kill them, as you know. It just slows them down." In one hand, he held a large, wooden bow. The carvings, which appeared to have been ornate at one time, ran down the length of the fine, heavily grained wood. It looked well cared for, with its satiny gloss and soft leather-wrapped grip.

In his other hand was a long, double-edged dagger with engravings along the edges of the blade. Like Griffin's dagger, though this one seemed a little smaller. She was certain it was just as sharp.

"And then I finish with this." He held up the dagger for her inspection. "This is the fate of every wolf, Mackenzie. Look on it well and see your future."

Standing behind the panting creature, he quickly punctured its neck, severed the head from the body, and tossed it aside. "This is always the outcome. Always. Otherwise, it will come back to life."

"Oh, my God!" Mackenzie cried, utterly horrified. Her stomach flipped over at the sight of the carnage. For a second, she feared she might throw up. How could he? What kind of man was he, exactly?

A cold-blooded killer, that's what. And she'd seen more

than enough to convince her that she wanted no part of him. "I'm out of here."

Christopher was on her in an instant. He clamped strong fingers around her wrist and dragged her closer to his body. "I can't let you leave just yet."

She tried to twist free. "Let go."

His gaze fell to her mouth. "In time," he purred. "When I'm ready. First, I need you to understand something. This wolf would have killed you, Mackenzie. Immortality does not mean invincibility. You can still die. And there's no loyalty among demon wolves." Christopher stepped back from the wolf's carcass. "You saw the bloodlust in its eyes. You know all about that overwhelming thirst. Understand your fate now. See your future. Look at the wolf."

The tone of his voice was low and compelling. Seductive. She did look, and then couldn't look away until the image had burned itself into her memory. And, like Daniel's shocked face, she'd remember the destruction of the wolf forever.

But this was her future?

Unacceptable.

She wrenched her wrist from his grasp, pushed both hands through her hair, and glared at him. "Not my future."

He nodded to the wolf. "It *is* your future, whether you believe it or not."

Before her eyes, it exploded into white-hot flames. She spun around, shielding her eyes with both arms, then stumbled and fell forward onto her knees, away from the sweltering heat and blinding light.

What made the wolf's body explode like that? And how could it burn so fast? Had it been Christopher? What was he that he might be capable of such dark magic?

Exactly what *was* an Eskarian?

In the distance, the screen door slammed. Sean raced toward them, baseball bat in hand. He was furious—she saw it in his eyes. He was ready to battle Christopher.

He skidded to a halt the second he saw the burning carcass. "What the hell is this? Kenz?" He scanned the area and found her still on all fours, in the shadows. "Are you all right?"

Mackenzie could barely hold back the tears. "Sean, please help me . . . Make him go away. I've seen enough . . ." This had become a nightmare and she was trapped inside with an Eskarian demon.

Sean immediately charged, shouting a throaty cry as he raised the bat.

"I don't think so." Christopher waved dismissively. "Goodnight, big brother."

Sean collapsed mid-stride on the grass.

Terror shot through Mackenzie. "Oh, no . . ." She let her head fall into her hands. "Shit . . ." Now what? There was no one to fend off the demon standing before her. No one.

Shit.

Looking at her brother, she could only pray he was all right. "Sean," she whimpered. She stayed on her hands and knees, afraid to move. What good would it have done, anyway? Christopher was so strong and fast, there was no way she'd ever escape. She was trapped. "You are the demon, I think. Not me," she whispered.

Christopher's gaze swung to her. "You know that isn't true. You also know that I speak the truth, don't you?" He twirled the large bow absently, as if unaffected by what had just happened. "Do you understand what I'm saying?"

Heartless. Soulless. Yes, he was definitely a monster and she hated him. How could he murder that poor animal like that? She looked at the wolf's smoldering remains. The carcass had ignited in a flash, then the flames just died, as if extinguished by the wind.

Gone. Just like that.

She had to figure out a way to escape. Wiping the tears away, she pushed off the ground and stepped back. Once. Twice. Was there any possibility of getting away? "How could you do that? It was just a wolf."

"This is what I do." He strode toward her, sheathing his dagger. "And no, it wasn't just a wolf. It was a bloodthirsty killer and you were its next target. Remember standing there, Mackenzie? You knew what was about to happen. Even you thought your life was over. I know what you were thinking." He drew closer.

She took another two steps back. "Don't you touch me, you cold-hearted son of a bitch."

He ignored her. Instead he set the bow against the house and, grasping her shoulders, guided her back against the side of the house. "Have you forgotten how the bloodlust feels? Has the image of Daniel's face faded from your memory already?"

His words stung bitterly. She leaned against his chest. Of course, she hadn't forgotten. His death would forever be on her hands, his terror-filled eyes forever etched into her mind. "I don't really need to answer that, do I?" She lifted her gaze to his.

He smoothed her hair back with his hand. "No, and I'm sorry I said that. I know it was harsh."

"It wasn't my intent to hurt anyone. I had no control over what I did."

"Neither did the wolf I just killed." He cupped her jaw and swept his thumb across her cheek. "Can you imagine what would happen if these wolves were allowed to live and propagate? I'm sorry, Mackenzie. I know it seems cold, but it has to be this way. They aren't just furry little animals. They're vicious. Relentless. And they're multiplying. They're killing people. Do you want to lose more loved ones?"

Her eyes closed. Daniel. Even she'd taken someone she cared for. "Okay, I see your point." She wanted to hate him, but didn't. Not really. She even wanted to remain angry with him for killing the wolf, but his explanation made sense.

The heat curling in the pit of her body didn't help at all.

"I need you to understand this. Despite their immortality, wolves do not live long." He pulled her closer. Catching her chin with the pads of his fingers, he tilted it upward and whispered his thumb over her lips. "I don't want anything like this to happen to you."

Despite her mind's desire to push him off, her body heated to the boiling point with just that simple touch. "S—Sean and I will find a way around this. Nothing will happen to me."

He shook his head. "I won't always be here to protect you. Be assured, Griffin *will* find you. Even if he goes back to the East Coast, another Defender will come. A Defender will always come. You can't remain a wolf and hope to survive. It simply doesn't work that way."

"Sean will build a cage for me, and I'll stay in it every night. I don't want to take anyone's life. I couldn't live with myself if I did. Don't you see that?" Somehow she knew she was pleading for her life, and was about to lose.

His sky-blue gaze bored into her, reduced her will to almost nothing. "Sean won't live forever. You will."

"I'll find a way." She just didn't know how. Yet.

"Mackenzie," he whispered. "I can't make an exception, and I won't allow anyone to destroy you." His fingers traced the line of her jaw.

Her heart raced with his touch and her body responded with liquid satin. God, she wanted to run. He frightened her.

The wolf frightened her. Her own feelings terrified her and now as she trembled, she pressed her hands against him and tried to push him away. Tried to get away. "You're touching me too much again. Can't you just let me go?"

"No, I can't." His grip tightened on her shoulders. Fierce blue eyes moved over her face, the hunger in them evident. "Understand what I am," he said, his voice low and hypnotic. "Eskarian. Not human, but not the monster you believe me to be, either. I am warm and alive, for all eternity. I can move without moving, see without seeing." Behind him, a tree exploded and then another followed, igniting quickly in white flames, just like the wolf. "See me, Beautiful. Trust me to take the wolf from you."

"You did that. You set the trees on fire." Her gaze darted from the trees to him, then to her sleeping brother.

"Yes." He leaned into her, pinning her body against the wall.

His erection pushed into her belly. Much as she wanted to ignore that, the fire shrieking through her veins and the wicked desire to feel every inch of that hard body wouldn't allow it.

He bent and whispered in her ear, "No one will come to rescue you. I can promise you that. Tonight, you belong to me."

She shook her head. "I don't want to belong to you and I don't want to be like you. Just leave me and Sean alone."

His gaze roamed over her face again, his eyes hot and hungry, his forehead and cheeks dotted with beads of sweat. "Now, you don't really mean that, do you? Please, Mackenzie, let me help you. I'm almost out of time. You heard what Griffin said. He meant every word. I can't lose you to him or any other Defender."

Mackenzie closed her eyes. "I'm not yours to lose. Get off

my property. Get away from me. Get lost."

"Mackenzie, this—" Christopher's muscles tensed. "Shit," he whispered. He caught her wrist and spun on his heel. "You're early."

The auburn-haired hunter, Griffin, appeared out of nowhere between Christopher and the blackened trees.

Mackenzie gasped. The man just *appeared.* Out of nowhere. Humans didn't do that. Nobody did that.

"So?" Griffin asked, a crooked smile on his face. "The way I see it, you're no closer to converting her than you were yesterday. She wants nothing to do with you. I suggest you let her go and move on. What's another hundred years to an immortal? You'll find another mate." Griffin drew his dagger. The blade caught slivers of starlight and glimmered, a stark reminder that she had no more time.

She remembered that blade. Last night it'd been meant for her, but Christopher had spared her life. Now she feared Griffin would finish the job.

"The wolf is mine," he said. "Step away, Christopher. I don't have all night."

Christopher pushed Mackenzie behind him. "I'm not letting her go and you're not going to touch her. I'll kill you first."

Griffin's eyebrows shot up. "Think so?"

Christopher snatched his bow. In the blink of an eye, he'd stepped forward, drawn an arrow, and nocked it. "Are we going to do this again? I'm ready anytime, asshole. Let's go."

Griffin's silver eyes glittered with amusement. "What do you think one small arrow is going to do, other than piss me off?"

Christopher grinned. "The tips are coated with Sendagi's wolf tranquilizer. I'm guessing it'll work fine on you, but we should find out for sure, don't you think?"

Griffin sheathed his dagger. "You have one more hour. Consider it a favor."

Christopher lowered the bow. "It's not a favor. You showed up too damn early. Go back to whatever festering shit hole you crawled out of, and I'll call you when I'm done."

Griffin peered around Christopher's shoulder. "Mackenzie," he purred. "I'll be back for you." He smiled and, a second later, dissolved into nothing. He was just there and then . . . gone.

Christopher faced her with the bow still in his hand. "*One* hour, Mackenzie. That's it. That's all I have to convince you how serious this is."

Mackenzie was still looking for remnants of Griffin. "Where did he go?"

Christopher took in a deep breath. "We do what's called phase-shifting. It means we split our molecules apart and become nearly invisible. I can still see him, because I know what to look for. I know he's still nearby." Christopher turned and looked behind him. "I'm not giving her up, Griffin. And a little privacy would be really nice. Take off." He faced Mackenzie again and shook his head. At once, his brow furrowed. "Do you understand what I've said? Is there any hope of convincing you what needs to happen, or should I just call Griffin back?"

She shrugged and tried to appear nonchalant. "No, don't call him back. I understand what you've said. I don't really have a choice, do I?"

Christopher set the bow against the wall and took her hands between both of his. "There's always choice. Some choices are just less appealing than others. Will you let me do this for you? For us?"

What? "Us? There is no *us*."

His gaze dropped to her mouth. "You know there is. You

feel the connection, the heat, don't you?"

Mackenzie nodded. "Yeah, I'm burning up. Are you doing some kind of demon magic thing to me?"

"No. We are simply . . . of the same essence. Already bound together, you and I. You have some sense of that, I know."

She closed her eyes. Did she have a sense of it? "Maybe. I'm not sure."

"Will you give me a chance to prove it to you? Please," he whispered, cupping her head between his palms. "I really don't want to lose you."

Mackenzie looked at him again. "I have to admit, you're a hard man to resist."

"Then, don't fight me," he said against her lips. "I have so little time . . ." He covered her mouth with his, enflamed her with a kiss that sent her spiraling out of control. How could a simple kiss do that?

But it wasn't just a kiss. It was his tongue sweeping into her mouth and fitting perfectly, as if it belonged there. It was his teeth, nipping at her bottom lip. Even his hands tunneling into her hair was as it should be.

But the bulge against her belly was the anchor that kept her there.

His mouth whispered across her cheek while he pulled her collar aside and his fingers traced a fiery path along her neck and shoulder. His mouth and tongue then retraced the same path.

She felt her resolve liquefy completely, as if it had never existed.

Slowly his head lifted, his blue eyes finding hers. "Do you see that I can't allow you to remain a wolf? Do you understand that Griffin means to come back and take your life? I can stop him tonight, but what about tomorrow, or the next day?" *What if he comes for you while I'm away?*

A soft whimper escaped her lips. "I don't know."

"No more time." Christopher's arms curled around her shoulders, pulling her tight against his body. He kissed her again. His tongue moved into her mouth, exploring urgently. Her body responded, knees so weak they could no longer hold her. In a single fluid movement, her legs gave out and he followed her down to the grass. His mouth again found her pulse.

"Mackenzie," he whispered against her neck. "I have to do this." His body moved on top of hers. "I have to. No one will hunt you, ever."

He'd said it earlier: he would make her like he was. Eskarian. Immortal. It would remove the curse, but what then? Her pulse shrieked inside her head. She was terrified to know her own life would end and she'd become something else: not human, not wolf, not herself anymore. Eskarian.

"I'm afraid." Her body trembled. Tears from closed eyes streamed along the sides of her face. "I don't know what it means to be Eskarian."

He raised his head to regard her. "It means you'll live forever. Do you understand I'm trying to keep you alive?"

She nodded, her eyes still closed. "I'm still afraid."

"Of what?"

"You. What you're going to do to me. What you do to me. What you are," she breathed.

He lowered his head to kiss her deeply with more passion than she imagined possible, as if her kiss were his very breath. "Don't be. I'm not ending your life. I'm giving you one that's stronger and better. Despite what you think, you would never outrun a Defender. It cannot be done, and I'm telling you now I will not have another Defender coming after you. I've told you what I am. You can feel it. I know you can. Tell me that I can save you now. I have no more time."

Captive now, she couldn't have moved if she wanted to. His words were almost a command. Choices? She had so few and didn't like any of them.

He leaned to her, his mouth so close she could feel the heat of his skin, his breath. The sky-blue eyes glittered even in the cover of night, and pierced through to her very soul. "I know what you're feeling. I know you have neither the strength nor the desire to fight me more than you already have. Your defiance is admirable and I applaud it wholeheartedly, but the time for it has ended. I know you're tired." His voice softened. "Let me finish this now. Give your life to me. I won't hurt you. I couldn't, Mackenzie. You belong at my side, always."

Her eyes closed. Slowly she tilted her head back, fully exposing her throat to him, silently giving her consent to do what he must. God help her.

"Thank you," he whispered. He brushed her cheek with his mouth. His head dipped, and long, sharp teeth pushed into her tender skin.

The pain was terrible. She squeezed her eyes shut and waited for it all to go away. She wished for time to go backward so she could make a different choice and avoid the wolf attack. Wished for Daniel to still be alive. For everything to be like it was.

But no one could do that for her. Moving forward now was her single, crummy choice. She silently hoped the wolf that had bitten her had already met a grisly end at the hands of a Defender. Even more, she hoped Griffin had been the one to do it. Slowly. With a dull blade.

Mackenzie shifted her focus to Christopher. His breath was quick against her neck, and his body, stretched out over hers, was hot. Every time he got close to her, she thought of a dozen erotic things she'd like to do to him. And as fast as those thoughts came to her, she pushed them away. Maybe she was losing her mind. It wasn't like her to think like that. His body wasn't just hot, it was *hot,* and something inside her ignited an inferno of wicked desire to meet that heat. No, not like her at all. It had to be Eskarian magic.

He swallowed her blood in small gulps. It didn't take long for the fatigue and nausea to claim her. Dizziness would soon follow, and then maybe the wolves would return. Maybe this time, she could go with them.

Lifting his head, Christopher spoke softly against her ear. His voice was a mix of hunger and desire, thick with need, rich and low. "I take your blood, your life into myself, Mackenzie Wallace, and in return, give you my blood and my life. Now and for all time, we shall be as one."

What was that? She knew she'd live forever, but what else?

She would be Eskarian.

Immortal . . .

As one . . .

The blackness once again reached for her.

"Mackenzie, drink. For me. For you. I'd lost all hope of ever finding you. You can't imagine the joy I'm feeling right now, but I will share it with you tomorrow and all the tomorrows after that." He raised her head and shoulders, pressed her mouth to the bleeding wound in his neck. "I am yours."

The morning sun pouring into the bedroom warmed her skin. Mackenzie woke slowly, stretched, and inhaled the scents of a new day. At once, she bolted upright. Frantically, she scanned the room to see where she was, and found herself absurdly grateful to be in her own room. How had she gotten there?

She looked beside her. *Uh oh . . .*

Christopher lay beside her above the quilts, sound asleep. The late morning sun washed his skin with warmth and light. His dark brown hair fell in silky strands over his face. Heavy muscles rippled underneath the T-shirt and black jeans as he rolled over onto his side.

She couldn't quite recall the night's events, but despite that, she was curious about him and what he was. Silently, she slid back down under the covers to watch him sleep.

Her fingers lightly traced the length of his arm. She wondered how he could stand the sunlight. And how did he stay so tanned? She thought vampires were supposed to avoid the light.

He stirred, and a moment later, his eyes opened. "I'm not a vampire." He reached for her hand and pressed it to his chest. "I have a heartbeat. See? Good morning," he said with a grin.

"Morning. Are you afraid of crosses or garlic?"

His brow furrowed. "No, of course not."

"What about stakes?" she asked.

"It wouldn't feel very good, but it won't kill me." He propped himself up on his elbow. "Silver bullets won't either."

"Aren't silver bullets for werewolves?"

"No such thing. They don't work on demon wolves, though. Or me. Neither do tranquilizer darts."

"Very funny." His words touched a memory. "I'm not a wolf anymore, am I?" She sat up, facing him.

"No, you're not. You're Eskarian. Like me." He pressed a kiss to the inside of her wrist.

She snatched her hand away. "How did I get here, and why are you in my bed? I don't recall inviting you to sleep with me."

"You didn't. I put you here so I could be sure you were all

right as your body converted to Eskarian. We're not quite the same as humans internally. The process can be unpleasant and takes a bit of time. I wanted to be here in case you needed anything. That's all."

Last night was starting to come back now. "What did you say to me? *Now and for all time*, what?"

"Eskarian men give themselves to their true mates as part of the binding process." He smiled. Evidently he liked the idea.

Her eyebrows shot up. "What does that mean? Are you telling me we're married?"

"Well, no, not really. Eskarians don't marry in the human way. Each of us has a perfect mate, one who was created from the same essence. We know that perfect other half by the heat generated between our bodies, and by the fact that we can sense their lifeforce pretty much anywhere, anytime. They are the ones who are perfect for us, and with whom we remain until one of us dies."

Her gaze narrowed. "What?"

"In a nutshell, you, Mackenzie, are my true mate. I gave myself to you last night."

Her eyebrows shot up again. "What? We're mated? Sounds an awful lot like marriage."

"If that's how you want to view it, then yeah, we're married." His fingers curled around her wrist, but she pulled away, and sprang out of bed. She found her sweatshirt in a heap on the floor. Tossing it over her head, she grabbed his shirt from the back of the chair and threw it at him. "I need you to leave now. There will be no more talk of marriage. I am not married to you. I don't even know you. And you know what?" She searched for her shoes. "That's not going to happen. I thought all you were going to do is make me Eskarian. You said nothing of getting married. I don't know what black magic you used to con me into that one, but I'm not going to be a part of it. Thanks for saving my life, but I think it'd be best if you just got the hell out of it now."

"Black magic? There was no magic involved. We were just made for each other. It's very simple, really." He sighed softly, his gaze falling to the shirt, now crumpled on the floor.

"Says who?" she snapped. Where were her shoes?

His gaze followed her as she found her shoes and stuffed her feet into them. "It's part of who we are, Mackenzie."

A horrible thought came to her. "Did we, uh . . . consummate . . . this thing?"

He smiled. "Not yet."

"Thank goodness for that." She folded her arms across her chest. "I want you to leave."

His brow furrowed. "Can't we talk about this?"

She shook her head. "I don't see any reason to talk about it." *You raving psycho.*

"Okay, I'll leave. But, sooner or later, you'll need me, Mackenzie. Eventually, you'll have questions that only I can answer." He pushed back his tousled hair. His blue eyes shimmered again with that eerie opalescence.

What else could she throw at him? She scanned the room for something breakable. "I can figure it out myself."

"But you're not the same as you were yesterday. There are things I need to teach you. Please, come with me. My home is on the other side of the island. Let me take you there." He rolled off the bed, picked up his shirt, and shrugged it over his bare shoulders.

His gorgeous bare shoulders.

"No," she told him.

His boots were on before she knew it. He brushed her cheek as he strode past to the stairway. "I'll leave my address on the table. You will change your mind, Mackenzie."

She struggled to keep up with his long strides, even though her own legs were strong. "I wouldn't change my mind if you paid me. If I do, I'll call Griffin."

He stopped in the doorway to face her. "He's not someone you want to mess with, Mackenzie."

She lifted her chin. "I'm not afraid of him."

"You should be," he warned.

Sean flew off the couch as Christopher tromped down the stairs with Mackenzie right behind him. He threw his hands up and glared at her. "What the hell, Kenz? You *slept* with this guy?"

"No, I didn't sleep with him." Well, technically she slept with him, but Sean didn't need to know that.

"What's he doing here, then?" He rubbed the sleep from one eye.

"Leaving." Christopher snatched the coat hanging over the kitchen chair and pulled a card from the pocket. He scribbled something on the back, then handed it to her. "Here's my address. You're welcome to come by anytime before sunset. After that, I'll be out hunting. Wolves."

"Good. Then I'll be free to marry whomever I choose," she said with a haughty toss of her head. The card fell from her fingers onto the table. "In fact, I'll start looking tonight."

Sean's jaw dropped. "What?"

Christopher shot her an angry glare. He spun around, clamped onto both her wrists, and backed her against the refrigerator, knocking several little magnets to the floor. Leaning close, his gaze roamed hotly over her face. "No man will touch you now. My scent is on you and in you. We belong to each other. It can't be undone."

"This isn't prehistoric times, Christopher. You can't come in here, drag me around by the hair, and then start calling me your wife. That's just not how it works. More importantly, you can't stop me from doing as I please," she said defiantly.

His eyebrows shot up. "I don't have to stop you."

Her eyes widened. "What do you mean by that?"

His mouth nearly touched hers. "Find out for yourself," he whispered. His opalescent blue eyes blazed with fire. Dangerous.

What had she done? Who was this guy? "You're hurting my wrists."

Christopher let go. He ran a single finger along her cheek. "I'll be waiting for you, Beautiful. Do yourself a favor and avoid Griffin."

She glared at him. "Get out of my house."

He smiled impishly, then spun on his heel to leave.

Sean stood behind him with the baseball bat already in motion, aimed directly at Christopher's shoulder. Without hesitation, Christopher's hand shot out to catch the bat in mid-swing.

"Did last night not teach you anything, Sean?" He snatched the bat from Sean's hands with seemingly little effort.

Sean's eyes grew wide. He looked at the bat in Christopher's hand, and paled. "Mackenzie doesn't want you around."

Christopher shrugged. "Things change." He set the bat on the kitchen table, then slipped his coat over his shoulders. "Later."

"Only by mistake," she snarled.

"We'll see." He laughed. With a casual wave, he stepped out the back door and let it slam behind him.

Mackenzie turned and rested her forehead against the refrigerator. She was livid. How dare he speak to her like that?

"Kenz, what were you saying about marrying whomever you choose?"

"It's nothing, Sean. Not worth repeating." What was that about no other man approaching her? She'd see about that, this very evening.

No, she'd not have any man telling her whom she'd marry, and it sure as hell wouldn't be Christopher.

The door chimes startled her. "Could you get that, please?"

"Sure." Picking up the baseball bat from the table, Sean headed out to the living room.

Still fuming at Christopher, she listened to the muffled voices in the foyer as she put ground coffee and water into the automatic coffee maker. The mundane task settled her jangled nerves a bit, and as the tangy aroma of fresh coffee filled the kitchen, she resolved to put Christopher out of her mind. She'd put up with enough nonsense about mating and choices.

Or lack of choice, depending on how one thought about it.

Sean appeared from the living room. "Kenz, Scott's here to ask you about Amy. She hasn't shown up yet." He leaned close and whispered, "I turned the cushions last night."

She'd forgotten about the bloodstained couch. Her hands flew to her throat. "Thank God, Sean. Thank you for doing that." Mackenzie started toward the living room, but stopped when she saw Scott's weary appearance. He looked as if he hadn't slept much since Amy vanished. "No word about Amy?"

"Hey, Mackenzie. No, I'm afraid not. I apologize for stopping by without calling first. I've been looking for her since we talked. I don't know what could've happened, and it's driving me mad."

"Please, sit down, Scott. I haven't heard a thing either."

She sat down in the chair. Sean took up a perch behind her.

Scott settled onto the couch.

"You know, it's just not like her to do something like this. Do you remember what time she left?" Scott leaned forward and rested his folded arms across his legs.

"It was early Friday evening, around seven, I suppose. I'm not totally sure about that. I was really tired that day."

"She didn't have any weekend plans, did she?"

"No. As far as I know, she was going to be here."

Scott looked away. "Did she ever talk about seeing anyone else?"

She shook her head. "No, of course not."

"Can you think of anyone who'd want to harm her?"

She frowned. Amy didn't have any enemies. "No."

Just then a horrible thought whipped into her.

Demon wolves.

Could they have gotten Amy? Alarm and dread filled her at the same time. Her mind raced with thoughts of Amy having been killed by a wolf, and then Christopher destroying the wolf and maybe Amy, too. Was that how it worked? That would explain how the great Defender came into her life.

"Kenz? Are you all right?"

"Mmm?" Mackenzie's thoughts scattered. Her gaze moved from Scott to her brother. "Oh, yes, I'm sorry. What was your question?"

She hadn't eaten since the night before last, and now found herself suddenly starved. "Excuse me, Scott, would you like some coffee?"

Scott shook his head. "No, thank you."

Turning to her brother, she placed a trembling hand on his leg. "Sean, would you get me some coffee? I just made a pot."

"Sure." He slipped from the back of the chair, and disappeared into the kitchen.

Her attention returned to Scott. “I’m sorry. Please, continue.” She smiled thinly, folding her hands into her lap so no one would see them shake.

“How was she feeling Friday night?”

“She seemed fine to me.” Until she went outside to be eaten by demon wolves.

“No arguments then?”

Sean returned with a cup of steaming coffee. She accepted it with a quick nod of thanks. “No,” she said over the cup.

She took a sip. Her stomach turned immediately, offended by the rancid liquid. “I’m sorry. I don’t really have anything more to offer, Scott. Everything was fine. I fell asleep on the couch and she evidently went somewhere and just didn’t come back. I have no idea what happened. I would hunt her down myself if I knew where to look.”

One thing was certain—she needed to know what had truly happened Friday night. Only one person had these answers—one whom she had hoped to not see again, despite the heat that curled between her legs whenever she thought about the dark silkiness of his hair and the ice blue in his eyes.

“Okay. Well, if you think of something, please call me.” He reached into his breast pocket and pulled out a card. “Here are my office and cell numbers.” Standing, he crossed the floor to give it to her.

“Thanks. I hope we can find her soon, Scott. I’ll call the police tonight, if we don’t hear anything,” she said, rising to give him a quick hug. She returned to the kitchen as Sean showed him out.

Her body’s reaction to the coffee had her completely baffled. She felt fine otherwise, save for a growing thirst. There was nothing wrong with the coffee, and yet she couldn’t tolerate a single drop. She pulled a fresh bottle of water from the fridge and took a tentative sip.

Awful.

What else could she try?

Orange juice had the same effect, as did milk, diet soda, beer, and iced tea. Now what was she going to do?

"What's going on, Kenz?" Sean leaned against the doorway, scanning the array of beverages and glasses with a puzzled look. "What are you doing?"

His voice startled her. "Yeah," she said, looking at the clutter. "I know this looks a little strange, but I'm fine, really. Having a little bit of trouble keeping things down."

"I'm worried about you, Kenz. First this wolf thing, then that Christopher—whatever he is. Amy is missing, and I don't even know what to think about all this." He surveyed the chaos on the countertop. "I'm surprised Daniel hasn't called yet."

"I'm sure he will, sooner or later. He was busy this morning," she lied.

"Daniel's never busy on a Sunday morning. Everything okay with you two?"

At once, she caught the scent of his blood. Sweet and intoxicating. Lovely. She inhaled deeply. "Yeah, fine."

"Then what's up, Kenz? Come on, spill." He folded his arms over his chest.

"I know this is weirdsville. Honestly, I'd probably think the same thing."

"So, you can see why I'm worried."

She took in the scent of Sean's blood, silently wishing she *was* drinking it. It captivated her such that she could almost taste it, wanted to taste it, needed it flowing in and through her. Reality came down hard then, as she realized taking her brother's blood was her foremost thought. "Yes, I can see it." She headed for the coat closet. "I need to go, Sean. Can we talk about this when I get back? I have to go."

He sighed, and shrugged his shoulders, resignation on his face. "Fine. You're leaving, no matter what I say, aren't you? Can I ask where you're going?"

"Mmm, no, I don't think that'd be a good idea." He'd throw a fit if he knew where she intended to go. She shrugged on a fleece jacket.

He picked up Christopher's card from the table. "Let me guess where you're going. Would it be," he read the address, "the other side of the island?"

Her head lowered. She pulled in her bottom lip and nibbled on it a moment. "Just to get some questions answered. He knows more than he told us. I'm certain of it."

Sean shook his head in disgust. "I can't believe you're doing this. Just for the record, Kenz, I think this is lunacy. You should be staying away from that one."

"I know you're right, and I totally agree." She wasn't sure she had any choice. "We'll talk when I get back. I just need to get this over with, before I lose my courage."

Christopher's huge estate sprawled out over a hill, high over the Puget Sound, on the northwestern edge of the island.

Mackenzie stopped the car in front of a heavy wrought-iron gate. She surprised herself by her sudden need to check her appearance. The leaves in her hair definitely had to go. Had they been there since last night? Damn. She plucked them from her hair and threw them out the window.

Then she thought about what she was doing, and laughed. She no more wanted Christopher's attentions than she wanted to be a wolf again, but there she was, like a teenager on her first date, ensuring her hair was just right and there was nothing stuck between her teeth.

As if on cue, the gate slowly opened.

She locked the car and walked past the gate, up the long driveway, past perfectly trimmed hedges, trees, and fall flowers in glorious colors. The brick house loomed before her with its expanse of windows and skylights, rustic wood trim, and dark-blue metal roof. To the right, a three-car garage housed three black vehicles: a Corvette, a Toyota Sequoia, and an Acura. Somehow the dark color seemed fitting for someone who was so comfortable in the darkness.

His home was an absolute palace.

"What am I doing here?" she asked quietly. She found herself afraid to take another step forward or back, so she just stood there in the light rain, and waited.

Her thoughts went back to the moment she'd first realized she'd wanted to taste Sean's blood. That's what it boiled down to, didn't it? Blood. Eskarian was just a fancy word for vampire.

Mackenzie spun around to leave. "This guy's a lunatic, and I'm a vampire." Great.

A crazed lunatic.

"You're an Eskarian. There's no such thing as vampires."

Startled, she turned to see him in a casual stance, with one leg crossed over the other, one hand in the pocket of his raincoat, the other behind his back.

Damn him. How did he move so quickly and silently? "Why do you always know what I'm thinking?"

"All Eskarians have telepathic and telekinetic ability. You have it, too. I'll teach you to use it." Christopher crossed the lawn to greet her, his blue gaze locked on hers, his steps long and sure. "You don't really think I'm a crazed lunatic, do you?"

Was he a lunatic? Maybe not. "Jury's still out," she teased.

He thought about that. "Well, then I'll just have to persuade them to decide in my favor. I wouldn't want to lose something so precious and beautiful because of a simple misperception." He produced a single red rose from behind his back. "For you, milady." He placed the flower in her hand and smiled. "Welcome to Canongate."

"Thank you." She raised it to her nose and inhaled. "Canon Gate? You named your house?"

"One word. The estate is named after an area in Edinburgh, where I grew up. It's a custom among Eskarians, especially the older ones from Europe."

"Cool tradition."

His smile widened, then he laughed. "Yeah, it is." He stepped up beside her and wrapped his arm around her shoulders. "Let's get you out of the rain. Come sit by the fire with me. I know you have lots of questions and, more importantly, you haven't fed yet. We'll take care of that, too."

"I won't stay long. I just have a few questions—but, thanks."

"It's my pleasure." He pulled her closer.

A huge Siberian Husky loped out to greet her. The black and white fur was brilliant, but what amazed her most was the dog's eyes. Same icy blue color as its owner.

Mackenzie let the dog lick her fingers. This she understood. Animals were good. She knew how to deal with them. Also good. "Who's this?"

Christopher ran his hand along the dog's back. "This is Ivan. Say hello, Ivan."

The Husky barked once.

Mackenzie nodded her approval. "Excellent. He's trained."

"I had to train him. He constantly chewed up my boots." He laughed again.

She smiled. "Well, puppies do that."

"Yes, they do," he said, nudging her forward again. "But,

my boots are four hundred dollars per pair. Ivan needed to learn that some things are off-limits, that's all. Things like boots, slippers, car keys."

She laughed. "Car keys?"

Christopher shrugged. "He went through a metal phase when he was about six months old. Keys and soda cans. Come inside. I can tell you're cold." He searched behind him. "Ivan, come."

"Thanks," she said with a nod. Pausing a moment, she thought about what she wanted to know first. "What's a Defender?"

Christopher's easy grin faded. "A Defender is a protector of life. See, the threat to humans is very real and always around. Sometimes it is easily taken care of, but most of the time, it's difficult and dangerous. And often deadly. Much as we like to think we're going to live forever, some of us don't. It's too easy to slip up, too easy to become overly confident." He opened the door for her. When she passed through, he scooped up her hand and led her through the house. "The idea of immortality is extremely seductive. You think it means you can do whatever you want, but that isn't true. Our enemies are skilled and fast. We have to be, too, or we die. It's that simple. In our profession, one mistake will get you killed. Sever the head or destroy the ability to breathe, and we're gone. Forever."

She winced at the thought. "Is it worth it, then, to become immortal? Seems like you'd live in fear all the time."

Christopher shook his head. "Not at all. I know my abilities so well. The minute I see what I'm facing, I can tell how long it's going to take to defeat it. When Blair tells me what I'm going up against, I know what weapons to take, whether or not I need armor, even though I've most likely never faced that particular enemy before. I'm not afraid at all. I've done this for so long, it's like breathing. I do it without giving it a second thought." He glanced back at her. "And yes, it is worth it to become immortal. Maybe you'll let me show you."

Mackenzie didn't think so. Her gaze dropped to her feet.

He took her to the living room. At the far end, a heavy stone fireplace enshrouded a small fire. Slipping her coat from her shoulders, he hung it up, then offered her a plush beige-colored leather chair. She sat down, silently grateful to be off her feet, and smiled up at him as he wrapped her snugly in a huge towel.

"Thank you," she said.

"You're very welcome." Taking the rose from her hand, he set it on the end table beside her.

Christopher shrugged off his coat and sat down on the couch. Ivan curled around his feet. "Thousands of years ago, seven prophecies were made by an ancient civilization that was demolished shortly after setting the prophecies to stone. Six of them have come to pass, and now the seventh has begun." He pushed a hand through his dark hair, and looked away a moment, as if to collect his thoughts. "The prophecy of the Seventh Dragon is the final, and perhaps worst, of all of them." His blue gaze returned to her. "Three men are coming. Among them is a sorcerer who, evidently, was once very great and powerful. According to the prophecy, he's protected by shadows and, upon his arrival, a war will begin and the land would be washed in blood. Vague, at best. My job is to stop them." Christopher stood, moving to the fireplace to stoke the waning flames. "The problem is that I don't know where they are or what they look like."

Chapter Five

Mackenzie sank back into the soft leather chair, wrapped the towel tighter around her shoulders, and watched Christopher stoke the logs. "Then how will you find them? Seems like it would be an impossible task."

"It's difficult, but not impossible. We have Defenders throughout the United States. Reports are coming in all the time, but most often, they conflict with each other. Some say they came from Asia and are making their way to America, and others think they're in Canada and intend to head up to Alaska. We know so little that it's hard to decipher what's around us. The only thing we do know for sure is that they have to be stopped, at any cost. Damned hard when we don't know where to begin."

She nodded and let her eyes close. Even though she'd come to Christopher's home to ask about blood, she was terrified to actually bring it up. She had no idea how she'd handle it. In her mind, what she'd need to do to survive was disgusting, wrong, and best left to shadowed vampires and predators who knew nothing else.

What it really boiled down to was that she just wasn't prepared to take human blood. Didn't want to take it and actually couldn't stand the thought of doing it. Images from cheesy vampire movies stuck in her mind, which didn't help at all, but she thought of them anyway. Even as she tried to use logic to work through her fear, she still couldn't shake the idea that there had to be another way. Surely she was not expected to rely *solely* on blood for survival, was she? It provided no nutrients. How was it even possible?

Certain there had to be more to this, she made a decision to wait. But even then, the word, forbidden and sacred, hung in the back of her mind. Tormented her.

Blood . . . Ick.

"I can't do this," she announced, opening her eyes. Her stomach rumbled loud enough that it caught Christopher's attention. Great.

It wasn't that she was afraid of it. Blood was a necessary component of her work. She didn't have a problem with that. But, drinking it? Just the thought made her stomach turn upside-down. Ick.

"Yes, you can." Christopher returned to the couch. "What you can't do is put off feeding anymore. Your strength has diminished, and that makes you vulnerable to attack. Your blood is extremely valuable now, as is your body. Humans will want to know how you work, and why you work. So, while we Defenders take care of supernatural threats, you must always be wary of human threats. Always. You will need the strength of the Eskarian to survive. Never allow yourself to weaken like this again." He toyed with one of the buttons on his white cotton shirt. "I'll help you feed. I can show you what to do and make it very easy for you."

Mackenzie wrinkled her nose. "And what am I to feed on?"

Ah, there it was. The question popped out before she caught herself. Time to face reality.

"You already know." He leaned back into the couch, stretching his arms across the back pillows. "Why do you fight it so much? It's not as bad as you imagine."

His deep, rich voice washed over her as gently as the fragrance from the leaves smoldering on the table.

"I can't take blood from another human being," she said. "Is there something else I could try?"

"No. You need blood to survive. Only blood. The first time is the hardest, but after that, there's nothing to it. I learned to do it myself, many years ago."

"Life was more difficult back then," she pointed out. She knew he was at least two hundred years old. He'd said so earlier. "You were more motivated, I'm sure."

He nodded. "It was. And I was. But that means nothing. It's still not a difficult thing to do. We never kill our donors. Does that make a difference for you?"

"Donors? Are you serious? You call them that? Who in their right mind would *ever* donate blood to a vampire?" Mackenzie almost laughed out loud.

"It's a symbiotic relationship. We provide protection from threats and they provide what we need to survive. May I remind you that I'm as much a vampire as you?"

She thought about that. "Yeah, and there's a huge difference between you and a vampire."

Christopher leaned forward and rubbed his forehead. "Mackenzie, you're making too much out of this. It's really very simple—"

She interrupted. "I'm not doing it. I'll go to a blood bank, or something. Squeeze rats, maybe, but I won't take blood from a person. That's just revolting. I'd feel like such a parasite."

His eyebrows shot up. "That's not how it is."

She rose, and tossed the towel on the chair. "What else would you call it? You suck blood from people's necks. Tell me you don't."

He couldn't argue with her, and she didn't bother waiting for him to try.

"It's repulsive," she said, her nose wrinkling in disgust. "I have to get out of here. I am *not* sucking blood out of someone's neck."

"Wait." His hand shot out to clamp her wrist. "You're too weak and vulnerable. I can't let you go like this. Stay and let me show you that you don't need to fear this." The easy demeanor he'd displayed only moments ago was replaced by something darker. More serious?

More fearsome, she thought.

He looked up at her. His blue eyes were intense, captivating. She could look at them all day and never tire of them.

"You can take blood from me," he said softly.

She tried to twist free from his grip, but it was like iron, solid and unyielding. "No, I won't do it. Let go, Christopher. You can't keep me here."

He pulled her closer, until she was on her knees and nose-to-nose with him. "Actually, I can." His gaze focused on her mouth. "Mackenzie," he said softly, his brow creased. "Why won't you let me help you?"

"Because I don't need help. I made a huge mistake coming here and I intend to rectify it this very minute. Now, let go," she said, her anger flaring. Did she really think it was a mistake? Maybe. Maybe not. It had seemed like a good idea earlier, but now that she was nose-to-nose with him, and his spicy scent and gorgeous eyes were assaulting her, she wasn't so sure.

She didn't like backing off, unless she had a good reason. And this was not a good reason. Her courage was extraordinarily high now that she was furious with him. Mackenzie Wallace was no one's doormat.

"I said, let go," she repeated. Mackenzie glared until his grip on her wrist softened; then she pulled away and sprang to her feet. "You stay the hell away from me, Christopher."

She headed for the front door, glancing back for one split

second—and barely avoided slamming into his chest. She frowned and looked back at the couch, then into his eyes. "How did you move so fast?"

His hand whipped around to grasp the nape of her neck. He bent his head and locked his mouth to hers. His tongue gently explored, while his thumb whispered back and forth across her neck.

Her anger dissolved, her legs quivered beneath her, and when he pushed her against the wall, she went willingly. It would lead to something she wasn't ready for, but her body had ideas of its own. His arousal, pressed against her belly, made her weak and hot. Made warm liquid rush to greet him. She wanted this, wanted to give in to the feelings. His spicy-sweet scent, which reminded her of thyme and mint, intoxicated her. She wanted to feel his heat against her body, his arousal inside her. How her body betrayed her, starting a wicked, slow burn that no one could cool but him.

"I can do almost anything," he whispered. "I *could* keep you here."

Her reverie dissolved. "No, you couldn't keep me here against my will. Eventually I'd find a way out." She should've been fighting to leave, but the heat of his touch lingered on her skin, and the liquid fire between her legs made it hard to move. His fierce, sky-blue eyes took her breath away, and his mouth, well . . . a soft, full mouth like that needed to be kissed, and often.

He leaned close enough so she could feel his breath on her lips. Sweet breath. "I'm not keeping you against your will." His whisper-soft voice seduced her, effortlessly, it seemed. Was he right?

No.

"Yes, you are." She closed her eyes.

His lips brushed her neck. "You like the feel of my body

against yours. You want more. Can you imagine me lying between your legs? Do you want me to tell you what I'd do to you, if I had the chance?"

Yes, she did, more than anything.

But not today. Her gaze dropped to the floor. "I need to get home." She pushed against him. "Sean's waiting for me." That wasn't completely true, but true enough.

He didn't move a muscle.

Mackenzie pushed against his chest. His body was all hard muscle and didn't budge. Not one bit. "Are you going to keep me here when I wish to be elsewhere? I believe that's called kidnapping. Just what the hell is wrong with you?"

"Nothing's wrong with me. This is your stubbornness talking, not your heart. You don't really want to leave, and yet you'd walk away from me without looking back, purposely destroying something that could be better and greater than either of us has known before. All that because you're one very rebellious woman. You hate being told what to do." He caught her hand and brought it to his mouth. Watching her, he pressed a kiss to the back of her hand. "I understand that. I know what you're feeling. I can see it in the beads of sweat on your forehead, in the rapid pulse in your neck, and in the fire that's burning your body. I know what you feel when I kiss you or touch you." Two fingers whispered down her cheek. "I know you're afraid of me. Terrified, in fact. Of me and your own feelings. You're so afraid that you'd run now and not stop. Ever. But I'm asking you, please, don't leave." He nuzzled her neck. "I'm not the evil monster you think I am. Stay with me."

The front door opened. Christopher and Mackenzie turned in unison to the muscular wall of a man with long, auburn hair and glittering liquid silver eyes, clearly a warrior from days gone by.

"You could have knocked, Griffin."

The silver-eyed titan shot Christopher a fiery glare. "You knew we were coming."

Behind him, an elegant man with long white hair and the most breathtaking pale green eyes followed. "Afternoon, Christopher."

"Ian." Christopher nodded. He took Mackenzie's wrist, then pulled her back to the living room, where they joined Griffin and Ian. "This is Mackenzie." He glanced back at her. "Ian is our leader. And I'm sure you remember Griffin."

Griffin's eyes drifted slowly over Mackenzie's body. "So the wolf becomes Eskarian. You haven't bound her to you yet?" An amused smile crossed his face, then the silver gaze snapped back to Christopher. "She's hungry. You haven't even shown her how to feed. Have you forgotten all our laws?"

Mackenzie's mouth dropped open. What had she gotten herself into? There would be no binding to anyone, thank you. And no feeding, either.

Christopher looked away. "No."

Suddenly, she felt like a caged animal and surrounding her were three keepers. No, she couldn't abide that. She rubbed her forehead, looked back at the front door, and resolved to get out of there as soon as possible.

How did Griffin know she was hungry?

If she could just leave, she'd be okay. Even if she couldn't, she'd be more than happy to show Christopher just how rebellious she was.

A quick snap of her wrist tested Christopher's grip. Without looking at her, he tightened his grasp.

Don't bother, Mackenzie. I'm not letting you go.

"Why haven't you attended her?" Griffin's eyebrows went up. "And why does she fight you?"

Christopher's eyes flashed. "How is this any of your business?"

Griffin smirked as his hands shot up, acquiescing to Christopher. "You're a much better Defender than you are a lover, my friend."

"Griffin, you're almost a thousand years old. I'm not sure it's me who's lacking knowledge," Christopher said with a smile.

"All the same, Little One, if it were me, there would be no question to whom she belonged. She would be well fed and well loved." Griffin winked at her.

Defiantly, she wrinkled her nose at him. But, just in case, she moved a little closer to Christopher, who tightened his grip further. Only one arrogant, macho man at a time, thank you very much.

Ian sighed, nodding to Mackenzie. "It's a pleasure to meet you, Mackenzie."

She smiled. "A pleasure, Ian." Now, can you just get out me of this place . . .

"We have new information about the prophecy, Christopher. It's time to formulate a plan." Ian sat down on the couch. "That is, if you've finished insulting each other."

Christopher turned to Mackenzie. "You and I need to talk as well. Let me finish with them and then I'll join you." He took her to his bedroom. "Look, I know what you're thinking. Running is not a good idea. You're too weak and you need rest. We need to get you beyond the fear of taking blood. Please, lie down here. Don't run until we've had a chance to talk."

She glanced at him, then looked away and said nothing.

"Please, Mackenzie, wait for me." Leaning to her, he covered her mouth with his, hands framing her face. "I'll come back as soon as I can." His mouth brushed her cheek and then he was gone.

His bedroom was masculine and inviting, decorated in soft colors of sage and teal. Thick quilts adorned his large bed, and his furniture, the bureau and bed frame, was maple. The room had been beautifully decorated with contemporary paintings and wall hangings. All from artists she didn't know, but they were lovely. Originals.

She stood near his bed. The king-sized quilt was masculine, yet intricate and appealing. Her mind drifted back to this morning, when he'd lain in her bed and the sunshine had washed his golden skin in warmth and light. Only now, hours later, did she allow herself to acknowledge that she'd enjoyed the heat of his body, the silky sheen of his hair. She longed to sift her fingers in it, to watch it whisper across his strong, wide shoulders.

If only he were human. If only she were . . .

She touched the quilt. Her fingers traced the detailed stitches of the moss-colored Celtic design. Yes, if things were different, if there was no blood involved, she might have stayed. He frightened her, though. The way her body reacted to him frightened her. She could melt into his strong arms, and stay there forever. She would. Everything about him was addictive. She suspected making love with him would be equally as addictive.

Mackenzie shook her head, both saddened and relieved by the choice she'd just made.

She headed for the window. It would be easy enough to slip out the window and be free. Then she'd take a long vacation and return to her business and to Sean. Back to the life that made sense.

Christopher would have to find another mate. She planned to forget about the dazzling blue eyes and voice as soft and seductive as velvet.

In time. He just wasn't someone you forgot overnight.

She scanned the yard. The iron gate was not far. Her stomach rumbled again. Her strength was fading, but she could get to the gate. She'd get over it or through it, no matter how hard it was. Whatever she had to do, by God, that's what she'd do. She was ready.

Reaching up to the lock, she unlatched it and slid the window open.

No, Mackenzie, please don't go. Wait for me. His voice echoed with pain, with fear of loss.

She couldn't help that. Even though his soft voice burned through her, left her hungry, once again, for the heat of his body, it just wouldn't work. She had no place in this world.

She wouldn't allow herself to be seduced by his hypnotic voice. This entire Eskarian thing, this blood thing, was more than she could handle and she was too tired to battle him further.

"I'm sorry. This just isn't for me." She wasn't sure if he could hear her, but it was the best she could do. "I really . . . *can't* . . . stay here."

Mackenzie, no . . . Damn it, wait for me. I can't leave yet.

She heard his words clearly in her head, but she wouldn't do as he'd asked. She couldn't. "Sorry. I can and I *am* leaving."

She removed the screen and slipped out into the rainy afternoon.

Sweet freedom at last.

Tumbling to the wet ground, she found her legs weak when she desperately needed them to be strong. But there was no way she'd give in to hunger or weakness. Sheer will pushed her off the ground and toward the front gate. How she'd get around it she wasn't sure, but there had to be a way. There was always a way, and all she had to do was look hard enough for it.

Rushing to the front gate, she was certain she had only minutes before someone came looking for her. Or, more specifically, came to haul her back into the house with all those blood-suckers.

She studied the gate to see how it opened. The swing arm was to her left, but if there was a manual release switch somewhere, she couldn't find it. Could she open the gate herself?

She tugged several times, but the locked wrought-iron gate wouldn't budge, no matter how hard Mackenzie pulled or pushed. Wasn't she supposed to have some kind of superhuman strength? Where was it?

Searching the gate and the surrounding area, she found no way to open it. The large spikes and concertino wire at the top were imposing enough to dissuade her from trying to climb over.

Finally, frustrated, cold and wet, she pressed her forehead against the metal bars and thought about her options. Anything but going back would be fine. Her grand escape attempt wasn't going so well.

On top of that, she was so hungry her stomach had stopped rumbling. Biting someone's neck didn't seem so bad now.

"You can bite mine."

Whirling around, she came face-to-face with Griffin. His auburn hair was wild and damp, and thick, well-defined muscles rested beneath a wet T-shirt.

His silver eyes scanned her face. "I see how hungry you are. Christopher has not treated you well."

She shook her head. "It's not his fault, it's mine. I'm not cut out for this kind of life."

"All the same, he should have taken care of this already, in whatever manner you needed."

She studied his face. Despite the smooth skin and glossy

hair, his handsome features seemed shadowed by something akin to sorrow. "You don't like him much, do you?"

"I don't like or dislike him. There isn't a place for emotion in my life," he answered with a crooked smile. "Duty comes first. No exceptions. Christopher's duty is now to you. He should've given you what you need to survive."

She shrugged. "I wouldn't let him."

Griffin raised an eyebrow. "If you're going to behave like that, he should've forced your compliance. You require blood to survive. Whether you like it or not, this is what you are now. Would you prefer to be dead?"

"No," she said slowly. "Not really."

"Then you must learn to do this. At any given time, there are several threats around who would love to see you dead or on a laboratory table. Neither is acceptable. No human can ever know what you are. To that end, you should never be so hungry that your strength is compromised. That isn't acceptable either. Christopher didn't do you any favors by allowing you to leave on an empty stomach. He's got a kind heart. Too kind, if you ask me. Fortunately, I don't have that problem. I'll show you what to do." He stepped forward, slipping his arm around her shoulder. "This will give us a little more privacy." He guided her away from the gate.

Alarms went off in her head. Privacy? "For what?"

"Don't be afraid. Remember, no one can know what you are. Some things are best done privately." He dropped down onto one knee in the soggy grass, and looked up at her. "I'll make this very easy for you. Just relax."

"No, I can't." She stepped back, but he reached out with both hands and shackled her wrists. Wide-eyed, she gasped as he brought her close enough so she could see the tiny freckles across his nose and cheeks.

"You will not move," he said softly.

His voice was amazingly suggestive. She'd never heard anything like it, and surprised herself by nodding compliantly.

He took out a small knife from his jeans pocket and slid the gleaming blade along the pulseline in his wrist. Blood instantly flowed from the wound, but dissolved quickly in the light rain. He raised his wrist, offering relief from the hunger. "Come closer, Mackenzie." His voice was low, seductive, and hypnotic. "I won't let you suffer another moment. Come now, and drink."

Mackenzie leaned forward, just a little. The scent of the blood immediately captured her with its wonderful richness. Sean's blood had done the same thing, she remembered. Was it always so powerful? She could almost imagine herself taking a little sip—just a tiny sample.

Would it be so bad?

"There's nothing wrong with drinking blood, Mackenzie. It's as natural to us as food was to you. Come closer, now. Let go of your fear." Griffin's voice drifted over her like a warm breeze. "You're a strong Eskarian woman. You can do this. Drink."

She found his words impossible to ignore. The call of the blood was so strong and just too difficult to resist. Or was it Griffin's voice? She wasn't sure, and perhaps it no longer mattered.

Now that she thought about it, she couldn't remember why she'd been so revolted in the first place.

She pulled her long hair to the side, twisted it, and held it out of the way. Her head descended and her fingers curled around his thick forearm. Delicately she tasted the blood, letting it rest on her tongue a moment before swallowing.

Not so bad.

She fully accepted the offer and closed her eyes to draw his blood gently.

Moments later, she straightened. "Thank you, Griffin." She dabbed at her mouth with the back of her hand.

"You're very welcome." He traced her shoulder with his fingers, his silver gaze once again on her face with such intensity, she found herself involuntarily stepping back. "You're really quite beautiful, Mackenzie. I would have done it already."

She frowned. "Done what?"

He stood, flashing a crooked smile. "Bound myself to you, of course. Made you mine. I wouldn't hesitate as Christopher does. And no one, no *thing*, would ever come between us." A glint of sadness shadowed his gaze. "Never. I'd protect you with my life, but if somehow I should fail, I'd follow you into death without ever looking back."

Her mouth dropped open. "I'm not really sure what to say to that."

He shrugged. "It doesn't require a response."

She studied his face. His golden skin bore the lines of one who had seen many things, and not all good. "What happened to you?" Reaching up, she laid a hand on his arm. "I see such sorrow in your eyes."

"I was young and foolish. It was long ago, but the price I paid was extraordinarily high." He looked away, seemingly lost in the memory.

"I'm sorry."

His body suddenly stiffened. He spun as the air stilled and became thick. Oppressive. Dangerous.

Christopher walked toward them, hands stuffed into his coat pockets. As he drew near, Mackenzie saw the fire in his eyes and felt the fury in his heart.

Get away from him, Mackenzie. Do as I ask, please. Now

would not be a good time to fight me. I assure you, I will not tolerate it.

Oh God, she gasped silently, finding cover behind a large Maple tree.

"What are you doing, Griffin?" Christopher's voice was low, whisper-soft, and full of menace.

"Taking care of your woman for you, since you have failed to provide her with what she needs."

"You took advantage of my position with Ian, coming out here to be with her when I could not. You're the second in command. What possessed you to do this?"

"I already know what the plan is. You're on the front lines for this operation. It was you who needed to work out the specifics with Ian." He cast a glance at Mackenzie. "And she was hungry. She was suffering."

"You had no right. I have spoken the traditional binding words. You can clearly see my mark on her." Christopher paced back and forth. "Why do you ignore Eskarian rites? What makes you think it's all right to do this?"

"I might ask the same of you. You should never have allowed her to become so weakened. What if someone other than myself had found her? Do you not realize how you have compromised us here? Why have you taught her nothing about our ways?"

Christopher's jaw clenched. "Back off, Griffin. You know nothing of what's happened."

"Why should I back off? You've failed her in the worst of ways." Griffin's head turned slowly to the tree where Mackenzie stood. "She deserves someone who will take the time to care for her, and teach her what she needs to know. You have spent too many years in the field hunting demons, my friend."

Christopher's face went utterly blank. Only the sheer fury

in his cold, blue eyes suggested any emotion. He looked away a moment, then returned to Griffin. "I chose not to impose my will upon her. It's that simple. If another man had found her, I would have killed him. I knew where Mackenzie was and what she was doing the entire time she was out of my sight. There was never a compromise." He spoke slowly, as if the anger just under the surface were barely contained. "She knows as well as I that she is my benekeda, but she wants choice anyway. She'll fight to get it, and fight if it's taken away. I will wait for her to come to me, even if it takes a hundred years. I have the time and I respect her need for choice. How long would you have waited?"

"I would have finished it, so there was no question. She'd have gotten over the shock of having her world change overnight." Griffin smiled, watching Mackenzie. "The words may have been spoken, but it's not yet done. How do you know she'll even come to you? It looks to me as if your mate doesn't want to be with you." He shrugged. "It happens. Things don't always turn out as you'd intended. Look at Jason, or Dominic. Perhaps you're mistaken about what the gods have willed. Maybe you're destined to be as miserable as they are."

Christopher's head lowered and he rubbed his chin with the back of his hand, then scanned the yard. "I don't think so." Turning to watch Mackenzie as she nervously chewed on a fingernail, he smiled, then turned back to the auburn-haired warrior. "Piss off, Griffin."

Without another word, he strode back to the house and disappeared inside.

Mackenzie waited until he was gone before she came out from behind the Maple tree. "I was afraid you were going to kill each other."

Griffin looked back at the house and smiled. "It wouldn't have happened. Might have been one or the other, but not both. I doubt it would have been either."

She nodded. "Thank you again for sharing your blood with me. My strength has returned."

"Do not allow yourself to weaken like that again. I mean it. You were extremely vulnerable tonight. The ramifications could have been disastrous, not only for yourself, but for all of us. You have more than your own life to consider now. Christopher should have taught you all this." He leaned forward to take her arm. "But since he hasn't, I'll teach you what you need to know. If you'll come with me, we can talk inside."

She stepped back. "Thank you, but no." She pulled a strand of hair, and twisted it around her finger, afraid that he might just drag her off somewhere as Christopher had, and she didn't have *that* much strength. "I can't. I'm sorry." Her gaze drifted to the house, then back to the tall, muscular Eskarian standing before her.

Christopher's blood burned in her veins. Griffin's did too, but there was something different about Christopher's blood. Something more deeply intimate, as if he'd given a piece of himself. Griffin had also shared himself, but there was nothing behind it. No heat, no fire. It was all very practical and unassuming. She realized then that Christopher was a part of her, and would always be a part of her life. "I'll never be free of this, will I?"

"No. It doesn't work that way for us. We're not like humans." Griffin placed his hand on her shoulder. "Christopher is your benekeda, your perfect, true mate, whether you like it or not. Everything that has happened to you, starting the moment you were bitten by the demon wolf, has led you to him. This is your destiny, the will of the gods."

She looked at the house again. "I'm not sure I want this destiny."

"It doesn't matter. He will never let you go. Wherever you run, he'll find you. He's a master at what he does," he said, following her gaze.

"Then I have no choice?" Christopher had been right about choice. She always fought for it.

"You can choose not to be a part of his life. There's nothing written in stone that says you have to be with him." Griffin shrugged. "But you should tell him now, if that's your choice. He deserves that much."

She nodded slowly. "I just don't think I'm cut out for this kind of life. It's just too much. I need to have my own life back."

"Even if you let Christopher go, you won't have your life back. You *are* Eskarian. You *do* require blood to survive. These are inescapable, unchangeable facts. Putting Christopher out of your life isn't going to make any of this magically disappear. The truth is, if you push him away, you're not going to be any happier." Griffin shifted his weight to the other leg. "In fact, you'll feel worse. You'll know that your perfect partner is out there, waiting for you, hurting as much as you do. And you *will* hurt, eventually. I know this for a fact, unfortunately."

"You don't make it sound appealing at all." She looked back at the steely-eyed Eskarian.

"It isn't. That's my point. He'll watch over you from the shadows and he'll keep his distance, but he'll always be around." His head tilted to the side. "And he'll never allow anyone else to love you."

She looked away. "That doesn't appeal to me either."

"Do what you must, but for what it's worth, I think you're making a mistake."

"Why?"

Griffin smiled. "Find out yourself. Go to him now. He's waiting for you."

She looked to the house, wondering if Griffin was right. Was she making a mistake? "Thank you. For everything." She reached up to touch his finely chiseled cheek, trailing fingers along his jaw, and then brushed his wild auburn mane. He leaned into her touch, a curiously tender response.

"You're most welcome," he said softly. "Now, go. Tell Christopher he owes me one."

She grinned. "We'll see if he owes you or not."

Heading towards the house, she felt increasingly anxious. Something deep within her needed to feel the heat of Christopher's touch, the press of his mouth upon hers. But she didn't know if she was ready. It just seemed easier to say goodbye and then get on with her life. Maybe she could find someone to love who didn't depend on blood to survive. Unless Griffin was right . . .

Chapter Six

Mackenzie stopped at the front door.

Uncertain and afraid, she closed her eyes and covered her face with trembling hands. She wanted her old life back so much, it hurt. She missed the simplicity. Missed the comfort and predictability of everyday life.

She missed Daniel.

In a matter of days, her life had spiraled completely out of control. First the wolf took her humanity, then Christopher took the wolf, all so quickly her head was still spinning.

And after that, to her complete horror, she took Daniel.

In her head, Mackenzie knew she wasn't human anymore, but her heart just flat-out refused to accept it. After all, there was no such thing as vampires. Or werewolves. She still wasn't sure what an Eskarian was, but was starting to think it sounded a lot like a vampire. Which didn't exist.

Mackenzie rubbed her temples. She'd taken Griffin's blood only minutes ago, just like a vampire, and now she felt better. Stronger.

Alive. Like she imagined a vampire would.

Solid evidence her heart couldn't ignore much longer.

Mackenzie let out a slow breath. What she'd give to just go back in time. If she could change the moment the wolf had attacked, maybe none of this would have happened, and she wouldn't be so torn by her emotions. By everything.

The worst part of all this—the part she desperately wanted

to ignore—she *wanted* Christopher's incredible body on hers. For a long time.

Forever.

The dark, seductive man with the sky-blue eyes was a force unto himself. Much as she tried, she couldn't push him from her mind. Like a shadow, he was always there, and part of her sensed he always would be, just as Griffin had said.

The attraction between Christopher and her was frightening. She'd never in her life known anything so intense. One touch from the dark-haired Eskarian, and she nearly dissolved. One kiss and she couldn't think straight. Grown women simply didn't act like this. She was *not* happy with her own behavior, but she knew it didn't matter. In the end, it wouldn't mean a thing. The deepest stratum of her being knew she had no chance of escaping her destiny.

Not a whit of a chance.

But that didn't mean she wouldn't fight. She hadn't chosen this destiny and didn't see any reason to accept it willingly. If she could change the odds in her favor, so much the better. How much could it hurt to try? And who said anything fated was cast in stone, anyway? She was certain that whatever the Fates had decreed as what would be was only probability and, at the heart of it all, choice still remained.

She was more than willing to find out if her theory was true.

Mackenzie looked behind her. Griffin was at the gate, talking to someone on the opposite side of the fence. She couldn't see the visitor well enough to know who he was, but there was little doubt he and Griffin were guarding the gate to make sure she didn't leave. Great. No escape. Had they not been there, she would've tried the gate again. Maybe now that she felt better, she could open it.

And what then? What about life with Christopher?

What about free will? her mind countered.

Made her dizzy to think about it.

Mackenzie's gaze returned to the door. Vampire or not, the only path she really *could* take lay before her.

Gathering her courage, she stepped inside, and turned before closing the door. Looking past the driveway, she found Griffin still talking with the visitor. "I don't like your world," she said to the auburn-haired warrior. "I don't belong here."

She saw his head turn, as if to face her. *Whether you like it or not, milady, you are already a part of it.* His voice echoed softly inside her mind. *Stop fighting what you can't change.*

Mackenzie cringed. "I hope somebody comes along someday and turns your life upside down. See how you like it."

A soft, male chuckle in her mind annoyed her. *I'd love to be turned upside down.*

"Yeah, you say that now. Easy, when there's no one around to make you think of doing things you normally wouldn't. I hope you come to understand just how hard it is to see your world crumble, and know that there's nothing you can do to save it." Shaking her head, she pushed the annoyance aside. Other, more important things beckoned, so she closed the door and returned to her task. "Leave us alone for a bit."

I'm sorry, Mackenzie. I do know how hard this is for you. I'll make sure no one disturbs you.

"Thank you." *I think,* she added silently.

Don't be afraid. Christopher will never hurt you.

His compassion surprised her. She'd just met him, and had thought him cold and aloof. Now, he was warm and caring. It was a startling, unexpected contrast, but not entirely unwelcome. His words brought her a little comfort, and that was more than welcome.

But, the fear was still there, and it wasn't just Christopher. It was the fact that no matter what happened, her life would be different forever. She finally understood now that there was no going back to the life she had. Not really. But where she'd go from here, she didn't know. Anything that was normal . . . or at least *almost* normal, if such a thing was possible.

She crossed the kitchen floor with measured steps. Her pulse thundered inside her head and outpaced the whispered tick-tick-tick of the grandfather clock. Even her breath was fast. Fear coiled tighter around her throat.

Fear of what she was about to do, or not do. The choice was so difficult. She knew he was nearby—she felt his lifeforce, his presence. Only seconds away, and still, she had no idea what she'd say to him. More importantly, she wondered how he would react. If she said goodbye, would he just let her leave? Could she just walk in, say goodbye, turn around, and go home? If she'd had to guess, she'd say, unequivocally, no.

No.

On the other hand, what would happen if she found the courage to stay? She didn't know.

She really didn't.

Mackenzie sighed again. "Damn it," she whispered.

At the edge of the kitchen, she stopped and clasped her hands. She brought them to her mouth, as if in prayer. She needed a miracle to get her through these next few minutes.

Christopher leaned against the mantel over the fireplace, seemingly engrossed in his own thoughts. His long hair was tousled, damp, and his shirt hung open.

She watched, not really sure how to proceed. He seemed lost, withdrawn, as if filled with a horrible sorrow. The atmosphere was heavy, oppressive. Thick.

It made her want to turn and run as fast as she could.

His head snapped up, turned slowly to face her. "Hi."

She cleared her throat. "Hello."

His eyes darkened. "How's Griffin?"

"Ah . . ." she began. "I don't know. Fine, I guess. Big."

"Yeah, I suppose." Christopher looked away. "What can I do for you?"

Her brow furrowed; terror gripped her so tightly she felt cold. Slowly, she approached and touched his shoulder.

His wild emotions had wrought havoc on his body. Beneath her hand, his body trembled and was hot. "Are you all right?"

"Sure," he whispered, looking at her.

"You're shaking," she said, reaching to touch his cheek. "It doesn't feel all right."

A storm raged within his glittering blue eyes. "Why are you here?"

She swallowed hard and discovered that she trembled as much as he. What had possessed her to do this? She should have found a way around Griffin instead. "Uh . . ." she cleared her throat again, "to say . . ." Her voice was barely audible. She paused, then shook her head. ". . . I don't know. I don't know."

He waited for her to say more. She didn't know if she could.

Mackenzie bit down on her lower lip. God help her. If she didn't get out of there soon, her nerves were going to shatter.

Tell him.

"I wanted to say goodbye." She swallowed again. "I want to leave."

His brow furrowed, and his mouth opened, as if he were about to speak. He caught a strand of her hair, and ran his fingers down its length, then lightly across the collar of her shirt, whispering over her heated skin, and down between her breasts. His blue gaze searched her face while his fingers set her skin ablaze.

Her heartbeat exploded. Her body betrayed her. Instantly, she was on fire, aching with raw desire for his hands, his body, his mouth. *Touch me . . .*

"What have I done to make you so afraid of me?" he asked softly.

His touch was potent and addictive, and she wanted to surrender to it, but she needed to keep her head. Say what she came to say. "It's not what you've done, it's what you are. I can't breathe when I'm around you," she told him. "All this benekeda stuff, I have no idea what that really means. If I'm going to get married, it will be to a man I choose and fall in love with. I don't want to be told you and I are perfect for each other and the universe has preordained it. That doesn't make sense. Only days ago, I had no idea who you were. How could I possibly be meant for you?

"Frankly, your world frightens me to death. I don't think I can be a part of it. I need my life, my business, my world. Not this dark world of blood and demons."

Christopher turned to fully face her. His fingers brushed her cheek. "Do you feel anything for me?"

She cleared her throat and she looked away. Her cheeks got warm. "I guess so."

"Tell me what you feel when I touch you." He grasped her hand, bringing her fingers to his mouth. His tongue traced her fingertips, then he took her index finger into his mouth and swirled his tongue around it.

Her gaze narrowed to what he was doing. She thought she might burn to ashes where she stood.

"I feel . . ." she paused, inhaled deeply, and allowed her tired eyes to drift shut. "Fire." Her legs threatened to give out on her. "What you do to me is simply amazing. And terrifying."

His fingers curled around her hand and brought it to his chest. He leaned closer. "Then why would you leave me?" His hot breath against her neck sent a flurry of chills down her back. He was trying to seduce her. "Feel my heartbeat. Don't you see how much I want you?"

Mackenzie looked at him and pulled her hand away. "This isn't about what you want. It's about what I want." Her pulse raced, her heart pounded in her ears, and it was all from the moist heat of his mouth on her skin. Like nothing she'd ever felt before. He simply stole her breath.

"Mackenzie," he whispered. His hands moved down her arms to grasp her wrists, as his mouth and tongue worked on her neck and shoulder. "Tell me what you want."

She turned to whisper what she knew she could never have again. "I want to be human, and I want my own life back. I want all this insanity to go away."

His head rose to capture her gaze. "We've spoken of this already. I would do almost anything for you, but I can't do that. No one can. I'm sorry the wolf took your human life away, but what's done is done."

Exhaling softly, she dropped her gaze to the floor. "I know. I wish it were different."

"You don't need to wish it was different, Mackenzie. You have the power to make your life greater than it would have been otherwise. You're assuming Eskarian life is less fulfilling than human life, and that's just not true. I'd be happy to show you what it can be, what it will be." His mouth found her neck again. "There's a lot I'd like to show you, if you'd let me."

"I don't know," she sighed. She was getting confused. Why did she want to leave him? Did she still want to leave?

Mackenzie pulled away to gather her thoughts without his

body heat distracting her. "This isn't fair. You're driving me out of my mind. I can't think straight."

He slowly released her wrists. "What isn't fair?"

"The way you make me feel. I don't think I like it. I mean, I do like it, but God . . ." She pressed her palms against her forehead. "When you touch me like that, all I can think of is how my body responds to you, as if it had its own will and I'm just along for the ride. This is insane."

Backing away, he kept his gaze focused on hers. "You're going to leave, aren't you? You don't want to be a part of my life." His eyes darkened. "That's it, isn't it?"

She didn't know the answer to that question.

"If that's your choice, then go. I won't keep you here against your will," he told her.

Turning away, she pressed her forehead against the wall, shivering, but not cold. She was so confused and aroused by his touch, she couldn't focus on what she needed to do. Her pulse pounded in her ears, and, truth be told, all she really wanted was to feel his body again, his mouth on hers, and his soft voice telling her it would be all right.

He touched her shoulder. "Tell me, is that what you want?"

"I don't know," she breathed. Rubbing her forehead, she inhaled sharply and faced him.

"Mackenzie, you look so unhappy. I'll have Matthew drive you home. If the decision is that hard . . . You should probably just go." He leaned against the fireplace mantel, watching her with a furrowed brow. His face bore a mix of anguish and misery, and it tore at her to see him this way, knowing she was the cause. He faced the mantel then, resting folded arms across it. He lowered his head to rest on his arms.

Mackenzie leaned against the wall beside the fireplace. "You'd let me go? Just like that."

He didn't bother looking up. "Yes."

That was what she wanted, wasn't it?

Wasn't it?

"But not 'just like that.' " His head slowly turned to face her. "Not at all. What I've given you is an amazing gift: life without the fear of disease or death. Once the threat of the prophecy has been eliminated, you'll be free to go back to your practice or do whatever your heart desires. *Anything* your heart desires. I'm not your captor. I'm your true mate, and I want you to be happy. If that means you're not a part of my life, then so be it." He pushed the dark hair from his face. "I want to show you the world, but if you'd rather go home to Sean, I won't stop you. Understand that your leaving doesn't actually change anything. There is still no one else for either of us. Never has been and never will be. Not until one of us dies. You'll be bound to me for as long as I live." He leaned closer. "And that *could* be a very long time."

She straightened. "Is there an implied threat in there somewhere?"

"No, not at all. You're one of us, and this is how we live and love. It's who we are," he said. "You need to fully understand what you're doing and the consequences. Our ways are very different from those of humans."

That's what Griffin had told her. She took a moment to think about it. "You really mean all that, don't you?"

Christopher nodded. "Absolutely."

Nibbling on her bottom lip, she approached him, and stood close enough to take in that wonderful spicy-sweet scent. Thick muscles rested under his open shirt. He was a Defender, and for the first time, she saw the power in and around him. And he was gorgeous, intelligent, and compassionate. And immortal.

And hurting.

He believed she didn't want to be with him, and why should he think otherwise? She'd come to him not knowing if she would stay or go. Even now, she hesitated.

He stuffed his hands into his pockets. His icy-blue gaze lowered to hers. *Choose freely, Mackenzie, without the heat of my touch. No distractions.* "I want you to choose me, but if you don't, at least know that you made this choice without any influence from me."

He was giving her the choice she needed. He couldn't restore her humanity, but he could let her choose what kind of life she'd lead from this moment forward. Now she had to decide.

She pointed to her left. "I can just walk out that door?"

His eyes closed. "Yes."

"And never come back?" she added.

"If that's what you want." Christopher opened his eyes, letting them rest on her. He really was letting her go, because he believed she needed that to be happy. His own happiness came secondary.

In that moment, Mackenzie recognized his real gift to her. His eyes reflected pain and fear, yet he waited quietly for her choice and, though he'd said nothing, she knew he'd have lived with whatever she decided. Griffin was right: she would make a mistake by leaving him.

She placed a hand on his shoulder, then allowed it to slip down to the front of his chest and stomach. Instantly, the fire started within her again. His golden skin was a powerful aphrodisiac, extraordinarily soft and warm. Facing him, she leaned in to taste the skin at the valley between his pectoral muscles, to savor his unique scent.

Christopher took in a deep breath, let it out, then sucked in another deep breath. "Can I assume this means you're not leaving?" His hands remained inside his pockets. She felt his body temperature skyrocket and his pulse explode beneath her searching mouth. She affected him as much as he affected her. The need was overwhelming for both of them, she could see it now in his hungry gaze, in his tense muscles and quickened breath. And still he didn't move. Not one muscle.

"Yes, you can." she whispered against his skin.

The difference between them was that he accepted the union as something magical and wonderful, ordained by the higher powers that seemed to govern his kind. She had fought until exhaustion threatened to claim her sanity as well her body.

But Mackenzie knew that the time for fighting had ended. She'd now surrendered her chance to leave to the dark-haired immortal, and discovered that it was all right. His gift had demonstrated to her the kind of man he was, and it amazed her. Astounded her, really. She'd had no idea of the depth and power of his emotions, or that he was capable of a sacrifice like that.

Christopher lifted his hands from his pockets. Cupping her face, he whispered his thumb across her cheek. "Do you understand what forever means?"

"I know what it means." She closed her eyes to shut out the hungry blue gaze resting on her. "All of this is a mystery to me. I think maybe you're the sorcerer your people are looking for. I don't understand how it happened so quickly or how it became so strong. What terrifies me is that I want this, too, and I don't understand why." She looked up at him. "I think you're the caster of spells. But, yes, I know what . . ." her voice faltered, ". . . forever means."

"I'm no sorcerer," he said, closing the small gap between them. His mouth whispered over her cheeks, her lips. "Stay with me tonight."

Stay and make love to him, her mind said.

"Yes," he whispered. "Make love to me."

She stepped back to regard him. "That makes all this permanent, doesn't it?"

"No, not really," he said. "We would be consummating the union, just like we would if it were a human marriage. It's the same principle. You and I are of the same essence. We're alike, perfect for each other . . ." He smiled. "Fated, if you will, to be together. You still have choice, though. There is always choice. You *can* walk away. Fate is not really any different from probability, if that's how you prefer to think of it."

She nodded.

He tilted his head, reaching to grasp her hand. "Will you stay with me tonight?"

Mackenzie studied his handsome face while she thought about it. "Doesn't forever frighten you? What if you get tired of me?"

"I think only about what I want to accomplish today. Forever really has no meaning. How could it? Most everything here has a beginning and an end. I could die tomorrow at the hand of any number of threats." He shrugged. "It'll drive you crazy if you think about it too much. I suggest you not worry about it. And I won't get tired of you. We're not like humans. Remember?"

"Hard to forget."

Christopher brought her against the solid warmth of his body. "Come with me, now." He nuzzled her neck, slid his tongue along her pulseline.

She raised her chin for him. The moist warmth from his mouth sent shivers down her back. His embrace was tender, reverent even. Under his ministrations, her residual trepidation gave way to something more primal and demanding.

He reacted to her need with a slow intake of breath against

her skin. "Mackenzie," he whispered, "I need you." His hands bunched fistfuls of her hair. "Really need you."

She loved the way he whispered her name.

His teeth grazed her neck and shoulder. Warm breath against her skin sent her body temperature higher. His hands framed her face as his fiery kiss set her mouth ablaze. "I want you in my bed, underneath me. I can't think of anything I want to do more than make love to you. Will you let me?"

"What about Griffin and the others?" she asked.

He shook his head. "They won't bother us. Don't give it another thought." He bent to grasp her wrist and tug her toward his bedroom.

"How do you know for certain?" she asked.

Eskarian telepathy is highly advanced. They can feel how much I burn for you. He glanced over his shoulder, a mischievous glint in his eye, and smiled. "I know."

Behind closed doors, she stood near him and watched several candles explode to life with brightly dancing flames. Silver-tipped leaves in four small ceramic pots sizzled and smoldered in unison. The scent wafting from the pots was familiar to her, but she couldn't remember where she'd first encountered it. Seemed like ages ago. "Do I know that smell?"

He smiled. "Yeah, you do. Think back to when we first met."

She first thought of the night Christopher and Griffin had cornered her. A chill whispered down her spine at the memory of Griffin's blade at her throat. Then she remembered the next night when Christopher had taken the wolf away. He'd carried a small pot of it in his pocket. "This is Livendium, right? "

"That's right. It's an Eskarian herb."

She nodded, remembering how the soothing fragrance, like a blend of sage and mint, had settled her nerves while he prepared to take her blood. "I like it."

"You'll find it works differently now that you're like us." He'd leaned against the bedroom door. Grasping her hips, he brought her close to his body, turning her around so she saw the room. "Watch the rest of the show," he whispered from behind.

The lamps flashed and then went dim, and the bedroom window opened, allowing a fresh breeze to bathe the room in cool pine-scented air. Music, a serene instrumental, emanated from small speakers suspended in each corner of the ceiling.

When it was calm, she faced him.

He traced the length of her nose with his finger, then whispered it across her bottom lip.

She caught the tip of his finger in her teeth. Her tongue teased it with little strokes and swirls while she watched desire take him—she could see the change—his lips parted, his breathing quickened, and his eyes smoldered with new fire. His response to her was fast and genuine: she turned him on.

Her own body ignited with a wild need to feel his mouth, his skin, upon hers. She let her eyes close, and savored the feather-light touch of his fingers sliding down the front of her shirt. He took the hem and lifted it over her head. "Mackenzie," he whispered. "You're so beautiful."

He pulled her close again, trailing his fingers down her back with a touch so soft, she shivered. "I've awakened so many times from a dream like this, only to find myself alone. Now, here you are, my dream made real."

He pressed a gentle kiss to her shoulder, while his fingers massaged the bead of her nipple through the taut cotton of her sports bra. Dipping to the top of her breast, he grazed the skin with his teeth. Pushing her bra aside, he took her nipple into his mouth, his long fingers curled around both breasts as he suckled her.

A soft moan escaped her lips. Such a simple thing set her body ablaze and scattered any remnants of thought from her head. She buried her fingers in the dark silkiness of his hair, giving herself over to him, to the power he wielded to unleash a firestorm in her body. Like no other, he drew the fire from her, mingled it with his own raging desire, and gave it back again. It was more than making love. It was a connection, a completion, the merging of two souls into one.

Trailing his fingers down the front of her stomach, Christopher quickly unbuttoned her jeans, kneeling at her feet to rid her of the last barrier to her body. He lingered with closed eyes, brushing his soft lips against the underside of each breast.

Her fingers slipped beneath the collar of his shirt. She pushed it off his shoulders, down the corded muscles in his arms, and let it fall to the floor.

He straightened. She leaned in, sucking his own small nipple as he had hers. He grasped her shoulders, clenching and unclenching his fists and whispering soft words in response to the warm path she traced with her tongue. Her pace measured, she followed the valley between the hard ridges of his stomach to the waist of his jeans. There, she stopped and looked up at him.

His eyes were closed, his head tilted back in complete trust. She knew the fire burned him, too. His nostrils flared and twitched in response to her ministrations. She liked knowing she had that effect on this amazing warrior, that her touch and words brought something primal to the surface. Made his body tremble with need.

He spoke softly in that language she didn't understand. Didn't matter. She understood enough. His voice soothed her, made her feel desired, loved. As if a part of him, she was fully attuned to his feelings, his raw, demanding need and desire. Knew how he wanted to be touched.

Without hesitation, she removed the last remnants of his clothing.

Kneeling before him, she caressed his body and erection with her mouth and hands. He let out a soft gasp, leaning back against the wall for support. "Mackenzie . . ." he whispered, a cry in his voice.

She cupped his fullness, taking him so deeply into her mouth, he cried out and tunneled both hands into her hair. He grasped a handful in each and held tight, as if he, too, needed an anchor to keep his trembling body from spiraling apart. "Mateña . . ." he said softly.

Beloved.

Abruptly, Christopher let go of her hair and caught her up in his arms. His mouth locked to hers in a fiery, consuming kiss, he carried her to his bed and followed her down to the soft blankets.

Beginning at her thighs, he kissed and nibbled a steamy path inward to the damp evidence of her need. He parted her legs, dipping to breathe warm air against tender, hot flesh. Her body tensed in anticipation. She took in a deep breath, held it, and waited, both anxious and desperate for his touch. He sampled her, delicately at first, then deeper and faster, as if his own need to become a part of her had been unleashed.

"Christopher," she breathed. Desire for this blue-eyed immortal overwhelmed her, a need to be one with him. Whole. Complete. "Please," she cried.

He lowered his body onto hers.

His tongue washed over her pulseline. She leaned back into the pillow, her unspoken consent allowing him complete access to her throat.

"Please," she said again. She didn't know why she needed this. Didn't care, really, because it would change nothing. She understood only that this was how it had to be.

"I won't hurt you," he whispered.

She knew he wouldn't. *Please . . .*

His mouth found her pulseline. He trailed a line from her ear to her neck with his tongue, then pushed long, canine teeth deep into her skin.

Her temperature skyrocketed. His powerful hips pushed his erection into her, and she cried out from the sheer power of his body as it fused to hers, and his mind and soul bound themselves to her forever. Sweat poured from his body to mix with hers. Wrapping her arms around him, she scored his shoulders with her nails and arched her back, allowing the pyre inside to completely burn her. To complete her. To bind. Forever and always.

Immersed in hot kisses and the soft caresses of his hands, she soared higher and higher. Her world narrowed until there was only him, and what he made her feel.

Higher . . .

Strong internal muscles erupted into spasms and coiled around him, pulling, as if to draw him deeper into her body.

Sharp teeth extended downward of their own volition. She felt them descend, felt yet another need erupt within her.

A need to complete the cycle. What was given out of love and desire would be returned.

"Yes," he whispered, lowering his head so his throat hovered just above her mouth. "Take from me, Mateña. I give it freely."

Closing her mouth over his pulseline, she pushed her long teeth into his skin and felt them immediately withdraw on their own. His body tensed and breath exploded from his lungs in long, raspy moans through clenched teeth. He filled her, physically, spiritually. Completely.

She swallowed his blood, her hand at the nape of his neck. Holding him still, she immersed herself in the perfect taste of him—rich and sweet and thick—and the wild scent of their lovemaking.

She swallowed as quickly as she could, then waited impatiently for her mouth to fill again.

More.

"Enough," he whispered.

More.

"Enough, Mackenzie," he repeated, cupping her jaw in his hand. "Always be aware of how much you take. You must never end a human's life to perpetuate your own."

Startled, she pulled away from his throat and swallowed the last of it. "I'm sorry," she whispered. She'd been carried away by it. The taste, feel, the warmth of the blood, all of it, had engulfed her in a maelstrom of power, love, and life. It was a complete and total connection with another living being.

"It's all right," he said softly.

But, it wasn't. She wanted to feel that again and again. Addictive.

He raised his head to press his lips to hers, to feed from her mouth, as if he needed her all over again. "I am yours, Mackenzie, now and forever." He drew back to trace the outline of her mouth with a finger. "Always. This is how just I thought it would be. Soft, warm, and perfect."

Mackenzie pushed aside her residual desire to taste more of his blood. She knew enough to understand the consequences of addiction. Need as intense as that could not be allowed to continue. "Me, too," she said absently.

She tamped down the need until it lay dormant. Never, never, never . . . *Never let it consume me like that again.*

A moment later, he eased himself from her body to lie at her side. Inhaling slowly, he closed his eyes.

She lay beside him for several moments, watching the rise and fall of his chest. When it looked like he might fall asleep, she propped herself up on an elbow, trailing a single finger along the ridges of his tanned stomach. "Benekeda," she said. "What does that mean?"

His eyes remained closed. "It means that you and I were made for one another, that the gods have decreed we should be together. Eskarians mate for life."

"So, *now* we're really married."

"In the Eskarian way, yes."

"Mmmm," she mused. She rolled over onto her stomach, and rested her chin on her fist. "I'm married." She didn't feel married.

His brow furrowed, but he smiled. "We don't look at it like that. Bound or mated are more common terms."

"Hmmm. And you don't celebrate things like this? Isn't this supposed to be a joyous occasion? As I recall, you said you weren't even sure you'd ever find me. Where's the celebration? Where's my wedding?"

He laughed and rolled onto his side to face her. "Benekeda means 'true mate.' It's left over from the ancient Eskarian language, which almost no one but the elders ever speaks anymore. I do, once in a while. But the joining of two souls is a wonderful, spiritual event. If you think about it, the whole thing is really quite spectacular. It encompasses so much more than human marriages. I knew you were the one for me when I first touched your fur. Do you remember that?"

She mostly remembered the blade at her throat. "Yes, I do."

"And that heat you feel between us? That never changes. We'll always be drawn to one another, no matter what tries to come between us. As for your celebration, the Eskarian women in this area know that you and I are together now. They'll stop by to bring you gifts to celebrate our union. They also know of your love for animals. Don't be surprised if Ivan gets a little sister or brother. The men will do the same for me. But we're not exactly party hounds. Especially the Defenders. There's simply no time for things like that. Most often, all I do is hit the shower and crash."

"Yeah, I can imagine . . ." Mackenzie's mind was half a step ahead of Christopher. "Wait till Aunt Bess meets you." She shook her head and smiled. "She'll have a coronary on the spot. Uncle Jake might, too."

"Well, I'll try not to scare them."

"As if there were a way you could do that." She raised her eyebrows. "Have you looked in the mirror lately? You're intimidating as hell."

Out of the blue, he laughed, free and easy, and so hard it brought tears to his eyes. She found his laughter infectious and giggled with him, even though she had no idea what struck him so funny. All the same, it was wonderful to see him happy.

After he composed himself, she sought to find out what had sent him into peals of laughter. "Okay, what was that all about?"

He rubbed his eyes with the back of his hand. "I don't feel intimidating right now. I feel like a kid who just found a secret treasure, something really rare and special. And I have, except I'm not a kid anymore. I just woke up from a very long slumber and found you."

His confession melted her heart. "What a sweet thing to say. Thank you."

"I'm lucky I found you," he said, turning onto his side. "Nothing good has ever come from a demon wolf. Until now."

Mackenzie nodded. "I guess the wolf bite was good. Thank God that Sean was there, or I might not have survived." She gasped. "Oh no . . . Sean . . ."

What was she going to do with Sean? "He's going to kill me. Or you."

"Yeah, I know. He doesn't like me much." He pushed a hand through his hair, and shrugged.

"He'll get used to you—eventually. He just thinks his territory has been invaded."

"He'd be a good Defender. He's very protective. I see how he watches out for you." Christopher leaned over to kiss her shoulder.

Her own protective alarms sounded. "Don't even go there. I don't want anything to happen to him. He's the only real family I've got. Bess and Jake are distant relatives and, while I love them dearly, they aren't like Sean. I *can't* lose him." It frightened her to think about the possibility. No, she wouldn't allow him to become a Defender. But could he become immortal? "Do you have rules about who you convert?"

Christopher nodded. "Sean would be a good addition to our family. We want those of strong character and integrity."

Then, something else occurred to her. "So, what happens if one mate dies?"

"Then the gods would provide another one, but it may be hundreds or even thousands of years down the road. It happens whenever it happens. Griffin's benekeda was killed when he was younger than I am now. With any luck, he'll find a new one soon. Maybe she'll improve his bad-tempered disposition." Christopher traced the line of her nose. "Now, no more talk of things that most likely won't happen. Come sit in the Jacuzzi with me for a while."

"Sure." She nodded.

He rolled off the bed and sauntered, still nude, to the

bathroom. In the doorway, he stopped, looked back at her. "Coming?"

Mackenzie wasn't quite as comfortable with her own nudity as Christopher. She swung her legs over the bed and, in one smooth movement, bent to pick up her T-shirt and toss it over her head before meeting him at the bathroom door.

His grin told her all she needed to know. "What?" she said, shrugging. "I'm not used to running around naked."

He laughed. "You'll get used to it, I promise." He draped an arm over her shoulders. Bringing her closer, he bent to kiss the top of her head. "I had this Jacuzzi put in three years ago after discovering, quite inadvertently, that even chlorinated hot water is beneficial to us. Of course, I wouldn't use it for total submergence, but partial seems to work well enough for little things."

Mackenzie studied his face. "Total submergence? What are you talking about?"

"We use hot, salty water to heal serious injuries. Normally, Jason or one of the other sendagis will submerge a wounded Defender in what we call a healing tank, which is essentially a whirlpool of hot water. Jason's very good about watching over them."

The Jacuzzi was massive, set just above the dark green marble floor. Christopher left her side to snap on the jets and check the temperature of the water.

She watched him move from the Jacuzzi to the cabinet, where he retrieved two large, thick towels and set them on the edge of the tub. His strong, graceful body was beautiful, like captured music in human form. His laughter was easy and free. Naked or fully clothed, he just always seemed to be perfectly comfortable with himself and his place in the world.

Christopher scooped up her hand and kissed it. "The

wounds heal quicker in the water, so Jason will keep the Defender submerged until he looks better. I've seen some guys come back from the grave. Jason's pretty good."

"How do they breathe if they're submerged?"

"We can breathe through our skin when underwater," he said, leading her to the tub.

She thought about that. "You're amphibians?"

"Technically, yes," he admitted. "But it's not that big a deal. It's not like we shift into frogs or salamanders. We just don't come up for air for awhile. Sometimes a long while," he said with a little shrug of one shoulder.

"Shift?" she echoed. "What does that mean?"

"Shape-shift. We can take most any form we choose."

"You mean change what you look like?" she asked, sitting on the edge of the tub.

"Yeah, we can. Do you want me to show you?"

Did she want to see him change his form? Sure. Why the hell not? "Yes."

A mischievous grin creased his face. "What would you like me to be?"

She thought a moment. "A cat?"

"Okay." He stepped into the center of the bathroom and closed his eyes. Two seconds later, his body compacted into a large, black cat. He circled her ankles, rubbing his soft head against her shins.

The black cat looked up at her with twinkling blue eyes. *What do you think of that?*

Shocked, she nearly fell off the edge of the tub. "Oh, my God. I wouldn't have believed it if I hadn't seen it for myself. All of you do this?" She bent to scratch behind his ears. He purred and danced between her legs, then returned to the center of the room.

He shifted back to human form. "Yes, we all do it. You can

do it, too. Any bird or mammal you choose."

She touched his shoulder, just to see if he still felt the same. "Incredible."

"It's easy," he said, stepping into the Jacuzzi. "I'll show you how to do it after things settle down a bit." He looked around the room. "So, tell me, what do you think of the place?"

"It's breathtaking. Simply amazing." She nodded her approval. The bathroom alone was as big as her bedroom.

"I'm glad you think so." He caught her hand, tugging her toward the water. "Come, sit with me."

Mackenzie discarded her T-shirt and followed him into the steamy, fizzy water. He took one of the seats, pulled her onto his lap, and locked his hands around her waist.

"I wish I had more time to spend with you. I could stay here forever." Christopher nuzzled her throat, trailing his warm tongue along her skin, kissing gently. "I love how soft your skin is."

"Why do you have to leave?"

"Blair needs me. I'm the fastest, strongest Defender we have. Lucky me," he said, shrugging. "Normally, I'd have left Service the second I'd bound myself to you, but the prophecy is huge. I have to be there in case something goes wrong." He slipped his hand down into the water to find the silken entrance to her body. "But I'd rather be doing other things."

Slowly he massaged her until her eyes closed and the pyre within her came to life again.

"What you do to me must surely be a sin." She raised her chin, and let her head fall back. "Are you ready to do this again?"

"It's not a sin. It's my gift to you." His mouth closed over her nipple and suckled gently. Two fingers slid inside her, moving slowly, driving her higher. Her breath quickened, her pulse following. She moaned softly, silently pleading with him to quicken his pace, but the rhythm never changed.

"And yes, I am ready to be inside you again," he said, removing his fingers. He slipped his hands under her thighs, lifting her enough to poise her over his thick erection. "I love the way you feel." He lowered her body onto his shaft, inch by delicious inch, until she was filled completely. He leaned back, closing his eyes, and moved leisurely in and back out again.

The languid thrust of his hips sent liquid fire racing through her body. She wanted him to move faster, to take her over the edge, but his strong hands just above her hips kept her still, prevented her from quickening the pace. "Christopher, please, you're driving me nuts. Go faster."

He looked at her through half-closed eyes. "I want to drive you nuts," he said softly.

"No, take me higher . . ." she whispered.

"I will." Christopher inhaled, then let out a moan. He pressed his thumb against her most sensitive nub and massaged. His voice lowered to a seductive whisper. "I will."

She shivered, moaned. Leaning forward, she took his mouth, poured her own passion into him. As the pyre consumed her, she surrendered to it, to him, to the connection that spun her helplessly out of control.

Seconds later, she whimpered softly. Muscles rippled in a tidal wave of pleasure. She locked her arms around his neck, holding tight while the last remnants of her orgasm shook her body.

He drew back to look at her, but his focus was elsewhere. His eyes blinked slowly, closed halfway, only to open again. He was lost deep within himself. Within her. Another thrust and his brow creased, then his jaw clenched and his bottom lip quivered. His eyes closed, and he softly pulsed inside her.

Chapter Seven

Mackenzie rested her head against a rolled-up towel on the other side of the Jacuzzi. She looked beautiful, lying amid a play of blue water and warm light, with flushed skin from the heat of their lovemaking. She'd fallen silent shortly after they made love, and Christopher was uncomfortable with it. He knew something wasn't right. A quick sweep of her mind would've told him what he needed to know, but talking aloud would be more comfortable for her, so that's what he'd do. Telepathic communication could wait for a while.

He watched her for a long moment. When she didn't say anything, he touched her shoulder. "What's going on? Are you all right?"

She nodded, her brow furrowed. "What happens next? You and I are married, or mated, so what does that mean? What am I supposed to do now?"

"It means I'll be with you forever. That I'll wake up next to you every morning, and lie beside you every night." He brushed her cheek with the back of his hand. Her skin was velvety soft, as was common to Eskarians. But hers was more than that. Extraordinarily soft and clear and beautiful. Perfect, to him.

"Here?" she asked. "In this house?"

"Yes," he nodded. "Here."

She scanned the room. "I'm not ready for that yet. I have my own house, my own life. You can't possibly expect me to just drop everything and take up with you, do you?"

Actually, he had. That's how it had happened for several Defenders who had found their true mates. "No," he fibbed, "I don't, though I hope you'll eventually warm up to the idea."

"In time . . ." Her voice trailed off as she looked away.

"This isn't a death sentence, Mackenzie. Whatever is upsetting you, I'm here to work through it with you."

"And what about tomorrow? Will you be there tomorrow?" she asked.

He held her close, wishing he'd already left Service, wishing he wasn't needed by his people. Anything so he didn't have to leave her. "I have to take care of whatever threat the prophecy brings, much as I'd rather leave it to Griffin or Blair. Once it's been eliminated, I'm done with Service. But, right now, getting rid of the threat has to take precedence. Once we identify who, or what, we're up against, I'll have to go wherever Blair sends me, and, honestly, it could be anywhere in the world. I just don't know yet. All I really know is that I will come back to you. I have to come back to you."

"How could you know that? You don't even know what you're up against," she said, a tone of disbelief in her voice. "Nor do you know how long it could take."

He drew back to look at her. "That's true, but I do know I've waited two hundred years to find you. Nothing will keep me away from you. Mackenzie, you have to believe that. I won't let anything come between us. I need you to believe in me, in what I can do."

"I don't require fairy tales or magic, Christopher. I don't need a white knight, nor do I need a hero. I can see that everyone's uptight about this prophecy. I know you're going up against something really big. I'm afraid to let myself care for you, if you're just going to get yourself killed. I don't think I can take that. I don't want to . . ." She fell silent again, studying the tips of her damp hair. Her brow creased in varying degrees and her fingers quickly picked off the ends of several aberrant strands of hair. "I just want the guy I'm with to be someone I can depend on. Someone I can love."

"What are you saying?" he asked.

Mackenzie shrugged, then looked at him. "Maybe I should just go home until this prophecy thing is over. I really should get back to Sean and my work. You could call me later, or something. You know, if you survive whatever you're going to fight."

"Eskarians are not that easy to kill. Plus, I'm not going to be fighting this thing alone, Mackenzie. Griffin will be there. So will Jason. Our strongest and finest warriors are here. Alex, Randy, Aaron. All of them. I wouldn't be surprised if old Nic showed up. Everyone here is an exceptional fighter. And they're all ancient and wise in the ways of strategy and battle. There's little chance that anything will happen to me." He smoothed back her hair. "Do you understand that? We have an army to stop the prophecy from coming to fruition. I'm out in front, but there's a battalion behind me."

She nodded. "Okay, that I can understand. It makes sense to me."

"Good. But, I still don't want you to be alone. You're new to our family, and so much can happen. It's a dangerous time for you. I want you where someone is always around to protect you, so that you're here, too, when I come back."

"If I need protecting, Sean can do it."

"Not anymore," he said. "You're much stronger than he is, and the kinds of threats you would face are not something he could begin to handle. It's far too dangerous."

She looked away, her nose wrinkling. "Honestly, Christopher, I don't really want to stay here. This isn't my home."

He scanned the room. "We can easily make it your home, Mackenzie. Anything you need or want to feel more comfortable, we can do."

She followed his gaze. "I don't know. It's awfully big and formal."

He softened his voice until it was like liquid satin pouring over her. "Then we'll change it. The important thing is I'm not leaving you alone."

She looked back at him, defiance in her emerald gaze. "Send someone to watch over me. I want to go home. My patients need me. Sean needs me. You don't."

"That's not really true. I do need you, Mackenzie, but I have to finish my job. I would do that, even if I were human. Won't you wait a few days for me?"

Her discomfort was palpable. He didn't really think she'd just happily turn her life upside down overnight, but his hope that she'd at least be amenable to the idea of living with him was beginning to wither.

Her gaze dropped to the bubbling water. "Sure," she said softly.

She didn't want to wait. He saw it written all over her soft face. "What if we stopped by the clinic in the morning to see how it's going, and then went by your place to pick up a few things?"

"So, you're going to make me stay with you?" she asked, returning a cold gaze.

Christopher sighed. "My home is our base of operations. Defenders will be coming in and out while we ferret out the Triad, all day and night. You'll be safe here." He searched her face for signs of acceptance.

She continued to study the effervescent water.

"They all know you're new to the family and will look out for you. It gives me a lot of comfort to know that they'll be with you. It'll let me do my job without wondering if you're all right or not. Please, tell me you'll stay here. I'll have the entire house painted and new furniture put in, if you need that to feel better about staying here. Anything, Mackenzie. Just tell me what you need."

Mackenzie looked up at him. "You don't need to go to such extremes, but thank you for asking."

"No problem," he said. He took some comfort in the fact she didn't look as annoyed. "Will you stay?"

"Yes," she answered.

Relief swamped him. "Great. That's what we'll do, then."

"I'd like that," she said with a nod. "I really do need to let Will know what's going on."

"Who's Will?" His stomach did an odd little flip.

"My partner. We co-own the business. Both of us have worked very hard to make it what it is. He's probably ready to choke me by now. I don't usually leave him alone this long."

He inhaled deeply to quell the tiny bit of jealousy that her business partner was a man. "I'm sure he's fine, but let's stop by first thing. Would that make you feel better? You could check on your patients, and I'll let Will know that you'll be unavailable for a few days."

"Let him know?" she repeated. "Or suggest that he be happy with his demanding workload?"

"Whatever works," he said with a grin. He drifted over to rest his hands on her thighs, just to be close, to feel the warmth and life within her.

She smiled. "Okay, but no hypnosis. Let him decide for himself."

Christopher raised his eyebrows. "Of course. I'll be on my best behavior."

"Sure, you will," she said. She paused a moment, seemingly deep into her own thoughts. "Do you . . . wear rings to show you're married?"

"No, not usually," he replied. He knew where this was going. "Shall I take you shopping after we visit Will? You can choose a ring—any ring. I'll put it on your finger and tell you that I'll be with you for as long as we're both alive. I'll tell you that until you begin to believe it." Christopher stood up and framed her face with both hands. "I did marry you, Mackenzie, in the Eskarian way. And every day I wake up next to you will be a celebration. I'll come back to you, so I can tell you all these things."

Her fingers curled around his forearms. "You must think I'm silly for thinking about things like rings and celebrations," she said softly. "If I'd known I was going to be whisked away by a pseudo-vampire, I would've planned differently."

Christopher nodded. "Most of us would've done something differently."

She tilted her head. "What would you have done?"

"I'll tell you some other time. It's not a happy story, and I don't think we need that at the moment." Christopher searched her face. "Do you feel better about all this now?" He took in a slow breath and held it.

"Yeah, I do. I just wish you weren't leaving to battle something you know nothing about. That scares me like you wouldn't believe. I don't know exactly what I could be losing, but I think it might be something really good. I hope you're right about your friends."

"I am," he assured her. "I know them all so well and trust them with my life. No hesitation."

"That's good to know." She put some distance between them. "Now, tell me what you do for a living, besides hunt down demon wolves and humans destined to destroy the world?"

Christopher let out his breath. Good. She wanted to know something about him. That one little thing released the tension he'd kept in his shoulders for some time now. "I'm an investor. I bought a lot of waterfront property many years ago all over this area, and just kept it for decades. I sold most of it, at a substantial profit, a few years ago. That's when I bought my first boat, a power catamaran. I call it *Maggie Blue*, after my mother. Her name was Margaret, and she had blue eyes. Maybe you'll take a ride with me some day." He paused to see what she'd say. When she didn't say a word, he returned to the original topic. "Anyway, I still have several homes in Seattle, some on Lake Washington, that I'll get around to selling eventually. I also have some commercial property along the downtown waterfront. There are some advantages to immortality. I was around to buy all that prime waterfront land."

"I can see how easy it'd be to become quite wealthy. And with so much time on your hands, you could weather the highs and lows of any market. I'm guessing you're all rich."

"Probably," he answered. "I don't really know for sure. We never talk about that sort of thing, but we do all have nice houses and cars. I counseled Michael when he became Eskarian, about a hundred years ago. He's my apprentice, so it was my duty. Otherwise . . ." He shrugged.

Mackenzie nodded, then looked out the French doors centered between the Jacuzzi and the large double-headed shower. "I should probably get home soon. Sean will worry. He thinks it's his job to baby-sit me."

"Your personal Defender."

"No, not a Defender, just a big brother who needs to get a life."

Christopher returned to the other side of the Jacuzzi to give her some space. "I'd like to think you wouldn't be opposed to spending more time with me. Maybe we could encourage Sean to move ahead with his life."

She looked away. "Maybe. Maybe it'd be better to talk about that after you've taken care of your wizards."

"I'm not worried about them. Your safety and happiness has my complete attention, though."

"I'll be fine. I just need some time. Admittedly, I am a little worried about Sean." she said, returning her gaze to his.

"Sean is a grown man. He'll survive without you."

"We've never lived apart for very long." She paused. "I presume I'm not your prisoner and can leave anytime. Is that true? I need to get home now."

"No, you're not a prisoner. I'll take you," he offered.

"I have a car here. I'll drive myself." She pushed by him, got out of the spa, and wrapped herself in a towel.

"I can take you. Really. I insist." He grabbed the remaining towel on his way out of the Jacuzzi. He dried his hair first, shook it out, then dried his body. Slipping on a faded pair of blue jeans, he turned to see she still stood in her towel. "Everything okay?"

She looked at the towel. "My clothes are still wet from the rain."

"No, they're not. They're dry and waiting for you on the bed." His thoughts drifted back to the moment she'd entered the living room. She'd looked so beautiful then, rain slowly trailing down her cheeks, emerald eyes dewy from confessional tears, and the touch of her fingers along his cheek had been so tender. He'd wanted to bury his face in her ebony hair and then lose himself inside her forever.

"They're dry?" She pulled the towel up, looking toward the door.

"Yes, they are. I have two people who take care of things for me. Sasha put your clothes in the dryer."

Her brow raised. "Sasha?"

Was that jealousy? He smiled, pleased at the thought. "One of the caretakers. The other one is Thomas. He tends the gardens, and does repair work whenever it's needed."

"Must make things much easier for you."

"Yeah, it frees me up to take care of investments, and hunt. Mostly hunt."

She headed for the bedroom, disappearing behind the door. "Do you like to hunt?"

"No, not really. In fact, once we defeat the Triad, my hunting days are over. I'm already looking for another apprentice to replace me, specifically. I have Michael, and he's good, but he doesn't have the speed I'm looking for." He sighed and leaned against the shower door. "I'm looking forward to making a change in my life. Some days it feels so chaotic. I might be in the middle of something, and have to drop it and leave to battle . . . whatever—it could be almost anything." He looked around the bathroom. "There were times I'd leave so fast, I'd forget to turn off the lights or music. I used to do it after I'd already left the house, you know, telekinetically. About two years ago, during a thunderstorm, I shut them off while Sasha was working. Scared the life out of her. We have a generator, so even if the island loses power, we don't. Anyway, she really let me have it when I got home." He chuckled at the memory. "I just leave them all on now."

"You let your housekeeper talk to you like that?"

"Sure. She was pissed. It just didn't occur to me." He shrugged.

"That was sweet of you." She paused a minute. "You seem like a nice guy."

He shrugged again. He was what he was. "I guess . . ."

"So, what do you think you'll do after your hunting days end?"

"I haven't a clue. In a way, I've been in limbo for a long time. You get up, every day, and it's the same thing. Fight this, fight that, get wounded, heal, and then do it all again the next day. It's what we're meant to do, but honestly, it's not much of a life. I get time off, now and again. It does little to offset the long stretches of time where everything's the same."

She wandered into the bathroom, fully dressed, a towel on her head. "Listen, I hope you'll forgive me for leaving so quickly. I just really feel like I need to get back to Sean."

Evidently they were done talking. "If that's what you need to do, I understand." He didn't, really. Sean was a full-grown man. She was an adult as well. Yet, they clung to one another as if they were still children in an unfriendly world.

"He'll be pounding on the gate if I make him wait too long, you know. As I've said, he's very protective."

He nodded. There was really no reason to keep her away from Sean, for now, he supposed. Sean would comfort her while Christopher dealt with whatever the prophecy had in store for them. After that, Mackenzie's relationship with her brother would change. Sean wasn't the only one who needed to move forward. "Yes, you said that. Will you let me drive you home?"

She looked up at him. Her emerald eyes reflected the uncertainty he knew she felt. "I guess so."

He closed the space between them to hold her face gently in his hands. "I'm coming back, Mackenzie," he whispered. He covered her mouth with his, and filled her with every ounce of passion he had. His kiss was long, deep, and little by little, he let her see images of love and family, happiness that spanned centuries. Eternity. "I am yours, Mateña. I could never leave you. Feel the truth in my words."

She glanced away a moment, then found his gaze again, and nodded slowly.

He kissed her again, then disappeared into the closet. Choosing a dark blue T-shirt, he pulled it over his head then shoved on his boots.

Back in the bedroom, he nudged her toward the door. "Now, come with me. I'll have your car driven home for you." As they headed to the front door, he snatched up both her coat and his, pulling her along without any chance for her to protest.

Outside, a large black limousine waited.

Mackenzie stopped. Her mouth dropped open. "We're riding in this?"

He laughed. "Yes, we are."

"How many cars do you have?"

"Seven. The Cobra's here now, but most of the time it's in off-site storage, along with the Super Bird, so they're always protected. I love American muscle cars."

Her mouth formed a perfect, silent O. He led her to the car, stepping aside so she could settle in at the far end of the black leather seat, then he followed. The moment he sat back, the engine rumbled to life and the car crept along the brick driveway until the iron gate had fully opened. Gliding through, the car turned and headed for Mackenzie's home.

She quietly stared out the window, chewing on a thumbnail. Watching her, he decided it was best to leave her to her own thoughts. Soon enough, he'd be taking her from all she knew, plunging her deep into his Eskarian world of blood and battles—the very one she feared. She was not ready to be left on her own and he, quite simply, would not lose her. To anything.

Several minutes passed in silence. She glanced at him once, but only briefly, then returned to the night scenery. When she spoke, it was solemn and measured. "I hope your battle is over quickly." She faced him. "How come you can't stay here? Let Griffin do all the fighting."

He smiled in an attempt to reassure her. "You know I can't. I'm the fastest and strongest." He brought her hand to his mouth, and pressed a kiss to her fingertips. "It may not take as long as you think."

Her gaze returned to the scenery. "Maybe. Maybe it'll take longer."

"It won't."

She looked at him again. "It might."

"What's really bothering you, Mackenzie? What are you afraid of?"

A soft sigh escaped her lips. "Losing."

He shook his head. "It'll never happen. Never."

The limousine pulled into the driveway. Christopher stepped out and offered his hand to Mackenzie. She took it, and he bent to kiss the inside of her wrist before he helped her out of the car. Her slow pace toward her own home was a measure of her weariness. As soon as it was possible, he would have her safely tucked in her own bed. Griffin and he would patrol the property to ensure she was safe. They'd lost new Eskarians before. It wasn't going to happen now.

Mackenzie opened the door and stepped over the threshold.

Sean sprang from his blue chair, beer in hand. "Kenz, I'm so glad you're back. I was afraid that Chris—" He stopped in his tracks, glaring at Christopher.

Christopher stepped in behind Mackenzie, filling the doorway. "You were saying? What about Christopher?" He completed the word for Sean.

"I was saying I'm glad Mackenzie is back." Sean took a swig from his beer. "Hello, Christopher. What brings you around?"

Sean returned to the couch. On the other end sat a young

man. His dark hair had heavy streaks of blond, which reminded Christopher of an Inyan Raider, except the Raider's humanoid hair was more like strips of leather.

Even from this distance, Christopher smelled the alcohol on Sean's breath. He'd been drinking for some time. "Afternoon, Sean. I wanted to be sure Mackenzie got home safely."

Sean straightened. "Why? Did something happen to her car?"

"No, it's fine. I wanted to see that she was safe."

"Okay. I guess." He set his beer on the wooden table. "Why would you need to do that?"

Christopher smiled. Alcohol did strange things to humans, made them docile and vulnerable to suggestion. He often found their drunken antics amusing, though more than once he'd rescued an unwary, intoxicated human from predators who searched for easy money, or an easy ride. "Because, like you, I care about her very much."

"Yeah, as if . . ." Sean countered.

Mackenzie interrupted. "Scott, what's going on? Any news about Amy?" She shook off her jacket and tossed it over the back of the couch.

"No news. I'm just hanging out with Sean. Waiting." He pushed a hand through his hair. Strands of blond hair mingled with dark brown. Eerie and fascinating at the same time. Strands of silk mixing with strands of glass. "I hate that there's nothing I can do to change any of this. I miss her."

"Have you called the police yet?" She fell back into the plush blue chair, one leg curled beneath her.

"Yeah, I did. I told them what I know, and Sean did, too. I'm guessing they'll want to talk to you next."

She nodded. "Not a problem."

Christopher moved behind her to keep an eye on both

Sean and Scott. He rested his hands on her shoulders, partially so he could enjoy the warmth of her skin and partially to annoy her brother. It was rude, but he rather enjoyed it.

Scott took a long swig from his beer. "I can't imagine where she would be, but I'm starting to think she's not coming back."

"No, you can't think like that. She'll come home." Mackenzie reached back to touch Christopher's hand.

"So, Kenz, not to be rude . . . well, maybe to be rude, but why did you bring this guy home with you?" Sean's gaze didn't waver from Christopher as he asked his question.

Mackenzie scowled at her brother. "Back off, would you? This is for me. I want to spend some time with him."

"Why? He's a jerk."

Christopher smiled, amused with Sean's candor.

"Sean, stop it. He isn't a jerk."

"Sure, he is," Sean countered. "Just ask him."

Christopher bent to her ear. "You need to call your partner. And Sean should probably know that you're coming back with me," he said.

Her shoulders tensed immediately. "I can't."

"I won't leave you here. You're coming with me, whether you've made your arrangements or not." His voice became his command. "Tell Sean."

She sighed softly and looked at her brother. "Sean, I'm going to spend a few days with Christopher, at his place. We want some private time together."

Sean grimaced. "Aw, Kenz, now why would you want to do that?"

"I like him. He makes me feel things I haven't felt in a long time," she said, looking up at Christopher.

What things? he wondered. Darned if he didn't want to scan her mind again. It was hard not to. He would have all the information he needed. Operating in the dark like this was driving him crazy.

Sean gripped his beer with both hands. "What about Daniel?"

Mackenzie's shoulders tensed again. "Sean, please . . ." Her eyes closed as she rubbed the center of her brow.

Christopher began a slow massage to relax her. Sean didn't need to know the truth right away. "Mackenzie and Daniel have parted ways."

Sean glared at Christopher, daggers in his gaze. "So you took the opportunity to swoop in when she was hurting?"

Mackenzie looked up at Christopher, apprehension in her eyes.

"No, I offered her friendship and understanding."

"You? Do I look stupid?" Sean stood up and headed for the kitchen. "I need another beer."

Christopher followed. He wanted to take the opportunity to make amends with Sean. "Look, I'm sorry we got off on the wrong foot. I'm really not some jerk out to break your sister's heart. I truly care very deeply for her. Like you, her happiness and welfare are foremost in my mind."

Sean pulled a bottle of beer from the refrigerator. He turned to Christopher and raised his chin in defiance. "I really don't want her hanging around someone like you. She deserves better. She deserves someone who's at least human."

"She's not—" Christopher suddenly felt Mackenzie's distress. He spun around, and rushed toward to the living room.

What the . . . ?

Scott had draped Mackenzie's arm over his shoulder and was dragging her to the front door. Her head hung forward, her body slack. He whirled around to Christopher. "Get lost. This doesn't concern you." He thrust out his hand. Immediately, a fiery, orange globe shot out from it toward Christopher with such speed and force, it slammed him back into the wall, scattering bits of drywall everywhere.

Christopher's clothes were either singed or burning. He dropped onto his stomach and smothered the flames, then looked up to see his adversary at the front door, ready to leave with Mackenzie.

Not a chance in hell!

With preternatural speed, he launched off the wall, and plucked her from Scott's arms. He shoved the smaller man against the wall and held him still with a solid grip around his throat. "It most definitely concerns me. What did you do to Mackenzie?"

"I do not answer to you." Scott's eyes blazed defiance.

"Then to whom *do* you answer?" Christopher purposely spoke in a measured, seductive tone, ensuring Scott's compliance.

"I am no novice, either. I hear the spell behind your words." He raised his chin. "I will tell you nothing."

Christopher frowned. How would Scott know there was subliminal force embedded in the words? His gaze remained locked to Scott's. "Sean? Take Mackenzie for me."

Sean hurried to his side. He took Mackenzie from Christopher's arms and laid her gently on the couch.

Christopher scowled at Scott, staring deep into his eyes. "Is that right? I think you will. Tell me, Scott, are you afraid to die?" His canines lengthened. "Hmm?"

Scott's eyes widened but he remained silent.

Christopher brought Scott's neck to his mouth and punctured the veins. The hot effervescence shot to the back of his throat and tasted sweet from the adrenaline that had surged through his body. Indeed, the young man was afraid. Good.

When he'd drained Scott of most of his blood, Christopher let him fall hard on the floor. "Oops, sorry," he said.

"What happened?" Sean's face was etched with concern.

"Scott attacked her. He was about to take her. Is she all right?" Christopher leaned over the couch to lay a hand on her shoulder.

"I think so. She seems to be sleeping." Sean brushed her hair back from her face.

Christopher returned to Scott, wrenched him upright, and slammed him against the wall. Splinters of drywall drifted to the floor. "Now, do you have anything to say to me? If I take any more blood, you'll die. I'm still a little thirsty."

Scott's dark eyes opened slowly. "Nothing to say."

Christopher took the Eskarian dagger from his coat pocket, positioning the tip against the sensitive area just behind Scott's jaw. "Are you sure? I only want one simple name. Tell me, Scott, who do you work for?" He pressed the dagger in enough to draw what little blood was left.

Scott winced. "I serve the great warlock, Uleah."

Christopher pressed harder. "What do you want with Mackenzie?"

Scott's eyes closed. "She will be the host for his return to the physical realm. You can't stop us, you know. You're not strong enough. You think you are, but you don't have near the strength of the Triad."

"Mackenzie's not going anywhere, Scott. I have her and I'm not letting go."

"You won't even know when we've taken her," Scott said, his eyes lighting up with this latest threat.

Christopher exploded in black fury. He dropped the dagger into his pocket, picked Scott up with both hands, and hurled him to the far wall. Scott's body slammed against it, breaking the interior frame and spraying drywall bits. "Who's not strong enough?"

He drew the dagger again as he approached the man he now considered nothing more than prey. Scott's head raised, and he murmured something that Christopher heard, but didn't understand.

A spear of lightning came from nowhere and pierced Christopher through the chest, throwing him several feet back into the front door. He slumped over, gasping for breath, then staggered to his feet, in pain but ready to finish the job. Scott raised a hand, waving slightly and whispering as Christopher charged. A second bolt of lightning came from nowhere and speared him again. The force threw him across the carpet and embedded his dagger into the wall behind him.

Griffin, I need your assistance. Christopher had no choice but to call for help.

Only a moment or two passed before Scott rose to his feet, seemingly no longer affected by the blood loss. "You won't win. You can't. She will die and Uleah will be reborn." Brushing bits of drywall and powder from his clothes, he spun on his heel and disappeared out the back door.

Griffin burst through the front door with wild hair, and sweat dripping from his face. "Christopher?"

"Scott went out the back door. He's got brown hair, streaked with blond. Somehow he's running on precious little blood." Christopher coughed, then winced from the pain in his ribs. "Don't feel too bad if you accidentally kill him."

Griffin disappeared into the kitchen and out the back door.

"Sean?" Christopher coughed again.

Sean raised his head from his position over Mackenzie's body. "Yeah?"

"Is Mackenzie all right?" Christopher wiped his face with the back of his hand. His muscles ached ferociously, but he'd seen worse. Much worse. If this was as bad as it got, they would do just fine.

"She's still asleep." Sean raised himself off his sister, and sat down on the floor in front of her.

"Good." Christopher pulled himself upright and rested his head against the wall. Every muscle in his body ached, but it would be only minutes until he was healed. Too many minutes.

His burnt raincoat and shirt hadn't fared as well. The large hole in this shirt where the lightning had struck him revealed blackened skin underneath. It was healing—he could feel it, but it was taking far too long for his comfort. Above his head, the dagger was solidly embedded deep in the wall. With minimal effort, he plucked it free and tucked it back into his coat pocket.

Moments later, Griffin returned to the living room. "He's gone."

Christopher spat a few choice Gaelic curses. His strength restored, he rose to his feet. "Who is Uleah?" Absently, he rubbed the new skin over his chest.

Griffin's head shook. "I don't know. Never heard the name."

"Scott said he served Uleah. He also said that Mackenzie would be the host and I couldn't stop them. He would have taken her tonight." More Gaelic curses.

"Them? How many?"

"I don't know. He said, 'We will have her.' " Christopher moved to the couch, checking Mackenzie's pulse. Leaning over her, he spoke, using the power of his voice to command her. "Mackenzie, wake up. I need to know that you're all right."

Her eyelashes fluttered a moment, and then she moaned softly, head lolling from one side to the other. Suddenly, she bolted upright.

Christopher caught her shoulders, eased her back against the pillows. "It's all right. He's gone. Tell me how you feel."

She turned to him with wide eyes. "Terrified."

He knelt beside her and held her hands. His thumbs whispered over her fingers. "He's gone now. You don't have to be afraid."

Her hands shook visibly. "I'm afraid not only for myself, but for Amy, too. I had no idea Scott was capable of such a thing. What if he hurt her?"

Christopher winced. She deserved to know the truth about Amy. "Mackenzie, I'm sorry," he began slowly. "Scott did nothing to Amy. She was taken down by a wolf last Friday night. I destroyed it myself."

"You knew about her all this time?" Mackenzie glared at him. "Why didn't you tell me?" Her voice was soft, hurt.

"Honestly, I haven't had a chance until now."

She studied him, as if she was thinking about what he'd said. Tears welled in her eyes, but he could see the anger behind them. "There was plenty of time to tell me. You chose not to." She slapped his face. "I can't believe you did that. Selfish jerk."

"She didn't suffer. The wolf was very quick." He rose to his feet, rubbing his cheek. Her temper was quicker than a Costa Rican Ghostcat's. Her strength was formidable as well.

"Christopher," Griffin interrupted. "We should find out who this Uleah is. We need to understand what kind of threat he, or it, poses. Bad timing, don't you think? If this prophecy turns out to be like the previous catastrophes, we'll have our hands full. Do you suppose the two events are related?"

"Haven't a clue." Christopher shook his head. "I need to know what they wanted with Mackenzie. Exactly what is a host used for? He said she would die and Uleah would be reborn. I don't understand how all that would work, but there's no way in hell I'll let her die. Where's Blair?"

"He's at your place, along with Ian."

Christopher turned to Sean. "I'm taking Mackenzie with me. She needs to be protected at all times. Can you pack some clothes for her?"

"Sure. Can I go, too? Maybe I could help?"

He sighed. "This is a very serious threat we're dealing with here. I can't have you challenging me at every turn. Understand that I will protect Mackenzie from now on. Give me any crap at all, and I'll have Griffin deal with you. Do you have a problem with any of this?"

Sean scanned Griffin's large, muscular body. The silver-eyed warrior smiled, his long, gleaming canines fully extended.

Christopher grinned. *Nice touch, Old Man.*

Sean's eyes widened. "Um . . . no."

"Fine. Go pack her things." Christopher waved dismissively.

Mackenzie sat up, rubbed her eyes, then pushed both hands through her hair.

Christopher knelt beside her, shackling her wrist to prevent any more outbursts.

She looked at him with fire in her eyes.

He didn't have time to deal with that now.

Two fingers caressed her jaw line while his thumb whispered across her cheek. "I chose not to burden you further with things you can't change. It was not meant to deceive you." He paused, waiting for any kind of reaction. All he saw was fire. "You need to call Will, now. Tell him you have to leave tonight. You're not sure when you'll be back. There is a family emergency." The power of his voice would ensure her compliance. "No more anger, Mackenzie."

Her gaze dropped to her lap. "You order me around as if I

were a child, Christopher." She looked up at him. "I'm not. Please stop it."

She should've accepted his command without hesitation, but she didn't. Her mind was strong, and she wouldn't be swayed unless she wanted to be swayed. "You're right. I'm sorry. I still need you to do these things, though, so I can have you guarded at all times. Now that we know someone wants you dead, we need to be certain they can't find you again. Will you do as I've asked, please?"

She thought about it, inhaled, and nodded. "Yes, I will."

He let out a sigh of relief. "Good, thank you." He stood up to let her pass. "Thanks for coming so quickly, Griffin. Were you nearby?" He turned to watch Mackenzie until she disappeared into the kitchen.

Griffin shook his head. "No, not really. Didn't matter, though. Traveling on four legs is much quicker than two. I like the power of the black cat. The speed is addictive."

"True." Christopher moved to the front window, peering out into the late afternoon light. "I hate to say it, but Scott took me by complete surprise."

"I see that." Griffin smirked at Christopher's burnt clothing.

"He had some power behind him, that's for sure. He spoke words to invoke the lightning. He controlled fire as well. The elements, I'm guessing. I don't know if that means he's a wizard or just clever. He said, 'Per tenebur mil advar.' I think that's it."

"It's not Latin. Not anything I've ever heard. Maybe Blair or Ian will have some ideas."

Sean came down the stairs with a suitcase in each hand and a book encased in glass tucked under his arm. Christopher frowned, his gaze focused on the bags. "I was thinking she'd only need a few things."

Sean raised the black canvas suitcase in his left hand. "This one's for me."

Christopher shrugged. "Okay. Go put them in the car."

Sean dropped the bags on the floor. "Here," he said, handing the glass case to Christopher. "This book is old as dirt and has been in my family since forever. My grandfather thought it was some kind of witch book. I have no idea, but since it looked like Scott was doing some kind of magic, maybe you guys could use something like this. Just take care of it. It's worth a lot of money."

"Thanks." Christopher accepted the case.

Sean nodded and hurried out the front door.

Turning it this way and that, Christopher studied the delicate contents within. He'd never seen anything this old. The pages were laced to a leather-like cover with a waxy-looking sinew. There was something odd about the book.

Something in the way it felt.

Warm.

The book had a vibration about it.

Magic. Christopher could feel the resonance now. "Griffin, this book is protected by magic."

Griffin crossed the floor and laid his open palm across the glass cover. His eyes drifted shut while he let the power speak to him. "You're right. This is an old power. I can't say how old, but it's not from my time."

Christopher sat down on the couch. He opened the case, picking up the book gently with both hands. The paper was thin, almost transparent. He didn't recognize what it had been made from, but suspected it was older than parchment. With great care, he turned page after page. His brow furrowed as he scanned the pictures and tried to find some words he could understand. The pale text was difficult to see, the words from a language he didn't know.

"Can you read it?" Griffin asked, peering over Christopher's shoulder.

"No, not a word. You?" Christopher handed the book to Griffin.

The old warrior scanned a few pages, then gave the book back to Christopher. "No."

Christopher put it in the case. "Maybe Ian can make sense of it."

Mackenzie returned from the kitchen.

Her weary face tugged at something within him. He sprang to his feet and wrapped his arm around her. "You'll be safe with us. Don't worry."

"The look in Scott's eyes really frightened me. I've never seen such evil, such hatred." She shivered. "I just had no idea."

"I didn't see it either, if that matters." Christopher led her to the waiting limousine, while Griffin checked the house and locked it. "But don't worry now. You'll be among family when we get home. They'll protect you—with their lives, if necessary."

"I really hope it doesn't come to that. I had a weird dream after Scott put me to sleep. I kept seeing you," she said, looking at him. "And you were calling to me, but I couldn't answer, as if I weren't there at all. It was kind of scary, and so vivid. I don't like dreams like that. They're too hard to figure out."

Christopher touched her forehead with the pad of his index finger. "No more bad dreams."

She smiled and wiped her brow with the flat of her hand. "What was that for?"

He grinned. "Eskarian good luck."

"Have I ever told you I don't believe in luck?" She turned and crawled into the back seat of the limo.

"No, you haven't. In that case, it was a subliminal suggestion," he said, closing the car door.

"Subliminals don't work either. That's just more nonsense." She smiled sweetly, evidently feeling pleased with her demystification.

"Okay," he said with a grin. "I spoke to your subconscious directly and planted the suggestion there."

Mackenzie thought about that. "I'm not sure I can comment on that one," she said, wrinkling her nose. "Do you mind if I lie down for a bit?"

Christopher shook his head. "Not at all."

Mackenzie laid her head in his lap. He stroked her hair, gazing out the window, and wondered who this Uleah was. What did it truly mean for her to be a host? With the Triad's imminent approach, they all needed to be sharp. His own mistake this afternoon could have cost Mackenzie her life.

Her presence distracted him from his duty, but it was her presence, *her life,* that had already given him so much joy. He looked down at her, brushing her cheek with his fingers. Her safety would not be compromised again. "I'll never leave you, Mackenzie. Never," he whispered.

Griffin leaned forward. "Blair and Ian will take good care of her. Perhaps we could send for Dylan. He's been in Alaska for months now. Could probably use the break."

Christopher continued to scan the forest outside. "Do we know for certain the trio isn't coming down from Alaska?"

"Not for certain, but the latest reports suggest they're in Northern California at the moment."

Christopher looked at Griffin and scowled. "I have no appreciation for their stealth."

"We'll find them. They cannot remain hidden forever." Griffin leaned back into the plush leather seat. He idly rubbed the back of his hand back and forth along his chin.

Several moments later, as the iron gate opened, Christopher leaned to Mackenzie. "Wake up, Beautiful. We're home."

She stirred, opened her eyes. Sitting up, she looked around. "Guess I fell asleep, didn't I?"

He smiled, once again feeling the elusive joy. It had been so long. "It's okay. I know how tired you are. Come inside to meet Blair and Ian; then I'll put you to bed."

When Christopher opened the door to his home, the scent of Livendium filled him with a welcoming calm. Burning in pots throughout the house, the spicy-sweet scent of the Eskarian herb permeated several rooms. He inhaled deeply, allowed its soothing scent to fill his mind and body. Mackenzie followed, still groggy from her nap.

Blair and Ian were in the living room, nestled in plush leather chairs in front of a crackling fire. Blair rose to greet Mackenzie.

"Good evening, Mackenzie. My name is Blair Atkinson. Welcome to our little family. Christopher speaks very highly of you." He hugged her briefly.

Mackenzie smiled. "Thank you, Blair. It's a pleasure to meet you."

Ian stood up and extended his hand. "Mackenzie, welcome. I'm so pleased to meet you, though I'm sorry to be losing our best warrior."

"Ian," she nodded, taking his hand. "I hope he makes it through this."

"He will," Ian assured. "There's no one faster or more cunning than this one." He smiled and rested his hand atop Christopher's shoulder.

Mackenzie looked at Christopher. "I hope you're right."

Ian tilted his head and smiled. "I am."

Christopher, embarrassed by all the praise, scooped up Mackenzie's hand in his. "Gentlemen, I'm going to put Mackenzie to bed, and then I'll join you. She's had a rough couple of days. Griffin, show Ian the book." He glanced at Mackenzie. "Come with me, Mateña."

He led her to his bedroom, where he settled her on his large bed. Pulling one of his T-shirts from the bureau, he laid it beside her. Then he turned down the quilts, closed the window, and pulled the blinds.

Mackenzie looked more tired with each transient minute. Christopher knelt before her and removed her sneakers. She leaned forward, surprising him by touching his cheek. Her long, slender finger traveled across his face, slowly down his chin, over his mouth, then whispered down the front of his throat. He waited for her to finish her exploration. It was such a tender gesture, he just couldn't bring himself to interrupt. Her eyes were filled with wonder as she explored his face, traced the tiny lines along his eyes and mouth.

When she laid her hand in her lap, he stood up and kissed her gently, one hand lightly resting on her shoulder.

"You need to sleep now," he whispered.

She unzipped her jeans, kicking them off to the side. She wore no panties, and he was surprised by his quick reaction to her scent. But this was not the time, he knew. He couldn't remain in the room and not make love to her. "I'll come back and check on you later," he said, backing toward the door.

Her brow furrowed. "You're not going to tuck me in?"

His jeans had become tight and more than a little uncomfortable. His erection demanded freedom and release. Now. He silently cursed his duty to Blair and Ian. Then he cursed the prophecy and Uleah, whoever or whatever that was. At the moment, he couldn't have cared less. It was their fault he had to leave. Their fault he couldn't make love to the most important woman in the world. "I really need to get back to my meeting."

She crawled into his bed, pulled the quilts to her waist, and waited.

And waited.

Silently he sighed and approached her, moving his hips as little as possible to avoid any friction. He dipped to hold her face with both hands and kissed her. His tongue pushed inside her mouth for his own languorous exploration. And dangerous. He wanted her.

Mackenzie's scent pulled at him again, momentarily overriding his sense of duty. His body tight with need, he ached to be inside her. Her hands dipped under his T-shirt to run cool fingers along the ridges of his stomach muscles. The gentle touch left chills dancing down his back.

Duty. The wretched thought came back to his mind.

"Mackenzie." He pulled her hands from beneath his shirt. "I can't do this now." He closed his eyes, tried to calm the unbearable fire burning inside.

"Why not?" Her voice was slow, soft with her own need. Her hands squirmed free of his grasp to caress his erection through the faded denim. She pulled him to her, and nuzzled the thick bulge with her mouth. "This would work better if your jeans were off."

"Please, Mackenzie, can this wait? I have to meet with Ian and Blair. You're driving me crazy with your touch, your mouth. I want so much to make love to you and I can't. Not yet."

Her sexy smile was enough to send him over the edge, and the way her mouth moved slowly over his hard-on sent white fire screaming through his veins. The heat in her emerald gaze drove every sane thought from his head. His breath quickened, and his body ached for her, needed her, begged for release.

"Let them wait. Please, I insist."

And he wanted to. By the gods, he burned to be inside her, burned to feel her tight muscles coiling around him, pulling against him, bathing him with her satiny cream. He wanted her under him, or over him. It didn't matter, as long as her hot skin was next to his. More than anything, he wanted her wild, passionate, and hungry. He couldn't remember *ever* needing someone this much. She'd become a temptress, and he was falling under her siren's spell. And he wanted to fall. Absolutely.

But now was not the time.

"You're killing me. Do you know that?" He rubbed his forehead. And she was. She might actually put him in the grave.

"No, I'm not. Please, don't go. I'm wide awake now and I want you to make love to me again."

Her voice, like pure magic, washed over him. His legs became rubber, ready to give out on him. "I can't, Mackenzie. Please forgive me." He spun around, rested a hand against the wall, trying desperately to regain his composure. "I'll be back for you. And then you'll know how much I want to make love to you." He left without a backward glance.

Damn it. Retirement could not come soon enough.

Palms pressed to his forehead, he whispered curses in the six languages he knew and waited in the hallway for his breath to return to normal.

A moment later, he stepped out into the living room. Heads turned, watching as he sat down on the couch with a grunt.

Griffin laughed at him. "Problem?"

Christopher shot his superior an icy glare. "Shut up, Griffin."

"Okay, so tell me this again." Sean paced the length of the large stone fireplace. "When Mackenzie got bitten by the wolf, she was infected and became one herself. Is that what you're telling me? She turned into a werewolf?"

"Not a werewolf, a demon wolf." Blair sat back in the soft, leather chair. "Werewolves are fictitious, but demon wolves are quite real. And quite deadly."

"I never saw her turn into a wolf."

"Would you like to see one?" Christopher shifted on the couch. His body still demanded satisfaction, yet he couldn't provide it. Anger was the only emotion he could allow a pittance of expression. "You saw only the smoldering remains of one whose intent was to kill your sister. Needless to say, I couldn't allow that, but I can show you a live one, if you'd like to see it."

"I'm not sure I do, actually." His gaze shifted back to Blair. "You said she's no longer a wolf, right?"

"That's right," Blair said.

"Okay, so what is she now?" Sean rubbed the back of his neck.

"She is Eskarian, like all of us here." Blair quickly swept the room with his hand.

Sean scanned the room. "All of you are vampires?"

"Not vampires," Ian corrected. "We're not undead and we don't kill those from whom we feed. We also have no sunlight restrictions. And, there's no such thing as a vampire. Pure myth."

"And, of course, you know that we have fangs, and we bite." Christopher stood, headed slowly to the fireplace. He was frustrated and knew perfectly well that Sean didn't deserve to be the target of his antagonism, yet he felt he would explode if he didn't vent his emotions somewhere. Sean just happened to be perfect for it.

"You're not going to bite me, are you?" Sean stepped back as Christopher approached. His gaze darted about the room, as if looking for an escape route.

"No." Christopher stoked the fire, placing two more logs into the ample hearth.

Sean heaved a sigh. "Thank God."

Christopher bared his teeth, extending his long, sharp canines. "But I could."

Sean's eyes widened. "But you won't, I'm sure. Not in front of all your friends."

Christopher pinned Sean against the wall, near the fireplace. "Actually, I *would* do it in front of them."

Sean lifted his chin to expose his throat. "Fine. Go ahead," he said. "Ian says you won't kill me, so go for it, jerk, if that's what you need to get off my case. Do it." Sean shoved his palm into Christopher's shoulder.

The move surprised Christopher. Very gutsy of Mackenzie's big brother to do something like that. He paused, then laughed. "Ian." His gaze swung around to the white-haired man frowning over the ancient black book. "I have chosen my successor. I will train Sean."

Ian looked at Sean, then glanced at Christopher. "He's human. Why don't you choose another Eskarian?"

"Because he's my benekeda's brother, and it would please me to give him Arden's Bow. I think he'll make a fine Defender. He stands up to me, even when terrified."

"I'm not terrified."

Christopher laughed. "Yes, you are." He was beginning to like Sean.

"And you're still a jerk." Sean stopped to think about what Christopher had just said. "Benekeda's brother? What's a benekeda?" He looked to Christopher, then around the room for his answer.

"Wife. Mackenzie is my wife, Sean." Christopher smiled, knowing Mackenzie's brother would not take the news well.

He was grateful she was in his bed, asleep. There was a good chance another testosterone episode was about to unfold.

Sean's face reddened. "You married her without telling me?" His blue eyes flashed, his fists clenched tight, and his body trembled visibly. "How could you to that to her? To our family? She doesn't even know you. She definitely doesn't love you. She still loves Daniel."

Christopher shook his head. "I'm not sure that's true, Sean." He knew better than to tell Sean what had happened to Daniel. "She and I are bound together, in a way that goes deeper than human bonds. But, essentially, yeah, I did marry your sister. This afternoon, in fact."

Sean shoved him again. "You had no right."

Christopher stepped back to avoid another shove. "I had every right. She is my true mate. I made her mine for all time after I converted her from wolf to Eskarian. You have to understand: she would have been hunted and destroyed. There was no choice for either of us. Not that I'm complaining at all."

"What? Mackenzie's a vampire, too?" Sean asked, firing daggers at Christopher.

"I found it." Ian's voice cut through the tension.

Christopher faced Ian. "Found what?"

Ian stood up, tucking the book under his arm. "Uleah was a warlock. He was one of the founding members of the Council of Elders, which was in power in . . . let's see . . ." He opened the book to a marked page. "Probably 2000 B.C. They governed all the wizards, warlocks, and witches then, ensuring no one became too proficient in the black arts, and they did well for about twenty years. But one by one, they all died off and no one was replaced. Why no one was replaced, I don't know."

Ian scanned the book again. "Uleah supposedly practiced

the black arts and was proficient when he shouldn't have been, since he was on the Council. It says here he was executed for his crime and supposedly sent to the Underworld of Toth, but before he died, he had a wizard protect his soul so that he could return some day. If Scott is serving Uleah, then it sounds like the old warlock has found his way back."

"To what end?" asked Griffin.

Ian shook his head. "I don't know. Revenge would not be an issue now. Everyone he knows is dead."

"We definitely need to find this Uleah," Christopher said.

"And we need to learn more about the Triad." Griffin rose to stretch. "Jason and Alex will be here in the morning. I hope we have more information about both threats by then."

"Griffin, see what you can find out about the warlock. Perhaps you can find Scott again and encourage him to offer up more information." Blair continued to write notes on a small tablet as he spoke. "Christopher, you find out where the Triad is now and see if there's a pattern to their movement." He stood to don his coat. "Let's meet again at noon tomorrow. Gentlemen." Nodding, he moved to the door and quickly left.

Christopher's brow furrowed. "Is it just me, or did Blair seem a little abrupt?"

Ian chuckled. "Anastasia is leaving tomorrow for a month in Europe. He's unhappy about it, and just wants to spend as much time with her as he can, before she leaves."

"I can relate. Well, if there's nothing further, I'll retire for a few hours, too."

"Christopher, I'd still like to talk to you about my sister." Sean folded his arms across his chest. Big brother was doing his best to defend his sister's honor.

"Sean, what's done is done. I can't undo it and I wouldn't, even if it were possible. Arguing with me will do nothing more than make you feel better, and I don't have time for that now." Christopher shrugged. "If you insist on pursuing this conversation, can I ask that we pick it up sometime tomorrow?"

Sean's anger deflated. "Uh, sure." He scanned the room. "Which room is mine?"

"Take the third door, down this hallway. On your right. Let Sasha know if you need anything." Christopher spun around to head for his own bedroom, glancing over his shoulder. "Stay out of trouble, Sean. I have plans for you."

Christopher opened the door to find Mackenzie asleep. He closed the door behind him, and headed for the other side of the bed, shedding clothes along the way. He slipped under the quilts, pressed his body against her, nuzzling her neck. His arm curled slowly around her waist as he savored the feel of her warm, soft skin.

She stirred, opened her eyes. Rolling onto her back to face him, she brushed hair out of her eyes. "You left me."

"I'm sorry. I had business with Ian and Blair. I'm back now. I have the entire night to spend with you."

"Great." She rolled away from him.

"Don't be upset with me." He laid a hand on her shoulder, but she shook it off. She didn't understand the importance of what was happening with Uleah and the Triad, didn't see that they all had to work together to defeat these threats. All she saw was her own need, and that he hadn't been there for her.

"It wasn't my intention to hurt you. I wanted to stay. You know that, don't you? Unfortunately, part of my job for now is to strategize with Ian and Blair."

She sat up, anger in her eyes. "What about my job? You had no problem dragging me away from it, did you? What am I to you? Some concubine you can keep in your room until you're ready to take what you evidently think is yours? Do I have no say in this—this, whatever it is?"

Her words stung. "Mackenzie, you don't understand. I could have lost you today. I'm not going to apologize for protecting your life by whatever means I see fit. Scott will be coming back for you. I need to be ready." He leaned back. "I don't really see why you're so angry with me."

"Because I needed you," she said quietly. "And you just left me here, all alone. You didn't say anything."

"Aw, Mackenzie. I'm sorry. Did you think I didn't want to be with you?"

Her shoulder shrugged lightly. "Maybe."

He propped his head up on his elbow. "Did you not see how I was burning for you? Could you not hear it in my voice? I was ready to explode just looking at you."

She pushed a hand through her ebony tresses and shrugged. "I was really hurt. I might not have been thinking clearly." Her eyes closed and she sighed.

"And are you thinking clearly now?" he asked.

"Yes, I think so."

"Look at me." He nudged her cheek with a single finger, so she'd face him. "I was hurting too. You were so beautiful, sitting there in my T-shirt. I love the way your black hair glistens like fine threads of silk, day or night, and the fire in your green eyes when you're angry takes my breath away. Looking at you, I could lose myself in those eyes forever and not care. And everything about you amazes me, including that temper of yours. You've got a quick wit, you're compassionate and intelligent, and you're mine. It's safe to say rejecting you was the *last* thing on my mind." He trailed a finger along her shoulder. "It took everything I had to walk out of here. But I *had* to meet with Blair and Ian. I had absolutely no choice in the matter. We have to figure out a way to defeat these threats, and I still have to be a part of that. Do you understand what I'm saying?"

She stirred. "I understand."

"Are you still angry with me?"

"I suppose not."

A slow smile crossed his face. He pressed a kiss to her shoulder. "I hope you'll give me the benefit of the doubt next time. Do you think you can do that?"

"Maybe." She toyed with a long strand of his hair. "We'll see."

"We'll see?" He leaned over to wash the inside of her elbow.

She grinned. "You still owe me an apology for bailing on me."

"I said I was sorry."

"Tell me how sorry you are with your body, not your words. I want to feel your apology." She lay back against the pillows. "Show me."

"Love to." Christopher kissed her, teasing her with long, slow strokes of his tongue inside her mouth. "I probably owe you a couple of apologies, don't I?"

"At least. In fact, it might take you all night to make it up to me."

His hand slid between her legs to push them apart. "Then I'd best get started."

Chapter Eight

Alistair McConnell stood at the window of the large estate. Ocean waves crashed steadily against the rocks below, sending a spray of salty droplets into the air. The sunset this evening was spectacular, but he didn't really care. He rubbed his chin idly, while seeing nothing before him.

"Alistair? You called?" A tall young man stood in the doorway.

"You've come back to us empty-handed, I see. Why did you fail?" Alistair turned to the man with tousled brown hair streaked with blond and bruises on his neck.

"I tried to take her—even had her in my arms and was almost out the door. But, she'd brought a man home with her, someone I'd never seen before. His mind and body were very strong—more than anyone I've ever known." Scott paused to rub his neck. "He took my blood. Felt like he took damn near all of it."

Alistair nodded. "A vampire, then?"

Scott shrugged. "I don't think so. He came to the house during the day. I threw fire and light at him and he still tried to stop me. When I had him down, he called for assistance telepathically. He called for Griffin."

Alistair's eyebrows shot up. "Is that right? Griffin, you say? Do you suppose this is the same Griffin we dealt with a decade ago?"

"I didn't get a look at the guy, but I remember Griffin, and he fought like this Christopher did. They're both incredibly strong and fast. I think Christopher is faster, though. Could be a problem."

"So there's another one, then. And he protects the host." He threw a hand up. "No matter. It may not be as simple as we'd hoped, but we'll prevail nonetheless. Our strength is formidable. Few, if any, have the power to stop us. Don't forget that, Scott."

"But if there are two of them now, I'm afraid our chance for success has been compromised. What if there are more than two? We should find out."

Alistair rubbed his shoulder. Long fingers worked the heavily-scarred tissue underneath his black linen shirt; a gift from the auburn-haired warrior. It had never truly healed. Even now, ten years later, it still ached when the icy winds came down from the north. "Don't trouble yourself with these thoughts. There are three of us. We'll succeed." He didn't know that for a fact, but felt reasonably certain it would be so. After all, he had the power of an ancient sorcerer behind him.

The heavy wooden door opened with a soft creak.

"Maya, good evening." Alistair's amber gaze wandered over the woman's body, drinking in every hollow, every curve. She was a vision, with red hair and legs that didn't quit. His mind slipped into a fantasy, where she pleased him instead of the young man she actually had chosen.

"Hello, Alistair," she said with no feeling at all. She sauntered across the office floor to Scott. "My love," she purred. She raised her face to receive his kiss, her long arms wrapped around his neck. "I missed you so. I just hate it when you leave me for that wretched woman."

He smoothed back her dark red hair. "Maya, my love, she is no more. One of Alistair's wonderful wolves has eliminated her for us. Now you don't have to be so jealous." Scott reached around to pull her close. "Though I rather like you jealous. You can be so amazingly sexy when you're angry."

Alistair cleared his throat. "If you have nothing more for me, perhaps you could take your love play elsewhere."

Scott cleared his throat. "Sorry, Alistair." He caught Maya's wrist and tugged her toward the heavy door. "We'll find out what we can about the other one—including what they are."

"Thank you, Scott."

Scott dipped his head lightly and pulled Maya to the hallway beyond the door, closing it behind him.

Left to his own thoughts, Alistair returned to the window. Dusk. The wolves would be coming out soon to feed. In the small town far below the estate, mothers would call for their children to come in before the sun set. Inevitably, there would be one who took too long to find his way home. The frantic parents would search for him, and when they found him they'd scoop him up, chastising the crying child vehemently as they hurried inside. Yes, the wolves were indeed a wonderful creation. Eliminated the foolish from the population.

"Yes, people, gather behind soft, wooden doors." He raised his eyebrows, thinking of what was to come. "You'll be safe from all evil inside those homes made of brick and mortar." A slow smile came to his mouth. "Until *he* comes for you."

He held out his hand, palm up. Closing his eyes a moment, he focused his energies until a small, clear orb, a glass-like, magical manifestation of a soothsayer, appeared just above his hand. The orb began to spin, humming softly. Alistair raised his hand so the orb was at eye-level.

"Tell me what is to be," he commanded.

Inside the orb, an image appeared, fuzzy at first, then

sharpened so that Alistair saw a small duplicate of himself inside it. He lay on his back, and kneeling beside him with a double-edged dagger to his throat was a tall, dark-haired man. With a quick swipe of the silver blade, the dark-haired man cut Alistair's throat and left him to bleed to death.

The scene never changed, no matter how many times or how many different ways he asked the question, *What is to be?*

Dreadful thing: to know how one would die, but not know when. Alistair closed his eyes, imagined the knife moving across his neck. How long would it take? How much would it hurt? Was there any way to change *what would be?*

He'd known about this fate for some time now. Some days he couldn't even get out of bed. The fear of death kept him under the blankets, terrified this day would be his last. And no one could tell him it would not. Too much of his life still was ahead. It was too soon to die. Uleah would change all that.

He snatched the orb in his hand and crushed it, leaving small shards of glass embedded in his hand. A quick shake of his hand sent the larger pieces of glass in every direction. Absently, he watched beads of blood form in his palm and along his fingers. "Unacceptable, this fate," he said. "I must find the book."

He spun around, grabbed a cloth for his bloody hand, and stormed out the door. Down the winding staircase he went, skipping every other stair in his haste to get to the cellar, deep inside the earth.

"Unlock the door," he commanded.

The heavily-muscled guard unlocked the thick metal door swiftly, then opened it wide so Alistair could pass through without interference.

He stopped before a small cell, his breath rapid from the rushed descent into the cellar. Inside, a man of the cloth huddled against the back wall. Dark eyes lifted when Alistair spoke softly.

"Allegra, where is your God now? Why, do you suppose, he leaves you in a place such as this?"

The priest rose to his feet, slowly. "Perhaps I have much to atone for. I cannot begin to know His reasons for this." He stepped to the front of the cell to face Alistair.

"Perhaps you're merely a fool, believing in beings who dabble in the lives of ordinary men. Hmmm?" Alistair raised an eyebrow. "Might that be closer to the truth, Father?"

"I did what I had to do. You have enemies, Alistair, and they wanted you off the Council. I regret that I placed myself in the unenviable position of being the one to carry out their wishes. However, it is done now. If I'm to die for that, then so be it." Father Allegra's chin lifted. "I'm ready to serve God in Heaven, if that's His will."

"If it's *my* will." Alistair smiled. "But that'll come another day. Today, the Fates are with you, for I've need of you. I'm leaving for Seattle tomorrow, at first light. You will accompany me. If I find what I'm looking for, I may need your assistance. You will, of course, not attempt to escape me. I'd have no problem taking your life. Indeed, I'd find it most . . . satisfying."

"I refuse to help the Devil do his work." Allegra frowned, stepping back.

Alistair tilted his head to one side. "The Devil has nothing to do with this. In fact, I'm not certain such a creature exists. But, more importantly, I must ask you: am I to believe that you're a man of principle? That you always strive to do what's right?" He leaned forward. "I know what you do, when you think no one watches," he said softly. "I don't believe the good sisters would approve of such behavior."

Father Allegra's eyes widened. "You know nothing

of me, or how I pass my time."

"Would you like me to show you what I know about you?" Alistair held out his open palm. An orb appeared and began to spin. "It's a simple thing to call up the memory." He looked at the spinning orb. "Does the young girl know you are a priest? Do you know how young she really is?"

The priest held up a quivering hand, a silent offer of truce. "Leave Annalissa out of this. I'll go with you tomorrow, and I won't escape. Say no more about my weaknesses, I beg of you. I'm already aware of the darkness in my heart. But I have redeemed myself, through her. She is my salvation." His voice broke with the confession.

"It would seem you're not well suited to your calling, Father. As a priest, I do not believe a woman can be your savior. On the contrary, I believe the lovely Annalissa has condemned you to hell." Alistair turned to leave. "A pity, to be sure. Do you not agree?" He inhaled deeply. "I'll collect you in the morning. Do sleep well, Priest. You and I have much work ahead of us."

As Alistair walked to his bedroom, high above the filthy cellar, he once again summoned a small, spinning orb, his own perpetual crystal ball. "Show me Allegra," he commanded.

Inside the clear orb, the priest fell to his knees and covered his face to weep. Alistair stopped to watch, a smile creeping across his face. When the priest sat back and cried out in anguish, Alistair burst out laughing. He lowered his hand, dismissing the orb. The image of the despondent priest faded then the orb itself dissolved.

Alistair awoke long before the sun was to rise. He hadn't slept much that night. With so much on his mind, he'd laid atop the blankets, turned frequently, unable to find the optimal position that would allow him to finally rest.

His thoughts drifted to the spellbook. They would need it to complete the spell once they had the woman. Uleah had said the ancient book had been brought to this area by the warlock's family when they emigrated from Scotland at the turn of the century. He was certain it was still in their possession. Yes, he most definitely had to have the book. His very life depended on it. The family would have no choice: hand it over or die.

Alistair sighed, rolled onto his side. The open window displayed a clear, moonlit night, but Alistair saw only the traitorous face of the Italian priest.

Allegra.

Father Ciro Allegra had all but destroyed Alistair's life almost fifteen years ago. It had been so fast. With just a few words, Alistair had been removed from his position on the newly-reformed Council of Wizards, taken to the dungeon, and beaten severely. So few words . . . They thought he'd broken the Cardinal Rule.

"Collaborating with the Devil, for the sole purpose of destroying this Council. I saw it myself, Sir . . ."

Alistair's eyes closed.

He'd been judged so harshly, without a shred of evidence, without the opportunity to defend himself against the accusations. He'd never seen the Devil, had never collaborated with him, and didn't actually believe he existed, if the truth were told.

He could have died in that place.

Now Alistair had a special plan for Allegra.

A special potion to stop his heart and lungs.

Yes, the potion he'd created only a month ago from a distinctive blend of herbs and powders. Alistair had ground the mixture into a fine paste, and then added a little water to make it liquid. Simple, and yet it had performed so beautifully on the servant he'd found stealing his powders—things meant only for an accomplished sorcerer, not some little servant best suited to mopping floors.

Once the book was in his possession, Alistair would open Allegra's mouth, fill it with the potion, and watch him suffocate. Alistair would have it no other way. The priest would pay for his deceit. Yes, an eye for an eye.

Alistair rose slowly. Sleep would continue to elude him now.

Joshua, prepare the car and wake the priest. Make certain he has bathed and wears clean clothes. I do not want his stench in my presence. He sent the thought clearly to the young servant.

An hour later, Alistair opened the main doors and stepped into the cool, crisp morning. Joshua leaned against the side of the limo. Father Allegra stood next to him, with wet hair and trousers that were a little too big, but the simple, white shirt seemed to fit well enough.

Alistair glided past him and stepped into the long car. "Come, Father."

Alistair sank back into the soft leather seat. He enjoyed these little jaunts. His home was far from civilization, and while he enjoyed that most of the time, it did sometimes get a bit lonely. He was grateful for the opportunity to serve a great warlock, and grateful for the company, truth be told. Even if the company was going to die, soon.

His gaze swung across to the priest. Allegra had taken the back-facing seat.

Joshua, we're ready to leave.

Joshua closed the door and started the car. The tires kicked up bits of gravel and dust along the rock-lined road that led downward. When they reached the main road, the interior of the car became silent, save for Joshua's soft humming.

Alistair leaned forward. "Were it not for the book, I would be tempted to kill you here and now." He sat back and smiled. "If you so much as think about seeking your freedom from me, I'll not hesitate. You'll remain alive as long as you serve my needs."

The priest turned to the window, looking perfectly miserable. He sat with his hands folded in his lap and legs crossed. His brow furrowed, as if deep in thought. Alistair supposed it was understandable, given the circumstances, but really couldn't have cared less.

"Yes, an eye for an eye," he whispered. He picked up his own spellbook and began to read from the middle.

The priest turned from the window to glare at Alistair. "I do not need your continual torment. I'll comply with your wishes."

Alistair lurched forward and locked a hand around Allegra's throat. "I'm not interested in your needs, unless they serve me. Speak again and I'll seal your mouth shut." Alistair shook the man's neck once. "Do you understand?"

Allegra nodded.

Alistair released his grip on the priest's throat, and sat back.

The priest rubbed the red marks on his throat, then cast a forlorn gaze out the window, returning his hands to his lap.

Alistair once again perused the spellbook. "We'll be there by mid-afternoon. Do not seek to annoy me further, Priest."

The wet air chilled Alistair's bones. He buttoned his coat, dipped his hands into the deep pockets. Allegra shivered in his lightweight shirt and trousers.

The limousine had stopped in an old neighborhood in the Magnolia section of Seattle. Large fir trees cast protective shadows over the brick home, shielding it from the elements. Allegra had quickly found the warlock's family history at one of the public libraries and traced it to the family here. It was a job very well done. The threat of an unpleasant death was useful, but love . . . ah, yes, love was the best way to ensure compliance.

Alistair stepped out of the car, surveying the finely-manicured lawn and perfectly-trimmed hedges. The rhododendrons had become dormant now that October had brought much cooler nights.

"Allegra, come with me. These people will surely have such a precious relic from days gone by."

The priest followed, arms crossed over his chest for warmth.

At the front door, Allegra knocked. Alistair stepped back, straightened his coat, and pushed a hand through his thick, tawny mane.

A large woman answered the door. "Can I help you?" She pushed a lock of salt-and-pepper hair from her face.

"Good afternoon, Mrs. Wallace," Alistair began. "My name is Alistair and this is my associate, Ciro. We're from the Scottish Historical Society. We apologize for dropping in unannounced, but we've just learned you have a very old book from ancient Scotland and we were beside ourselves with excitement. Do you know the book I'm speaking of?"

"Of course. It's a tattered old thing. You can't hardly read the words. I couldn't read it anyway. You know, it's so old, they didn't even speak English back then." She smiled broadly. The afternoon sun danced in her brown eyes.

"You wouldn't happen to still have it, would you?" Alistair returned her warm smile.

"Oh, no, I gave it to my nephew years ago. He went through a phase where he was interested in his heritage. His parents, my brother-in-law and sister, were killed when he was quite young. He traced the family line all the way back to as far as you can trace these things."

"I'm sorry for your loss." Alistair's brow furrowed in mock concern.

"Thank you. We practically raised Sean and Mackenzie from birth." She smiled, as if recalling fond memories.

"Do you suppose he'd mind if we contacted him? We would love to see such a wonderful treasure from so long ago."

"I don't know. I'd have to ask him." Her brow furrowed slightly. She raised a pudgy hand to touch her cheek.

"Let me give you my card. We just want the opportunity to see it, perhaps take some photographs for our records. It's such a rare and exciting find. We'd be most appreciative if you could have him call us." Alistair pulled a card from the inside pocket of his blazer. The card contained only his name and phone number, but with a wave of his hand, anyone who looked upon it would see that he was indeed a member of the Scottish Historical Society.

"I sure will." She accepted the card. "Thank you. It was nice to meet you both. Have a good day, now."

"Thank you, Mrs. Wallace. It was a pleasure. Good afternoon." Alistair dipped slightly and turned as she closed the door. He almost floated to the waiting limousine, giddy with excitement. The book was at *her* house. It was more than he'd dared hope for. Uleah would most certainly be pleased.

He slid onto the leather seat and moved to the side to make room for Allegra.

Joshua, take us to Vashon. "It won't be long now, Priest. Call Scott and get the address for Mackenzie Wallace. We're going to pay her a little visit."

While the priest spoke with Scott, Alistair gazed out the window. If the two warriors were not with the woman—Mackenzie—they would be able to get the book and take her at the same time. But concern about the auburn-haired warrior persisted in his mind. He remembered the battle between Griffin and himself. The warrior's strength was impressive. He'd rammed a double-edged dagger clean through Alistair's shoulder with seemingly minimal effort. What was it about him that he was so strong?

Uleah, give me the strength to defeat them, should they present a problem for us. Alistair rubbed his forehead with the palm of one hand.

Always, my child.

His eyes closed, relaxed to the soothing words of his dark master. The ancient warlock, now only a shadow, would return in this time to take his place as the king of warlocks. Alistair would provide the host for the warlock's new life. And in return . . .

"It's on the east end of the island, not too far from the ferry docks."

Alistair nodded. "Excellent. She and the book will be ours by this evening. I'm certain of it."

Allegra turned his gaze to the window.

Two hours later, they found no one home.

"Open the door, Allegra." Alistair scanned the forest around Mackenzie's house, while Allegra fumbled with the lock. Several minutes passed, and still the door remained locked.

"I'm working as fast as I can, Alistair." Allegra sounded nervous. As well he should have. Alistair was not a patient man.

"Competently would be far more effective, Allegra." Alistair moved down the steps, strolling around to the back porch. The back of the house was well-kept, comfortable, with Adirondack chairs and large pots of ferns, and greenery. The old house had probably been painted over several times, but the dark green color it bore now was complimentary to the architectural style. Alistair liked old things, the simplicity of the times long ago. Like old books with ancient spells inside. Yes, spells that could change what is to be.

"Alistair?"

Allegra called from the front of the house. Alistair trotted down the back porch stairs and around to the front door. Allegra waited with the door wide open.

Alistair waved his hand toward the entryway. "You go first. The book must still be here. She will return at some point and, if we haven't found it by then, perhaps we can encourage her to assist us. Either way, we will wait for her. I do not want to be this close and leave empty-handed."

Allegra let a soft sigh pass his lips and stepped over the threshold. Alistair followed. His gaze swept the living room for evidence of the book. It had to be here somewhere. The priest immediately headed upstairs.

Alistair began his search in earnest. He searched the two bookcases in the living room, then moved to the dining room and kitchen, not that he expected much, if anything, from those two areas. Still, one had to be sure. When he'd finished searching the first floor, he sat on the couch to wait for Allegra.

Upstairs, the priest rummaged through closets and drawers. Alistair heard the contents of drawers dumped onto the floor. He chortled quietly when something fell and broke, and Allegra cursed in a very un-priest-like manner. He searched through each room, but after several minutes, Allegra appeared at the top of the stairs. "It's not here, Alistair."

Alistair waved dismissively. "It has to be here. Tear this place apart. I want that book found."

"I've searched everywhere. It isn't here."

Alistair felt the rage pulsing through his body. "What do you mean, it isn't here? It has to be here."

"It isn't. Look at this floor. It's in ruins. I've turned over mattresses and rugs, looked behind pictures for a safe, searched closets and cabinets. The book is priceless. It's going to be in a place where it would always be safe and protected. It is not here."

Alistair's temper flew out of control. He kicked over the coffee table and turned over the blue chair. Turning to a large tree in a pot, he pulled it out by the roots and hurled it across the room, swearing loudly.

Allegra had failed him. Alistair whirled around, found Allegra still watching him from the top of the staircase. Silently he bounded up the stairs and grabbed Allegra by the throat, slammed him up against the wall.

"You didn't look hard enough. The book is here," Alistair snarled.

"It isn't here," he whispered. "I've nothing to gain by keeping it from you. I've searched every inch of this house."

Downstairs, the front door opened.

Alistair released Allegra's throat and glided silently to the edge of the hallway where he could see the living room.

The auburn-haired warrior stood at the entrance, surveying the demolished home.

Griffin. The same Griffin who'd speared him ten years ago. The Griffin who didn't look any different than he had ten years previous.

Alistair silently exhaled, distraught at this turn of events. Within the span of mere seconds, his plans had been utterly shattered. Griffin would never willingly allow him to search further for the book. They'd be lucky to get out alive, let alone alive with the book.

Allegra peered out from behind Alistair. "Do you know

who that is?" he whispered.

Alistair silently motioned for Allegra to be quiet, but it was too late.

Griffin turned to face Alistair and a slow smile came to his mouth. "I see we meet again, wizard. Is this your work?"

Alistair raised an eyebrow. "Does it matter?"

Griffin sauntered to the base of the stairs, resting his forearms on the railings. "Not at all. Did you find what you're looking for?"

"Is it not possible I found the house in this condition?" Alistair asked.

"No, it isn't. Do not attempt to distract me, Alistair. I'm in no mood for your inane games."

"What I'm doing here is not your concern. Get out of my way and you'll not see me again." Alistair was fully aware the warrior could be quick and unpredictable.

Griffin's head slowly shook. "Now, you don't really expect me to do that, do you?"

"I have more power behind me now than when we last met. It wouldn't be nearly as easy to spear me as before."

Griffin smiled. "That means nothing to me. You were *very* easy to spear. Now, as I know the people who live here, and I'm certain you do not, I think I need to know what you're up to. Either you tell me willingly, or I'll take the information by whatever means would amuse me most."

Alistair decided a better strategy would be to concede to the warrior. "I was looking for Mackenzie. She and I are old friends."

Griffin suddenly appeared at the top of the staircase, his nose only millimeters from Alistair's. "You insult me with such a pathetic excuse." He slammed Alistair up against the wall and leaned closer. "Not for a second do I believe that. You're looking for something. What is it?"

Alistair could hardly breathe. The warrior's silver eyes blazed. There would be no reasoning with this man.

"Uleah, lend me your strength."

"It is yours, my son."

"Allegra, prepare to leave." Alistair croaked out the command, gathering his energies. "Now it's my turn to walk away and leave you bleeding and in pain." He waved his hand across Griffin's chest. "Im plurio danon."

Griffin's clothes burst into flames. Alistair gave him a quick shove and the warrior toppled end over end from the top of the stairs. He hit the carpet with a heavy thud and thrashed about to extinguish the flames.

"Allegra, run, now!" Alistair flew down the stairs and out the front door in a mere heartbeat, with Allegra at his heels. Sliding into the opened limousine, they both sighed with relief as Joshua sped away.

Alistair leaned into the soft leather and closed his eyes. "Of all the people who could have shown up, why did it have to be that damned Griffin?"

Chapter Nine

Slivers of light splayed in ribbons across the bed. Mackenzie opened her eyes and stretched lazily. Christopher lay behind her with an arm over her waist, his face nestled in her hair. His warm breath whispered across the back of her neck.

It felt good to have him close to her. Felt right, and somehow, as if it had always been like this. Daniel's memory was drifting farther and farther away, and that, too, was all right. She saw now that he'd never been the right one for her.

Christopher was.

"Good morning," he said, pulling her close against his body.

"Morning" She laid her hand on his forearm. His golden skin was soft, and so warm. The heat that sparked between them reminded her of last night, when he'd made love to her more than once. Now she felt wonderful. Loved. Sated. Happy. She smiled at the memory of his body on hers, and then beneath hers. "Did you sleep well?"

"I did," he answered. "You?"

She turned to face him. "Very well. I could get used to this."

"Me, too," he said, brushing the tangle of wild hair from his face.

He propped himself up on his elbow. Morning sunlight splashed across his face, lighting up his eyes like a summer sky. Amazing, the opalescent ring around the outer edge of his irises that shimmered in the light, and the kaleidoscope of blue within blue. Those eyes melted her heart every time he looked at her.

He looked happy—relaxed, finally, after all that had happened the last few days. She realized it meant something to her that he was happy. His well-being and happiness were important.

She cared for him.

"Later this afternoon, I want to teach you some things you need to know." He paused to run a finger from the base of her throat down to her navel while his gaze remained on her face. "Have I told you yet how beautiful you are?"

Her gaze dropped to inspect her hands. "I believe you told me that last night, but I'll admit, I like to hear it."

"I like to tell you." His hand caught her chin and raised it to capture her gaze. He leaned forward, fixing his mouth to hers in a fiery kiss that curled her toes. "I like waking up next to you."

Her stomach turned upside down. His eyes were blue flames, alive with hunger and desire.

For her. She exhaled softly. "You have the most amazing blue eyes. An ocean with a million shades of blue. They're so amazingly expressive." She pushed a wisp of hair from his face. "You're strong, compassionate, and brave. How fortunate I am that you were meant for me. And that you actually found me."

"It was fate that I happened to be hunting with Griffin when he found you. We usually hunt alone." He cupped her cheek in his hand as he leaned to her. His hand whispered down the side of her neck and caught in the thick chain around her neck. The vial of iridescent green liquid at the end of it captured his attention. "You wear this all the time, don't you? What is it?"

"I'm not sure. My aunt Bess gave it to me about five years

ago. Apparently it's been in our family for a long time. Kind of interesting, isn't it? It glows a little in the dark."

He inspected the small, dark-green glass tube encased in black, metal webbing. "It is interesting. I wonder if there's any way to find out where it came from."

She shook her head. "The only thing I know is that it's always been in our family. Who the original owner was, I haven't a clue. A relative, but that's it." She shrugged.

"The metalwork is detailed and delicate. Good workmanship. It must mean a lot to you." Christopher looked from the vial to Mackenzie.

"Yes, it does. That's why I keep it on such a heavy chain. I like knowing it's with me, sort of like a talisman," she said, her gaze dropping to the vial.

"Don't you worry about the chain breaking?"

"No, not really. It's quite strong. I haven't taken it off or had it break in the five years I've had it. I might remove it at some point, but not just yet." She touched the vial with her fingers. She'd never opened it, though she'd been curious about the shimmering liquid inside. There were times when she'd wondered what it was, and had considered opening it, but, truth be told, she couldn't figure out how it opened, or even if it *could* open.

"Well, you might consider putting it in a protected environment. The safe in the basement is both fireproof and waterproof and where my most sacred possessions are kept. I'd be happy to safeguard yours, too," he said.

She wasn't sure she wanted to do that. It was more than a good-luck charm. It was a link to her heritage. "I'll give it some thought. Thank you for the offer. Now, may I ask what you're going to teach me today?"

He exhaled softly and sat up. "I know you're not going to like this, but first and foremost, I want you to learn to take blood from someone besides me."

Blood. It always came back to blood. "I'm not sure about all that."

"I'll take you out to the park today and show you how we move in and out of a group of humans and take a little from several of them. If you can't do it, you're free to continue to feed from me, but eventually you must learn to not be disgusted by it. The first time is always the hardest, but with practice, you'll come to see it as quite natural." He paused to smile. "Today, I ask only that you try."

Mackenzie's gaze drifted to the window. In the heat of a passionate moment, she'd taken his blood, but the memory was fuzzy at best. Had she been afraid then? Repulsed? No, she hadn't. She'd latched onto his neck with scarcely any thought behind it. How had she come to terms so quickly with her objection to taking blood?

A frown creased her brow. Her gaze shot to his. "You made me do that, didn't you?"

"I didn't make you, no," he said. "I eliminated the apprehension you felt and let the rest happen on its own."

She glared at him. She had no idea he'd invaded her thoughts and emotions. How many times had he done this? Private thoughts were meant to stay private. And her emotions were hers alone. Not his to do with as he saw fit. "I don't like that you can control me like that. It's not right."

He rubbed the center of his forehead with two fingers. "Mackenzie, I'm not going to apologize for what I did. I'll do it again if I have to—without hesitation. You don't seem to understand that terrible things can and will happen to you, if you're not careful. You cannot behave as you did when you were human. We won't allow it, for your sake and for the sake of our people. Griffin did the same thing to *encourage* you to drink from his wrist."

She clutched the sheets to her neck, becoming increasingly annoyed with the liberties he'd taken with her mind and body. "You're taking away my free will."

"No, I'm helping you adjust to your new life."

"By taking away my opportunity to learn in my own way," she argued.

"Mackenzie . . ." His tongue slipped out to wash his lower lip. "You're not really at the top of the food chain anymore. Humans would kill to be what you are. They would kill you to find out what you are. I *won't* let that happen. If you need to be angry, then be angry. It won't change anything."

"Are you always going to do this? If so, I want out. Now," she told him. "I don't like it."

He shook his head. "No, I won't. I'll back off the second you're ready."

Good to know. Maybe she wouldn't have to bail then. "Great. I'm ready."

His eyes darkened. "We'll see."

"We'll see? Arrogant son-of-a- . . ."

She pressed her palm to her forehead. It was clear she wasn't going to win by fighting him. Maybe there was another way.

"There isn't."

She glared again. "Stay out of my thoughts."

"Make me," he said, grinning.

She slapped his arm.

He laughed and caught her shoulders. One quick turn and he had her pinned beneath him. "I only want you to understand, Mackenzie, so I can be with you a long time. I swear, I'm not the ogre you think I am.

"You're a hell of a fighter. You know that? Griffin saw that you would have fought him, too, despite your hunger. He chose to avoid a confrontation, so he took the revulsion away, just as I did. It's never meant to take your free will. It's to make it easier for you to learn. Taking blood is a part of Eskarian life you'll need to come to terms with. I don't want you to be dependent on me or anyone else."

She watched him a moment, her anger starting to fizzle. His blue eyes were fringed with thick black lashes, shining in the morning light. Those same eyes were fire and ice when he was angry, but when he looked at her, they smoldered, dark and gray, teasing and hungry at the same time. Mesmerizing, those eyes. Did he see the same fire within her? she wondered. Benekeda or not, she felt something for him—something hot, burning, and alive. "Okay, I understand."

"Good." He rolled to her side and lay on his back.

She grinned. "Bet you never thought your mate would challenge you this much."

"Um . . ." He rested his arm above his head. "No, not really. It's okay, though. I can handle whatever you throw at me."

"You sound just like Sean. He says the same thing." Her brow furrowed. "Just what I need."

He laughed. "You do need me."

"Think so?" She studied his face, amused by his statement.

"Absolutely. You like what I do to you."

Her eyes widened in mock surprise. "Oh, really? I don't recall telling you that. What makes you so sure?"

"First of all, you did tell me, in so many words. More importantly, I'm your benekeda and, as such, we are connected, you and I." He leaned toward her. "So, I *do* know what you like, even if you think to keep it from me."

"There's that thought invasion thing again," she said, her nose wrinkling. "You have me at a serious disadvantage."

"I'll teach you how to hear the thoughts of others. Then

you'll be able to hear all the wicked things I plan to do to you when I get you behind closed doors." He laced his fingers through hers. "Things I already know you like."

"Things you *think* I like," she teased. "Nonetheless, I can't wait to know what's going on inside your head."

"I'll be happy to show you what's going on in my head. Anytime." His eyebrows raised. "Do you want to know what I'm thinking right now?" He pressed a kiss to her shoulder.

"No," she teased. "I need to check on Sean and . . . *feed,* I guess." Mackenzie made a sour face as she said the word and thought about what it meant. Yes, she definitely needed to get over her disgust of taking blood. She knew that already. Didn't make it any easier.

His thumb whispered lazily across her palm. "Mackenzie, there's something I'd like to ask you." His blue eyes darkened a little. He sat up, leaning on an elbow. "How do you feel about Sean being made like us?"

Mackenzie sank back into the pillows, surprised he would ask such a question. "Why would you do that?"

"I think he should have Arden's Bow and replace me as a Defender. The sooner I convert him, the sooner I can begin his training, and then I can figure out what to do with myself. You said he should get a life. Does this qualify?"

She looked away. The idea made her stomach do a little flip. In truth, she didn't want to lose Sean and she could, if he were an immortal warrior, like Christopher. "I guess so. Maybe. Not really. No. I don't want him hurt. Or killed. Have you already talked to him about it?" If he wasn't converted, she would lose him to old age, eventually.

"I mentioned it last night. I'll tell him what he needs to know this morning and, if he agrees to it, we can begin tonight. He can rest during the night and complete the process.

I'll begin his training after we deal with Uleah and the prophecy threat."

She hated the idea. "Could you choose someone else to replace you?"

"I could, yes, but I was hoping to keep Arden's Bow in the family. It's a very old weapon, and I'm somewhat protective of it. I'd rather give it to someone who will respect it for the great thing it is. Someone like Sean. I've found him to be courageous and strong. I think he'll make a fine Defender. Perhaps later on, our son or Sean's son will have it."

She gasped. "*Our* son? *If* I have a son, he will *not* be a Defender. Absolutely not! I forbid it!" She hadn't thought about having children yet, but at the mere mention of it, her blood pressure shot up. She couldn't—wouldn't—imagine her son fighting demon wolves . . . or worse. She grabbed his forearm and gave it a good squeeze. "Tell me it doesn't have to be that way. Tell me, Christopher. I'm not going to have a son only to lose him in some hideous battle."

"Relax, Mackenzie. All I meant was that he could have it, not that he would necessarily be a Defender."

"Oh." She released his arm. Her impassioned grip left red imprints on his golden skin. She wrinkled her nose in apology, feeling a little bit embarrassed. Of course, he didn't mean his own son would be a Defender. "Sorry."

His gaze dropped to the red fingerprints. "Perhaps our son will be destined for something other than hunting." Idly brushing the prints with his fingers, his eyes grew wistful, as if he were considering the possibility. "Let me talk to Sean this morning and find out if he's interested. He can have time to think about it, if he's more comfortable with that. I can wait until after the battle."

"I suppose." She turned away. "I don't like all this battle stuff."

"It has to be done, Mackenzie." He shrugged, but she could tell he was concerned about it.

"I know, but I have a really bad feeling about all this," she said, her brow creasing. She did, too. Something awful was about to happen.

"I've never lost a battle. I'm very good at what I do." His fingers curled around her arm. "I've gotten a little beat-up before, but never anything too serious."

"That doesn't mean you're not in danger," she said quickly. "And you said this prophecy thing was really huge. Your very best may not be good enough."

"That's why Griffin, Alex, and Jason are up to help. These guys are our top warriors. But I don't think you should worry about the battle for now. We've got Defenders searching the countryside, and they report all unusual activity to Blair. They can't remain hidden forever. We'll find them. And when we do, we'll destroy them." He waved dismissively, as if it meant nothing. "Shall we get up and do that *feed* thing?"

Her brow furrowed. "Feed. I do *not* like that word."

"You'll get used to it." Christopher rolled out of bed.

He glided to the bathroom with such graceful movements. His body simply amazed her. How someone so tall and muscular could move like that was truly beyond her comprehension. He almost floated across the floor.

He stopped at the bathroom door and nodded towards the Jacuzzi, smiling mischievously. "Come sit in the Jacuzzi with me."

"Again?" she asked.

"Yes, again." He raised his eyebrows in invitation. How could she refuse such a gorgeous face and body? How could anyone?

She got out of the warm bed and found her sweatshirt on the floor. Slipping it over her head, she trotted into the bathroom. He was already in the water, dipping underneath to wet his hair. Several pots of Livendium smoldered around the ample tub, immediately setting her mind at ease.

She scanned the bathroom. Pots were everywhere. "You burn this stuff a lot, don't you?"

"Yes. It's relaxing, but it also enhances our telepathic abilities, so we can communicate with each other from great distances. You'll be able to do it too, in time. I'll teach you."

She lowered herself to the seat. "So I can always find you."

He smiled. "You *could* do that." Moving to her, he brushed his mouth against her neck and shoulder, then moved down to nuzzle her breast.

Suddenly his head shot up. "Griffin?"

Her eyes snapped open, her reverie shattered. "What?"

"Something's happened to Griffin. He's not in the house and he's not answering anyone's call. I'm sorry, but I have to find out what happened to him. I have to leave for a bit, but first, I want you to remember this moment." He offered a sly grin. "I'll be back to do more of this to you. Do you understand that? I *will* be back to finish what I started."

She nodded. "I understand. I'll be fine."

She watched water sluice off his golden, muscular body, and swept her disappointment aside. There would be time for love play later. In truth, all these distractions were driving her crazy. Was his life always this hectic? Just the thought of living at his pace made her tired. No wonder they were immortal. No human could keep up.

Christopher snatched a plush white towel, dried himself quickly, then slipped into a pair of faded, torn blue jeans, zipping them carefully over the impressive bulge.

"Are you going out like that?" she asked, stifling the urge to laugh.

"What?" He looked at her, confusion on his face.

Her gaze dropped to his tattered jeans. "Don't you have a lot of money?"

"Yeah. So?" His brow creased, as if befuddled by her statement. He found a black sweatshirt in the closet and threw it on.

"Can't you afford nicer jeans?" she asked.

He relaxed. "Oh, yeah, I could. I'd rather be comfortable. These are my favorite jeans. See this rip here?" He pointed to a tear along his outer thigh. "That's from the claw of a Costa Rican GhostCat. He caught me just before I . . . well, you probably know what I did."

She raised an eyebrow. "It's not hard to guess."

"I've worn this pair for years." He turned to show her another rip just below the knee. "This one was from a Crystal Dragon. They're actually blue and have two sets of talons on each foot. I was lucky to get away with this little scratch."

"See? I *knew* it! You could be in danger." She tossed him a maternal glare.

He nodded sheepishly. "I could be, I suppose."

She shook her head in exasperation. "Arrogant. That's what you are. You're in danger from yourself, I think."

He caught a strand of her hair. "I like that you care so much about me. I'll be back, Mateña." He spun around and disappeared out the doorway before she could launch on him again.

It was true, but did he have to point it out so arrogantly?

Mackenzie lay back, letting the bubbling water rock her from side to side. It felt good to just relax. To just be.

Her thoughts turned to Griffin. Anyone able to bring down someone like him would have to be something awful to contend with.

"Kenz?" Sean called from outside the door.

Startled, she stood up quickly, spilling water over the edge of the Jacuzzi. She'd hadn't heard him come into the bedroom. "I'm in the spa. Can you wait a minute?"

"Sure."

She dried quickly, wrapped herself in a towel, and went to look for some clean clothes. Rounding the doorway to the bedroom, she found Sean seated on the edge of the bed.

"What's going on?" Mackenzie pulled out clean undergarments, jeans, and a sweater from the bureau where Sasha had placed them earlier.

He shrugged one shoulder. "They all left. I have no idea where they went. Is it true you're Eskarian, like they are?"

She pursed her lips together, somehow thinking she needed to hide her long teeth. "So it would seem. I'm not sure what that means. I feel better than I used to, and I'm stronger. I see and hear better. Evidently I have a long life ahead of me." She moved to the window and spread her arms wide to allow sunlight to bathe her. "And, as I don't seem to be a vampire, I must be Eskarian."

Sean's gaze dropped to the carpet. "I've been thinking, Kenz. I want to be one, too."

Mackenzie's jaw dropped. "One what? Eskarian? Why? Wait. I need to get dressed." She brought her clothes back to the bathroom and dressed quickly. Returning to the bedroom, she sat down in the chair near the window. "Okay, now why do you want this?"

He rubbed the back of his neck. "Because otherwise I won't have anything in common with you, and eventually you'd leave."

"But it's a chance for you to do something else with your life, Sean. You wouldn't have to spend every free moment protecting me. I want you to be happy, too. I feel bad that you've spent so much time watching over me."

He shrugged. "It was as much for me as it was for you. We

were really young when Mom and Dad were killed. I mean, I'm glad Bess and Jake were there to take care of us, but to me, family was just you and me. Yeah, I could run off and do my own thing, but I'd rather stay here. Alan and Bill spend a lot of time with their girlfriends these days, and I'm not ready to hook up with anyone new, so I kind of feel left out there, too." He shrugged. "Truth is, I don't know where I belong and, until I figure that out, I'd just as soon stay here with you. I'm guessing Christopher doesn't need any help protecting you, does he?"

Mackenzie shook her head. "I don't think so. He's quite confident in his abilities to keep me out of harm's way."

"I suspected as much," he said, looking every bit as lost as he'd said he felt.

His expression tugged at her heart. He felt left out already. Much as she was opposed to it, maybe both her brother and Christopher had a point. Maybe she needed to set aside her fears for Sean, so he could live a happier, better life. "Well, Christopher said he'd like you to replace him as a Defender, so if you're up for that, then I guess you'd be made Eskarian."

His blue eyes lit up. "Yeah, he was talking about that last night. Said he wants to keep Arden's Bow in the family."

"Yeah, I think he really likes that idea. I just don't want to see you get hurt. Are you sure you want to become a Defender?" *Please say no.*

He nodded. "Yeah I do."

With a soft sigh, she rose to her feet and walked back to the bathroom. "Figures you'd say that. I'll be right back." She dragged a hairbrush through her tresses, winding the glistening strands into a thick French braid. Finally having a little time to herself, she lined her eyes with a charcoal liner, applied a couple coats of black mascara and fresh lip-gloss, and pulled a few wisps of hair out to frame her face.

"Ok, I feel civilized again." She returned to the bedroom to find him standing at the window, seemingly lost in his thoughts. "Are you okay?"

He turned to her and smiled. "It's kind of amazing that I'm standing here, thinking about letting go of my humanity."

"I know what you mean. At least you have a choice. I didn't," she said with a grimace.

"Would you change back if you could?"

She nodded. "If I could."

"I don't know if I would." He inhaled deeply. "Is there a good reason why I shouldn't become Christopher's apprentice?"

"Yeah," she said quickly. "Because you could be killed or maimed or something."

"Maybe. Maybe not. You don't know that for certain."

"Neither do you," she pointed out.

"True, but I'm willing to find out." He leaned against the wall, folding his arms over his chest. "Tell me what it's like to have someone take your blood."

She thought about it for a moment. "It hurts and yet it doesn't. There's nothing like it, though I can't stand the sound of it. I can't even describe that to you."

"Then show me."

"Excuse me?" Had she heard him right? Was he asking her to drink his blood?

He nodded. "I want to know what it feels like, before I commit to this thing. Will you do it for me? I can't stand the thought of one of those guys sucking on my neck. That's just disgusting. But you could do it. Will you?"

"Sean, I don't know. I have a hard time taking blood. The whole thing kind of sickens me." She pressed a hand to her stomach. Just the thought made her tummy do a flip.

"But you've done it, right?"

"Yeah, I did. Reluctantly. Christopher says both he and Griffin changed my thoughts, so I wouldn't be so grossed out. But, they're not here now to help me with that."

"So, I'll help you and you'll help me. It's a fair trade." He moved to the bed and sat down with an impish grin. "Come on, Kenz. Bite me."

Her nose wrinkled at the thought, but she ignored the butterflies in her stomach and approached him. "I don't know about this, Sean."

His legs parted to allow her easy access to his neck. It seemed bizarre to think about taking blood from her own brother, let alone doing it.

"Come on. You can do this." He nudged her closer with a hand to the back of her thigh. Looking up at her, he smiled. "I want you to do this for me. You should be my first."

She laughed uneasily. "You'd be my first human." She rested a hand on his shoulder. Could she do this on her own? Her gaze focused on his pulseline; the steady beat slowly spoke to her. The scent of his blood then drew her closer. Her fangs lengthened.

He bared his throat to entice her further. "I'm ready now, Kenz. Don't make me wait all day."

"Shhh. Don't rush me. This is so . . . disgusting. I don't know if I can do it," she whispered. She brushed his neck with two fingers, gathering her courage.

"You can. Come closer to me." Another nudge to the back of her thigh.

Cautiously, she descended to his neck, stopping when her mouth met his warm skin. His breath quickened. "Don't be afraid, Sean. It doesn't take very long."

"Hurry up," he whispered. "And don't take all of it."

Closing her eyes, she found his pulse with her tongue, then

pushed her teeth into his skin. He gasped, and his hands shot out to grab her hips, as if he would push her away, but she wrapped an arm around his neck and held him to her, knowing her Eskarian strength was far superior to his.

She drew his blood slowly, so he wouldn't hear that awful sound, wouldn't be revolted as she had been, but the blood called to her, seduced her with its rich, bubbling heat, filled her, nourished her, replenished her parched veins. She found herself humming softly as she drank and realized then she felt no revulsion at all. Quite the opposite, in fact.

She enjoyed it, and so she drank more, pulled a little harder.

From far away she heard him whispering to her. He pleaded with her to stop, but she wasn't ready yet. Her thirst was not quite sated. Soon.

A firm hand to her shoulder spun her around, ripped her from Sean's throat. Shocked out of her reverie, she opened her eyes to face Christopher's hot, angry gaze. "You're killing him. Do you know that?"

Chapter Ten

Mackenzie whirled around to her brother. "Sean? Oh, no!" Her hands flew up to cover her mouth.

Sean had slumped down onto the bed and now lay perfectly still. She tugged at his leg. "Sean? Wake up, please."

No movement.

She faced Christopher again. "I didn't mean to hurt him, I swear it. Oh God. Can you help him?"

Christopher bent over Sean and placed two fingers on his throat. He shot her another angry glare over his shoulder, then removed the dagger from his coat pocket and cut a deep slit in his wrist. As the blood escaped from the opened vein, he slipped a hand under Sean's neck and tilted his head back so the blood would flow down his throat. "Drink, Sean. You need this to survive."

Sean didn't move. He looked dead to Mackenzie, but somehow Christopher must've known he was still alive. He'd felt the weakened pulse and seemed unconcerned.

Christopher's blood dripped into Sean's mouth impotently. Mackenzie watched him, then Christopher, and tried to gauge Sean's condition from Christopher's expression. It was impossible to tell. The crisis didn't seem to affect Christopher at all. His palm remained flat against Sean's chest while he periodically scanned Sean's body, as if telepathically assessing the damage.

If her brother died, she'd never forgive herself. Never.

She'd never be able to live with the fact that she'd taken his life needlessly.

Sean's blood had caught her up in a vortex of desire and life.

"Never again," she whispered to herself.

Christopher glanced at her but said nothing. He'd probably have plenty to say after Sean was in better shape.

A moment later, Sean's eyes fluttered, and he swallowed, slowly at first, a mechanical response to the liquid in his throat, then pulled harder as the blood strengthened him. Christopher allowed him only a little. "If I give him more, his body will change. We can't do that without his consent."

Mackenzie brushed a strand of hair from her brother's forehead. "He was considering the conversion when he asked me to take blood. He wanted to know what it was like. He said he wanted to be like us, and I think he'd still like that, even after this. Can you ask him, to be sure?"

Christopher's wrist took only seconds to heal. He watched it absently until no sign of the wound was left. "I could do that, yes. Are you sure you're okay with this?"

"No," she said slowly. "But, I'll have to respect his choice and hope you'll train him well enough that he doesn't get himself killed."

"I will train him to the best of my ability. I promise you that." Christopher knelt beside her brother. "Sean, wake up. I have a question for you."

Sean's slumber would be very deep with the blood loss, but Christopher's powerful voice would rouse him.

He'd told her he had learned long ago that sound could affect the brain patterns and make a human susceptible to suggestion. Eskarian training included learning to control the voice, in order to control the human or the unwilling

Eskarian mate, when circumstances called for such a thing. Christopher had mastered it and could manipulate not only humans, but animals as well.

His voice was a powerful weapon.

"Mmm?" Sean inhaled deeply, then his eyes opened. "What happened?"

"There was a bit of an accident. The call of the blood can be very persuasive and seductive and sometimes those new to it will forget they're drinking from a living being. Mackenzie just took too much." He shrugged. "It happens. Now, I've given you enough to survive. You'll need to rest for some time, but your sister thinks you might want to be converted to be like us. I'm willing to do this for you, if that's your choice. However, once it's done, I'll want to train you as a Defender. You'll take Arden's Bow off my hands. When the time comes, you'll pass it on to someone else. I know this is a lot of information to digest all at once. Do you need some time to consider your choice?"

"What? Yeah . . ." Sean turned over onto his side with a soft exhale. "God, I'm so tired." He rubbed his eyes with a trembling hand. "Where am I?"

"You're at Canongate—my house—trying to decide if you should become Eskarian. Take your time and think about it. I'll be back." Christopher straightened and crossed the floor to Mackenzie. "Come with me."

Mackenzie followed Christopher, but at the doorway she stopped in her tracks, wide-eyed, when she saw Ian and Blair tending Griffin. The ancient Eskarian had been blackened, as if by fire. Ian held a cup to Griffin's mouth, while Blair gently peeled away what was left of his clothing.

"Mackenzie?" Christopher grasped her hand and tugged. "Come."

She followed him to the end of the hall. He unlocked a

door there and opened it wide, to reveal a large solarium with frosted glass.

It was gorgeous.

The air temperature there was distinctly warmer and more humid than the rest of the house. Huge trees and ferns were scattered throughout, and pedestals with large pots of smoldering leaves surrounded a black granite slab in the middle of the room. Shale tile on the floor was protected by white area rugs strewn about. Near the granite slab, two plush white chairs stood as silent sentinels, guarding the heavy structure.

Christopher went to an electrical panel on the other side of the room. Opening the door, he pressed two buttons. The granite slab split into two pieces, separated by silent hydraulic lifts that rotated the top piece ninety degrees to its side. Inside was a pool of steamy, iridescent green water that swirled wildly from the small jets embedded in each end.

Christopher walked to the granite structure and studied the water. "This is hot salt water mixed with liquefied Livendium. It'll help Griffin heal faster."

Ian and Blair followed, dragging the unconscious Griffin to the structure. They set him on the floor in front of it. His entire body, now naked, had been burnt. His flesh reeked of smoke and charred skin.

Who'd done this to him?

Blair took Griffin's legs, and Ian took his shoulders. Together they lifted him over the edge of the slab into the hot water and submerged him completely. Blair held him under with a hand pressed to his chest until his lungs had filled with water. With that done, he nodded to Christopher.

Another button lowered the granite structure over the pool, sealing Griffin inside.

Blair and Ian left the solarium in silence.

Mackenzie and Christopher were once again alone.

She sat in one of the plush white leather chairs and inspected the condition of her fingernails. Certain some kind of admonishment was coming for having taken too much of Sean's blood, she waited quietly. It was more than obvious she'd made a serious mistake that could have cost her own brother his life. The thought of losing him hurt her stomach and her heart. Any reprimand of Christopher's would only add to what she'd already done.

Instead, he knelt before her, and laid warm hands over hers. "I know you didn't mean to take so much blood from Sean. There is a bit of a science to it, or at least a method. I'll take you to the park now and show you how it's done." He smiled. "I assume you won't have any problem taking blood from a stranger after today's event. If you can do that to your own brother, you should be just fine."

"He wanted me to take his blood. Perhaps not as much as I actually took, but I was only doing as he'd requested of me. I know I screwed up, though. I'm sorry." Her gaze returned to her fingernails.

Christopher raised her chin with his fingers. "Look at me."

Reluctantly, she did.

He shook his head. "I need no apology, but your brother might."

She looked away, tears burning her eyes. That didn't make her feel any better. *Nothing* in this world could have made her hurt Sean on purpose. "I feel just terrible about this."

He stood up. "It's over, Mackenzie. There's no value in feeling bad about it. I'll teach you how to do it properly, and then this problem won't arise again. It's as simple as that. Now, let's see if Sean is ready to make a decision, shall we?"

She pushed a hand through her hair. "Okay."

He smiled and took her hand, pressing a soft kiss to the

inside of her wrist. "I'm sure he'll forgive you. He loves you."

She nodded. There was no one she loved more than her brother.

Back in the bedroom, they found Sean standing at the window, seemingly engrossed in his thoughts. Though still pale, Sean looked better.

"Have you had enough time to make a decision?" Christopher asked, leaving Mackenzie on the edge of the bed. "It's not a problem if you need more time."

"I don't. I've made my decision. I want to become like you," Sean said with a slight nod of his head.

"Great. Let's finish it, then. Lie down." Christopher waved a hand toward the bed, indicating Sean should lie there. "I'll have to take more of your blood. All of it, actually, and then you'll get some of mine."

Sean lay on the bed beside Mackenzie. She decided there would be time later for her apology.

"Ready?" Christopher asked, approaching him.

Sean bolted upright. "Whoa, wait a sec! You're not going to bite me, are you?"

Christopher nodded. "Well, yeah, that's how it's done."

A knock on the open door drew their attention. A gorgeous blonde-haired woman stood at the threshold holding a heavy silver chalice.

"Thank you, Sasha. Please leave it on the dresser." Christopher remained by the bed. "Sean, you do know how this works, right?"

"Yeah, but I don't want *you* to bite me. Kenz can do it." Sean grimaced as he spoke. "Just her."

Christopher rubbed his forehead. "Fine. Mackenzie, this time it will be all right to take all his blood. Stop when his heart stutters." Christopher withdrew his dagger from his coat pocket again. "Start whenever you're ready."

Mackenzie rolled off the bed and moved to the side where Sean lay. She glanced tentatively back at Christopher. "You won't let anything happen to my brother, right?"

He looked up briefly. "Of course not."

She turned back to Sean. "I'm sorry about what I did," she blurted. "I never meant to hurt you."

Sean smiled. "I know." He patted her forearm.

Mackenzie nodded, grateful for her brother's understanding. She pulled her hair to one side, holding the thick braid so it was out of her way. His eyelids drifted down. He raised his chin to allow her complete access to his throat and took a deep breath. She dipped slowly, finding his slow pulse without effort. Her tongue swirled around it, and then she pushed her canines deep into his skin. Once again, the hot blood captured her, drew her to the sound of his heartbeat, which slowed further. It would not be long.

As she drank, she heard the sound of liquid dripping into the chalice. She opened her eyes to see that Christopher had cut a deep gash into his wrist and was filling the chalice with his blood.

He glanced at her a moment, then focused again on the chalice. "That's enough, Mackenzie. Did you hear his heart flutter?"

"Yes," she admitted.

"That's when you need to stop."

"Okay, I will." She straightened right away and stepped back to allow Christopher to finish the process. Sean lay pale and still on the bed, his breath shallow and slow.

Christopher grasped the chalice and approached the bed. "Sean, this is my blood. I need you to drink all of it." He raised Sean's head and held the chalice to his mouth. "You can't sleep yet. Drink."

Sean's lips parted. Christopher tilted the chalice and

poured some liquid into Sean's mouth, massaging his throat until he swallowed. Little by little, he took every drop. When it was over, Christopher covered Sean with a quilt, then bent close to his ear. "Sleep well, my brother, and heal. I look forward to giving you Arden's Bow."

Mackenzie stepped forward. "Now what do we do?"

"We wait. I need to be sure Griffin has healed and your brother has completed the conversion. After that . . ." His voice trailed off. He shook his head. "We're still not getting definitive reports on the whereabouts of the Triad. It's unheard of for us to take so long to track a threat, but . . . I don't know. There's something we're just not seeing, I think." He rubbed the bottom of his chin with his fingers, as if lost in thought, then laced his fingers in hers. "Come. It's a beautiful day. I can take a little time to show you how to feed."

A limousine waited outside. She crawled into the back seat, scooting all the way to the end. Christopher slid beside her and closed the door. He nodded to the driver and the car quietly started, then crept from the driveway.

Christopher captured her hand with his own. "We'll go to the park on the east end of the island. There are usually people there, but it's seldom crowded this time of year. Don't be afraid. I'll show you what to do. I want you to practice a few times while I'm with you, so you get the hang of it. Then I'll leave you to do it on your own."

Mackenzie looked away. "I'm not sure I'm ready to do this."

"It's a matter of survival. Get ready," he said.

She supposed he was right. With a heavy sigh, she turned her attention to the scenery and tried to think of anything but what she'd have to do today.

Christopher wouldn't allow her fears to get the best of her. On the way, he spoke of learning to control the thoughts of others, that most of the time, the mind was overrun with constant gibberish. He would subdue her first donor, if she so chose, but she would have to approach them on her own and take the blood quickly. They'd do it in broad daylight and no one would notice. It was a simple process, a matter of making oneself nearly invisible, calming the donor, leaning in to take the blood, then quietly slipping away. Quick. Painless. Easy. Not disgusting or repulsive, but just how it was. Life. Precious.

He made it *sound* so easy, but once the car came to a stop and Christopher was scanning the small crowd of people, she became frightened, wholly uncertain about whether she could do it.

He grasped her hand and brought it to his mouth, kissing the inside of her wrist. "It doesn't matter if you choose someone in a crowd or someone who's all alone, as long as you're quick. When you've made your choice, imagine that you are invisible. Your mind is stronger than a human's. It's easier for you to create reality from thought. Making yourself invisible is called phase-shifting." He released her hand. "I'll show you first."

In one graceful move, he slipped on dark sunglasses and was out of the car, walking toward a group of teenagers. Her heart leapt at the thought of taking blood from any of them, but he seemed calm, walking around them casually with his hands in his pockets.

Then, he just dissolved. Not completely. She could see movement in the air, but couldn't tell it was him. He moved into the group and no one seemed to notice how he dipped his head to several teenagers, and drank quickly. Somehow they all seemed fine, as if they had no idea what he was doing. They probably didn't, she guessed.

Now, she would be the one to tell them they were to feel

nothing. She wondered how often blood had been taken from humans without their knowledge. Had it happened to her before? She'd had no idea—a sign they'd been exceptional at disguising their entire existence.

He became solid again, and turned to her. With a quick toss of his head, he motioned her to the group. She signaled back that she wanted to choose someone else. Truth be told, she couldn't bear the thought of taking blood from such young people. Why that was so, she didn't know. And maybe he had no problem with it, but she would have preferred an adult.

Actually, she preferred not to do this. She realized she was stalling, since she wasn't hungry at all, but she supposed that the point was to complete the exercise.

No, she stalled because she didn't want to do it again. Sean had been different, somehow. Less intimidating, maybe.

Her gaze dropped to inspect her shoes. Asics. Runners' shoes. She'd love to go running now.

In the opposite direction.

"I want you to do this, Mackenzie. Choose your donor."

He remained within the crowd of teenagers. She scanned the crowd, felt indecisive. Perfect strangers, and she couldn't do it. Not one person seemed like an appropriate choice.

"Mackenzie?"

She whirled around to face him. His sky-blue eyes flashed over the top of his dark sunglasses, icy and hot at the same time.

"Don't bother trying to stall further. You *will* do this. I can keep you here for as long as it takes." He shrugged. "Griffin will sleep for some time, as will Sean. We have other Defenders patrolling for any and all threats. At the moment, I *do* have the time to wait. Be assured, you're not leaving until you've taken someone's blood. Choose your donor or I'll do it for you."

She remained silent. A young dark-haired man on a park bench caught her attention. He sat quietly, reading a book, with one leg crossed over the other. He would do as well as anyone, she thought. Not an imposing presence. "Fine. I've chosen."

Christopher's gaze followed hers. "Do you want me to send him to sleep for you?"

"No, I don't."

He nodded, a hint of a smile on his lips. "Then do it. I'll wait here for you. Don't forget to phase-shift." He absently pushed his sunglasses farther up on his nose. "And take only a little blood. You don't need that much to stay alive. Your body manufactures most of what it needs. All you're really doing is providing the gas that makes the manufacturing system work. Does that make sense?"

"Yes, it does. Okay . . . here I go . . ." She headed for the dark-haired *donor,* astounded they were actually called that.

Mackenzie decided it would be easier if she stepped behind the donor and then leaned in to his neck. And no, she wouldn't forget to make herself invisible.

Her thoughts snapped back to Christopher. "I'll make you invisible," she grumbled. No, she definitely didn't like this part of Eskarian life.

You'll get used to it.

"You could stay out of my thoughts," she whispered.

She heard laughter inside her head. Was he laughing at her?

Yeah, I could. It won't happen, though.

With a half-hearted shrug, she ignored his comment, and hoped her flash of annoyance wasn't noticeable. Her privacy was important, damn it. She didn't need him in her head, on top of everything else.

She scanned the small pockets of people around her to see if she'd attracted any attention, but no one seemed to know or care that she was there. A good sign, she decided. They wouldn't notice, then, when she just dissolved into thin air.

With the image firmly set in her mind, she concentrated on becoming nothing. Only seconds later, she felt the cool breeze pass through her.

Through her?

I can barely see you. Good job.

She splayed her fingers in front of her. Damn, it worked! She *was* nearly invisible.

With that under her belt, she came up behind the dark-haired man and bent to his neck. At the same time, she silently assured him he would feel no pain. She took in the rich scent of his blood, and summoned her long, sharp teeth. "No pain," she whispered. "You feel nothing but the breeze."

He drew in a deep breath.

Pausing a moment to focus on the steady beat of his pulse, she pressed her mouth to his neck, then plunged her teeth in, thinking only that she couldn't lose herself in the heady taste of this man's blood as she had with Sean.

She mustn't take too much.

Beyond that, it was best to not think about what she was doing. Such poisonous thoughts would only increase the likelihood of failure and she didn't need to deal with that either. Speed was of the essence. She closed her eyes and drew the blood hard, and swallowed as quickly as she could. A moment later, she finished and withdrew from the man.

As if she'd overcome a major hurdle, she backed away with a smile on her face, and started back for Christopher, when she began to feel sick to her stomach. Maybe it was just nerves.

This was her moment, and no matter what she felt, she

would not be denied. She stood in front of him, a smirk firmly planted on her face. "I did it."

"Yes, you did. Very good! I'm proud of you." He bent to kiss her forehead. "Let's go find another donor now, while you're feeling confident. It should be easier for you next time." He slipped his hand inside her arm and guided her toward another group of people.

No, something was not right. She spun around, and knew with absolute certainty she was being watched. Malevolence surrounded her, thick and suffocating.

The dark-haired man had risen to his feet and, quite obviously, stared. Rudely.

Mackenzie met the man's gaze, horrified that he knew what she'd done. "Christopher, that man—the one I just drank from—is watching me."

He glanced over his shoulder. "No, he's not. He has no idea what just happened."

She glared at Christopher. "How can you say that? He's looking at me."

He stopped and regarded the man for a moment, then shook his head. "Mackenzie, he's not even facing us. He's looking at the water. I know what he's thinking. He doesn't know what happened."

She looked back at the man. He *was* facing the water. "Okay, I don't understand. He was looking at me. I felt sick, too, as if he wanted to hurt me or something."

Christopher grinned, his eyebrows raised. "And how do you feel now?"

Her gaze instantly dropped to her shoes. "Fine." The sense of dread had passed, just as quickly as it had come. "I'm not crazy."

"I know." He draped an arm around her shoulders and nudged her forward.

★ ★ ★ ★ ★

Mackenzie sat on the couch, engrossed in a novel. Two pots of Livendium smoldered nearby on the end table. She felt sated, having taken blood from four donors over the past several hours, but the first man from whom she'd taken blood still haunted her. Christopher hadn't seen him. The man really *had* been looking at her and his thoughts had been dark. He knew. She was certain.

They're coming for you.

The spicy-sweet scent of the Eskarian herb had eased the tension in her shoulders and given her a sense of well-being. Now the voice inside her head disrupted the peace of the evening.

The thought was not her own.

It wasn't Christopher's either. He was in his office with Blair and Ian. Alex and Jason had arrived earlier in the afternoon, and now they were strategizing again. The newest reports from the field said the trio had come from the edge of the coast, and that they were in the Seattle area already. Christopher's battle would be on his home turf.

He keeps secrets from you.

She scanned the room. Had she heard the voice inside her head, or was someone talking to her? What secrets? Who was keeping them? Sean or Christopher? They hadn't known each other that long, so secrets weren't a complete surprise. But still . . .

Her quick scan of the room revealed nothing. She was alone. Jason's voice carried well, and she could hear him speaking behind the closed office door. He was arguing about something, but she couldn't tell what it was.

Christopher sounded agitated as well.

Other voices she didn't recognize. She knew only that they weren't the same voices as the one in her head.

She stood up, suddenly curious about the reason for the argument. Pushing a hand through her hair, she walked silently to the door and pressed an ear to it, but the voices were still muffled. She couldn't decipher a word. Odd.

They will lock you away soon.

She rubbed her forehead, now annoyed. Something was going on in this house, and she didn't like it. Not one bit. And she had no intention of dealing with it. After all, it wasn't her house. More importantly, she couldn't be sure the thoughts weren't her own. Who would be talking to her? No one. Maybe the stress of the day had affected her more than she realized. There had to be some rational explanation—hopefully something better than foreign thoughts in her head, telling her things she didn't want to know. Either way, she wouldn't tell Christopher about them. Nothing good could come from *that*. He hadn't thought her crazy earlier in the day, but with this latest bit of information, he might reconsider.

Inhaling deeply, she stretched and decided some fresh air would help. She moved through the house quickly, ready to be away from the stuffy indoor air. Even the spicy-sweet fragrance of Livendium bothered her now. The closer she got to the door, the more it seemed important that she be away from whatever was happening in the house. Or what was *in* the house.

Something definitely was in the house. She could feel it.

Once she was out under the full moon, the tension in her shoulders melted away. She headed away from the malevolence, out to the perfectly manicured lawn and surrounding foliage. Feeling better, she strolled around the gardens.

Away from the estate, a massive rock wall cradled a large pool, fed by a gentle sheet of water spilling from the center. Lily pads floated leisurely in the pool, and the surrounding vegetation, flowers and ferns, dipped toward the pool as if to drink.

Mackenzie stood there, watching the lazy fall of water, content for the moment to be alone with her thoughts, grateful they belonged only to her. The night was quiet. The wolves were silent, though they would most certainly be awake by now. Only the distant sound of the ferry horn intruded on the tranquility of the night.

"Good evening, Mackenzie."

Startled, she spun around to face a tall, muscular man in a black coat. She glanced back at the house, away from the most intense amber eyes she'd ever seen, and sent a silent call for help to Christopher. Her internal alarms shrieked their warning to get away before it was too late.

But it already *was* too late, wasn't it?

"No one will hear your call tonight, my dear. They're all busy arguing among themselves. By the time they realize you're gone, it will be far, far too late." He smiled, slipping a hand into a deep pocket. "Allegra?" he called, looking to the side. "Take her."

Mackenzie's eyes widened. She whirled around and took off at a dead run for the house. The one called Allegra was right behind her. With every ounce of strength she had, she tried to go faster. A second later, a strong hand caught her wrist and wrenched her backward into the hard wall of his body. She swung her elbow back into his stomach and knocked the breath from him, but he held on tight.

Her Eskarian strength should have sent him to the ground. Why didn't it have an effect on him?

Another strong hand clamped onto her other wrist; then he brought her arms up behind her, tight against her own body. She was his captive. In this position, he could easily have wrenched her arms from their sockets if she tried to escape.

Allegra pulled her closer to his body and bent his head to her ear. "What a luscious mouth you have, bella. You can suck on my neck anytime."

Allegra's soft Italian accent sent chills racing down her back. He was the one she'd taken blood from earlier today.

He *knew.* She'd been right about him watching her. He knew what she'd done.

The tawny-haired man faced her. "I should tell you, it's useless to try to escape Allegra. He's not what you think."

"What do you want from me?" Mackenzie tried to pull away, despite the warning that she couldn't. She wasn't giving up that easily.

His eyebrows raised. "Your life. I want your life." His head tilted, and he smiled. "Good night, pretty Mackenzie. When you awaken, you will belong to me."

He spoke words she could not understand, in a language she'd never heard before. In his open palm was gray powder.

Before she could utter another word in protest, he'd blown it into her face.

And she'd inhaled.

Dear God, what was happening? Her vague recollection of Scott trying to take her from her own home came screaming back to the forefront of her memory. Why was she being taken? And where?

She couldn't keep her eyes open anymore.

Leaden muscles would no longer support her legs.

Allegra spun her around to face him, but she couldn't focus enough to see what he looked like. She tried to hold on to him, to consciousness, but she couldn't think and her strength was gone. Just gone.

A moment later, her knees buckled and gave out. Strong arms kept her from toppling to the ground. One thing kept running though her mind. *This one isn't right.*

"Scott, I want you and Allegra to put her in one of the chaise lounges on the back deck. Make it look as if she just fell asleep. They mustn't suspect a thing."

Someone brushed the powder from her face.

Allegra continued to hold onto her shoulders. Somebody—did he say Scott?—lifted her by the ankles. They were taking her somewhere.

Time passed erratically, for only a second later, or was it more, she found herself in a chaise lounge, with warm male breath close to her face.

Scott's voice was soft, low. "I knew we'd get you. Your macho boyfriend can't stop us. He's simply no match for Uleah. The greatest warlock who ever lived will soon return to power—in your body. Your boyfriend will pay for his interference. In fact, I'll be the one to kill him. And I'm going to enjoy that. Oh yes, Mackenzie, your precious Christopher is about to die. And so are you."

Chapter Eleven

Christopher paced the length of his office, chewing irritably on a toothpick. He was angry that the Triad hadn't been found yet. All they had was speculation and that just wasn't good enough. Why were these people so hard to find?

Thomas, who patrolled western Canada, speculated that they had been in the Seattle area all along, but Jason and Alex insisted they were coming up through Oregon. Christopher was certain they had it all wrong. Thomas's information made the most sense.

The thick forests of the Pacific Northwest were home to many a meth lab. It stood to reason that a wizard and his crew would also seek the protection and seclusion of the vast woodlands. They would need absolute privacy and secrecy while concocting their strange brews, powders, and potions. They had a tendency to stand out, whether in a crowd or alone. Wizards were just different.

All the wizards Christopher had known—three of them to date—had been odd fellows indeed. They muttered incessantly, lashed out at people for reasons known only to themselves, and often had less than optimal hygiene.

Wizards were best left in the shadows of the forests.

Jason and Alex were livid that Christopher and Blair did not take them seriously.

Ian stood and raised a hand to silence the din. Jason's mouth closed immediately, but Alex continued to bark at Blair.

Alex's blond hair had been pulled back into a long tail and secured with a leather tie, but as his gaze shot from Blair to Christopher, wisps of hair tumbled loose, and, with green eyes blazing with anger and hands locked into white-knuckled fists, he looked every bit the madman. "I am unaccustomed to having my information questioned, Blair. Why would you do this now? I have served you for over five hundred years. Why now?"

He was Old World, and had kept his ancient accent because he didn't want to lose the last remnant of what he considered his time. He'd told Christopher many years ago that this was an age of heathens and barbarians, and he would most certainly *not* adapt to their uncultured ways. His only concession was allowing his Eskarian brothers to call him Alex, rather than his full name, Alexandario.

Christopher and the others had long since adapted their speech to this day. Blending in was more important than holding onto things that had long since passed. Alex was an old dinosaur and sometimes a risk to their kind. Had he not been Ian's cousin, Christopher was sure Alex would not be here today. Stealth was their motto. Alex was anything but.

"Alex," Blair spoke quietly. "We will speak of this privately. Now is not the time." He glared at Alex for a moment, then gave his full attention to Ian.

Alex brought his green gaze to the Eskarian leader.

Ian scanned the group. "Why is it we know so little about the Triad? We learned about the prophecy several days ago, and yet we have no information about who these people are, where they are, and exactly what the prophecy means."

Christopher leaned back against the bookcase. "The prophecies were all riddles, Ian. How did you solve them before?"

"The threats were more obvious," Ian began. "It was not as

difficult to deduce what was happening. For example, the Sixth Dragon came to pass at the turn of the century. The prophecy read that an eruption would blacken a mighty king's land. We already knew there was a group of subterranean Water Demons in Australia."

Christopher had been just outside Cairo then, along with Griffin. Together they had battled an Egyptian Sandraptor, while the others battled the Water Demons.

The Sandraptor's voracious appetite for human life precluded Christopher's involvement in such an important event. He had wanted to be a part of it, more than he'd ever let on, but the Sandraptor had other ideas. And he'd been a young Defender then. So arrogant and full of himself. The Sandraptor had shown him just how fragile life really is.

He'd spent a day in Griffin's makeshift healing tank. The Sandraptor had nearly severed him in half.

That was just before the Priestess had foretold his future: She bears a small scar on her high cheekbone, and you will come to love such a small imperfection in otherwise flawless skin . . .

Mackenzie had such a scar. It was a tiny thing just under her left eye. Even without it, Christopher knew she was the one.

"There must be something we're not seeing, Ian." Christopher paced again, and pulled the toothpick from his mouth. "The Seventh Dragon says that three men are coming. Among them is a sorcerer, protected by shadows. We've already determined that a sorcerer protected by shadows would probably not be seen, unless he wanted to be seen."

"How would he be protected by shadows?" asked Jason. "Is there some significance to the word 'protected'?"

Ian's rubbed his chin idly. "Maybe. Could it be that these two men protect the sorcerer and they are the shadows? Perhaps they are servants to the sorcerer, following him like shadows."

Blair continued with more questions. "And how would he start a war? With whom? Is he so great a sorcerer that he could take on a country? If that's true, shouldn't we know of him already?"

A scant minute passed as each man considered the questions; the old clock that sat on the wooden bookshelf thumped its soft rhythm, as if to break up the silence in the room.

"Perhaps we do already know of a great sorcerer." Ian raised the tattered old book, Uleah's spellbook and journal. "We have this book, from a once-great sorcerer who may have returned from the dead. This has to be it. Uleah must be the sorcerer from the prophecy."

"Then is Scott one of the men who protect him?" Christopher tossed the old toothpick and plucked another one from his shirt pocket, his mind working as he absently popped it into his mouth. "Could this have something to do with someone burning Griffin at Mackenzie's house? Not just anyone could have accomplished such a thing. Griffin is a seasoned warrior and very used to watching for threats. If we assume that Griffin interrupted something, we would have to consider that there was something in her house that someone of great power, like a sorcerer, wanted very much. Enough to kill to get it. If Uleah was at Mackenzie's house, perhaps he was looking for the spellbook. Do we have any information yet about who did this to Griffin?"

"No, we have nothing." Blair shifted in the plush leather chair. "But it could be that Scott or this Uleah came back to Mackenzie's, looking for the book, and found Griffin instead. Or he found them."

Christopher looked at Ian, then Blair. "It makes sense."

Blair nodded. "I think we're onto something here. I don't know about the shadows, but according to the journal here, Uleah was an adept sorcerer. Evidently, he intends to come back from the dead, though I have no idea how he would accomplish such a thing. The prophecy says after his return, the land would be washed in blood, which means his reasons for coming back are not for the benefit of humans. It seems logical that we should follow this path, and that we should consider Uleah the most serious of threats."

"I agree. Who else could be a member of the Triad?" Christopher scanned the room, though his gaze fell on blank expressions. No one had any ideas. "Griffin should be able to tell us something. I'll check on him in the morning to see how he's healing. Maybe we'll have our answers then."

"I'll take my leave of you then, gentlemen. Until tomorrow." Ian dipped his head once to the group, gathered up his coat, and left.

Blair glanced at Christopher. *I would like to speak privately with Alex.*

Christopher nodded. *Of course.*

Leaning back, with one leg crossed over the other, Blair regarded the stout, ancient Eskarian. "Perhaps you and I should continue our discussion."

Christopher nodded to Blair and Alex. "I'll leave you to your business." He quickly left, with Jason following close behind. Once in the living room, Christopher smiled and gave Jason a good swat on the shoulder. "How's Phoenix these days, Jason?"

"Hot as ever, my friend. I'll admit I'm glad to be up here. It's October, and until yesterday, I was still taking nightly dips in the pool to cool off," he said, shaking his head.

Christopher laughed. "I'm not surprised to hear that. Do you still make it down to Mexico to see your family?"

"Not often enough. It's been almost a hundred years since my parents passed on. All I ever really do is check on the great-grandchildren. It's nice to see them, though. They all speak English well already. I had to learn it much later in life. Times change, I guess."

"That they do." He stopped, his senses at once scanning the interior of the house. Something didn't feel right. "Where's Mackenzie?"

"Can't you feel her?" Jason asked.

"No, I can't. I sense one raccoon, Griffin in the tank, Alex and Blair, and an owl out front. No Mackenzie. Something's wrong, Jason." Christopher frowned. "Very wrong."

Jason looked around. "Last time I saw her, she was on the couch."

Sean appeared at the hallway entrance, with tousled hair and wrinkled clothes. "What's going on?"

Christopher swung around to meet his gaze. "Well, good evening, Sean. How do you feel?" He scanned the perimeter of the property as he waited for Sean's answer. He couldn't feel Mackenzie's lifeforce.

"I think I need a beer." Sean ran both hands through his hair. "I feel like I've been asleep for a hundred years."

Christopher raised a brow. "No, you don't need a beer. You need blood. Jason, can you take Sean out and show him how it's done?"

"Blood? Oh . . ." Sean looked from Christopher to Jason. "Blood. Kenz took my blood, and then you gave me yours."

"And I gave you enough to convert your body to Eskarian." Christopher smiled thinly. Alarm raced through his veins. He couldn't feel Mackenzie at all. No matter where she was, he should be able to feel her. "I need to find her. Jason, take care of Sean." Christopher spun around, heading for the bedroom, leaving Jason to his assigned task.

Sean stepped forward. "Um, excuse me?"

Christopher stopped with an annoyed sigh. He didn't have time for this. What was done was done. The last thing he needed was another argument. "Yes, Sean?"

"I'm not human now? Am I like you?" Sean asked.

"Yes, you are. Jason will explain everything to you. Not only is he a Defender, but he's a sendagi, or healer, as well. He can answer all your questions. I'm sorry to leave you hanging like this, but I don't know where your sister is. I can't feel her," Christopher said, hoping he didn't sound as impatient as he felt. New Eskarians needed patience and understanding, not annoyance.

"She's missing? I should look for her, too, shouldn't I?" Sean looked from Christopher to Jason, then stuffed his hands into his pockets.

"No. You're in no condition to do anything but feed. Jason? Take care of this." Christopher waved a hand dismissively, leaving the sendagi with Sean.

Christopher searched every room in the vast estate. She simply wasn't in the house. Finally, he went out to the back porch. By then, he was frantic.

She was fast asleep on a chaise lounge.

Why was she sleeping outside?

He knelt beside her, brushing ebony hair from her face. "Mackenzie?" His voice was soft, subtly commanding. She would hear him, no matter how deep her slumber.

Her mouth twitched. She inhaled deeply, stretched, then opened her eyes. "Hi," she said softly.

He held her face in his hands. "Are you all right?"

A frown creased her brow. "I'm fine, I think. I feel lightheaded, but essentially fine."

"Why are you sleeping out here? It's much warmer in our bed."

She looked around, confusion on her face. "I don't know. I must've had a reason, but it escapes me now. I'm don't know how I even got out here. How long have I been asleep?"

"I'm not sure. I was in the office for about two hours." His acute sense of smell detected something on her skin. "Mackenzie, come inside with me. Let me have a look at you." He needed better lighting, needed to see that she was all right.

He helped her stand, then grasped her hand. She quietly followed him to the kitchen, where the lighting was the brightest. Once he'd seated her at the kitchen table, he thoroughly inspected her face. "There is something on your skin." His fingers brushed her cheek, over the tiny scar he'd thought about only moments ago. A soft fine powder dusted his fingertips. "Powder, I'd guess, but what would it be?"

"I have no idea."

"Do you remember what happened tonight?" Christopher wrapped his hands around hers, kneeling at her side.

"Well, I remember I was reading a book." She paused, as if she was thinking about what she'd done. "I got up for something." She looked back toward the office. "I heard you arguing, but there was something in the house that scared me. I had to get out."

"What frightened you?" he asked.

"Someone told me you were going to lock me away. Would you do that to me?" Her frightened gaze clawed at him.

Christopher shook his head. "No, of course not. Who said that to you?"

"I don't know."

"Was someone in the room with you? Did you see anyone?"

She nibbled on her lower lip. "I was alone. I think the voices were in my head."

"Do you remember anything else?"

"I remember you waking me up. That's it." She brushed her cheek then looked absently at her fingers. "It's a little unnerving that I can't remember what happened." She continued to gaze at her fingers, as if they held some special interest for her.

"Mackenzie?"

"Mmm?" She looked at him, shadows in her emerald eyes.

"Are you all right?"

"Oh, sure. I'm sorry. What were you saying?" she asked, a smile creasing her face.

"Nothing, really. You look lost in your own thoughts."

"Oh. Yeah." Her gaze drifted down to the hardwood floor. "I fell asleep."

Christopher's brow furrowed. "What? When did you fall asleep?"

"I was reading my book and then I fell asleep. Outside. I don't know why I was outside."

Christopher sat down beside her. "Honey, we just talked about this. Don't you remember?" Fear curled in the bottom of his stomach. Why didn't she remember what they'd just discussed?

She pushed a hand through her hair. "No. My head's a little foggy, though. I kind of feel like I'm in a cloud."

"Maybe you should lie down. Let me take you to the bedroom." He straightened.

"Okay." She rubbed her eyes with both hands, then sighed softly.

"Come with me," he said firmly.

With his palm on her elbow, he guided her through the house to his bedroom. Setting her down on the bed, he took off her shoes and sweatshirt, and started to remove her T-shirt, but she protested.

"What's wrong," he asked.

"I'm feeling out of sorts. I'd like to keep some clothes on." She crossed her arms over her breasts.

"No problem. I just want you to be comfortable. Can I get you anything?" he asked. She looked so confused, his heart went out to her. At the same time, he wanted to know who'd done this to her.

Her head shook slowly. "No, I don't think so."

"I'll be back in a few minutes. Lie down. Get some sleep, if you can."

He pulled the covers over her legs, then quietly stepped from the bedroom and closed the door behind him. Leaning against it, he pressed his palms against his forehead and tried to suppress the wild emotions running through him.

The powder . . . it had to have come from a wizard. No one else would have something that powerful.

The realization sent the breath rushing from his lungs.

The Triad was after Mackenzie.

His fists clenched with the thought. They couldn't have her. He would find them, and they would pay with their lives. There was no doubt about that.

Oh yes, they would pay.

Christopher headed for the office, and burst in on Blair and Alex, having yet another heated discussion. "My apologies, gentlemen, for the disruption. Blair, something has happened to Mackenzie. She's not herself. I believe it's the Triad, and I'm getting really pissed off." Christopher paced the office again, his hands stuffed deep into his pockets just to keep from breaking furniture.

Blair stood, stopping Christopher in his tracks. He gripped Christopher's shoulders tightly. "Calm down. Now. The first thing we need to do is see what Griffin knows. We must verify it's the Triad. We can't do anything until tomorrow. Do not hasten a mistake, Christopher."

"I can't wait until tomorrow." Christopher sighed. "I need to know what happened now. I can't bear the thought of losing her."

"You don't know yet what's really happened," Blair said. "I know you want to keep her safe, but there just isn't anything we can do, yet. We need more information. At first light, we can see how Griffin is doing. Get some rest, please. We'll handle it in the morning."

Christopher closed his eyes and rubbed the bridge of his nose with two fingers. "By the gods, I *will* find out who did this to her."

"I know you will. *Please,* get some rest. Be ready when she needs you tomorrow."

Christopher sighed. "I'm sorry for the interruption. Goodnight."

He spun on his heel and left quickly, still angry and frustrated. In fact, his head pounded so much, he feared it might explode. He needed to release it before he returned to Mackenzie. Before he really did explode. Ignoring the startled looks from Jason and Sean as he rushed by, he hurried out to the back deck. There, he bent over and rested his palms on the tops of his knees, trying desperately to collect himself, to calm the raging emotions boiling inside him.

Something was happening to her, and he didn't know how to stop it.

Unleashing his fury, he picked up a wicker lounge and hurled it out into the back yard. It twisted through the air, cracked solidly against a large Maple tree, and shattered into a thousand pieces. Not satisfied with the destruction, he put his fist completely through one of the heavy posts holding the porch roof, splitting the wood in half. The roof sagged ominously, but held.

He pressed his palms against his forehead. A thousand deaths to whoever did this to his beloved Mackenzie.

With a long sigh, he gathered his wild emotions and went back into the house. She would be waiting for him. The house was quiet now and he was grateful for the silence. With any luck, everyone had retired for the evening. The last thing he needed was anything, really, that kept him away from her or raised his blood pressure further. Anyone foolish enough to approach him now risked their life.

Morning could not come soon enough.

Stepping into his bedroom, he eased the door shut. Mackenzie lay on her side under the quilts, just as he'd left her. With a thought, he ignited several pots of Livendium and candles along the dresser and nightstand. The room blazed to life with fire and smoke, settled his emotions a little.

Just a little.

As he dimmed the lighting, he shed his clothes and crawled in beside her. Against her body, he trailed a hand along her waist and hip, down her thigh and back up again. The feel of her skin alone beneath his fingers soothed his fiery emotions more than the Livendium. "Are you still awake?"

"Yes," she answered.

"How do you feel?" He pressed a lingering kiss on her shoulder.

"Fine."

He exhaled softly. "I'm relieved." His eyes closed as he nuzzled the back of her neck. "Seems like I've waited forever to feel your skin next to mine. I just need to know you're all right."

"I am, Christopher." She regarded him with a slight crease in her brow. A single, slender finger traced the line of his jaw and then her emerald gaze met his. "Have you always been Eskarian?"

"No, I was made Eskarian when I was just twenty-three years old." He smiled. "Do you want to hear the story?"

She nodded. "Very much."

Her smile warmed his heart, eased some of the fear that curled around his throat.

"I lived in Scotland then, just a ways out of Edinburgh. One night, I was out with my brother, Colin." He paused. Inhaling deeply, he propped his head up on his elbow. "It's been so long since I've thought about this . . . So, we were at my parents' house, near the barn, and there was a nasty thunderstorm. Lots of thunder, lightning, and wind. It was an eerie night, I remember. An Eldorian War Demon attacked us. They have claws . . ." He measured seven inches with his hands. "Like this. Vicious fighters. I was lucky to have survived. Colin wasn't quite as fortunate."

"I'm so sorry."

His head shook and he waved his hand idly. "It was long ago. Anyway, Blair found me bleeding to death and was impressed that I was still alive. Because of that, he offered me immortality. And here I am, two hundred years later, thinking about passing Arden's Bow off to someone else."

"The cycle continues," she said thoughtfully.

"Yes. Always."

Her brow creased further. She watched him silently for a moment, nibbling on her lower lip. "I don't remember where I was born. Or when." Tears glittered in her eyes, and a single drop trailed slowly down her cheek. "I think I should remember that much, don't you?"

"You were born here, almost thirty years ago." His voice was strong, sure. She needed his strength, and, by the gods, he would not fail her. His thumb whispered across her face and down to capture the tear and whisk it away.

"I don't know what's happening to me," she confessed

softly. "There are black spots in my memory that I don't think were there yesterday. It frightens me."

"Whatever it is, we'll see it through together. It'll be all right."

She sat up against the pillows, her gaze cold. "You can't possibly know that. Do not placate me with idle statements, Christopher. I won't tolerate it." Tears streamed down her cheeks and she wiped them away with both hands. She kicked the blankets down and rolled from the bed.

Christopher rose up on his elbow. "Wait, Mackenzie. I'm sorry. I didn't mean it like that . . ."

Without a word, she padded to the bathroom, slamming the door shut behind her.

"Damn it," he said. He lay back, fingers drifting over the ridges of his stomach. She had a point. He didn't truly know if she would be all right, and it tore at his insides to think it was possible he might lose her, but damn it, he wouldn't give her up without a fight. No matter the adversary, he would fight—and die, if necessary—to save her.

Several minutes passed before he threw off the quilts and got up. Tapping softly on the bathroom door, he waited for Mackenzie to respond.

Nothing.

He tapped again. "Mackenzie? Are you all right?"

No response.

He scanned her mind and knew she was near, but something wasn't right. Her thoughts were jumbled, her emotions wild.

Fear wrapped around his throat. "Mackenzie?" The alarm in his own voice surprised him. "Answer me. I need to know if you're okay."

Silence met his question.

He waited only a minute longer before trying the door

handle. Thankfully, it was unlocked. Stepping inside, he scanned the bathroom to find that she was nowhere in sight, but one of the French doors was slightly ajar. A cool breeze slipped in and, as he approached, it chilled his skin and sent a slight shiver down his back.

He opened the door and found her sitting in one of the patio chairs with her knees pressed up against her chest, and her arms curled around them. The cool rain had dampened her thick fall of ebony hair and plastered the T-shirt to her skin.

"Mackenzie?" He leaned back casually against the door.

Her gaze moved slowly to his, but she neither moved nor blinked.

He tilted his head. "Why are you sitting in the rain?"

"I had to. I was suffocating in the house. Needed some air. My own space." She pushed her hair back with both hands. "Sometimes, I have to be where there are no walls, no constraints, and no harnesses. I need the cover of the night around me."

"But it's cold and wet out here. Come inside with me. Let me warm you up."

"Warm me up out here. I don't want to come inside. The open space is comforting and I need it right now."

Christopher exhaled softly. "As you wish."

"Come here. Warm me up."

In the golden haze from the patio lights, she was exquisite. Her face was wet from the rainwater, and her parted lips, soft and full, beckoned him with silent promises of need answered with fire and passion. She rose to her feet and, locking her gaze to his, slid her satin panties down long thighs. Stepping out of them, she sat back down in the chair, slowly parted her legs, propping one foot on a chair, and the other one on a heavy planter. Propped back against the wet cushions, she raised her chin, watched him with half-closed eyes. Now a wild vixen, she grasped the chair back behind her head and arched her back invitingly.

She was fully open to his view. Her hips tilted, and she beckoned, her body calling to him in a soundless plea. To torment him further, her tongue came out to wash an already-moist lip. No other woman had ever come so close to bringing him to his knees. Even the Priestess, for all her knowledge and sexual power, was a rank novice compared to Mackenzie.

His breath quickened as hunger for her body drove every sane thought from his head. His erection was already thick, heavy, and screaming for release. "What are you trying to do to me?" He stepped out from under the eaves and knelt beside her.

"Take you over the edge," she purred. Her slender hand whispered across his cheek.

"Mmm, dangerous. I could so easily lose control." Christopher laid his hands on her thighs, thumbs caressing her heated skin. "Can you imagine what might happen?"

"I suppose I can." She leaned forward and caught a strand of his long hair, running two fingers down the length, over his chest, then down farther. "I'll just have to take that chance. I'm not afraid of you."

Ah, yes, he would play her game.

And win.

A slow smile crossed his face as his gaze dropped to the dark juncture between her legs. "No?" He gently pushed her back into the chair. "Is that right?"

Her eyes closed. "That's right. I'm not afraid."

Her leg muscles tightened as her hips sought to invite him inside her. "You should be." He stood up. "You're playing with fire." He was ready to explode and he hadn't even started yet. She'd become the wild temptress again, and he didn't know how much longer he could wait before he really did lose control.

Not much longer, he thought.

He lifted her from the chair by the waist and set her in front of the heavy metal patio table. With a palm pressed to her back, he bent her over the table and pinned her flat against it. "Fire, Mackenzie. You will feel *my* fire."

"So, burn me." She stretched out over the table. He thought he might lose it right there, when she grasped the opposite edge of the table to give herself to him.

Though the rain was cold, he felt only the heat of her body against his hands. Such a wonderful, silky seduction, her body. He pushed the T-shirt up, exposing her backside and the small of her beautiful back and narrow waist. Slowly and deliberately, his hand trailed the delicious smooth lines of her back, down her hips to her thigh, then to the inside, nudging her legs a little farther apart. She was fully open to his inspection.

And what a sight she was.

He needed her. *God,* how he needed her. He loved everything about her. She was hot-tempered, independent, and she belonged to him. His benekeda. True mate.

And he loved to drive her over the edge.

Captured by her musky scent, he dipped down to take her into his mouth, to sample her sweet honey. Every inch of his body screamed for release, fire raced through his veins, and his erection pulsed with such hunger, such need, it hurt. So much effort it took to slowly—ever so slowly—set her aflame as she had him. Ah, she'd captured him unmercifully with her scorched heat and wild desire. He loved the way she coiled around him, doused him with fire.

Only a moment later, her body tightened and she released her pleasure in soft moans, gripping the edge of the table and shuddering. Rapid-fire spasms rippled over her body.

Beautiful.

He straightened and leaned over her, so that his mouth was against her ear. "I want you to explode once more for me. I want you so hot, you can't think of anything other than me inside you." His voice shook with his confession.

She shuddered. "Please . . ."

She was ready. He was ready to explode.

But he wanted her as close to the edge as he'd found himself: just a breath away from disintegrating into a million bits.

He took her wrists and held her captive. "You're mine, Mackenzie. For all time. No matter what you do, where you go, I will find you. I'll protect you with my life and give it up for you if necessary. There is no other for me." He savored the moment, then thrust himself deeply into her searing, tight fire.

She moaned through clenched teeth. He pulled back, then thrust into her again with driving force. His eyes closed, the heat took over, possessed him, and hunger tore at his insides, shrieked for release. The rest of the world faded away. There was only her body and his, melded together as one, a burning pyre of blue steel and red flame. For all time.

Slowly his sharp teeth lengthened. His breath was quick, ragged, and still he pushed into her, hard, demanding. His mouth pressed against the top of her shoulder, his tongue washed the hot, salty skin, and then his teeth pierced into her tender skin. Mackenzie tightened, trembling and pulsing around him.

He drank of her fire, her essence and blood, and it was like nectar—perfect, hot, and sweet. As if it were his last meal, he relished each precious drop of her lifeblood.

He raised his head and pressed a kiss to each puncture wound. They would heal in a matter of seconds.

Christopher released into her. He was exhausted, spent. Sated.

"I need you, Christopher." Her voice was raw, vulnerable. "I want you to do this to me again."

He smoothed the back of her hair. "I will. I promise you."

He allowed himself a moment to rest before withdrawing. Carefully pulling her up from the table, he wrapped his arms around her. "I meant what I said."

"As do I." She looked up into his eyes, smiling for the first time this evening.

"Are you ready to come in from the rain?" He brushed the wayward strands of ebony hair from her face.

She nodded slowly, yawning. "I think so."

He nudged her toward the door. "Come. Let's get you to the shower. Your skin is getting cold."

The shower, encased in glass, had two golden heads and an assortment of smaller sprays that could be maneuvered to pulse water over any body part. He selected a warm temperature, removed her shirt, then brought her under the spray. Starting at her shoulders, he gently scrubbed her skin with a soft sponge and soap.

"That feels so nice," she said softly.

He smiled. "It's my pleasure."

Her eyes drifted shut as she allowed him to take care of her.

He scrubbed her from head to toe, then rinsed her thoroughly. When he was done, he dried her body with a large, plush, white towel. "You'll need something warm and dry to wear."

"I'll take one of your T-shirts." She walked to the closet and chose a blue shirt, quickly swapping her wet towel for the new, dry shirt that came down to her knees.

"You look great in my shirts." His eyes roamed the length

of her body, drinking in the beauty of her strong, tanned legs, slender hips, and full breasts. "You look great out of my shirts as well."

She laughed. "Blue is my favorite color. I'm keeping this one."

His eyebrows shot up. "You're keeping my clothes now?"

"Sure, why not? I like it and it fits. Sort of. You go buy more," she said, nodding.

"So that's how you're going to be?" He snatched her up by the waist and carried her, laughing and squealing, to the king-sized bed. Protected by heavy quilts and plump, large pillows, he pulled her close to his body and kissed her cheek. His time with her was precious.

At that moment, he didn't know how he'd survived all those years without the warmth of her body against his. Now, he couldn't imagine a more bleak existence.

He loved her. With everything he had, he loved her.

As he nestled into the fall of ebony hair, he extinguished the candles and snuffed out the smoldering Livendium leaves, all with a single thought. Glancing at the lamp, he snapped it off with another quick thought and settled in against her back.

He hadn't told her yet, but yes, he absolutely, completely loved her.

It was well past sunrise when Christopher bolted upright, knowing with absolute certainty that something was not right. He felt it down to his very bones. His mind immediately flared out to find her, to feel her lifeforce.

She wasn't in the house.

He threw off the quilts and rolled out of bed. Dragging on a pair of black jeans and a T-shirt, he burst into the living room, clearly startling Sean and Blair.

"Have you seen Mackenzie?" Christopher asked as he raced past.

"She's out front." Sean bounded out of the chair and followed Christopher. "What's going on?"

"Something's not right. I need to find her." Christopher's mind scanned the premises and found her at the edge. "There." He hurried out the front door, into the cool morning.

She leaned against the gate it as if waiting for someone or something to show up.

Christopher trotted up beside her. "What are you doing out here? You scared me."

She met his gaze and smiled. "Hello. Sorry about that. Beautiful day, isn't it?"

"Yeah, it is. Why didn't you wake me when you got up?" He pushed two hands through his hair, smoothing it back.

She inhaled deeply and smiled as Sean joined them. "Morning."

"Hey," Sean said, stuffing his hands into his pockets.

She turned back to him. "You looked so peaceful lying there. I just didn't have the heart to wake you. It's no big thing, really. I'm fine by myself."

Christopher leaned in to brush her cheek. "Are you feeling okay?"

"Yeah, I feel just fine." She tilted her head to the side, scanning the house and yard. "Can you tell me whose house this is?"

Chapter Twelve

"You don't know where you are?"

She took a closer look at the man who stood before her. His dark brown hair glistened like threads of fine silk in the morning sun. She reached up to touch it, to bunch a fistful in her hand, and wondered if she'd done this before. His long, thick hair sifted through her fingers, settled across his broad shoulders. He leaned into her touch just a little, as if he enjoyed her fingers tangled in his mane.

His intense blue eyes softened, then closed when her fingers whispered over his cheek. He knew her and cared about her, that much was plain.

"No, I don't." She had no idea who he was. Or where she was. In fact, she didn't know who she was, either. It hadn't always been this way, she guessed. How could she wake up one day and have no idea who she was or which people were important? Was she like this yesterday? Obviously, these questions needed to be answered, but where to begin?

It seemed unlikely that she could've been in some kind of accident. There were no scars or bruises, no pain. No evidence, no clue. Maybe she fell or . . .

No, she had no idea what had happened.

The blond-haired man who stood beside her frowned. "What's going on?"

The dark-haired man's crystal blue gaze swung to the blond. "I think the Triad cast a spell on Mackenzie."

"Who's Mackenzie?" she asked.

Both the men looked at her as if she were crazy. Great. Just what she needed. "I'm sorry. I should know that name, shouldn't I?"

The dark-haired man frowned. "Yes, you should. You are Mackenzie," he said flatly.

She nodded. Mackenzie. The name didn't sound familiar at all. They could've said her name was Byron, for all it meant to her. She studied the blond to her left. His face showed similar concern, but he didn't look at her like the other one did.

"Kenz?" The blond looked at her. "What's going on?"

He knew her.

Kenz was a nickname. "I don't know," she admitted. "But, if this man says it's a spell, then I think I'm in no position to disagree. I honestly have no idea."

The dark-haired man placed a hand on her shoulder. "This man? You don't know who I am?"

Her gaze met his. "No, I'm sorry I don't. I should know that, too, right? Please tell me what it is." He was the one who'd slept beside her last night. Was he her husband or boyfriend?

His brow furrowed and his mouth opened, but he said nothing right away. He seemed genuinely concerned—alarmed, even—that she didn't know him. "Christopher."

It was obvious she should have known his name, yet even when he said it, there was no recollection. Nothing she could use to figure out what had happened. Nothing to tell her what kind of life she had.

God, she wanted to run. She couldn't have been more uncomfortable.

"And you?" She turned to the blond-haired man.

"What the hell is going on here?" In his face, she saw outright alarm, and it frightened her to her very bones.

"Now is not the time, Sean. Tell her your name and who

you are. Do it." Christopher's voice was firm, harsh. "You're scaring her."

"Is this some kind of sick—"

"Sean, *not now.*" Christopher's eyes flashed. The blond-haired one had angered him.

The blond looked at her, confused and . . . what? Angry? Why? "I'm Sean, your brother. Our parents were killed when we were very young. I was four and you were barely two. Aunt Bess and Uncle Jake raised us."

Sean. She had a brother. He had no idea what had happened to her, either.

Sean looked at Christopher. "What makes you think it's a spell? There's no such thing as magic spells. Is there?"

"Yes, Sean, there is. There are also demons, wizards, and an infinite number of threats that humans have never known about, simply because of what we do."

"Oh, yeah, Defenders. Got it." Sean nodded.

"I'll train you to be one too. Now, can we get back to Mackenzie's issue?"

"Of course. I'm sorry." He draped an arm around her shoulders and pulled her close. "Don't worry, Kenz. We'll figure this out. Christopher is pretty good at this stuff."

"That's encouraging, because I certainly have no idea. That bit about demons and wizards sounds like nonsense to me. Next you'll be telling me there are dragons. I might be missing pieces of my memory, but I'm not stupid. Dragons don't exist. Neither do demons."

Christopher raised his eyebrows. His gaze darted first to Sean, then back to her. "No, you're right. I was just yanking Sean's chain. No such thing as demons, dragons, or vampires."

"Thought so," she said. He didn't look like he was messing with Sean, but maybe it was best to just leave it for now. She could keep that information in the back of her mind and summon it again when the opportunity presented itself.

Mackenzie had to decide what to do next. She needed time to think, to sort things out, and figure out what had happened, if that was even possible. If it was a spell, who'd cast it and why? Had she done something to cause it?

Of course, the biggest question was, should she trust these people? She couldn't be certain one of them wasn't the perpetrator. Now wouldn't that be rich? Dancing with scorpions, she thought.

But, first things first.

If she left, where would she go? Not only did she not know where she was, she didn't know where she lived. Was it here?

Mackenzie sighed again. "Do I live here?"

"In a manner of speaking, yes. I'm your benekeda, your true mate. You and I are of the same essence." Christopher spoke softly, staring at his bare feet more than her.

She frowned. The same essence? "What the hell does that mean? Are we married or not?"

He looked away for a moment, as if he had to think about the answer. "Yes, we are." His gaze met hers and his blue eyes were shadowed with . . . what? Sadness? Despair?

She couldn't be sure.

"Are we happily married?" He certainly didn't look happy at the moment.

He nodded, his gaze dropping again to his feet. "We just got married yesterday."

"Oh . . ." That explained the look on his face.

Christopher looked at Sean a moment, then back at her. "And I love you, more than you could possibly imagine."

Mackenzie stepped back from the men and glared at Christopher. Exactly what was the point of that? Was it meant to jog her memory? There was *nothing* to jog.

"Mackenzie," he said, reaching for her. "No, wait . . . I'm sorry."

She launched, suddenly angry. Furious. "For what?" she demanded. "For looking at me as if I were some kind of freak or someone to be pitied? Do you think your pretty words will bring back my memory? Did it ever occur to you that I'm fully aware that something is terribly wrong with me? I *know* you two should be very familiar to me, and yet, I tell you, I know nothing about either of you. Nothing. I've tried to bring back the memories, but there's nothing to bring back and I don't know what to do to change it." She pushed angrily at the hair that had fallen into her eyes. "I've lost my entire life . . ." Rubbing her suddenly-throbbing temples, she looked at Christopher first, then Sean. "I *hate* this!"

"I didn't mean to make you feel bad, Mackenzie. I wanted you to know I'm here to help," Christopher said, stuffing his hands into his pockets.

Her brother smiled. "Me too, Kenz."

She sighed. Now she just wanted some peace and quiet, away from everyone. "Listen." She looked from one to the other. "I've just got to have some space right now. I might never get my life back." *God, what an awful thought.* "What am I to do then?"

"No, don't think like that. We'll find a way to bring your memories back. There has to be a solution," Christopher said. "We just have to find it, that's all."

"You don't know that," she countered.

"Yes, I do." His eyebrows raised. "I *will* find a way. I always do."

She shrugged, uncertain if she should believe him. How would she know if he meant what he said, or if what he said was even possible? She knew nothing about him.

Still, she knew there was something between them. She

felt a connection to him and sensed that it was unusually strong. Different.

Maybe he would find a way. "I hope you do," she said softly.

He nodded. "I will." He leaned in and kissed her cheek. "Stay close, so I know you're all right."

Sean watched her, but said nothing. His face was impossible to read. What kind of man was her brother? What about their parents? They'd had an accident? What had happened? Why? A million questions ran through her mind. If she could just get the answers to a few of them, she'd feel a little better. One or two, even.

She looked at Christopher beneath a furrowed brow. "Clearly, I'm not all right." Offering her companions a thin smile, she regarded them both for a moment, then headed for the house. Mackenzie needed some time. Lots of time, actually, just to get her bearings and figure out what to do next.

Her head still ached. She stepped into the house and searched several rooms for a place she thought might be unused, far away from everyone. How she thought she would figure any of this out, she had no idea, but the solitude felt good now. Felt right. It was a start, anyway.

Several moments later, she chose a room at the end of a long hall. Opening the door, she stepped into a brightly-lit, large solarium. Inside, she surveyed the exquisite décor of the formidable room. Tall trees reached for the sky and lush ferns sat atop marble pedestals. Her surroundings were lush, opulent, and clean, just what she needed. A large, black granite table lay in the exact center, surrounded by foliage, and flanked by two white chairs, an odd contrast to the verdant greenery surrounding it.

She had no recollection of this place, but it appealed to her, with its dark, shale tile and frosted-glass walls. Here, she felt protected and safe from all the wickedness outside, and hopefully safe from those who had taken her memory, her life.

Safe. For now. She relished the thought. Safe . . .

Mackenzie took a deep breath and strolled around the room, brushing the leaves of various plants with her fingers as she passed. The scent of something pleasantly spicy-sweet permeated the room. She found it soothing and calming. What herb was so powerful that she could forget her cares, and just surrender to its power? For now, she would just enjoy the most welcome reprieve.

Wandering farther, she found a large pool with a beautiful rock fountain near the outer wall. Water bubbled up from the center of a small tower of flat stones and sluiced down into the clear pool. Lily pads rimmed the edge of the pool, and delicate water plants swayed beneath the surface. Water dripped off the smooth stones to become a part of the pool again. The simplicity of it melted the tension from her shoulders, and left her, if not calm, at least not utterly overwhelmed. With a soft sigh, she felt ready to resume her investigation.

A low-pitched humming caught her attention. She spun around to see the black granite table split into two and the top piece turn onto its end, exposing iridescent green water. Mackenzie watched, uncertain about what purpose such a contraption might serve.

A man burst through the water's surface. Water sloshed onto the tile floor, the peace of the solarium now shattered. She nearly jumped from her skin, and backstepped until her head bumped into a large Weeping Laurel and the tree threatened to topple over. She steadied the plant; then her gaze returned to the gasping man. He hung over the side of the marble structure, coughing up water and taking in huge gulps of air. From the little she could see of him, he looked like a big, muscular man.

Really big.

After a moment, he seemed more composed. His gaze shot to hers and his silver eyes, like white steel, harsh and unforgiving, bored through to her very soul. She had no idea who he was, but every instinct she had told her he wasn't someone to mess with.

He didn't seem to recognize her either. He just watched without a word. What was he thinking? His ice-cold gaze chilled her bones and sent shivers down her back. This one seemed different: wild, untamed, and unpredictable. Not like Christopher, who seemed strong and confident. This one was dangerous.

She backed away. Was he another one she should have known? Did it matter? She wasn't sure she wanted to find out. He looked lethal and unforgiving.

With that thought, she bolted for the door. For all she knew, *he* was the enemy—the one who had done this to her.

The sudden slosh of water to the floor sent adrenaline through her veins. He was in pursuit. The solarium was large and the exit so far away. She couldn't get there fast enough.

A second later, he was on her. He clamped onto her shoulder and wrenched her back against the solid wall of his body. Thick, powerful arms curled around her waist and throat, making her his captive. The heat radiating from his body was intense enough to make her sweat.

"Please . . ." she whispered. Her pulse raced. What was he doing? What did he want? She tried to pull free, but her arms were pinned to her sides. She kicked against his legs as hard as she could, but he didn't budge. Didn't even flinch.

The silver-eyed man burrowed his face into her neck, and inhaled deeply. "You smell nice, Wolf." Then he straightened to pull her up with him so that her feet were completely off the floor. "I love the scent of fear." His voice was liquid satin, pure and deep.

"Please, put me down." She was terrified. His hot breath and liquid voice sent chills dancing down her back. She squirmed in his arms, hoping to persuade him to comply with her request, but his grip was firm and steadfast.

"I'm not done with you yet." He pressed a lingering kiss on her neck.

"What do you want from me?" she asked.

"Blood." With no further delay, his mouth pressed against her neck, then searing pain shot down to her shoulder.

She screamed in terror. This demon from hell was surely going to kill her. Panicking, she fought wildly to free herself. She had to escape or die trying, but there was just nothing she could do.

Nothing.

His grip was like iron, solid and unmovable. The harder she fought, the tighter his hold, until she could scarcely breathe. And no matter how much she tried to twist free, his mouth remained locked to her neck.

Seconds later, dizziness washed over her; she could no longer fight him. Her eyelids drifted down as the nausea overtook her.

He'd taken too much blood. Bastard . . .

The fight left her weakened and exhausted. He'd won.

"Griffin, put her down. Now." Christopher's voice was slow, soft, with just a hint of menace.

Mackenzie opened her eyes halfway to see him standing in the doorway, with Sean and another man behind him. His anger was evident in the hard set of his jaw, and in the steely gaze riveted to the behemoth who'd captured her.

Griffin. Good name for the titan.

"Put her down," Christopher said again.

Griffin held tight but raised his head to regard Christopher. At least he listened. Well, that was something. Maybe he'd be reasonable.

"Let her go. Listen to me, now. We'll get you all the blood you need, but drinking from Mackenzie is not appropriate. Do you understand? You are never to drink from her again."

"Christopher." Griffin eased her back onto the floor. "I know the rules. I *wanted* the wolf's blood."

Christopher stepped forward, his blue eyes blazing with fury. "Don't do it again. I won't be so forgiving if you do, my friend. Consider this your only warning."

Griffin shrugged. "Guard her well, then. I like the way she tastes."

Christopher glared at the titan. "I'm sure you have better things to do than provoke me. The battle wouldn't be nearly as easy as you'd like to think, Old Man."

Mackenzie gathered whatever strength she could muster and flung herself away from Griffin, landing solidly in Christopher's arms. Her body trembled visibly, but Christopher's warmth and his arms around her afforded some comfort. "Please take me away from here." At the moment, she didn't care where he took her, as long as it was away from Griffin.

Christopher locked his fiery gaze onto the nude man. "Remember my words, Griffin. You leave her alone. I'll send Sasha to tend to your needs."

He turned and ushered her out of the solarium. Sean and the other man remained behind. She looked back to see why they'd stayed behind, but the door closed before she had a chance to see what happened next.

"Pay no attention to them." Christopher nudged her forward.

"Why?" She wondered what would happen to Griffin. If

they were smart, they'd lock him up forever.

"He's not himself right now. They'll take care of him."

He led her to another part of the house, a room washed in soft colors of teal and light moss. This room she recognized. She'd slept here last night, beside him.

"Lie down, Mackenzie. Griffin took a great deal of blood from you. I'm sorry I didn't get to him sooner. It is difficult," he paused, closing his eyes, "to feel you since . . . your mind is different now. I didn't know what he was doing to you. I'll change that as soon as I can. It's important to me to be able to feel you, to know where you are and that you're all right."

She shrugged one shoulder. What he'd said didn't really make much sense to her. She wasn't willing to discuss it, though. She was tired and needed to rest. Kicking off her shoes, she burrowed under the heavy blankets.

He settled down behind her with his head propped up on an elbow. "Do you remember Griffin?"

"I remember nothing at all," she said flatly. "Should I?"

"Yes, you know him. He's an associate of mine."

"He called me Wolf. Why?" Instead of waiting for the answer, she thought about the blood he'd taken. "Is he a vampire?"

Christopher nodded. "Sort of."

"Then is that stone table a coffin?"

Christopher smiled, idly trailing two fingers along her shoulder. "No, it's a healing tank, filled with hot salt water. It speeds up the healing process significantly. Griffin was seriously injured yesterday, and unfortunately his wounds were so severe, he required quite a bit of time to heal. He was submerged for more than twenty-four hours and was somewhat disoriented when he attacked you. I should have been there when he awakened. At least, Jason should've been around. I don't know where he is . . ." He furrowed his brow.

Mackenzie nodded. "I think Griffin is . . . not someone you want to mess with, no matter his condition," she said.

Christopher agreed. "No, he isn't. Griffin is strong and aggressive—one of our best."

"Our best what?" she wondered. She sensed Griffin did things without considering consequences.

"Defenders. Warriors who keep us safe from things that go bump in the night," Christopher said.

Mackenzie smiled. "I thought he *was* one of those things that goes bump in the night. He's frightening. Did you know he bit me?"

"Yeah, he did. I'm sorry." His finger touched the hot punctures on her neck. "It won't happen again."

"Hurts."

"Not for long." His voice soothed her.

Her lashes drifted down. "Will you stay beside me?" She rolled over and nestled against his chest. His scent was faint, musky, and she loved it. "I feel so out of sorts, and I'm *so* afraid. There's so much I don't understand. But there's something about you—I can't put my finger on it, but I feel something when I touch you. It's like electricity, hot and alive. You, I can trust. I'm sure of it."

His arm draped over her shoulder. "Of course, I'll stay with you. Until the day I die, Mackenzie Wallace. Trust in that."

The afternoon sun hung above the mountains when she awoke. He snored softly beside her, with both an arm and a leg draped over her, as if to protect her. *From what,* she wondered. He looked peaceful lying there, so she eased from the bed with minimal movement. It seemed unnecessary to wake him.

She wasn't sure if it was the temperature of the room, or

just the fact that she was no longer close to his body, but now she was cold. She found the closet inside the massive bathroom and stepped in to find a sweater. After some searching, she found only one sweater and one shirt that seemed like it would fit. Was this her home? she wondered. If she truly lived here, why did she have so few clothes of her own? Did she not like clothes? Did he not allow her to buy clothes? In a house this big, she didn't think money was an issue.

She wrapped a white cardigan around her shoulders and padded softly from the room. Her intent was to explore this home on her own, to gather information based on what she gleaned herself, not from what other people told her. A nagging sensation made her think that all was not as it seemed.

In the kitchen, she found the granite countertop clean and inviting, but the stainless refrigerator was oddly sparse. Did they eat together? Even the maple cupboards were bare. Perhaps he had his meals catered. Somehow that didn't seem likely. He didn't seem like the sort of man who would have every meal brought to him. Not that she knew, of course.

Now that she thought about it, she couldn't even remember his name.

What was hers?

She stopped and pressed her fingers to her mouth, letting the words sift through her mind. *What was her name? What was his?*

Oh, Lord, what was going on? She had no idea how she'd gotten into this room. Where was she? Who was the man she'd slept with?

How in the hell would she find the answer to *that* question?

A bowl of apples on the kitchen table caught her attention. Her stomach had been rumbling earlier and, though it had quieted, she was still hungry. An apple would hold her over for a while. She chose a bright red one and brought it to the sink to wash it off.

As she dried it, she heard voices down the hall. It sounded like an argument, but she couldn't be sure. She had no intention of becoming involved, especially since she most likely had no idea who they were. Best to stay out of sight, she thought. Too many questions.

A door slammed and the sound of footfalls filled the hallway. A tall, heavily-muscled man glided in and stopped at the edge of the living room, running both hands through his wild mane of auburn hair. He sighed audibly, then spun to face her, as if he'd just realized he was not alone.

"Well, Mackenzie, how nice to see you again. I trust Christopher is treating you well." He smiled the devil's smile: perfect, insidious, secret, and dark.

This one was of the dark. She knew that much. She felt it.

Mackenzie nodded without a word, clutching the apple to her chest. Who was Christopher? Was she supposed to know him?

He strode toward her, his silver eyes unblinking.

Holy crap, the man was big.

She thought he looked amazing, with that long, wild hair and fiery silver eyes. Her gaze moved higher as he approached. Tall. Huge. Muscular. He placed his hands on her shoulders, brushed back the strands of hair that had pulled loose from her braid.

"Do you mind if I ask you a question?" His voice was soft, deep, and whispered over her, through her.

"No, though I'm not sure I'll be able to answer you."

"I understand completely. Whatever information you can offer will be appreciated. Do you know a man named Alistair?"

Searching her memory, she sought anything that might

trigger recollection, but there simply was nothing. Not a damn thing. "No, I don't think so."

"I ran into him when I was looking for the keys to your car. Christopher thought you might want it here. We think Alistair was probably looking for something at your house."

"Really? Maybe I should go see if everything is all right. He could have stolen something from me." Sounded good, but she had no idea where she lived or what she owned. This man had called her Mackenzie. She would accept that as her name until she learned more, like why she couldn't remember anything.

"It's not likely. Alistair has no need of anything. I've known of him for years and despised him for most of that time. He is an accomplished wizard. And utterly devoid of a conscience." His gaze rested on the apple. "You're not going to eat that, are you?"

She looked at the dark red fruit. "Sure, why not?"

A slight frown creased his brow. "Because your body won't tolerate it."

"Why not?" she asked. "I like apples . . . I think."

"Trust me. You won't enjoy it." His silver gaze drifted lazily over her face. His amused smile annoyed her.

Her eyebrows raised. "Is there something I can do for you?"

"You don't know who I am, do you?"

"No," she answered. "Should I?"

"Mmm-hmm." His hand whispered across her cheek. "Do you have any idea how beautiful you are?"

A slow smile creased her face. "Thank you," she said softly. Her cheeks and ears burned with embarrassment and her gaze dropped to the apple. The man was strong, it was obvious, and with golden skin and eyes to die for, she'd be thrilled to be with him. Maybe she was already, but, to save her life, she couldn't bring herself to ask.

She rolled the apple from hand to hand as his gaze roamed over her face. The man's eyes were hot, intense, like liquid metal, surrounded by long, black lashes. They were the eyes of a demon.

A red demon.

"Tell me your name." She needed to know who he was.

"Griffin. At your service, milady." He leaned forward, his head tilting. "Just once, allow me to taste your lips." His eyes closed as he descended. "Just once."

Her hands came up against his chest, but she didn't stop him. She couldn't. She wanted to know what his body felt like close to hers, and what his mouth felt like as he explored hers.

Maybe she should have, but she didn't know. Really didn't know. She wasn't sure what to think of Griffin, but his body felt amazingly hard. And nice.

His full mouth pressed gently against hers and she gave herself to him, accepting the tender strokes of his tongue inside her mouth. He held her face in his hands; his kiss became deeper, more passionate, as if he poured his very essence into her. Had he done this before? Were they together? Was he her lover? If so, who was she sleeping with earlier today?

Why couldn't she remember him? Why couldn't she remember anything?

At once his head snapped up. He glanced behind him, then returned to her and smiled. "Thank you, milady. I won't forget this."

And then he was gone. Just like that. She looked around, but he was nowhere. Gone.

His taste lingered upon her lips. She brought two fingers up to brush her mouth, remembering his passion, and wished she could remember something about him, about anything in her life.

With a soft sigh, she set the apple on the table and tried to figure out what had happened to her life.

A door opened and closed down the hallway.

She looked up to see another man enter the living room. This one, also tall and well-muscled, crossed the living room floor with a smile on his face, and fire in his blue eyes.

He stood close to her and dipped to catch her wrist, to kiss the inside of it with soft, full lips. His mouth left trails of fire where his skin touched hers. Unlike Griffin, this one made her heart race and breath quicken without doing anything special. She didn't know him, but instinctively knew this one was different.

This one was hers. She knew it without being told.

"Do you feel better now?" he asked.

Better than what? "Yes," she replied softly.

He searched her face, a slight crease in his brow. "You don't know what I'm talking about, do you?"

Her gaze lowered. "No, I don't. I'm sorry, but I don't remember anything. I'm so confused by all this. I don't know what has happened to me?"

"Aw, Mackenzie. I'm so sorry." He leaned in to hold her, but stopped. Catching her chin with his hand, he tilted her head upward, so he could fully examine her face. This one also had the fierce eyes of a demon and now they blazed, an inferno of indigo and ice.

She looked up at him. "Tell me your name."

"Christopher." His gaze focused on her mouth. "Griffin came to see you, didn't he?"

"Yes, he did. I thought . . ." Maybe she shouldn't say what she thought. The look on Christopher's face told her keeping quiet about Griffin was the best choice.

His eyes blazed. "What, Mackenzie? You thought what?"

"He was quite pleasant, actually." She stepped back, feeling the explosive anger build around Christopher. She knew at that moment that allowing Griffin to kiss her had been the wrong thing to do. Very wrong. "I'm sorry. I didn't know."

Anger flushed his cheeks. "It's not your fault. I'm not blaming you. Griffin's the one who should have known better. He took advantage of you." His voice was whisper-soft, unsteady, and his breath had quickened. "Stay here."

He spun around, strode to the living room, and grabbed a large, wooden bow resting behind the front door. A quiver held several long, white arrows. He snatched one and headed toward the door at a furious pace.

Shit. He was going to kill Griffin. "No, Christopher, wait—" Nothing good could come from this.

Too late.

He was gone.

Two other men immediately trotted out from the hallway and called for Christopher to reconsider, but he either didn't hear them or he'd chosen to ignore them.

Something terrible was about to happen. She ran after the two men. Though she knew nothing about most of what was going on, she still felt partially responsible and didn't want Griffin getting hurt. Didn't want Christopher hurt, either.

Christopher made her feel things deep inside her soul. She knew that one was special.

Griffin and Christopher faced each other on the lawn, several feet apart. The other two men caught up and surrounded them.

A black-haired man spoke. "Christopher, you can't do this. There has to be another way."

"Why not? Griffin has been after Mackenzie since she

came into my life. He knows the rules. He knows she belongs to me, and now I come to her and find his scent on her mouth. *On her mouth,* Blair," Christopher snarled. "I've had it with him. It ends, here and now."

Griffin smiled. "Rules are for idiots, Christopher. Who says she can only belong to you? Perhaps she would choose someone else, if you gave her the chance. After all, I can tell you for a fact the wolf enjoyed my kiss. Perhaps you should allow her to choose her own mate."

Mackenzie frowned. Wolf? When did a wolf come into all this?

"She's under a spell, Griffin. She doesn't know either you or me at the moment. All you did was prey on her, and she reacted without knowing what kind of a man you are. I doubt she'd give you more than the time of day, if she knew as much as I."

"Christopher, calm down." Blair stepped between the two men. "Griffin, you back off. Now. There's nothing to be gained by this kind of discussion. You both need to settle your nerves, and then we can find a resolution to this problem."

Christopher growled. He shook his head, sending strands of dark hair about his face. He pushed them back angrily. "No, Blair. I'm done trying to reason with him. There is only one resolution at this point."

Griffin raised his chin. "And what would that be, Little One? Hmm? Do you really think you could take me on and win?"

Christopher moved forward. "I surpassed you long ago as a Defender, Griffin. I'm stronger and faster. You're bloated with your own warped self-image."

"Christopher, that's *enough!*" Blair turned fully to Christopher. "You must come to your senses. This is *not* how we settle our differences. We must discuss this as rational beings, not as animals."

Christopher's fury focused on Blair. "Stand aside, Blair, or face my anger as well. I meant what I said. This battle between Griffin and me ends now."

"No, I will not stand aside," Blair said. "How would you have it end? With Griffin's death? Is that what you want?"

"Yes." Christopher's eyes were flat and cold.

"You haven't the stomach for cold-blooded murder, Christopher," Griffin said, grinning.

Christopher's gaze shot to Blair. "I'm sorry. Not this time . . ." In one fluid movement, Christopher dropped, and swung one leg out to catch Blair behind the knees and send him toppling to the grass. He spun about, brought up the wooden bow with his movement, and cracked Griffin across the side of the head as he spun.

Mackenzie's hands flew to her mouth.

Griffin spun around from the force of the blow, but he recovered quickly. Raising a hand to wipe away the blood, he looked at his hand first, then down at Blair and back up to Christopher. "So, it comes to this. You're ready to kill for her. Is that it, Little One?"

Christopher snarled. "Shut up, Griffin. I'm tired of your blather. More importantly, I'm tired of you fucking with my life."

The blond-haired man backed away from the scene and took Mackenzie into his arms, pulled her back to the patio. "Come on, Kenz. We need to get you away from all this."

Griffin's gaze was riveted to Christopher. His body shimmered for just a second, blood trickling from the deep cut on his head, then he blurred and shifted. In his place stood a long black leopard, with silver eyes and sharp teeth.

"No, wait, please," Mackenzie begged. "I don't believe

what I just saw. Griffin can change his shape, just like a vampire. Did you know they could do that?"

"No, I didn't. How would I know? Kenz, this isn't going to end well. You don't need to see this. One of these guys could die today. Now. Come inside with me. *Please,* come inside."

The huge leopard, with glistening, black fur and thick, rippling muscles, padded slowly around Christopher on huge, clawed feet. Its long tail twitched as it moved and its silver gaze never wavered. The leopard knew what the stakes were. No doubt about it.

"I can't leave. Please don't take me inside. I want to know that Christopher is going to survive this. There's something about him that makes me think he's very special to me."

Sean let out a slow breath. "He is, Kenz. He's your husband. Let's just avoid this confrontation, just to be safe."

"My husband? I can't leave . . ." Mackenzie grasped Sean's arms for support. "Something's not right. I don't feel . . ."

Christopher glared at the black cat. "Is this how you intend to win your battle with me, Old Man? Do you think the leopard can beat me? Are you really that stupid?" Christopher laughed. "You've made a fatal mistake, my friend. You've made this *way* too easy for me." Christopher raised the bow, nocked the arrow, and aimed for the body. "Even in the cat's body, you're not as fast as I am. There's no way you'll even get close to me. My arrows are tipped with Sendagi's poison, Griffin. Once you're paralyzed, it's over. You have no chance of winning. No chance of surviving. No chance at all."

Chapter Thirteen

Alistair plucked a tiny piece of lint from his wool pants and watched it flutter to the wooden deck. The view from the back of the house was spectacular. Nothing but sky, ocean, and the jagged ridge of the Pacific coast. His home was a fortress—a paradise, enriched with the best décor money could buy, but a fortress nonetheless.

He brought the fine crystal to his lips and sipped the golden nectar. The vintage wine, a California Chardonnay, was old; he drank to the success he was certain was at hand. He needed success desperately. Failure meant his own death at the hands of a dark-haired man. There was simply no alternative. "Where is the traitor?"

The Italian bodyguard stepped through the sliding glass door and sat down beside Alistair. His lean body betrayed the strength he possessed, the speed he was capable of attaining, and the agility he exhibited so easily. The former priest was truly a work of art. Genetically enhanced art.

Alistair smiled. Uleah's magic, powerful enough to change a man into a veritable machine and humans into wolves, had been worth the price.

Alistair's daughter.

The restoration spell called for a female host from the symbiant's lineage. They didn't know, then, about Mackenzie. Her parents had been killed when she was very small. She and her brother had been raised by relatives, her past erased.

They had tried to use Sarah, Alistair's daughter, as the host. The results had not been what they'd expected.

Alistair closed his eyes, fighting to tamp down the bite of his loss.

She'd been a beautiful girl.

But greatness required sacrifice, and so Alistair had given up the one woman who meant everything to him.

Sarah . . .

"He's coming." Allegra glanced up once, then resumed an inspection of his fingernails.

"Excellent. I need to know what that woman or her brother did with the book. Is it with her, or is it still at the house? The traitor can tell me, I'm certain. The success of the spell depends on that book. I won't accept failure, Allegra. This is too important," he said, his impatience growing.

He leaned forward to brush the legs of his pants, removing remnants of a powder he'd been experimenting with earlier in the day. He'd been startled, and had spilled the powder down the front of his coat and pants. *Foolish mistake,* he thought. Next time he'd lock the door when tampering with the formulas he'd already perfected.

Still, if he could alter Allegra just a little more, the man might become invincible—a warrior capable of taking on Griffin. Capable of winning. Engineered to win.

"If it had been there, Alistair, we would've found it. I turned the place upside-down, looking for that book. It isn't there," Allegra said, leaning against back into the soft outdoor chair.

Alistair ignored him. "That damn Griffin. I have enough to consider without him interfering in my plans." Alistair sipped his wine while he recalled the intrusion. Griffin was a bitter enemy. He rubbed the scar, evidence of Griffin's amazing strength. "However, I think we've seen the last of him, since I summoned the hottest of fires for him. I'm sure he was burned extensively." He suppressed a smile at the thought.

"No doubt," Allegra said.

"Still, I worry." He brought a finger up to touch his mouth. "What if he survived the fire? I can't see how, but that one is so strong. Ten years ago, when he pierced my shoulder with his double-edged knife, the force of it was unreal. The knife went completely through my shoulder and pegged me to the wall. And he wasn't even trying very hard. It was *nothing* to him. I can't imagine that kind of physical power.

"Scott says he was the one who figured out how to kill the demon wolves. Can you believe that? I don't know what it is about him, but something's different." Alistair took a long sip from his glass, then continued. "He looks the same as he did ten years ago, I swear. I don't know how that could be, but I know what I saw with my own eyes. I think he has a secret that might be of interest to us."

Alistair mused, more for his own benefit than anyone's. "There's something about him that isn't quite right. I'd love to find out."

"Most people have secrets, Alistair," Allegra said, his bored gaze shifting to the ocean.

"Yes, most do. The issue is not whether they have them, but whether we can discover who they are and exploit them. I'm most pleased that we now have another one to study. This Christopher appears to be just as strong as Griffin. As long as they don't get in my way, I'll allow them to live. But if they so much as think about interfering, I'll be forced to kill them. It's that simple, Allegra. I'll have no choice at all." The thought pleased him. Yes, no choice but to take their lives.

A knock at the door drew Alistair's attention. Another

man, an albino, spoke quietly with Allegra, then left as silently as he'd come.

Georges, one of Alistair's many servants, slipped out behind the albino and refilled Alistair's glass from the decanter on the table. "Thank you, Georges," Alistair said quietly.

"Bien sur," Georges said with a slight bow.

"The traitor is here. Are you ready to see him?" Allegra asked.

"Yes," Alistair said, reaching for his glass.

Allegra turned and motioned for the traitor to be brought out to the deck.

Alistair returned his glass to the table, rose, and walked to the edge of the deck. Resting his hands on the railing, he gazed down at the waves crashing against the rocks below.

He would've felt better if they'd had the book already, but time had run out. He'd have to take a chance that they'd find the book in time. The woman, Mackenzie, would be ready tonight for the second part of the spell. Her body would be an empty shell, ready for a new inhabitant.

Uleah, of the Valley of Toth. The dark underworld of sorcerers.

The spell required a new moon, for it would invoke the restoration of a soul. Bring back to life the dearly departed. Bring back a deadly warlock.

The Great Change would begin then, starting with the impregnation of the host. Mackenzie would give birth to a new species. Stronger, faster. Imbued with the Power of Shyalla Nar.

The Circle of Shyalla, twelve sorcerers who had combined their powers once they realized the Council was against them. They would give up their lives, only to be reborn after the bloodbath. After fear of the black arts had faded. They'd trusted Uleah with their most prized possession. He'd had it converted to droplets of a liquid so powerful, it alone could change the world.

And then he betrayed them. He secreted the Vial of Power away where no one could find it, and then gave himself up to the executioner's blade.

Betrayal was a harsh pill to swallow.

Yes, for the moment, they needed the traitor. Maybe he could tell them where the book was. They desperately needed the spell to succeed.

If it did, Uleah would be reborn tonight. The greatest and deadliest of all the wizards would be reborn. The wizard with the Power of Shyalla Nar.

It was truly an exciting time.

"You asked to see me, Alistair?" The traitor stood near the doorway.

Alistair turned to face him. "I required your presence, yes. I'm looking for a book of spells. This is a very old, priceless book and it's been in Mackenzie's family for many, many years but belongs to the great sorcerer, Uleah. I don't suppose you've seen it, have you?"

The traitor thought for a moment. His gaze, black as obsidian, scanned the horizon as he considered the question. "I would have to search Christopher's house again to be certain."

"I'm out of time, traitor. I need to know if the book is there. If we can't find it, this effort will not succeed. Neither you nor I can afford such a thing. Tonight is the new moon, and our only chance to make this work. If we have no book, the spell cannot be completed and Mackenzie dies. You can see the predicament we're in, can't you?"

"Yes, I can."

"Do you think you might search Christopher's house this afternoon?"

"Of course, Alistair. Right away."

"Good boy. Now, go." Alistair waved him off.

The traitor headed back into the house, with Allegra close behind. Alistair watched with narrowed eyes, then returned to his chair and wine.

A moment later, Allegra returned. He sat in the cushioned chair next to Alistair's. "Do you think he knows where the book is?"

"I'm not certain. I do believe I've convinced him of the need to find it, however. The rest is up to him," Alistair said, studying the etching on his wine glass.

Allegra tilted his head. "You trust him?"

"His need is as great as mine. Yes, I suppose I do trust him. For now." Alistair inhaled deeply. "Has Maya returned yet?"

"Yes, she's with Scott."

"Ask her to mix up the potion and administer it to you, then rest for a while," Alistair ordered. "I'll need you strong and alert tonight, priest."

"Yes, Alistair." Allegra rose and disappeared into the house.

He took a long time to finish his wine.

When he was ready, he stood, straightened his garnet-colored blazer and tossed his long hair over his shoulders. He stepped inside the glass doors, cast a quick glance toward Scott and Maya in the living room as he passed. Maya was on the couch with Scott at her side. She would be tired from invoking the spell and Scott would be angry. He always was—he knew what the spell was really doing. She did not. Blackmail was a wonderful tool.

The thought amused Alistair.

The spell transferred her lifeforce to Allegra, extended his life, and imbued him with great strength and stamina, rather like Griffin. Alistair hoped the night would bring a confrontation between Griffin and Allegra so he could see how the priest had grown in strength and agility. It would be Allegra's final test. If he wasn't ready, though, Allegra would find a quick death at Griffin's hands. If he was, Alistair would administer the potion himself. Either way, Allegra was a dead man. He'd served his purpose by finding and capturing Mackenzie.

Now, Alistair required revenge. Too bad, but that's how it had to be.

Alistair hurried downstairs to the dank cells below. The guard snapped to attention, unlocked and opened the door without being told. Alistair passed through and skidded to a halt before a young woman behind the cold, steel bars. She hugged her knees against the back wall.

"Open the cell."

The heavy guard lumbered into the holding area and slipped a thick key into the keyhole, turned it, and opened the door.

Alistair rushed in, kneeling before her. Soothed by this vision of beauty and grace, he gently brushed a strand of her blonde hair back. "Lissa, my precious, it won't be too much longer. I'll come for you tonight after Uleah has made his transition. Allegra will be dead by then, and we'll be free to be together."

Her gaze slowly lifted to his face. "I've waited a long time for this night. I'm more than ready to be free of Allegra and the wolf. It is a curse, you know." In the dull light of the cell, her eyes flashed olive green. A tiny furrow creased her brow. "Remember your promise."

"I'm so sorry. I had no idea they would multiply so quickly. I really didn't. And I never thought a wolf would find you. Not you, Lissa." He touched her cheek. "But I shall find a way to relieve you of such a burden, my love. I have promised you that, and I'll keep my word." He laid a hand on her thigh. "I want more than anything to feel you in my arms at night. Every night."

"I'm holding you to that, Alistair."

"I ask only for your patience. Just a little longer. I'm quite certain that Uleah can help you as well, but we must finish the spell first. When he has taken the body of the woman, he'll help us, I know it."

"Just make it happen. I don't care how you do it." She sighed softly, pushing a hand through her hair. "Now, please leave me. I'm tired and I want to be ready for tonight. You said you'd let me out to roam free, and I'm so looking forward to feeling grass beneath my feet and the wind on my face."

"Yes, I will set you free tonight, before we leave. And when you return to me tomorrow morning, I'll have such a surprise for you."

She smiled. "I can't wait."

"Until tomorrow, then." He leaned forward to kiss her. His hand whispered down her shoulder to her arm, and he sought to caress her breast, but she stopped him cold.

"Please, don't. Not here." Her eyes darted from one side to the other. "This isn't a place where love would, or should, be found."

"Perhaps you're right." Alistair stood. "Enjoy your night, Lissa."

Leaving the cell, Alistair stopped at the guard station. "Set her free three hours before midnight. Make sure no one harms her as she's leaving. And," he scanned the hefty guard, "watch yourself. She will be quite thirsty."

"As you command. Thank you, Alistair." The guard dipped his chin.

Alistair climbed the stairs with much less enthusiasm than

before. She was his light, his haven of tranquility. The beauty of her face and body amazed him to no end. He really did want to feel her next to him at night, wanted to feel her long, blonde hair tangled in his hands as he made love to her. Inhaling, he remembered her scent with complete clarity, as if she were still near. Yes, she was light, peace, and all that was good. All that he was not.

The added bonus was that she had once belonged to Allegra. And Alistair had taken her. Allegra had had no choice but to give her up.

He stopped to check on Allegra. The Italian priest slept on a small bed. His face buried in the pillows, he lay on his stomach, and snored lightly.

Yes, he and the priest went way back. Fifteen years. When Allegra had slandered him so badly, had him removed from the newly reassembled Council of Wizards, Alistair had vowed revenge. And tonight he would have it.

Finally.

Allegra loved Lissa. Enough that he was willing to trade his life for hers when Alistair had threatened to take her. He'd told Allegra that her life was in danger, which was true enough. Alistair *could* have killed her. Instead he'd fallen hopelessly in love with her. But he'd told Allegra that his compliance would guarantee that Lissa's life would continue. And, the priest had acquiesced so easily, believing every single lie Alistair had thrown at him.

When the experiments began, Allegra had clung to the belief that he and Lissa would soon be freed. But there was always a reason for keeping them on. Lies, of course, but they worked. That was the important part. The lies worked.

And then, within a very short span of time, Allegra became an efficient killing machine and a fine assistant as well. His loyalty was to Lissa, but he served Alistair well. As long as

Lissa remained imprisoned, Allegra could be controlled.

Too bad Alistair would require a new assistant after tonight. He almost regretted having to end the priest's life. Almost.

He strolled out to the back deck and leaned on the railing, inhaling deeply. Time was not on his side and too much was at stake. He wasn't happy about having to rely on the traitor for such a crucial element of the spell. He didn't know what had motivated the large man to make his bargain with Uleah, and that concerned him. Could he trust the traitor? Maybe. Maybe not, and that was what upset him the most. He didn't like not knowing for certain.

What did the oracle have to say about the outcome?

He opened his hand, palm up, and focused his energies. The air shifted and a clear blue orb appeared. "Tell me what happens tonight with Uleah and Mackenzie."

White smoke filled the orb, clearing to reveal a large black leopard and a smaller gray one—a demon wolf, presumably. But what did they have to do with Uleah or Mackenzie? The animals were running together. It wasn't clear if they were running to or from something.

The image faltered and faded to Mackenzie standing out on the back deck. Her eyes were closed, her face raised skyward. In her outstretched hands were a black book and a chain with a long pendant at the end. As she raised her arms, both the book and the pendant exploded into flames. The black tome would be Uleah's spellbook most likely, but he knew nothing about a pendant. He could only speculate about any importance it might hold.

Still, he wanted to know. The image seemed to be a symbolic representation of something, but what? He couldn't begin to decipher such a puzzlement. Perhaps it wasn't Mackenzie at all, but Uleah in command of her body. Perhaps it was best that he not trouble his mind with useless speculation. The answer would be revealed tonight. With a heavy sigh, Alistair rose to his feet and stepped inside the house.

Alistair seldom left the protective walls of his secret hideaway. There were other people to do his bidding for him. As money was not an issue, he could easily afford to have them at his beck and call, allowing him the comfort of knowing his enemies would likely not find him, at least not without significant effort. Indeed, the world did not even know him as Alistair McConnell. To the business world, he was Benjamin Brooks, a wealthy European antique collector and trader. He knew more about fine English furniture than anyone. Bar none.

Alistair meandered through the various rooms, inspecting the activity in each. Maya and Scott were in the studio, mixing powders for Alistair's potions. In another room, the albino, Milan, polished a large pentacle he'd carved from a slab of black marble. Such a gifted sculptor. The pentacle's lines were not solid, but instead were a series of words—incantations for health and prosperity held together by tiny wires in the ancient language Uleah knew when he'd been alive. The beautiful carving was a gift for the sorcerer, who would soon be able to run slender fingers along the smooth, cool stone.

In the kitchen, Alistair stood behind one of the many servants he employed to take care of the massive house and grounds. She peeled potatoes against the kitchen sink, and paused to push a strand of dark brown hair from her face.

Alistair picked up a shiny green apple and bit into it. "Anything new to report, Elizabeth?"

"No, Alistair. She still won't eat." The cook spoke without looking at him. "She's angry with you for confining her."

"It probably won't matter after tonight."

"Of course, sir." She smiled, as if she knew what he meant.

"Lissa will be just fine. I'm letting her out tonight. Be sure to stay inside after the sun goes down." He casually brushed a finger against her cheek. "She needs to run a little, you know." He thought of his love, the beautiful Annalissa de Biasi. How she hated being confined in the cellar, but it was necessary, for now. Tomorrow she would be freed, after the sorcerer had been reborn and Allegra was dead.

"Yes, sir." Elizabeth gathered the peeled potatoes and dropped them one by one into a large pot.

Elizabeth was a good employee. No matter what he said or did, she took it all in stride, without complaint. He could use more people like her. Patting her shoulder, he left the half-eaten apple on the countertop and wandered out from the kitchen.

He hated waiting for time to pass.

Alistair eventually returned to his office, where he sat in a large black-leather chair. Rolling the chair toward the huge picture window, he studied the lines of the horizon for several moments. How long would it take for the traitor to find the book and return? Too long, he supposed. He inhaled deeply and closed his eyes to rest. Yes, time sometimes passed too slowly.

Hours later, Alistair awoke to the sound of a soft tap on the office door.

"Yes?" he asked, stretching his legs.

The albino poked his head around the heavy door, pulling his dark sunglasses down the bridge of his nose. "Sir, the traitor has returned."

"Bring him to me."

A moment later, the albino returned with the traitor, bowed lightly, then closed the door behind him.

Alistair poured himself a glass of wine from a new bottle, left by a staff member, and stretched out in the plush, cushioned chair. "I'm going to presume you have good news for me, traitor. I can bear nothing else. What do you have for me?"

"Before I tell you anything, I'm curious about something. How do I know my request will be honored?"

"You don't. Neither do I. We must both trust that Uleah will provide for us as we have asked, but it's true: we *could* both be denied our hearts' desires."

"I'm not certain I wish to share my information, then. I need a guarantee. My information comes to me at a price. I don't wish to give it freely." The traitor stuffed his hands into deep coat pockets.

Alistair shot up out of his chair and snagged the traitor by the throat. "I need that book. If you have it, you will give it to me now, or I will strike you down where you stand."

The traitor's face remained calm. Dead calm. The black eyes were flat and almost lifeless. He grasped the hand around his throat and removed it without so much as a flinch. "Do not threaten me, as you would be unable to deliver on your threat. I am Eskarian. Your words have no meaning."

Alistair was shocked by the physical power of the traitor. "Eskarian? What is that?"

"Immortal." The traitor pushed back his black hair and straightened his coat.

"Immortal," Alistair echoed. "Are there more like you?" His mind was quickly putting together the missing pieces. What an exciting new twist to this little mission. His hands clasped together in anticipation.

"Yes, there are many."

He had to know. "Is Griffin like you?"

"Yes."

"And Christopher?" *Was it possible?*

"Yes."

"I understand now." This was valuable information indeed. "Can you make me like you?"

"I'm capable of such a thing, but I will not do it. None of us will. Few are chosen to become like us. Most are born unto it. Like humans, we are as old as time itself."

"I will find a way to make you do this for me," Alistair told him. He would defeat the dark-haired man by becoming immortal. It was a perfect way to foil what Destiny had in mind for him.

"No, you won't. I'm certain you feel you must try, but I will not do it. You can do nothing to force me to concede."

"We'll see about that, traitor. Now, I must ask you: do you have the book?" Alistair held his breath as he waited for the answer.

"Yes, I do."

He'd almost been too afraid to hope the book would be found. So much relied on it, and he'd been more worried that he'd cared to admit, even to himself. But now, the book had been found, and was nearly within his reach. He savored the moment as if it were his last, breathing a sigh of relief. Alistair returned to his chair, taking a long drink from the wine glass. "Where is it?"

"In the car. I'll get it once you assure me my request will be honored."

Alistair's irritation rose to the surface. "Have we not already discussed this? Uleah has agreed to it, and so you will have what your heart desires. He is not one to go back on his word. Now, my book?"

"Of course. I will return momentarily."

Alistair was once again alone with his thoughts. He felt better now that he was reasonably certain the spell would be completed tonight.

If not, if something unforeseen should happen, he still had the traitor and these Eskarians. Now, he felt that if the spell failed, he had an ace in the hole to defeat the dark-haired man who would come to slice his throat. Yes, things were definitely looking up.

Nonetheless, he needed to learn more about these Eskarians. Immortals.

Clasping his hands together, he pressed them to his mouth and inhaled deeply, thinking about what he might do with such a species. There was simply no end to the havoc he might wreak. No end. On the other hand, what might he do with an *immortal* species? How might he work it to his advantage? What if he had one that could be studied, dissected, what then? So much could be learned. He shivered with the possibilities.

The albino appeared with the traitor in tow. "The traitor returns with your book, sir. Shall I take it from him and send him away?" He stood in the doorway, keeping the traitor behind him.

"No, I wish to speak with him further. Thank you, Milan."

The albino bowed slowly. His long black coat, covered with black marble dust, swirled around as he turned to leave.

"Tell me, good sir, how is Mackenzie?" Alistair waved his hand to offer the traitor a thickly-cushioned patio chair.

The traitor's head lowered as he sat. "Her spirit is gone. It's sad, really. She was a beautiful, vibrant woman. Christopher is distraught and vows to find you. Let us hope he isn't successful. He is a master at what he does, so I doubt you'll elude him very long."

Alistair nodded. "Mmm. I see. Yes, we will hope, then. Leave the book and be off." Alistair glanced once at the Eskarian traitor and waved dismissively.

The traitor scowled for a moment. "Be off?" he asked, eyes widening.

"I'm quite certain you don't need me to repeat myself."

"What about my request?"

"Uleah will decide when he is ready to grant your request, Traitor. Until then, you must be patient. Uleah has other, more important matters to consider at the moment. Be *off,*" he said firmly.

"Then I suspect our business here is finished. Call me a traitor again and I'll bleed the life from you without trying very hard. My name is Blair."

"Leave now, *Blair,* before I change my mind and have you killed for your insolence. I'm sure even immortals can die." Alistair smiled. "Uleah decides when our business is finished. Not you."

"Perhaps you're right. Nonetheless, I have finished with *you.*"

The traitor rose slowly, his eyes remained solidly on Alistair's face. So much the better. Alistair would show that he wasn't intimidated by the immortal. His gaze followed the traitor as he opened the door.

Allegra appeared in the doorway, forcing Blair aside. He stepped over the threshold and stopped, glaring at Blair. Neither said a word for several seconds.

Blair looked past Allegra. "Your priest reeks of weakness, Sorcerer. He's no match for any Defender."

"Would you like to see what I can do?" Allegra asked.

"You mean, besides capture young women? No, I don't want to see it. I don't care." Blair pushed by the priest and left.

Allegra leaned against the bookcase. "We should be leaving soon. The powder you gave the woman was quite effective, evidently. She's as good as dead. I don't think you need to worry about Christopher, though. I'm ready to take them both." Allegra stretched with casual ease, muscles rippling beneath his white T-shirt.

Alistair was unsettled by the Eskarian's defiance. He didn't like admitting it, even to himself, but this *Blair* was no longer someone Alistair felt he could trust. S*omething in the eyes,* he thought. "One or the other, priest, but I don't think you can take both."

"Then let me start with Christopher. He's the smaller of the two. I'm ready. I want to do this."

"Fine. Once we have Uleah in place, you finish Christopher and, if possible, kill Griffin too. But, do not approach him unless you know you can do it. If you have any chance at all, it will be only a second. You'll need to be quick."

Allegra nodded. "I know. I can do it. I'll bring you their heads on platters."

Alistair chuckled. "Yes, of course. Well, I suggest you prepare, then."

"Thank you, Alistair." Allegra dipped his head once and left.

He carefully picked up the old, worn book and began leafing through the heavy parchment. The tome, bound in black leather, detailed Uleah's experiments in black magic and his subsequent dismissal from the Council. No wonder the ancient sorcerer had selected Alistair to lead this effort. They had a great deal in common. Moving to the section that detailed each of the ten spells of restoration, Alistair read with great interest. The parchment was so old, and the language was dead to most, but Alistair could read it perfectly. He loved the ancient ways and spells, loved the fear that the dark magic had incited. It was as if he had come home. His fingers moved over the parchment, lovingly tracing the letters of the old language. Yes, he'd definitely come home.

Turning the pages, he found the spell he would invoke tonight, which was actually two spells. The first spell, to rid Mackenzie's body of her soul, had already been cast. Now, she was an empty shell. She would be catatonic, unable to move or speak or even think. She would no longer be Mackenzie Wallace. For all intents and purposes, she was indeed dead.

Alistair read further, learning the words to the spell and the items required for its success. "Oh, no . . ." he whispered.

Suddenly looking up, his body pulsed with alarm. How could this be? He didn't have everything he needed. "Oh, dear God."

Chapter Fourteen

"Oh, God! Somebody *help me!*"

Christopher's gaze shot to the patio. "What the f—"

Sean held Mackenzie's limp body in his arms, her eyes open and unfocused. "Please, help me. I think she's dead," Sean said, looking at Christopher. "Please . . ."

"Mackenzie," Christopher whispered.

He turned to the black leopard. "I'm not done with you yet, Griffin. Do yourself a favor and stay out of my sight." He slung the bow over his shoulder and hurried to her side. Behind him, Griffin's body cracked and shifted back into his waking, or human, form again.

Setting the bow against a chair, Christopher lifted Mackenzie from Sean's arms and carried her to a chaise lounge. Her body was like ice and, as far as he could tell, she wasn't breathing. Setting her gently on the soft cushions, he crouched beside her.

He curled his fingers into fists as the fear coiled around his chest and squeezed. He couldn't breathe like this, much less think logically. Closing his eyes, he struggled to harness the vicious emotions swirling inside his gut. He needed a clear head.

He needed Mackenzie, alive and well. "Mateña, can you hear me?" he asked softly. He could only hope his voice was powerful enough to pull her from the deep abyss into which she'd fallen. Or been taken.

She didn't respond, didn't move. Not one muscle.

Nothing. He touched her face.

So cold.

Please, no . . .

This had to be a dream. The gods couldn't possibly be that cruel, could they? Would they do that? Would they give him such a gorgeous, perfect mate, only to yank her from his grasp a few days later? He couldn't stand the thought. Lowering his head into his hands, he fought his emotions again. Fought the urge to demolish something, as if that would somehow hurt the perpetrator, or make any difference at all. "Don't do this to me," he breathed.

Blair bent to Christopher's ear. "Have faith," he said quietly.

How? Christopher nodded, then steeled himself long enough to take her hand and search for a pulse. He found it strong and steady. She was alive.

Thank the gods for small favors.

He pushed back a lock of hair and looked at Sean. "What happened?"

"She just collapsed. One minute she was awake and talking, the next it was like the life just seeped out of her. I mean, I could see it in her face. Like something came along and snatched her away." Sean's eyes drifted shut. "I was terrified that I was watching her die."

Christopher studied her face. There was nothing to tell him she'd heard either of them say a word. *Mackenzie, look at me.*

Nothing.

He let his eyes close. Reaching deep into himself, he gathered all the power he could muster and sent his mind into her. Sent his arimé—his essence—into her. Became a part of her.

Became *her.*

He breathed as she did, his heart matched her rhythm,

though his own body seemed far away.

Beneath him, the cushions of the chaise lounge were soft and comfortable.

He opened his eyes. *Her* eyes. Through her, he saw Sean, Griffin, Blair crouched over her body, concern etched on their faces. He looked at each of them. Then he lifted her head to look at himself.

He was sweating. It was difficult to be in this body without an anchor. He had nothing to grasp, to keep himself inside her. Similarly to swimming upstream, he had to fight to keep his position.

"She gone," he said, using her voice. Had she been there, he would have tied his arimé to her and then he could've stayed for awhile.

Not now.

He closed her eyes before preparing to return.

Christopher inhaled deeply and stood up, wiping his brow with both hands. He was exhausted.

His gaze swung around to find his tactical commander. "Is there anything you can do?" he asked.

Blair knelt beside Mackenzie. He examined her closely for several minutes, touching her hand or her face as he whispered to her in the language of the elders, even leaning over to listen to the rhythm of her heart. He laid his hands on her upper arm, sending himself inside her to try to reach her as Christopher had. Still, she lay as if already dead.

Deep in his heart, Christopher knew she wasn't going to wake up anytime soon. This was a spell and nothing was going to break it. But that didn't matter. He'd still try, and he'd hope that Blair knew something no one else did.

Christopher stepped off the patio and headed out into the yard. Just as Ivan loped up to him, he pulled a toothpick from his shirt pocket and rolled it from one side of his mouth to the other. "Ivan, good boy," he said softly, brushing the Husky's head. "How you doing?"

Normally, spending time with Ivan was relaxing, but now all he could do was pace and hope for a miracle. "Anything, Blair? Tell me something—anything. This is tearing me apart."

Blair's gaze remained focused on the task. "No, Christopher, nothing. Give me another moment or two. I need your patience."

Griffin came up beside Christopher. "I'm sorry about what's happened to Mackenzie."

Blair threw a stern glance behind him. "Griffin, don't anger him further. We don't need anymore battles today. Christopher, I mean it. No more battles. We have enough to worry about."

Christopher ignored Blair's warning and glared at the silver-eyed Eskarian. "It amazes me how stupid you can be sometimes. What were you thinking?"

Griffin shrugged and smiled—a crooked smile that angered Christopher all over again. "That you were fortunate to have found her and, more importantly, you didn't deserve her." He turned to watch Blair for a moment. "Nevertheless, she didn't know who I was. You're right. I did take advantage of her. She'd never have allowed me to touch her, let alone kiss her, if she'd been herself. I know that for a fact. She's a good woman."

"And yet you insisted on pursuing her." Anger raged inside him, demanding a resolution, demanding retribution. Wanting blood. It didn't matter that they'd been friends for almost two hundred years. This was different.

Griffin had stepped over the line.

Christopher could barely control his temper. He folded his arms over his chest simply to restrain himself. His first instinct was to reach for the bow and plant an arrow between those soulless, gray eyes. Then he'd plunge his dagger into Griffin's throat and pop off the head as if the old man were nothing more than a common demon wolf, a pest who deserved nothing more than extermination.

Now *that* was a perfection solution.

Griffin nodded. "Yes, I did."

"She's not yours to pursue."

"I know." Griffin's gaze returned to Christopher.

"And yet you would have tried to take her away from me?" Christopher glanced at Mackenzie, and the thought of another man's hands on her raised his blood pressure until he felt it in his cheeks. He spit out the toothpick.

"Absolutely. She's beautiful, intelligent, feisty, and—"

"Mine," he snapped. "Leave her alone, unless she speaks to you first. Let me remind you that I'm done trying to work this out with you. Make certain you keep your distance."

Griffin turned to Mackenzie. His gaze softened as he watched Blair examine her. Silently, he pushed a hand through his auburn hair and fixed his gaze on something out in the yard. "I'm sorry," he said, his gaze returning to Christopher. "It was never really you, my friend, but rather my own envy. I grow tired of days spent in an empty bed, nights spent hunting one threat after another, and nothing but time in between."

Christopher's eyebrows raised. "Do you think a hasty apology is going to spare you from Arden's Bow?"

"No, I don't." Griffin's heated gaze softened with the admission. "But I know I was wrong. She truly belongs to you. I should have kept my distance."

Christopher brushed the elder's mind quickly. Griffin spoke the truth, from the heart. So, the old man did have emotions. "Then you'll stay away from her?"

Griffin nodded as his gaze dropped to Mackenzie's lifeless form. "Yes."

Christopher's anger fizzled. He knew the pain of an empty bed, day or night. "Then it's over." He offered his hand to Griffin.

The silver-eyed leviathan accepted it. "You win."

"It wasn't a contest," Christopher said flatly.

"You still won."

He laid his hand on Griffin's shoulder. "All things change with time, as you well know. She'll find you."

"Of course." He offered a thin smile, then headed for the house.

"Christopher, I'm astounded," Blair said. He stood and touched Christopher's arm. Behind him, Griffin slammed the door. "I've never seen Griffin apologize for anything."

Christopher glanced toward the door. "I was ready to kill him today." He rubbed his forehead impatiently. "It's possible that apology saved his life. And mine, I guess." Eskarian law forbade taking a life without reason. The punishment for such a crime was death. Pure and simple.

"I refuse to believe you'd really have killed him."

Christopher's gaze swung around to Blair's. "I might have."

Blair shook his head. "I don't believe that. You're impulsive, but not stupid. You had time to release the arrow you drew on him today. You didn't. You're just not that kind of man." He paused to exhale slowly. "Now, we need to talk about Mackenzie. I honestly don't know what's happened to her, but you're absolutely right. There's no spirit inside her."

"Can anything be done?" Christopher's fear spiked. Blair *always* knew what to do.

"I don't know what it would be. Mackenzie appears to be in a state similar to a coma, except there's nothing going on in her head. No matter how deeply I probe her mind, I hear nothing. I can't even force her into wakefulness." He paused to pat Ivan's head. "I'm truly sorry. I have no idea if anything *can* be done. But, I'll discuss this with Ian. Perhaps he'll have some ideas."

"I can't wait, Blair. She needs help now. We can't just leave her like this. *I* can't leave her like this." He slumped back against the post and glared at his commander. The hope he'd been clinging to was fading fast. In its stead was a rising anger that someone had done this to her, that she'd purposely been taken from him.

Blair threw up his hands. "What would you have me do? I *don't know* what's happened. I can't perform magic, nor can I bring back the dead. There are limits to my power. I need you to understand that."

"Ivan, stay with Blair," Christopher said to the Husky. He tossed the worn toothpick into the grass as his anger and frustration detonated. He walked out onto the yard with his hands deep in his pockets. In the center of the well-manicured landscape, he closed his eyes, unable to hold the fury back any longer. Trees and bushes burst into white-hot flames, exploding seconds later. Water in the pool boiled, sending billowing steam into the cool night air. At the same time, the ground beneath the rock wall rumbled, dislodging the heavy stones. The entire wall crumbled to the ground to reveal the water pump and filter underneath the structure. The pipes bent as if made from plastic and snapped apart at multiple points. Water shot into the air, fanned out like rain, and tumbled down upon him.

He stood perfectly still, absorbing the sound of the destruction. It wasn't enough. It would never be enough. Tears burned his eyes.

A wizard's power had done this to her. "I'll find you,

wizard. You'll wish you'd died long before I finish with you," he said softly.

He raised his face to the downpour, allowing it to wash away the tears he could no longer hold back.

No matter how long it took, he would find that wizard. No matter how far he had to go, the wizard would pay. A thousand times over.

Christopher opened his eyes and turned a hot gaze to Blair and Sean. He knew by their sudden alarm they'd both felt his rage.

Leave, he demanded.

Sean heard the telepathic command and headed for the door without hesitation. Blair stood his ground, his hands raised in acquiescence.

"Christopher, please . . ." Blair began.

"Back off." Christopher faced his commander. "Leave me alone with her."

"We'll find a way to get her back."

"Will we? How could you possibly know for sure? We have no idea what was really done to her. You can't be certain I'll ever get her back." He looked at Mackenzie. "I know that this is the work of a sorcerer. I also know his days are numbered and his death with be slow and painful. I will see him beg for mercy before I tear him to shreds."

"I understand your anger, but you need to calm down."

"Why? After two hundred years of fighting threats, being so tired I could hardly stay upright, I find her, this vision of beauty and intelligence. Had I not been hunting with Griffin, he would have destroyed her. Instead, I found her. I'm allowed a paltry few days with her, and then she's taken away. Tell me, Blair, why should I calm down?" His brow raised. "Hmm?" He strolled back to the patio, every muscle tight and ready to explode. "How should I approach this, Blair?

Logically? Methodically? With casual indifference? As if she were just another victim of a threat?" He stopped only inches from Blair's startled face. "I don't *think* so. Now leave."

Blair inhaled, backed away from Christopher. "Fine. You know where to find me."

Christopher knelt beside Mackenzie. "I'll bring you back, Mateña. I'll search this entire planet, if I have to, for the cure to whatever has been done to you. So help me, I will." His voice faltered. "I won't let you go," he whispered. Pressing trembling lips against her cool cheek, he closed his eyes over burning tears. "Never." He leaned his head against her shoulder, rested a hand on her forearm.

Oh yes, the wizard would pay.

Gathering his explosive emotions, he rubbed his forehead and sighed. He slid his arms underneath her body, straightened, carried her through the open door, and, with only a thought, slammed it shut with enough force to crack the hardwood down the middle.

In the bedroom, he laid her down on the bed, removed her shoes, and covered her with a thick quilt. With quiet reverence, his fingers whispered along her cheek. His anger melted as he savored the feel of his benekeda's flawless, creamy skin. Kneeling beside her, he saw that her breath was slow and steady, her heart still strong, though her skin was cold. She was alive, but he couldn't feel her lifeforce, couldn't feel a thing, save for the ache in the pit of his stomach and remnants of a deadly rage.

A knock on the door startled him. "What?"

The door opened and Sean poked his head in. "I'm sorry to disturb you, but I think maybe we should take the amulet off Kenz. I don't know if it has anything to do with the book, or what happened to her, but maybe it'd be best if we put it someplace else. When they were given to us, we were told to keep them safe because people would want them. Both are priceless. I get the feeling their value doesn't have anything to do with money."

Christopher turned to Mackenzie. "I'd forgotten about that. She said she's never taken it off." He caught a strand of ebony hair, sifted it through his fingers.

Sean stepped inside the room. "No, she never has."

Christopher bent and found the clasp to the old pendant. Unhooking it, he slid the chain off her neck, then dipped to brush her cheek with his mouth. "You'll wear this again." He dropped it into his palm, and closed his fingers over the thick chain. He wanted to keep it himself until he could clasp it around her neck again. But, he knew it wasn't right, much as he wanted any part of her close to his heart. "Here," he said, his voice gruff. He planted the pendant in Sean's hand. "I want you to keep this. It might be safer with you."

After a moment, he added, "Take good care of it."

Sean nodded. "I will."

Leaning to Mackenzie, he kissed her forehead. "I'll be back soon." He headed for the door. "Stay with her until I return."

"Christopher?"

At the doorway, he looked back.

Sean sat down beside Mackenzie and studied Christopher with soulful eyes. "I have faith in you. If anyone can bring her back to us, it'll be you."

He nodded. He would find a way. He didn't know how he'd do that just yet, but somehow, he would. After all, Mackenzie needed a champion. He couldn't let her down. *Wouldn't* let her down.

He hurried toward the office. No doubt Blair would already have a plan and, with any luck, Ian would be there. Perhaps he could shed some light on what had happened today.

Ian leaned against the heavy oak desk, with his arms folded over his chest. Blair leaned against the wall next to the window. Griffin and Alex sat on the dark leather couch.

Christopher sauntered in and sat in a corner, away from everyone. He was suddenly so tired, and though he needed to focus on what was being said, he found that his thoughts migrated back to finding the one who had done this to Mackenzie. The one who would die. He pulled his Eskarian dagger from his pocket and lifted it from the sheath. The silver blade, with two holes at the base and engravings along the length, glittered with menace in the soft light. The wizard would know what a mistake it had been to anger a Defender. Damn straight, that bastard would die. He would feel the full impact of Eskarian rage.

Christopher ran the tip of the blade lightly along his palm, and imagined what it would be like to slice open the wizard's throat.

"Christopher, are you listening to me?"

Christopher's head snapped up. "What?" He looked sheepishly around the room. All eyes were on him, including Griffin's. The elder Eskarian didn't bother hiding his amusement.

"No, Ian, I'm sorry. I wasn't." He rubbed the bridge of his nose, then sheathed his blades. "Was there a question?"

"Have you seen the book?"

"No, not since we spoke of it last, whenever that was." Seemed like years ago. "Why? Is it missing?"

Ian glanced at the group. "Yes, it is. No one else has seen it either. For hours, evidently."

Griffin scanned the room. "Jason isn't here and neither is Blair. Does anyone know where they are?"

"It's been hours since I saw Jason. Was he on an assignment?" Alex looked from Griffin to Ian.

"No, he wasn't," Ian said, looking to the group for answers.

"Blair was here less than an hour ago," Christopher added. "But I haven't seen him since."

No one knew where they'd gone.

"I refuse to consider the possibility that Jason could have taken the book. That would make him . . ." Ian paused. "No, I won't even say it."

"A betrayer." Griffin finished the sentence. "To us, and the humans."

"Has this ever happened before?" Alex asked.

Ian nodded. "It has, but never when the consequences were so serious. It'd be one thing if Jason decided he no longer wanted to associate with Eskarians. It's quite another if he's aligned himself with the sorcerer. Should we find that has happened, he will suffer the same fate as Uleah. It would be unprecedented, but he would force us to consider him a threat."

"Now that I think about it, Jason was the one who said the trio was migrating here from Oregon. It was not information I had obtained, but rather something I accepted from him without question. What if it was not true at all? What if he deliberately tried to lead us in the wrong direction?" Alex looked around the room for answers.

Griffin shook his head. "We can't think like this. I refuse to condemn Jason with circumstantial evidence. I've known him for hundreds of years."

"I agree. Blair and I will pursue this further. Do not concern yourselves with it, until we are able to find some solid evidence to substantiate the claim. For now, let us work to find a way to bring Mackenzie back to us and Uleah to his death."

"Do you know what's happened to her, Ian?" Christopher's ears perked up with the topic change.

"No, I'm afraid I don't. I understand you found the remains of a wizard's powder on her face. Is there anything more you can tell us about that?"

Christopher searched his memory. "Only that it was extremely fine, and smelled a little like almonds."

Ian smiled. "Almonds. If this were one of Uleah's spells, the powder would be made from something ancient. I don't know what that would be. I can't say I know much about the black arts."

"I'll pay my old friend Alistair a visit tomorrow. Perhaps he can tell me what the powder does. No doubt I can convince him to share any information concerning spells," Griffin said with a small grin.

Christopher stood up. "If you don't need me, Ian, I'm going to retire for the night. It's after midnight and I'm more than ready to be done with this day."

"Of course, Christopher. Rest well." Ian nodded his consent.

Christopher left the office and walked back to his bedroom. He pushed the door open and found Sean asleep in the chair near Mackenzie. Tapping lightly on Sean's shoulder, Christopher waited for the newest Eskarian to awaken.

Sean blinked and looked around, finally meeting Christopher's gaze. He yawned. "What's going on?"

"Nothing. Go to bed now."

"Great. My back hurts from this damn chair." Sean rose and stretched, hands pressed against his lower back. A soft grunt passed his lips. "Did Blair or Ian have any suggestions for helping Kenz?"

"No," Christopher said, shaking his head.

"Nothing?"

"Nothing," Christopher echoed.

"Christ. What are we going to do?"

Break something, he thought. "Wait. For now. When I find that wizard, I'm going to pull his heart out through his mouth."

"I'll hold him for you."

Christopher smiled. "I appreciate the support."

"It's the least I can do. Let me know if anything changes."

"I will. Try to rest now. You'll be the first to know if anything changes."

Sean closed the door behind him.

Christopher kicked off his boots and sat down on the bed opposite Mackenzie. Running both hands through his hair, he sighed softly. She hadn't so much as twitched a muscle since this happened. He lay down beside her, whispering two fingers along her porcelain jaw. "I'll find a way." Grasping her cool hand, he brought it to rest next to his heart.

There just had to be a way to bring her back.

Christopher was sure he was dreaming. Not yet fully awake, he felt a gentle hand slide under his T-shirt, along his waist to the ridges of his stomach. The soft crush of full breasts against his back brought him instantly to full arousal.

She leaned over to nibble on his ear, her hair falling over his face.

Black hair.

Mackenzie.

He rolled over to face her. "Mackenzie? How? What happened? Are you all right?"

She smiled. "Of course I'm all right."

He held her face with both hands, and rained kisses over her mouth, nose, and face, astounded that she was really awake. "Do you know who I am?"

"You're Christopher, my benekeda, a wealthy investor with a *very* dark secret," she said with a wicked smile.

Odd that she used the Eskarian term for mate, instead of husband, a term she preferred. No matter. He was thrilled she was alive and well. "What happened to you? Who did this?" His hands roamed her body. He wanted to feel every inch of her, just to be sure he wasn't deceiving himself.

"It was a man with the strangest eyes. Like liquid amber. He blew powder into my face and I breathed it in before I realized what had happened. Then I wasn't able to tell you what happened. I was so far away. It felt like I was dreaming everything around me."

"He will die for what he did to you. I promise you that. I'll find him and he'll die."

"Nothing would please me more. Except . . ." Her fingers trailed down the front of his body to the top of his jeans. "I don't think you need these anymore, do you?" She sat up and pushed the covers back, watching him with a dark gleam in her eye.

He grinned. "I assume you have something in mind."

She straddled his thighs. "Oh, indeed I do."

He laced his fingers together behind his head, raising his brows. "By all means, continue."

With exquisite languor, she teased the button of his jeans open, her gaze riveted to his. "I'm so hungry. It's been too long since I had you inside me. I need to feel this—" She traced the length of his erection. "Do you think you could help me out?"

"Absolutely," he said softly.

"I want you to feed me. Not with your blood. No, I want something else from you. Dim the lights," she commanded. "And set the Livendium on fire. Please."

He leaned back into the pillows, half-closed his eyes, and obeyed. The lights softened to a warm glow. Several pots of Livendium burst to life, and tendrils of the spicy, sweet smoke wafted into the air. As powerful as the Eskarian herb was, it did nothing to soothe the raw hunger that burned him from the inside out. That was just fine with him. He wanted to burn. Was ready to burn. Just for her.

Her emerald eyes glittered in the soft light. Her own arousal was evident in the quickness of her breath, the slight tremble of her fingers.

She bit down on her lip and held it, her gaze drifting over his body. "Have I ever told you how amazingly sexy you are?"

"No, I don't think you have." Her soft voice washed over him like a favorite melody, sweet and warm, and his heart melted with her words. He loved that she thought he was sexy.

"You really are. I have something for you." She rolled off the bed and disappeared into the bathroom, returning a moment later with two silk ties. "Now, I want you to take hold of the headboard railings and don't let go. You're mine tonight."

He reached up to grip the wooden railings. "I'm yours every night."

She grinned as she bound his hands securely with the two black ties. "Tonight is special."

He tugged on his restraints, testing the strength, and was surprised they held so well. "But, now I can't touch you."

"That's all right. I'll touch you. Just relax." She leaned over him and grasped a bottle on the nightstand.

"Yes, Ma'am," he said with a grin.

Mackenzie smiled. "I like the sound of that." Straddling his hips, she poured a small portion of the bottle's contents into her palm and rubbed her hands together. Starting with his stomach, she massaged the slick liquid along his stomach and up to his chest and neck. The faint scent was vaguely familiar.

"What is that?" he asked.

"Massage oil," she answered. "This one is my favorite. It's very relaxing, don't you think?"

"Yeah, I like it. Where'd you get it?"

"I had Sean bring it over. Now stop asking so many questions. Just lie back and let me work."

When? "Yes, Mistress."

She laughed.

His eyelids drifted shut as she leaned forward to kiss his neck and chest. Her full breasts, crushed against his body, sent his body temperature higher and higher. He could think of nothing more than making love to her, whispering her name, and running his hands over every inch of her body. Making her come for him.

The wild temptress was seducing him again. Her moist, warm mouth against his skin was deliciously agonizing. His hips pushed against her and he moaned softly, wanting, needing to take her. The restraints were driving him crazy with anticipation. His need became a screaming demand to be a part of her, to feel her heat coiled tightly around him, to thrust into her pyre, to possess her again and again. "Mackenzie," he whispered, his breath catching in his throat. God, how he needed her. "Please . . ."

She sat up and twirled a strand of hair between her fingers. "Do you want more?"

"Oh yeah. I want to touch every inch of you," he admitted.

"Maybe I'll let you have me," she teased. "Maybe not." She tossed her hair back, and raised her chin.

He shifted restlessly. "You will." If the anticipation didn't kill him, finally making love to her surely would.

She trailed slender fingers down her breasts, bringing both nipples to small peaks. "I want you to burn for me." She cupped her breasts, feathering her thumbs across both to keep them erect.

His gaze was riveted to what her hands were doing. "I'm beyond burning for you, Mackenzie. You're dancing with cobras, girl."

"Even better." Bending over him, she locked her mouth fully to his. He tasted oil and something spicy, magical. Her tongue swept into his mouth, probing, searching. He loved the way she poured her own fire into him, but he needed more. So much more.

His painful erection screamed to be bound by her coiled heat. It shrieked for it, controlling his breath, his mind, every part of him. She was all he could see. His need and her body were all he could feel.

Need. An understatement.

There wasn't a word for what he felt.

She pulled back. "Where's my pendant?" She paused, her fingers searching her neck and shoulders.

"What? Why are you asking now?" He was shocked she'd ask about a necklace while they were making love.

"I need my pendant. Where is it?" Her eyes had gone cold, just that fast.

He studied her face. She was angry. "I gave it to Sean earlier tonight."

"You shouldn't have done that. It wasn't yours to give away."

"He wanted to ensure its safety. You can get it later."

"I need it now." She swung her long legs over the edge of the bed.

Without any effort, he ripped one silk tie from the headboard. His hand shot out to clamp onto her wrist. "Why now? Can't you wait a few minutes? I thought we were sharing something really special."

Her gaze snapped to his fingers shackled around her wrist, then up to his face. "Release me," she said flatly.

"You don't need the pendant this very minute, do you?" He saw the anger in her eyes, but his erection still scorched him, still demanded release. She was unreasonable now, and he would not let it end like this. Her anger made no sense. Why did she need the pendant *now?*

"Of course I do."

"Why?"

"It is mine to protect. I must have it with me."

"No, you're being unfair. Sean is capable of protecting it. What's so special about it that you have to guard it all the time?" There had to be a reason for her madness.

She pulled free of his grip. "It is powerful."

"How?" he asked.

She shrugged. "I don't know. It just is."

He kicked off his jeans, hung his legs over the side of the bed, and snaked an arm around her waist. Pulling her back in between his legs, he trapped her against his body. "That doesn't answer my question at all."

"Let me go," she demanded.

From behind, he slipped his free hand between her thighs. "Are you sure you want to leave?" His fingers moved slowly along the outside of her panties. "There's just so much I want to do to you. I want to make you to feel things you've never felt before. Maybe you could wait just one more minute?"

Her eyes closed. "Maybe."

Christopher reached up to caress both breasts, to whisper his thumbs over her nipples, just as she had done. "I don't think you really want to leave, do you? Say you'll stay with me for a while."

She rested her head against his shoulder. "Okay," she said softly.

"I want to make love to you," he whispered.

Mackenzie turned to face him. "There's something I want you to do for me first."

He nodded. "Anything."

She looked at him with blatant hunger. Her emerald eyes were a mix of fire and lust. Her teeth lengthened. "Feed me," she said softly. "I want your blood in my veins."

Christopher frowned. "You want to take my blood?"

"Oh yes," she said with a smile. "Very much."

Something in her words made the hair on the back of his neck stand up. This wasn't right.

"I need you, Christopher." Pulling him closer, her mouth found the perfect spot at the base of his neck. She kissed it, then drew the skin in to suck on it, as if to leave a mark.

His thoughts scattered. Her mouth was pure magic.

Her teeth teased the area she'd chosen until he shivered in anticipation, then she pushed them into his neck, and drew hard. It felt so good. Perfect. Warm. She curled her arms around his shoulders and held tight as she drank.

And drank more.

He grasped her arms to push her away. "Enough, Mackenzie. Remember what I told you."

I remember, she answered. Her grip on him tightened. *You taste so good.*

He pushed harder. "Stop . . ."

She was taking too much blood.

Why was she doing this? Why couldn't he pull her off his neck? "Mackenzie, please stop."

Way too much. If she took it all, he'd fall into the dream state, and that's where he'd stay until someone fed him enough blood to awaken him. It was a waking hell.

He couldn't let her take him there.

"Get off me," he ordered.

The room started to spin. With surprising strength, she pushed him back on the bed while she remained at his neck and pulled more blood from his body.

Something was very wrong. He couldn't move his arms or legs.

He was paralyzed.

"Mackenzie, you've taken too much."

She released him. "I know." Her eyes were cold as ice. "That was my intention. I told you tonight was very special."

"I don't understand." Alarm shot through his heavy, immobile body.

Something about her . . .

Not right. Not Mackenzie!

She rolled off the bed. "You will." Dragging on her jeans, she extinguished the smoldering Livendium leaves with a flick of her hand. "I hate that smell. What possesses you to burn such a ghastly weed is beyond my comprehension." She smiled. "I have pressing needs to attend to, but I thank you for the blood. I like biting you." She headed toward the door, stopping to glance back. "By the way, you won't be able to move for awhile. I must have time to complete the spell and will not tolerate any interference from you."

It became perfectly clear at that point. "Uleah."

Mackenzie nodded. "When did you finally figure it out? Perhaps when I seduced you? No? Was it before or after I took your blood?" She smiled, but it was a mixture of amusement and hatred. "Not too smart, are you?"

Christopher's anger flared. "I can't wait to put you in your grave again. This time, I'll make certain you stay there."

Mackenzie looked away, seemingly bored. "I do not think so. You see, I have all the power now, and you have nothing. And once the spell is complete, I'll have more than you could possibly imagine." She trailed her hands down the front of her body. "After almost four thousand years I will, once again, be alive."

"Not for long." He struggled to keep his eyes open. His muscles were tense, exhausted, achy, but utterly immobile.

"Oh? And you think you'll stop me?" Mackenzie raised her brows.

"Count on it, asshole."

She waved dismissively. "I've wasted too much time with you already. You may think whatever you like, but your time has come to an end, as has that of your people. When the spell is complete, I'll return to take your life. I find you Eskarians more of a bother than I care to tolerate. This body I'll keep, but you . . ." She paused. "Are quite expendable. I've already taken everything you had that was of value." She turned and headed out the bedroom door. "Prepare to meet your gods, Christopher."

Christopher gathered his strength as best he could. *Griffin, Uleah has taken Mackenzie's body and paralyzed me. I can't do anything.*

There was no response. Had something happened to Griffin as well?

Griffin? he called again.

It seems I will be unable to assist you or affect this situation at all. Griffin's telepathic voice was muted. *I too have been paralyzed, and Blair is dead.*

Chapter Fifteen

Christopher didn't believe what he'd just heard. *What do you mean, 'dead'?*

I'm not sure how I should answer that, Christopher. What language would make the most sense to you? He's no longer among the living. Do you Scots have another name for it?

Christopher ignored the barb. *What the hell happened? The prophecy unfolded right under our noses and none of us even realized it? We're supposed to keep the world safe from things like this. How did we fail so badly?*

He sighed. They *had* failed. Miserably. He couldn't remember any time in the past when they'd been beaten by a threat like this. And no one, not even Ian or Blair, had a clue.

Really, how had that happened? It made no sense.

The painful truth was, Christopher hadn't paid attention too much, aside from spending time with Mackenzie. He'd told her duty came first, but it hadn't. She'd come first.

That was it, wasn't it? He'd been distracted by love. It was easy to see now why Ian made it mandatory that newly-mated Eskarian males retire from Service. He'd been more concerned with Jacuzzis and feeding his two-hundred-year-old hunger than with the awakening of this century's deadliest sorcerer.

Griffin laughed. *You're taking more responsibility for this than you need to. We all had a hand in this. Truthfully, we've never been this closely involved in the fulfillment of a prophecy. Our place has always been in the shadows. It could be no other way, though. You were destined to meet your true mate, and she, apparently, was destined to destroy the world.*

Had there been no choice, then? Was it all preordained and they were just pawns to the will of Fate?

The hell with that. Even if this path was preordained, he had no intention of sitting back to watch it happen. Hell, no.

Maybe, he said to Griffin. *But it hasn't happened yet, which means there's still time to change the course of things. It's not over yet.*

Not yet.

Great. Any ideas how to get out of this? Griffin asked.

Still working on that part, he admitted. Damn. He'd gotten himself into quite a mess. He'd been so relieved that Mackenzie was alive. It just never occurred to him that it wasn't really her. Not once. *What would I have done differently?*

Nothing. You would have reacted differently had you seen a reason to do so.

Christopher's acute hearing caught the crisp snap of twigs and dried leaves beneath a booted foot. He turned his attention to the window and struggled to force his body to move. Nothing. Not even the twitch of a finger. *Griffin, someone's coming.*

Do you have any telekinetic ability yet?

Christopher tried to extinguish the lights, but they did little more than flicker. *No, I can't do anything.*

Not looking good, Little One.

The intruder crept along the side of the house, edging steadily closer to Christopher's window. *I know.*

I'm not sure how we're going to get out of this. Uleah's power is unparalleled. I've never seen anything like it. Griffin's voice was tired. Resigned.

Don't give up on me, Old Man. I'm going to need your strength soon. You damn well better be there for me. Christopher sighed, annoyed that the ancient warrior would give up so easily. Or seemed to give up.

Warrior, hell. The Old Man should be put out to pasture. Useless old fart.

Tough talk for such a young pup. I'll be ready.

Christopher's attention snapped back to the intruder just outside his window.

Both the blinds and the window were open. Christopher caught the scent of soap and masculine sweat. And fear. The intruder was probably human, but Christopher wasn't entirely sure. There was something different about him.

With surprising stealth, a tall, muscular man hopped over the windowsill, hunkered down, and crossed the floor to Christopher's bed.

He pushed a lock of black hair from his dark eyes and spoke softly. "My name is Ciro Allegra. You can call me Allegra. I'm an associate of Alistair McConnell's, or at least I was until now. Alistair is one of the three you're looking for." His black gaze darted to the door and back. "In fact, I personally know all the people you are seeking."

Christopher scanned his mind and body. "What are you?"

"I'm the product of genetic engineering through magic," he said, his gaze dropping to the floor. "An aberration of nature, really."

"And you know about the prophecy?"

"Yes, I do, unfortunately. It was discussed among the students at my seminary school—covertly, of course. Obviously, I never thought I would be involved in such a thing. But, here I am."

Christopher's eyebrows shot up. "You're a priest?"

He nodded. "I was. Then I became Alistair's underling—not by choice, mind you. It was a wretched position to be in, but it's over." He paused to glance back at the open window.

"Now, I'm here to assist you. I have a message from your commander. He told me to deliver it right away, so that you would know not to kill me."

"Blair is dead. As I'm unable to move, killing you is not really an option. You wouldn't have gotten inside my house, if I had all my strength."

"Yes, I know. I understand you immortals are quite strong."

"Quite," Christopher repeated.

Griffin interrupted. *Christopher, Uleah is returning to your room. He's searching for something and is pissed that it hasn't been found yet.*

"Leave now, Mr. Allegra. Uleah's coming. He should not find you here."

Allegra turned at once and cleared the windowsill without a sound. Christopher listened for footsteps, but there weren't any. The priest remained just outside Christopher's window.

He cleared his mind just as the door opened. Mackenzie sauntered in, twirling a lock of ebony hair around her finger.

Her emerald gaze raked his body with raw hunger. "Aren't you a sight? There is nothing so fine as a sexy, naked man just lying there, waiting for something to happen."

"What do you want now? I'm afraid you'll find me less than cooperative, if you're looking for more than conversation."

"Where is my brother?" Mackenzie flopped onto her stomach beside him. She studied the ends of her hair while she waited for her answer.

Christopher looked away. "Sean? I have no idea. If he's smart, he's long gone."

Her gaze swung back to him. "Well, we both know he's no rocket scientist. He spends too much time protecting me, when he should be doing other things. I think he's around here somewhere."

"I couldn't say. Try looking in the kitchen. He likes beer," Christopher suggested with a grin.

"Do you think me a fool to be toyed with?" she asked. "I know how to make you suffer. I am a master at causing pain, among other things, and when I'm at full power, I will hear you plead for death." She leaned forward. "But you won't get it, vampire. Not until I've turned you inside out. Further attempts to deceive me will not benefit you in the least, when it's your turn to die. It would be effortless for me to prolong your pain for a long time. Days, weeks . . . Who knows how long it might take? Now, is there something you want to tell me?"

Christopher considered the sorcerer's words. He was in no position to fight. Yet. "Perhaps I can help you, after all." He'd wait until he found the sorcerer's weakness. Everyone had one. It was a matter of looking in the right place.

And when he found it, he'd strike, hard and fast.

Mackenzie nodded. "I thought you might. Where is Sean?"

"I don't know for sure, but he's probably in his room, in the north wing."

"Thank you." Mackenzie pressed her mouth to Christopher's. Her lips were cold, and her tongue inside his mouth was unwelcome, but he accepted it to avoid a confrontation with the powerful sorcerer. She trailed cold kisses down his chest, stomach. Lower.

His eyes closed. *Not now,* he thought.

She ignited a flame within him against his will. Her lips deftly took him to a fevered pitch, but he remained silent, with a clenched jaw, the only way he could protest her invasion.

His mind drifted back to just moments ago, when he made

love to her, and she'd screamed when she climaxed. And he'd loved it. Loved her.

What now?

She raised her head. "I hear your thoughts. You make love to me even now. And, as you seek to destroy me, you still think of my body wrapped around yours."

"I think of Mackenzie's body. Not yours. This isn't making love." His upper lip curled into a sneer. "I can't wait to get my hands on you."

"You'll never get that chance." She paused. "And even if you did, you won't kill me. Do you want to know why?"

"No," Christopher snapped. "I will kill you."

"Ah, but I don't think you will. You see, your seed is still within me. As we speak, new life is beginning. Immortal life." Her lashes drifted down. "I look forward to being fully alive again. I will build an army of sorcerers who live only to serve me. Your technology will crumble at my feet. Your kings will kneel before me. The new race I will create will be vastly superior to even you, vampire." She laughed softly. "And you can't stop me. No one can. We will dominate this planet. For eternity."

Her mouth returned to drive him higher. Her hands lay across the ridges of his stomach, fingers drawing light circles in his skin.

Like Mackenzie.

It was about to happen. He didn't want to, but there was no way to prevent it. The mechanics of it were simple. Cause and effect. Her mouth was sheer magic. Her hair tickled his thighs and abdomen. Even her fingers tracing the ridges of his stomach affected him.

He missed her.

"Mackenzie . . ."

Christopher moaned, a soft cry ripped from the back of his

throat as he released. He couldn't help it. Didn't want to do it. She just took his control away, much as she took his breath away. Even now.

Mackenzie wiped her mouth with the back of her hand. "Nice, vampire. Very nice."

"Get out," he whispered.

She laughed. "What's the matter, love? Didn't you like that?" She stood up. "I'll be back for more. You taste sweet." She left the room without a backward glance.

Christopher closed his eyes. "Shit," he whispered.

Allegra climbed over the windowsill. He knelt beside Christopher, his black gaze on the door. "Uleah was the cruelest of the Shyalla Nar—the circle of twelve. Even after his transition to the Underworld of Toth, he was feared."

Allegra continued. "Alistair discovered all this quite by accident. After the newly re-formed Council banished him, he made a pact with Uleah, though what that is, I don't know. What I do know is that we can't fail to remove him from your beloved's body. He has to die. Tonight." The priest sat back. "Blair gave me a message for you. The spell is not complete until Uleah drinks from the vial where the Power of Shyalla Nar has been kept for thousands of years, and the words are spoken to restore his soul. Until that is done, he's still vulnerable."

"Where is this vial of power?" Christopher asked.

"I don't know," the priest said. "We can assume Alistair has it. The only thing I ever saw was the spellbook."

Christopher thought about that. "Great. How much time do I have to find this vial?"

"Not much. Mackenzie has to have a soul in her body by midnight, or she'll die. Two spells are needed for soul restoration. The first one drives the soul from her body, and the second is completed just before midnight on the first night of the new moon. The second spell is what puts Uleah's soul in her body forever. If he drinks from the vial, it's too late. For all of us."

"What time is it now?"

Allegra found the clock on the dresser. "Eleven thirty. You have a half-hour."

Christopher let out a flurry of Gaelic curses. "I can't even move yet."

Allegra removed the vial from his breast pocket. "This will counteract the effects of Uleah's spell." He removed the stopper. "I suggest you drink quickly. It will take a few minutes to work."

Christopher studied the vial. "Why are you doing this?"

The priest rested his forearm on his knee. "Alistair took everything I had. Most importantly, he took Lissa. I've been her guardian for almost three years. I've loved and protected her as if she were my own daughter. Alistair keeps her in a horrible place in his basement and I can't get to her. He won't let me see her. I'd do anything to get her away from him. He's a twisted man, Christopher. He talks about her as if she were his lover, and that just makes me ill." Allegra rubbed his brow and sighed. "After tonight, he really has no reason to keep me around. I may or may not be able to stop him from taking my life. Not only does he have the power of the Triad, he may also have the Power of Shyalla Nar. I just need to make sure Lissa is safe first." Allegra shrugged. "After that, who knows . . ."

"How do you know Blair?" Christopher asked.

"Blair came to see Alistair a few days ago. I saw it as a potential opportunity to free Lissa, so I offered to help him and your people. We have a common need to see Alistair die. Obviously, Uleah needs to die as well, but I'm not sure what I can do to help. I offer whatever I have, though. Use me as you see fit."

Christopher saw sorrow in Allegra's black eyes. He scanned the priest's mind quickly, just to be sure, and found he was telling the truth. "I'll take your serum."

Allegra dumped the contents into Christopher's mouth. "Uleah is not as strong as he'd have you believe. The Triad is holding him in Mackenzie's body. They're using all their power to keep him there. As I've said, the Power of Shyalla Nar is the key to his remaining in her body. He doesn't have very much time left."

Christopher nodded. Swallowing, he grimaced at the rancid taste, and worried for a moment that it might not stay down. "I understand. Where is the Triad?"

Allegra tilted his head in the direction of the back yard. "Near the rubble in back, under the Willow tree. They'll stay there until the spell is complete."

His stomach churned a moment, then accepted the potion. "I need blood. I have to be ready for this battle. May I have a little of yours, Allegra?"

The priest sat back. "You won't take all of it, will you?"

Christopher's legs tingled. "No. You'll feel a little weak, but it won't last long."

Allegra was quiet for a moment, then stood. "For Lissa." He bent and leveled his throat over Christopher's mouth. As Christopher's long teeth punctured the skin, the priest gasped. "God in heaven . . ." he whispered.

He took only what he needed, then pulled back. "Thank you, Allegra."

The priest straightened, then gripped the headboard with both hands to steady himself. With a quick smile, he looked down at Christopher and covered the puncture marks with his hand. "No problem." He looked at his fingers.

"The punctures heal almost instantly," Christopher said. "There's a gland in our mouths that secretes a kind of glue to seal the punctures. No one can know of our existence." His arms tingled. Good. It was starting to work. "Do you have any more serum?"

"Yes, I have one more vial." Allegra dipped his hand into his pocket and retrieved a second vial.

"I need you to find Griffin and give it to him. Can you do that?"

"Yes, I can. I know Griffin," the priest told him. "We . . . ah . . . met at Mackenzie's."

The image of Griffin's blackened body rushed back into Christopher's mind. "You burnt him."

"Alistair burnt him. I was there because he demanded it of me. I traded my life for Lissa's. All this—" He spread his arms wide to indicate the genetic manipulation of his body. "I do it to keep her alive one more day. He threatens, daily, to take her from me. Given that, you can see why I chose to help Blair."

"Yes, I can," Christopher said. *Griffin, where are you?*

I'm in the living room. Why?

Help is coming. Trust the priest.

"Griffin is in the living room. Find him quickly, give him the serum, then get out of the house. After I get my strength back, all hell is going to break loose. Tell me I don't need to worry about you harming Griffin while he's vulnerable. So help me, if you do—"

"Don't worry," Allegra said. "My allegiance is to you. I swear it."

"Find Griffin, then." Christopher nodded toward the door. "Turn left at the door and head straight. Go." He thought a moment. "Allegra?"

The priest looked at him.

"Thanks for your help. My people are indebted to you."

The priest smiled and dropped the second vial back into his pocket.

Alone again, Christopher waited for Allegra's serum to work. Uleah had been looking for Sean, which meant he thought Sean had something of value. What was it?

Christopher tapped his fingers on the bed sheets, then looked at them. Excellent. Not much longer.

Then it hit him.

Mackenzie's pendant. The Power of Shyalla Nar was contained in that tiny vial? Had to be. Mackenzie and Sean had been the keepers of the book. Now that it was missing, it stood to reason that Alistair had acquired it. All they needed was the vial.

They weren't going to get it.

A minute later, Christopher was able to move his legs.

He swung them over the side of the bed, and raised himself up on trembling legs. After a moment, they were strong enough to support him so he could walk. Bending to pick up his T-shirt from the floor, he lost his balance and stumbled. Damn it.

He steadied himself by holding onto the back of a chair.

Seconds later, he put on the shirt, then found his jeans and boots. Securing his dagger in its sheath, he was finally ready, and felt strong enough to finish this job.

Christopher swung his legs over the windowsill and slipped into the cool night. *Griffin, has the priest found you yet?*

Yeah, I remember this one. He was with Alistair when that damned wizard burned me. I should crush his throat here and now.

Save your anger for Alistair. I need you to go out back and find the Triad. They're near the pool by the old Willow. Break their connection with Uleah however you can. Mackenzie's life depends on it. Christopher needed Griffin's strength for this battle.

As soon as I'm able to move, it will be done.

We have until midnight, my friend. Do not fail me.

Not a chance. This old fart is ready to kick some ass.

Christopher grinned.

He moved in silence along the side of the house, staying in the shadows to avoid being seen. The Triad—Alistair, Scott, and some woman—were huddled together beneath the old Willow, not all that far from him. It would be so easy to just change shape, and rip out a throat or two.

His own primal shape, a large timber wolf, applauded the thought. It never tired of the hunt.

Or the slaughter.

Christopher inhaled softly. Much as he wanted to interfere, he needed to find Uleah and the vial. The wolf would have to wait.

He glanced at the Triad, then back, to ensure no one followed him.

Continuing the path to Sean's room, he kept an eye on the Triad. As long as they remained in their trance, he was fine. They would keep Uleah inside Mackenzie's body until the spell was complete.

So far, so good.

Sean's bedroom window was closed and securely locked. He could open it, but the amount of noise it might make was a concern. His only other choice was to enter through the adjoining bathroom door.

That was a better choice. No noise.

Easing the sliding glass door open, he stepped inside, and silently shut the door behind him.

"I have no time to battle with you, Big Brother. Where is the vial? I know that you took it from me earlier today." Mackenzie's voice held anger and hatred inside a veil of seductiveness.

Christopher stood on the other side of the wall and peered around, careful to remain unseen. Sean was held in midair by the sorcerer, a good four feet off the ground. His outstretched arms trembled as if exhausted.

Sean sneered at the sorcerer. "I won't tell you anything. Go ahead and kill me."

"Oh, I will, but I'll do it at my leisure. Until I'm ready, I'll just make your life an unending hell. Let's see . . . how might I entice you into telling me where you've hidden the vial?" Mackenzie bit down her lip and stepped forward, looking up at Sean. A slow smile crossed her face as her hands moved to the button of his jeans.

"Oh, God." Sean's eyes snapped shut.

Mackenzie pulled the zipper down. "Your culture frowns on incest, doesn't it?" She laughed, a lighthearted song that sent pangs of remorse through Christopher's heart for what he was about to do.

At this moment, he hated his job more than anything he could imagine.

Uleah had to be stopped by whatever means necessary. If it meant he had to kill Mackenzie, well, that's just how it had to be.

"No, please, not that." Sean's voice cracked. He was afraid.

Christopher rounded the corner, stepping fully into the bedroom. "Hello, Bitch."

His dagger was already in motion by the time Mackenzie whirled around to face him with wild fury in her eyes. The blade embedded solidly at the base of her sternum.

She stumbled backward, fury replaced by shock. "I swear you'll pay for this, vampire. You'll know pain as no other man on this planet has ever known."

He ignored her. "Where's the vial?" Christopher asked Sean.

"In my coat pocket behind the door."

Christopher found the vial in Sean's denim jacket. He studied the vial a moment, then grasped the ends and gave a good tug.

The filigree netting around the vial crumbled, leaving only the glass vial with a metal stopper. He pulled the stopper free.

Mackenzie clutched the dagger, screaming her outrage. "No! Give that to me! It's mine!" She staggered toward him, her hand extended, fingers curled into a claw.

"Not anymore. I know about the Power of the Twelve, Uleah. And it's mine now. Thanks for the blow job, by the way. Nice." He raised the vial. "My life for Mackenzie's. You lose, Uleah." He tipped the vial, emptied the contents into his mouth, and swallowed. "Sean, find a way to bring her back."

What effect it might have on him, he couldn't know. Didn't matter. Uleah had to be stopped. If it cost Christopher his life, then so be it.

He hoped like hell Sean would be able to save Mackenzie.

The liquid burned with ferocious intensity, searing his insides. It made him so hot, he feared he might melt right there. His legs weakened and gave out, dropping him to his knees. Suddenly, his vision changed. He frowned and blinked, astounded that he could see color—vibrant blues and reds. They swirled before him in a violent cyclone that encircled Mackenzie and Sean. Was that cyclone the power of the Triad, holding Uleah in her body?

The rush of wind was deafening, or was that the rush of blood in his veins?

Was that Mackenzie screaming and putting her fist through the wall?

Who was spinning in the air?

What time was it? He turned toward it, but he couldn't see the clock. Couldn't focus. Was there any time left?

His gaze moved to his beloved. Blood spilled from the cavern he'd created in her stomach. She'd pulled the blade from her body and now teetered where she stood.

Good. The sorcerer would be too weak to use his power.

Now, he had to wait for Griffin to do his work. Had to wait, and watch his beloved bleed.

He leaned back on his legs, pressed his palms to his forehead. Adrenaline pulsed through his body and made his stomach burn. No, everything was already burning. He was going up in flames. The Power of Shyalla Nar seemed strong enough to tear him to shreds.

It probably would tear him to shreds.

His head hurt so much, he thought it might explode.

Mackenzie, I'm so sorry . . .

What had he been thinking? He'd just driven his dagger into her beautiful, beautiful body. His thoughts swirled like the color around her. Had that been the only solution? Could he have done anything different? His gaze dropped to the floor. He didn't think he could bear another minute of this. The guilt and sorrow of what he'd done overwhelmed him. Like a tsunami.

"I'm sorry, I'm sorry . . ." he whispered.

His body was so hot. Sweat trickled into his eyes. He swiped it from his forehead then looked up. Mackenzie was crossing the floor to him with the dagger in her hand. The red and blue cyclone swirled around her as she approached, and the rush of air deafened him. Sean was shouting, but Christopher couldn't hear a word. Only saw the agitated movements of his mouth. The terror in his eyes. It happened so slowly. In fact, he wasn't sure it was even real. Seemed like a dream. Felt like a dream.

All he had to do was wake up.

Mackenzie slammed into him, pressed him up against the

wall. She thrust the dagger into his chest, in between his ribs. The blade penetrated his lung. He could feel it deep inside.

So much pain. Had he ever felt this much pain?

How much time was left?

Blood seeped from the beneath the dagger and streamed down his shirt.

She leaned close, her emerald eyes brilliant flames of hatred and bloodlust. "You die first, then Sean. You didn't stop me, vampire. You didn't do shit," she sneered. "You lose."

Chapter Sixteen

"Christopher, get up."

"Get off me," he said, pushing a hand off his shoulder.

"Get. Up." Someone shoved him.

His body ached from head to toe. What the hell had happened?

"Christopher, get your lazy ass off the floor. You got no time left."

Sean . . .

Inhaling, he stopped abruptly when pain seared his lung. He clutched his chest. "Jesus. I was stabbed," he recalled. "With my own blades." His eyes opened slowly, his brow furrowed. "What time is it?"

"You've got three minutes to bring her back. Get up," Sean said, stepping back. His shirt had been sprayed with blood. Why?

Allegra stood behind him, Mackenzie in a crumpled heap at his feet.

"What? I'm bringing her back?" His thoughts were clouded, but the words *bring her back* caught his attention. "How am I supposed to do that?"

Mackenzie stirred. "No . . ."

Sean's gaze shot to his right.

Christopher turned to his left.

Mackenzie was awake and had propped herself up on her elbow. "Help me up."

"Mackenzie," Christopher said. She was awake!

Sean knelt and placed a strong hand against the center of Christopher's chest, pinning him against the floor. "Don't move. You don't know who that is."

"It's Mackenzie." He pushed against Sean's hand.

Sean brushed Christopher's hand aside and held him firmly in place. "You don't know for certain. The wizard is clever and manipulative."

"Christopher," Mackenzie pleaded. "Help me up." She reached for him.

Christopher snatched Sean by the neck and swung him over his body to the floor. "Don't fucking tell me what I do or do not know." He sat up and pushed both hands through his hair. Every muscle screamed in protest of the simplest of movement. Didn't matter. The pain was of no consequence.

He stood up and approached. "Back off," he said to Allegra.

The priest raised both hands and stepped back without a word.

Smart man. He knew when to keep his yap shut.

Christopher knelt beside Mackenzie and cradled her to him. "Are you all right?" he asked softly.

She placed a trembling hand on his shoulder. "I can't," she whispered. "I can't . . . keep him out." She gripped him tightly. "Don't let him win. I have never known such vehemence, such violence." Tears filled her eyes. "I am no one's victim, Christopher. I don't know why things happen as they do. I wish I'd had more time with you, but if this is how it must be, then I implore you, have the strength to end it. End the prophecy."

She was saying goodbye. Christopher struggled to remain calm. She couldn't give up like that, damn it. He wouldn't let her. "Mackenzie, hold on. Stay with me . . ."

Her eyes closed.

Ian handed him a piece of paper. "Read this."

"What is it?" Christopher asked.

"It's the spell to restore Mackenzie's soul. You have one minute before it's too late. Speak the words now."

"I don't know how to pronounce them." He didn't want to lose Mackenzie because the words were foreign.

"Do it," Ian said. "Just read. It doesn't matter if the words aren't pronounced quite right. You have the Power of Shyalla Nar within you, Christopher. Very little can stop you from doing whatever you want."

Allegra stood beside Christopher, a black velvet pouch in his hands.

Christopher's gaze returned to the sheet of paper. "E para nos cindaro. Nostra cindarion re ten alaros sinto. Sheltor de ler diar eternala." His fingers tingled.

White smoke wafted in tendrils from Mackenzie's nose and open mouth.

He looked at Ian. "What does it mean?"

Ian held the spellbook. "As I understand it, it's something to the effect of, 'I grasp you out of darkness. Here you will remain in this body. Now and forever, always.' It is a binding spell, in the truest sense. You've bound her to this body for all time."

"Now you must sprinkle this powder on her." Allegra handed him the pouch.

Mackenzie's eyes snapped open. "Get away from me," she said flatly, pushing free of Christopher's arms.

The smoke escaping her nose and mouth turned dark blue.

She raised her hands. "Tarruna dosfor carrume." A cyclone of hot, fetid air blasted Christopher, Sean, Ian, and Allegra, knocking the breath from each man as he smashed against the wall.

"Did you think I would give up so easily?" She stood and reached behind her to retrieve the dagger she'd used on him. Reaching out, she plucked Allegra from the floor and brought him close to her body. She raised the blades to his throat. "You are holding my wizards. Bring them to me," she ordered.

Christopher felt the malevolence of the ancient wizard inside Mackenzie's body, but now she was there too. Her lifeforce, strong as ever, was a part of him once again, but that meant the wizard now had an anchor—her soul—and could remain.

The restoration spell had failed.

Christopher had the Power of Shyalla Nar at his beck and call. He peeled himself from the wall and faced Mackenzie. "Uleah," he said softly, his voice a mixture of velvet and menace. "You can't hope to win. *I* have the power now, and you have nothing. The wizards will remain where they are."

Mackenzie glared at him. "I can still destroy you all. The Power of Shyalla Nar is nothing in the hands of a fool." She smiled and lowered her head, fixing hateful green eyes on Christopher. "You will not send me back to Toth. My destiny is to bring a new order to this planet. I am to rule it for all time. I must begin. Now, one more time. Release my wizards or the priest dies."

"So kill him," Christopher said. "We accept that there are casualties of war. Regrettable, but necessary. Your choice is this: you can rule the underworld, or you can rule nothing. *That* is your destiny." Christopher summoned his power. He *was* going to send the sorcerer back to the underworld. Toth was the only place for someone like Uleah.

"No," Mackenzie said, hurling Allegra to the side. She dropped the knife and reached toward Christopher. Sparks cracked and sizzled around her fingers. "I'll see you dead first."

The cyclone kicked up again. The power of the vortex was deafening, the force enough to crush Christopher against the wall.

He couldn't breathe.

Without oxygen, he wouldn't survive.

I will not be denied, Uleah said in Christopher's head. *You will die.*

Christopher closed his eyes to the whirlwind of destruction. Ian and Sean might survive, but Allegra would be crushed to death. It would be a bloodbath.

"No," Christopher mouthed to himself. "No prophecy." He summoned the Power of Shyalla Nar and let it build around him. Tighter it coiled until his body was wired from its energy. His muscles trembled and cramped. The wound in his chest opened.

Blood seeped from his body, only to be lost inside the vortex.

He couldn't think.

No oxygen.

"No," he said again. The wizard would not win.

Forcing his arms to spread wide and his mind to focus, he used the Power to surround himself with a pocket of calm air. All the knowledge of the Shyalla Nar, the circle of Twelve, was his. "Tularen obridae."

He spoke the words to create his own vortex.

Her eyes widened. "No," she said. "You can't."

"I can and will," he answered.

Wham!

Christopher let the blast hit Mackenzie full force. It struck her hard, sending her flying backward into the far wall. Drywall exploded around her.

Uleah was gone. Forever. Christopher hadn't sent him back to Toth. He'd obliterated the wizard's soul into a thousand tiny particles of energy, which scattered in the waning whirlwind.

Christopher released his vortex and fell to his knees, coughing and gasping for air.

Ian pushed off the floor and dusted his clothes. "Well done," he said with a nod.

Sean and Allegra hadn't moved.

Neither had Mackenzie.

Ian bent to check Allegra's battered body for a pulse. Looking back at Christopher, he shook his head.

The priest had passed.

Ian turned Sean onto his back and inspected the young Eskarian's body. "Sean, time to wake up now," Ian said softly. "Get up, son."

Sean bolted upright. "I'm up, I'm up . . ." He looked around, confused. "Where's Mackenzie?"

Christopher straightened and crossed over the rubble to where she lay. He brushed the hair from her face. "Mackenzie?" He pressed his fingers against her pulse.

She was alive.

He wanted to stay with her to be sure she was all right, but couldn't. Duty came first, and this time, it really did have to come first. "Sean, take care of Mackenzie for me."

"Yup," Sean said, rising to his feet.

Outside, Griffin lay motionless on the ground, charred and covered in blood. Nearby, a woman lay with a dagger protruding from the base of her neck. To the left, Jason held Scott with a dagger to his throat and Alex held another man with tawny hair and golden eyes at bay, both hands held securely behind his back.

Ian pointed to the captives. "These two are all that remain of the Triad. The woman was Maya. She was an accomplished witch whose expertise was manipulating emotion."

"Who's the one with the orange eyes?" Christopher asked.

"That's Alistair, the leader," Ian said. "His specialty is genetic engineering. With a twist, of course. A little magic is involved."

"You're the one who cast the spell on Mackenzie, aren't you?" he said to Alistair.

"Yes, I am. What a lovely creature, too. I should have taken her before I gave her back to you."

Christopher glared at the wizard. "It would only make your death now that much more painful." He eyed the dagger protruding from Maya's throat. It would be such a simple thing to plunge that dagger into Alistair's throat, turn it in and . . .

"Did you know Alistair created the new strain of demon wolves?" Ian asked. "He's the one who made them so hard to kill."

"Really?" Christopher stuffed his hands into his pockets. "Mackenzie was a wolf when I met her. It was a horrible, painful process for her to change from human to animal, and she felt terrible about the people she killed and fed from. People she loved. You did all that?" he asked Alistair.

The amber-eyed wizard raised his chin. "I did. It was a beautiful combination of magic and engineering. A feat accomplished by no one else."

Sean came up beside Christopher, Mackenzie tucked under his shoulder. She was pale but alive. "You black-hearted, scum-sucking pig."

Alistair shifted under Alex's restraints. "Your insults are meaningless. My wolves were a magnificent creation. I am proud of them all."

"Your magnificent creations killed people. They themselves were terrified of the night. They knew we were waiting for them. As quickly as they propagated, we snuffed them out. Your wolves lived short, miserable lives," Christopher pointed out.

"And all that is about to change. We know all about you now," Alistair countered. "You had a betrayer in your midst. He told me what you are before Uleah killed him. You'll soon find yourselves on a laboratory table, or worse. Perhaps you'll find yourselves hunted, just as you tried to exterminate my wolves."

"What makes you think you're going to survive long enough to tell anyone about us?" Christopher asked.

"And what makes you think Uleah killed Blair?" Ian stepped up beside Christopher. "Eskarians are *very* hard to kill."

Alistair's eyebrows raised and his mouth opened, but he said nothing.

"The prophecy is no more. Uleah, gone. Forever." Christopher shrugged one shoulder. "It's over," he said to Alistair and Scott. "You lost."

"Yes, it was a complete waste of power and life. How utterly sad." Blair stepped off the patio and out into the yard.

Alistair's amber eyes widened. "You. Traitor. How could you survive Uleah's attack?"

"We heal very quickly," Blair said. "Uleah stopped my heart, but he did no other damage. It healed after only a few minutes."

Christopher turned to his commander. "Allegra has passed."

Blair rested his hand on Christopher's shoulder. "I know. I'm sorry. Now, let's finish this."

Christopher focused his considerable energy. "Yes, it's time."

In the front yard, the mechanism to open the wrought iron gate sprang to life. Slowly the gate opened, a dim scrape of metal against metal signaling the activity.

Christopher searched for all the demon wolves in the area. *Wolves, come to me. I have an offering for you, and the promise of a new beginning.* Christopher crossed his arms over his chest and turned to the man with amber eyes. "Alistair, some friends of yours are coming. I'm sure they'll be quite happy to see you."

Moments later, a dozen wolves appeared from the front yard. Large and small; black, gray, tan, and multi-colored ones came to fill the back yard.

Scott and Alistair looked at each other, then surveyed the throng of wolves milling about. Both men knew of the bloodlust and would realize they had no chance of escaping. Christopher would make certain they couldn't escape.

He stepped close to the pack. "Some of you, I can tell, have lived like this for a long time. You've suffered so much and some of it has been due to the fear of the nightly hunt. I know your loss has been great. I am a Defender and have hunted wolves for a long time, but that all stops tonight. Return here tomorrow as men and women, and we will find a way to heal the bloodlust. No more killing. No more hunting. This, too, is over." Christopher looked at Alistair. "As a gift to you, here is the man who made you what you are. No doubt you have a great deal to say to him."

The wolves surrounded Jason and Alex and their captives. In a sudden implosion of white feathers and wind, the Eskarians shifted into large white birds of prey, and launched into the air, carried by massive wingspans.

Alistair and Scott were alone—and terrified.

Alistair's brow furrowed. He scanned the pack of wolves, his gaze finally settling on a small, gray wolf. "Lissa, no. Surely you don't mean to partake of this madness."

"He is yours to devour, my friends. See you tomorrow

morning." Christopher turned to leave the wolves to their business.

He scooped up Mackenzie in his arms and kissed the top of her head. "Welcome back. How do you feel?"

"Okay, I think. Glad it's over." She inhaled and smiled. "Thank you."

"All in a day's work." He looked at her brother. "Sean, can you pick up Griffin? We'll put him back in the healing tank." The power of the great sorcerer remained within him, but he was unsure how long it would be his to command. For now, he would use it for good. Healing the demon wolves would be his first project.

"Christopher, I don't think we can do that. Look." Sean pointed at Griffin.

The wolf Alistair had spoken to had moved away from the pack and headed toward Griffin. She approached with trepidation, dipping her head first to scent his hair and body. Then her tongue darted out to lick his face.

Griffin stirred, then awoke with a start, no doubt surprised to find a demon wolf in his face. Despite his injury, he drew another, smaller blade from his pocket with lightning speed.

No demon wolf would ever approach a Defender. Instantly, Christopher understood.

"Griffin, *stop!*" He barked the command before the elder could do any damage.

Griffin's gaze shot to Christopher. "Have you lost it, man? This is a demon wolf. What would you have me do with it?"

"Touch her." Christopher knew the feeling, knew what Griffin would find.

You have no need for blood tonight. We will provide later, he said to the wolf. The strength of his thoughts were enhanced by Uleah's essence.

I am no demon wolf, Defender. Just a wolf. The small, gray wolf turned her head to look at Christopher. *Just a wolf,* she repeated.

Christopher took a step back. Not a demon wolf? His brow furrowed, then he smiled. Griffin was going to be so pissed. "Go on, Old Man. Do it," he ordered.

Griffin tentatively reached out to stroke the wolf's fur. His hard features softened as he realized what was happening, then a grin creased his face. He tilted his head to her. "What's your name, Wolf?" Waited for her answer. "Annalissa. What a beautiful name."

"Come, Griffin, and bring your wolf. I think we've seen enough bloodshed for a while." Ian headed for the house.

Griffin rose to his feet, ambled toward Christopher and Mackenzie, Ian, Sean, and Blair. Annalissa trotted behind him, her tongue hanging out and bushy tail wagging.

"Does anyone know what happened to Uleah?" Sean looked at Ian and Christopher.

Blair nodded. "The Power of Shyalla Nar kept him chained to this level of existence for many hundreds of years. But Christopher chose not to send his soul back to Toth. Instead, he shredded Uleah's soul. There is, quite simply, nothing left."

"So, what happened after I got staked?" Christopher sat on the couch with his bare feet up on the coffee table. Mackenzie had curled up next to him with a blanket over her legs.

His gaze dropped to his shirt. The large rip revealed the tender area where his own dagger had penetrated him. He whispered a finger along the aching flesh. It had healed, but it still hurt like hell.

Sean had changed into a new shirt and now sat on the fireplace hearth. "Griffin found the Triad outside. His intent, I think, was to take the witch out first. She surprised him by slicing him with her own knife, but that broke the connection. And by then, Mackenzie had put your own knife inside you." He glanced at Mackenzie, who shrugged.

"Wasn't me," she said quietly.

"Anyway," Sean continued. "When Griffin dropped his knife, I picked it up and stuck it into Maya. It was hard to do with them moving so quickly. I got her in the neck, but I was actually aiming for her body. Guess it worked out okay."

"I know it's hard to take a life," Christopher said.

Sean nodded, his gaze dropping to his feet. "Yeah, it was, but I was sure it had to be done. It was us or them."

"Yes, it was," Christopher agreed. "Always is."

"But what I don't get is how you guys pulled this off." Sean's gaze swung up to Christopher.

"Oh, jeez," Jason said, inhaling on his pipe. "Here we go. You'll never get Mr. Strategy here to shut up now. We'll be listening to this all night." He exhaled two perfect smoke rings.

"Like you have anything else to do, Sendagi, besides blow rings," Christopher teased. He curled his arm around Mackenzie's shoulder.

Jason emptied the contents of his pipe into a large ashtray. "Yeah, whatever," he said, his cheeks flushing.

Griffin laughed. "Harsh language, Sendagi." He leaned forward to brush the fur of the small wolf curled around his feet.

Jason waved dismissively. "Go on, Chris. Explain your strategy. Bore us all to tears."

Christopher smiled. "Uleah knew we weren't human, but he had no idea we were so strong. He just didn't know what he was up against at all.

"Blair knew that if Uleah was able to take the Power of Shyalla Nar, he'd be a formidable enemy. Blair was with

Griffin when he was burned at Mackenzie's, but Alistair didn't know that. He intercepted them at the ferry docks before they left the island, and admitted that he was with Griffin and knew what had happened. He said he knew they were looking for the book and that he had it. Of course, Alistair had to have the book, so he was receptive to whatever Blair said. He told Alistair that he wished to strike a bargain with Uleah, that his need was great and he would trade the book for help from Uleah. Alistair sought to verify what Blair was saying and consulted his little orb, which Blair manipulated without much effort. Alistair saw what only Blair wanted him to see." Christopher turned to Jason. "You bored yet?"

Jason faked a yawn. "Total snore-fest, Chris. Wake me up when you're done."

"You wish," Christopher said, grinning. "Anyway, Alistair knew nothing of our telepathic or telekinetic abilities, but we had to assume Uleah would. That meant that I couldn't speak with Blair once he left to deliver the book. I had to believe that he would find a way to heal Mackenzie. When she went down, I almost couldn't go through with it." Christopher shook his head and tightened his grip on Mackenzie. "I had to trust that Blair had found a way when everything around me screamed utter failure. I felt as if I were a blind man standing in the middle of a busy highway and I had to get to one side or the other."

Sean nodded his understanding. "So, they never really had a chance."

Ian tilted his head. "They had a chance. We had to ensure Uleah would never drink from the vial, which meant one of us had to do it. The problem was that we had no idea what might happen afterward. If it had killed the one who drank it, we could have failed. It was a very risky plan."

"Definitely." Christopher's gaze moved to Griffin. "And what happened to you?"

"After Maya was staked, Scott was outraged, and unleashed his power. Scott had the ability to control weather. I went down under a shower of fire and ice." Griffin leaned back in the chair. "I only spent two hours in the tank this time. Yeehaw . . ."

Christopher laughed. "Well, gentlemen, I hope you'll survive without me. As of this moment, I'm officially out. Sean, Arden's Bow is all yours."

Sean looked at the old bow in the corner of the room. "You're going to train me, right?"

"No, we're going to send you out with no training at all. If you come back, then we'll make you an official part of the team," Christopher said with a perfectly straight face. "That's your initiation."

Sean's mouth fell open. "Huh?"

Christopher laughed again. Felt good to relax, especially with Mackenzie at his side. "I'm kidding. Of course you'll be trained. Jason will do it."

Sean rubbed his chest. "Man, you guys are cold."

Christopher, Jason, and Griffin laughed this time. Sean was a welcome addition to the Defender ranks. Initiates were fodder for just about any prank.

Maggie Blue was nearly ready. The power catamaran had food for the dogs, and plenty of fuel and water.

Christopher escorted Mackenzie onto the boat, then led her to the lavishly-decorated salon. "This will be your new home for a few months. What do you think of her?"

Mackenzie surveyed the living area with wide eyes. "It's incredible. I can't believe my eyes. This thing must be worth a fortune."

He grinned. "No. I *paid* a fortune, but they don't really keep their value. Not like land, anyway."

"Well, I love it."

Ivan joined them, followed by his new little brother, Artemus, a black and white Malamute. Artemus had been a mating gift from Blair's benekeda, Anastasia.

Sean followed the dogs and stopped abruptly in the doorway, as amazed as Mackenzie had been. "Whoa . . ." he said, looking around. "Score, Kenz. This guy must be loaded."

Mackenzie's eyebrows shot up. "I think so, too, but I'm just using him for sex."

Christopher burst out laughing.

Sean looked surprised until he realized Mackenzie was teasing him. He giggled, then fake-punched his sister in the arm. "I'm going to miss you, Kenz."

"I won't be gone long. Jason's going to keep you very busy anyway. You won't have time to miss me."

"All the same, I'll be glad to see you home again." He leaned forward and scooped her into his arms. "Have a great time, little sister." He pulled back and kissed her forehead.

"I will," she said. She blinked several times. "Now go, before I get all mushy."

The intercom crackled to life. "We're ready, Christopher." Jeremy, chauffeur and captain, was at the helm.

"Time to go," Christopher told Sean.

Sean waved awkwardly. He'd never been apart from his sister for more than a few hours. Now it would be weeks. Christopher thought he was handling it well, though.

He'd make a fine Defender.

As the boat headed away from the dock, Christopher took Mackenzie to the bow of the boat. "We'll have company for a few weeks, until we get to Alaska."

"Oh?" Mackenzie looked behind her. "Who?"

"Alex," Christopher said, pointing upward. "He wanted a lift. Hope you don't mind."

Perched atop the radar arch was a huge, beautiful Bald Eagle.

"No, I don't mind. I think." She studied the bird, looking uncertain.

"Shape-shifters, remember?"

"Yeah, I remember. I was thinking about our privacy." She looked back at him. "This *is* my honeymoon, after all."

Christopher loved the way her mind worked. "Don't worry. He'll just take off while I make love to you."

"Then I don't think we'll see much of him," she said, a sly grin on her face.

Christopher studied her face, his smile slowly fading. She completed him somehow. Everything about her was perfect, including the little scar under her eye. He lifted a finger to trace the scar, then kissed it. "I love you, Mackenzie."

"I love you, too. I can't imagine what my life would be like without you in it. I don't want to imagine that. I just want to wake up next to you. Always."

"Forever," he whispered.

About the Author

Tyler Blackwood grew up riding horses in the Arizona desert and lounging in the family swimming pool. Most often, though, she spent free time writing short romantic fantasies. After graduating from college with a degree in business and information systems, she dabbled with other creative outlets, such as sculpting, pottery, and mixed media, but nothing came close to feeding her like telling a story. Once she started writing again, that was it. She was hooked.

She lives in Seattle with four cats and a husband. Summer weekends are often spent aboard their boat, either reading or writing, or sometimes just doing nothing. You can reach her at tylerb@tylerblackwood.com or visit her website at www.tylerblackwood.com. Find out more about the Eskarian Defenders at www.eskarian-defender.com.